AN ARROW THROUGH TIME

FOREWORD

Foreword written by Arthur Cole, Co- Author of the Terry McGuire series of Crime Thrillers and Poet.

I have known Maggie for well over forty years, we were both members of the South Wales Police Force. Little did we know that at the time we were both interested in poetry, and English Literature whilst at school, though neither of us did anything with it until later on in our lives, and after we had both retired from the force.

Maggie was born and raised in Llantrisant, a town steeped in legend and folklore, situated in South Wales midway between Bridgend and Pontypridd.

Although Maggie did pen a few poems as a child, her writing didn't really take off until she was fifty-six with one of the main drivers behind this being the Covid pandemic. Maggie had time on her hands, and she decided to make the most of it and put all her energy into writing.

At that time Maggie also became an avid watcher of the television series Outlander, and a reader of the books from which it was adapted and as a result was inspired to write poetry based on the characters within. Maggie then published a series of books of poems relating to her thoughts and images that came out of the series. These were and still are sold to raise money for Riding for the Disabled, a charity close to her heart.

Having read Maggie's poetry, I would describe her writing as imaginative, artistic, and emotional, with a unique style.

'An Arrow Through Time' is Maggie's first full length novel and begins in 1364 at the Battle of Crecy in which archers from Maggie's hometown Llantrisant fought to the death.

This her first novel is gripping in its entirety and will transport you on a journey from the bloody Battle of Crecy, and subsequently through the centuries. It is a real page turner, absorbing in the extreme, weaving its way through, murder, mystery, time travel, romance, witchcraft, myth, and legend throughout mid Wales.

The novel itself is beautifully written and is a true work of originality. I have no doubt it will keep readers deeply engrossed. Maggie has used historical events, combining them with her own imagination and has created a novel of absorbing fascination and fulfilment, taking Sybil the main protagonist in the novel on a voyage of mystery because of who and what she is. You will not be disappointed, I guarantee.

Being an Author/Poet myself I know how difficult it is for an individual to put pen to paper and create a body of work that they can be proud of. I believe that Maggie has really nailed it on this occasion, bearing in mind 'An Arrow Through Time' is her first attempt at writing a novel.

I would like to thank Maggie for giving me the opportunity of writing this short foreword, and I must say it has been a pleasure. I am confident that readers will enjoy the novel and gain true inspiration if they themselves have any thoughts of writing.

Arthur Cole
Author/Poet

CONTENTS

PART ONE

AN ARROW THROUGH TIME

CHAPTER 1- TWO DAYS AFTER THE BATTLE OF CRECY
August 28th, 1346

The archer was well hidden. The forest was dense, the oak trees old and gnarled, their branches thick and in full leaf. The vanguard had moved on, along with the baggage wagons and the trappings of the camp followers.

The battle had been won and the enemy put to flight through the French forests, and apart from the occasional skirmish of a rear-guard action being fought more for the sake of saving face than any hope of a victory, the French had gone, it was time for many of us to head back for the coast, and home.

The whole of the Kings army was beginning to set camp in a large clearing amongst the oaks. Sentries would be posted, and fires lit. There would be merriment and singing and a little respite after the hard-fought victory on the field at Crecy.

The French had suffered the majority of the casualties. Yes, ours had suffered, too, but that was the cost of war. Morale was high, the men in high spirits and eager to enjoy some rest and recuperation in the rich French countryside before continuing on.

Seated astride his fine chestnut horse and dressed in all his splendour, golden helmet and red and yellow shield, surcoat of red and yellow emblazoned with the family coat of arms, unscathed and unmarked by battle, Sir Hugh de Audley surveyed the landscape and congratulated himself on keeping well out of harm's way. He was not a brave man. In fact, he was an abject coward. Forced to ride with his men and serve his King he was now impatient to get back to the safety of England and leave the fighting to the young pup alongside him.

He hoped that he had done enough to bring himself to his sovereign's notice, to find some favour at the royal court which would restore what he saw as his rightful place amongst the courtiers to new King Edward III

He longed to leave the backwater to which he had been consigned. Wales. Not even a prosperous part of this godforsaken piece of the kingdom. What had he done to so offend the King that he was to spend the rest of his days in Llantrisant, a hilltop town beset by raiders, swept by the wind with its draughty castle and ill-educated barbarous people?

And the dried-up stick of a wife that the old King had saddled him with? He had married purely for what came with her - her reinstated fortune and the prospect of the Gloucester lands to come.

Little more than a child, the rider who sat alongside him atop the hill had proven himself a true leader in battle astride his fiery black charger. The fighting done, he wore no armour this day, his thick black leather jerkin covered only by a light coat of chain mail and a tabard bearing his father's colours. The Kings colours.

Relaxing In the warm August sunshine, Edward Woodstock, Prince of Wales tipped back his helmet to show his bright blonde hair and the beginnings of the stubble of manhood. He was but sixteen years old and had already proven himself an able leader of men, and a ruthless combatant. Yesterday he had won his spurs, earning himself the moniker "The Black Prince" for the colour of his battle armour, his manner of fighting and his skill in battle. On this morning he chose to ride amongst his men wearing little protection enjoying the warmth of the French weather and the feeling of a great victory.

It was Edward of Woodstock Prince of Wales who broke the silence. 'Come Sir Hugh, let us show ourselves amongst the men. There are heroes amongst them who should be recognised'.

He wheeled his horse in front of Sir Hugh's and the two riders descended the low rise into the throng of the men gathered below them. Sir Hugh followed his Prince, reluctantly. He hated the stench of the unwashed soldiers his Prince chose to ride amongst. He hung back allowing the throng of men to close around the huge black charger in front of him, seeking to create distance between himself and the rank-and-file he despised.

In the clearing ahead, men were building fires, the women of the camp followers were foraging for fresh food in the abundant woods, a hunting party was beating slowly through the bracken and underbrush in search of fresh meat. The forests of Northern France when not reduced to burnt earth by the French themselves, were plentiful hunting grounds and the men hoped to eat well tonight.

Just a little closer, just a few more yards and he's mine, the archer mentally counted the yards between arrow and target. The arrow was nocked, and the bow drawn by a practised hand, the eye was steady and patient for the right moment.

The archer did not hear the rustle in the leaves at the base of the tree. Senses focussed, did not see the huge black shape. Disturbed from its sleep it shook its hairy black head grumpily and ambled out into the clearing then trotted slyly towards the two horses making their way down the slope.

Now! The arrow was loosed and flew straight and true.

The chestnut mare, handsome but not truly battle hardened and still unused to its surroundings, spooked, reared, and took flight back up the rise, instinct taking it out of danger, nostrils flared and snorting, eyes out on stalks, it's rider completely unable to keep control. Sir Hugh de Audley was nearly unseated by the animals' haste to leave the arena. The rudely awakened boar lowered its tusks and charged into the melee. A hunter's arrow took it straight behind the shoulder and it fell, squealing and trembling just feet from the unsettled charger.

The first arrow, still true in its flight was now on course for the black horse and its rider.

Gwyn ap Meredith was hard by his Prince's side among the crowd milling around the black charger. He walked by design close to the rider's leg, his ears tuned to the noises of war, his face turned towards the line of the arrow's flight, ears alerted to the familiar sound of death in the air.

The archer in the branches of the tree saw the tall man turn, saw his face, and recognised it as well as Gwyn recognised the face of the archer. Gwyn flung his arms upwards and taking him in a bear like embrace pulled his Prince half out of the saddle turning his own back towards the oncoming missile. The arrow struck Gwyn ap Meredith in the back of his shoulder.

Both he and the Prince fell to the floor under the pounding feet of the battle charger as it stamped and plunged in an attempt to get clear of the crowd.

Sir Hugh de Audley having regained control of his own mount rode into the middle of the confusion. He waved his arms in panic and stared about him unsure of what to do. In the few seconds that followed, men had pulled the King's son from the crashing hooves, bringing him and his saviour to safety.

All had happened in a matter of seconds.

Sir Hugh looked back towards the forest from where the second arrow had come. He knew the tell-tale wind of an arrow in flight, but he did not see the third. The bodkin point pierced his armour and his mail, the poison at its tip pierced his heart and he fell from his horse. He was dead before he hit the floor. An arrow fletched with the black, red, and white plumage of the woodpecker protruded from his chest.

High in the oak tree the archer took his time, and then, when all below was in the chaos of the moment, his slight figure climbed carefully down from the branches of the oak, quickly donned the clothing left in a neat pile at the base of the tree, then on soft booted feet ran swiftly to the rear of the column and the baggage wagons with one eye watching for the boar or its relatives.

Sir Hugh de Audley was dead, and that was all that mattered.

Gwyn ap Meredith was carried to the Prince's tent. He was still conscious. The arrow had lodged in the muscle of his shoulder. He could not see it, as it had struck him from the rear, but he knew in his heart who had fired it. He knew whose arrow it was.

And there would be questions, many questions. An attempt on the life of a Prince: heads would fall for this.

'Fetch the healer, there is one with the men', the Prince called to his page.

Elgan materialised on command and on the swift feet of a messenger ran to where he knew the healers would have made their place.

Gwyn felt himself placed face down on a pallet bed, his arms hanging limp over the sides. He felt the strong hand of his Prince on his shoulder and then the jolt of pain as the Prince himself tried to pull the arrow from his flesh. Under well-meaning but unskilled hands the arrow snapped leaving an inch of shaft and the armour piercing arrowhead in the wound.

'You have saved my life this day, I pray to the Gods we can now save yours'. Edward the Black Prince of Wales dropped the arrow on the floor under Gwyn's nose. The feathers were, indeed, black, and white and red, just as he had suspected.

'Iesu Mawr, what have you done!'

As this thought left his head and the darkness of oblivion engulfed him he heard voices shouting,

'Sir Hugh, Sir Hugh is dead!'

Elgan, the Prince's page, had run like the devil was after him, weaving through tents and wagons, pushing through gaggles of serving women and the occasional nest of whores until he eventually found Marged the healer at the rear of the convoy with the laundry women and the other camp wives. He grabbed her by the arm and dragged her to one side.

'Come, you are needed most urgent, there has been trouble, Gwyn is wounded, a hidden archer tried to kill the Prince. And Sir Hugh ... 'He did not have time to finish the sentence.

She ducked back inside the shelter which the women had just erected for some privacy, straightened her dress and her composure, and stuffed the bundle of old rags at her feet under her pallet, grabbed her bag of salves and ointments, needles for stitching and the brutal looking tool she used to remove stubborn arrow heads and followed Elgan the page to the Prince's tent.

Marged saw with horror the unconscious body of her husband Gwyn lying on the bed in front of her, the arrowhead still embedded in his flesh. She could remove it, but she knew without doubt that without the help of another she could not heal him, but neither would he die.

She set to work with able hands. The Prince himself held Gwyn's shoulders still while she enlarged the hole made in his flesh by the arrow. She carefully removed the arrowhead from the wound, cleaned it with a good slug of the Prince's brandy and closed the hole with three carefully placed stitches. She then applied a salve of comfrey to the wound; this was as much as she could do.

Then, addressing Elgan, the page. 'Do not move him, let him lie face down, and let him sleep, when he wakes call me and I will strap the wound for him'. She knew he would not wake.

Sir Hugh de Audley was dead his body sewn into a rough canvas shroud and placed on a cart. A coffin would be found or made at the next town, and he would be taken back to England for burial as befitted a knight of the realm.

Edward had duly noted that the same style of arrow had killed Sir Hugh as had wounded Gwyn ap Meredith. When Sir Hugh's body had been brought to the tent the coloured feathers were still waving at the end of the arrow's shaft that proudly protruded from his brand new and undented armour.

He kept his counsel. Had that arrow been meant for him? Who was the archer? One of skill no doubt. The treacherous rogue must be found and dealt with, and soon. 'Healer, you will stay with my friend here, for friend he is, I will not have him left alone, call for what you need, my page will bring you all you ask for.'

A voice at the back of his mind all the while telling him quietly that there was more to this than murder!

Enquiries would be made, he knew that there were people in the camp who would talk, those that would provide the information he needed, at a price.

He swung open the flap of the tent and walked into the encampment, to the smell of unwashed men, ale, fires baking bread and roasting boar, the sounds of singing accompanied by homemade whistles and flutes, makeshift drums, and the occasional lute.

He would enquire of the men. Who used such a pretty hunting arrow, distinctive in its construction, almost feminine in appearance, but lethal in its intent.

Edward Prince of Wales was happiest amongst his fighting men. He walked among the fires flanked by Sir Kenneth the master at arms and sought out the company of his own Black Army, the longbow men of Llantrisant. If battle honours were deserved, these men deserved them all and honoured they would be!

Gwyn ap Meredith foremost, he had been at the head of the bowmen. It was he who had coordinated the volleys of arrows, wave after wave, each man, twenty-four arrows a minute at their peak. Until they ran out of arrows, then he had drawn a sword, not a weapon common in the archers ranks and had fought his way to Edward's assistance, standing alongside the Prince's standard bearer as they repelled the attack by the Count de Alencon. Gwyn, the same age as the Prince himself had stood his ground with one other of his archers and proven himself brave indeed.

23

His standard bearer, where was he, was he amongst these brave men? Owain they had called him, Owain y Mynydd, Owen of the Mountain, and a mountain of a man he had proven himself. And what of Sir Hugh de Audley in the fight? Well, what of him? He had proven noticeable entirely by his absence.

Tomorrow they would break camp and start the long ride for home. He had faith that he would find the archer with the woodpecker arrows. There would be no mercy, a fine and brave man had been laid low today, and he did not mean Sir Hugh.

PART TWO

CHAPTER 2 - ST HARMON THE YEAR OF OUR LORD 1873- RED
St Harmon, Wales, 1873

There were few visitors to Hengwm and most of those who visited had somehow lost their way. It was an isolated spot, a long low house set into the shadow of the mountain. The woodland behind sheltered it from the worst of the driving wind and rain. The hillside rose steeply through the woods and upwards to mountain pasture and moorland with rough scrubby grass and gorse, punctuated with rocky outcrops. The mountain levelled out at the top into a flat green field surrounded by squat black trees which were grouped like a posse of old men bowed by age and wind and deep in never ending conversation with each other and with their surroundings.

A stream emerged from just below the summit and bubbled down through a steep sided valley bounded by gnarled oak trees on either side, the sides of the valley so steep as to be nearly inaccessible. The stream levelled out just below the house and flowed through fields of flat pasture and then on down the valley to the village below.

The house was now accessed by a cart track, but this was a relatively new addition and led down from the rear yard which was at the sheltered side of the house and joined on to the rocky parish road about half a mile down the hill towards the village.

The house had been occupied by the Meredith family since, well since forever. The original foundation stones had been laid in the days of King Edward II.

Edward of Caernarfon had come to the throne of England in 1307. Then Hengwm had been a single roomed cottage with an earth floor, animals, and humans both occupying the living space around the single fire. This part of the cottage had, either ingeniously or due to a lack of stone, been partly built into the rock face and descended into a rock walled cellar made by making use of a cave situated behind and below the back of the house.

The presence of the cave was known to very few people and those that knew of its presence were glad that it was now walled off from the house. It was an eerie place. It exuded a sadness from its walls. Whatever it contained, or it had witnessed was best left to its own devices. Over the many years the cottage had been extended and expanded and was now a comfortable but spartan residence whose occupant was still a Meredith and a confirmed bachelor. The oldest part of the house was no longer used, the steps into the cave having been walled off together with its secrets, years before.

CHAPTER 3 - A FOUNDLING

10th June 1873

It was a Tuesday, the day had been blisteringly warm, the scythe men had quit their unrelenting exhausting cut of the first hay crop in the meadow rolling down to the stream.

The sun had already begun to dry the fallen grass and the air smelled of sweat and cut grass, with just a hint of horse from the pony and trap tied loosely to the gate post at the top of the field.

The stone bottles of homemade cider and ale were passed round and drunk by the farm workers, men and women who sat on the ground taking their ease of a job well done.

If the weather held there would be another field to cut tomorrow, the cut fields to be turned by the women with their hay forks, and once dried to be heaped high on the Haywain and stacked in the barn.

As the sun set behind the mountain, groups of men dispersed to the Sun Inn to continue to slake their thirst, indulge in outbursts of spontaneous singing and eventually stagger home to their cottages to sleep the sleep of the just, ready for the next day's labours.

Edward Meredith was not one of those men, he drank sparingly, everything in moderation, he would drink his quota in mugs of ale and talk with his old friend Idwal Lewis the innkeeper and then make his way back to Hengwm and his solitary bed.

Edward Meredith was a stern looking man. He had turned forty years of age that January. He was stocky, broad shouldered, barely five feet and eight inches tall and with a wild mop of red hair now shot through with white. His hair was not the dark red of a deer's pelt or a squirrel's tail, but a brighter altogether more ferocious shade of ginger, it was well – shocking, and his eyes were a piercing light blue, and he was renowned for his incendiary temper.

It was not unusual for him to be involved in the fighting which sometimes broke out at the Sun Inn when too much ale had been consumed and tempers flared over the most minor of disputes. Edward had a reputation for being able to hold an argument with his own toenails. When roused he rarely lost a fight, he had fast fists and the natural balance of an athlete. He was strong from manual work, chopping logs, handling sheep, and hefting the stone to build the dry-stone walls which neatly divided the fields behind the farmhouse. The farm was called Hengwm and as far as Meredith was concerned it truly was a jewel in the hills.

Edward Meredith farmed the Hengwm well. It was his pride and his joy. The stock was well kept, the fields

30

walled and fenced, and the long low farmhouse built into the shelter of the hill was well maintained.

He was financially well set up. The farm was not rented ground like many in the area, the house and surrounding fields were his, he owned the grazing rights to the vast acreage of mountain and woodland behind. Passed down by royal decree to generations of his family who had all farmed the same land before. If it hadn't been for his irascible nature, he might have been quite a catch, but at forty years of age he had no wife, no live in housekeeper, no children that he knew of and no wish to have any. He was a confirmed bachelor.

Meredith sat by the bar in the Sun Inn on this warm summer evening, his ale before him in his old and battered pewter tankard, listening to the men of the village talking amongst themselves. The topic of conversation seemed to be Helena Lewis, the Innkeeper's daughter, she of the neat figure, long white-blonde curls, and morals as loose as her petticoats. The village gossips said she had grown up for too long without her mother and in the company of men. The same small group sitting at the same table by the window cradling their mugs of warm ale, musing amongst themselves in voices just loud enough to be overheard.

'Like mother like daughter, isn't it?'
'Mother wasn't any better than she should be,
'Reckon the daughter will work out the same.'
'Sad for old Idwal mind, no luck with women, most careless to lose the two of them!'

Idwals wife Bron had disappeared when Helena was ten. Little Helena had spent her formative years helping her father in the bar, in the company of men, listening to the bawdy stories they told around the fire of a night, basking in the adoration of the younger boys who sat on the wall outside and who would do just about anything to get her attention.

Idwal Lewis had lost his wife, Bron. Not dead, as far as the village knew, she was just gone. One day Idwal had woken to his daily life and found that his wife of ten years had disappeared, leaving him alone with their ten-year-old daughter.

Bron Lewis had taken nothing with her, her clothes, her small items of jewellery, her books, for she loved her books, were all still in the small attic room above the Inn where she liked to sit and read. Her perfume was still in its tiny bottle on the dressing table in his bedroom. Surely if she had run away with another man, then these things would be gone. But they were not. Every day Idwal prayed for her return, his Bron, his silver blonde elfin lass. Her daughter was so, so much like her.

Every anniversary of the day that Bron had gone missing, he walked the hillside above Hengwm and prayed, for something drew him there. He did not like to believe that Edward Meredith was anything to do with his wife's disappearance, yet when his daughter, Helena, had gone to work for the man he called his truest friend, he had felt a chill run down his spine. He was good friends with the man, in fact Edward Meredith was probably Idwal's closest friend. He trusted the stubborn intractable old bastard. He would trust him with his life, but why on earth had he remained single all his life? Something was not quite right, but Idwal could not figure out what. Rumours, there were always rumours, a village was like that, one day you would be the toast of the whole valley for some action or deed, the next you could be branded as the anti-Christ and directed to the stocks or the gallows if there still was one.

Helena, the apple of her father's eye, wild as the hills and pretty as a picture. The village gossips risked a black eye to speculate on what had become of her.

It was true, Helena had an eye for the lads, and she had lodged at Hengwm for several weeks at the end of last summer, the least said of that the better in Edward's mind. She had thrown herself at him in fine style, installed herself as impromptu housekeeper, done his washing and ironing, cooked, and cleaned, and warmed his bed, and not only with a warming pan if it had been up to her. He was a man after all. Then, unsuccessful in her mission to seduce him into marriage, she had, like her mother before her, disappeared. Gone, the gossips said to work in service at a big house over the mountain, in Rhayader.

Idwal did nothing to correct this assumption He had no better idea where Helena might be, he stood quietly sentinel behind his bar, talking with the older men, and with Edward.

One ear listening for trouble and one hand on the pistol he kept primed and loaded under the counter, the ceiling bore witness to Idwal's method of restoring order if necessary. Helena had been sixteen then and Idwal forty.

No man would speak ill of Idwal's wife or of his daughter and stay alive to live another day.

CHAPTER 4 - DEAREST DADA – ST HARMON - HELENA

The letter was written in a hurried and scrawling hand:

31st October 1872

Dearest Dada
By the greatest stroke of luck, I have gained employment as a lady's maid in the home of Mrs Eliza Jones at Pen y Banc over by Rhayader.

I did not want to wake you, so have left early this morning with Mrs Jones' servant in their gig to travel with them to Rhayader. The position was put my way whilst I was at the herbalist's shop in Rhayader, it is an opportunity not to be turned down.

I shall write once I have established myself in her employ.

Your daughter,
Helena

I had propped the letter on the mantle shelf above the kitchen fire and in the darkness of that chilly October morning had left the Sun Inn and my home of sixteen years carrying my belongings such as they were in my mother's old carpet bag, a culf of bread and cheese in my hand and a stone bottle of small beer from behind the bar. I left.

I could not stay. I loved my father too dearly to shame him so. I loved Uncle Edward too much for him to face the ridicule of the village, the rumours which would rip two families apart. For no one would believe the truth, I barely believed it myself.

Mr Isaias Rees the Apothecary had told me of Mrs Eliza Jones. I had met her then one day when she was in Rhayader at his shop buying herbs and remedies. She was in need, she said, of a general servant who wanted to learn her art and also to help her maid Hannah with the heavier chores. Mr Rees had given me a reference. He knew me and of my family and so I had agreed to start work for Mrs Eliza Jones.

There was no servant, no horse and trap, I would be walking wherever my journey was going to take me, but there was Mrs Eliza Jones. I had heard that Mrs Jones could help me out of my predicament, I needed to get away from the village and all that went with it.

On foot I headed down the lane out of the village of St Harmon heading for Rhayader and the house at Pen y Banc.

CHAPTER 5 - THE TRUTH WILL OUT - HELENA

I had been at Pen y Banc for about four months when Mother Eliza as she liked to be called took me one side. She called me into her library, that most enthralling of all places where she kept her books and papers, the room smelled of book, and leather, and slightly musty. A severe looking woman, but quite kindly and very forthright in her way, she did not mince her words.

'You are with child Helena'. It was not a question but a statement which required an answer.

'I am, 'I replied, and burst into a flood of pent-up tears.

'How far along?' she queried.

'About four months' I mumbled into the apron with which I was wiping the tears and snot from my face. I felt that I had in some way let her down.

'Please tell me you did not think that I would help you out of your predicament.'

'Well... My dear child, even if I could, I would not, my husband when he was here had some skill and some custom in those matters, but in my eyes it is a sin before God to end a life.'

She sighed deeply and called Hannah to fetch tea.

'My husband did not mind that the gossips believed that it was I that disposed of the unwanted babies of the town, that they came to see me as some form of witch. You must go back to your home, to your family. If you stay here then it will bring shame on my house. Yes, you must go.'

I had pleaded with her. She had asked me who the father was and when I had remained silent she had placed a hand on my belly, a smile had crossed her face, but she had said nothing.

Hannah had told me that she had 'the sight' and could see things not visible to others and had knowledge of other worlds than ours. Yet, if she knew anything at all that might have helped me, she said nothing.

That night I packed my bag and left. On the long walk back over the mountain, I imagined what my reception would be at the Sun Inn. All hugs and welcome at first, then the village would find out that I was with child and the witch hunt would start. Who was the father? Assumptions would be made, and wrongly.

The gossips would brand me a whore. Idwal would try and silence them, Edward would be stuck in the middle. I would be called to the church and shamed in front of the congregation. No, I could not go home.

I took to the road, I found work where I could and for as long as I could, I walked to the coast to the seaside town of Aberystwyth and skivvied for an old lady called Nan Jenkins who lived on the outskirts of the town in a run-down old cottage. When my time came, she helped me to give birth to my daughter, it was she who wrote down the details of the birth in her own family bible and tore out the page for me to keep. Kind old soul she would have been happy for me to stay with her, her eyesight was gone, and she had no one else to do for her.

On the morning that I left I did not hear the tap of her old walking stick on the flagstone floor of the cottage as she made her way from bed to the outside privy. I made her tea and toast as usual and took it through to her room. The old lady was dead.

I bundled up my belongings and I left, pushing a note under the door of the first house I came to telling them what had happened. Then with my baby wrapped in Nan Jenkins's red shawl I faced the journey back to St Harmon.

I could not face the shame of it. So, I took refuge in the only place that I could think of. It was June I had been gone nearly a year.

CHAPTER 6 - THE PRODIGAL RETURNS - HELENA

I pulled my cloak about my shoulders and the hood over my head and crept slowly from doorway to doorway, keeping out of sight of the street, limping in the darkness for my boots had worn through and had blistered my feet. Carrying my precious bundle in my arms I paused in the doorway of the Sun Inn and checking that all was in darkness, I left a package in the porch, in the darkness and moved on.

I could so easily have let myself in using the key I knew would be under the large stone which held the door open for customers all day.

I could have let myself back in, but to what?

Through the village, onto the stony parish road which wound up the hill towards Hengwm. Past the farm gate for I would not burden Edward Meredith with my circumstances, and on into the woodland, through the brush through the prickly gorse bushes where the woodland gave way to mountain and through the narrow gap in the rock into the druid's cave.

The cave was at least dry, invisible from the track its entrance was sheltered by the yellow gorse, the entrance opened into a small cave which legend said had been used for practice of the dark arts of magic and pagan ritual. At its centre was a large almost circular stone balanced upon another large stone giving the appearance of an altar. I knew this cave well.

When the sun rose on certain days of the year, the feast days, then the light would shine through the cave entrance and strike the stone table at its centre. This was the time that the Druid Stone came to life – according to the stories handed down by the grandmothers of the village. These days no one paid any attention to these tales, they were old wives' tales, superstitions not to be taken seriously. Yet not even the local children went exploring in this particular rocky fissure. I knew without doubt that all they thought of as superstition was without doubt true.

Exhausted I placed my daughter wrapped in her warm red shawl on the druid stone. I felt the heat rise in the stone as it seemed to sense that one of its own was returning. I wanted no sanctuary from the stone for myself, I made a small fire in the back of the cave from where I could watch and wait and see if my faith would be rewarded. I remember a warmth coming over me and a calm and a terrible sadness. My ears heard him call and my body followed him. I truly thought that my child was with me, how could he leave her there to face life alone? Without her mother.

As the dawn broke over St Harmon casting its light into the entrance of the cave, bringing new life to the day, a long sigh left the body of Helena Lewis, an accompanying tear running down the hollow cheek of the wild child lost. Lying in the pool of sunlight on the druid's stone and wrapped in a red blanket was her child.

CHAPTER 7 - SHEARING TIME

It now was the end of June 1873. It was a warm summer. One crop of hay had been gathered and there was a possibility of a second cut in August. A good year for the farm.

Time now to gather the sheep for shearing, Edward's flock numbered some seventy hardy mountain ewes, they ran the mountain behind the house. Grazing on the mountain turf, tough survivors of the harsh winter weather. This weekend the men of the village and the surrounding farms would gather all the sheep in and pen them in the meadow for shearing. Once shorn of their wool they would be unceremoniously washed in the dip made by damming the stream below the house. A total of over a hundred sheep to be shorn and returned to their grazing. First to round up the sheep.

Edward saddled his tough Welsh cob Copper and rode off up the mountain. Whistling to Floss, his grey and white sheepdog, he headed for the top pasture. Up through the woods along the rough parish road and through the gorse bushes the sun was just lighting the mountain side, its light cast on the mouth of the druid's cave. Following the shadows made in the grass, the dog arrived at the fissure in the rock. Floss began to bark and whine at the entrance, unmoved by her master's calls and whistles. Her high-pitched bark demanded he pay attention.

Dismounting from Copper and tying the cob to a gorse bush at the cave's entrance, he manoeuvred his wide shoulders into the cave to be met by the whimpering of a baby, the barking of the dog and the sight of the wasted careworn body of Helena Lewis lying wrapped in her cloak. His stomach churned and he felt slightly sick with fear. She looked dead. There would be hell to pay for this.

The child was small, only a few weeks old. Fitting it snuggly into one of his saddle bags he slung the child and the bag in front of him, abandoned the sheep for the morning and rode for the village. How would he tell Idwal? What could he tell Idwal? It would break the man's heart. He knew what his daughter was, but like any doting father he wanted to believe the best of her and to know that she was safe. She had written, hadn't she. Of her good position and improved prospects?

In the depths of the darkness in the cave a shadow stirred heard only by the pale, wasted figure on the floor, a voice whispered. "I am here, follow me!"

CHAPTER 8 - A PLACE IN THE SUN

Idwal had risen at his usual time, had his breakfast, visited the privy, tidied around the bar area, scrubbed down the tables and the counter, washed the stray left-over tankards, fed the horse, the dog and the large grey cat which had been his late wife's constant companion, a useless mouser it spent all day sunning itself on the bedroom windowsill.

He put a saucer of milk out for the ginger feral cat which cleared up the vermin, but which never came indoors That was a proper cat, according to Idwal.

Then he opened the front door which led into the porch. There was a letter wedged in the door jam, a folded document, and a single sheet of paper. The note was brief, only three words.

Dearest Dada
I am sorry.

The document was the flyleaf torn from an old-fashioned family bible. The details filled in with homemade ink in a faint spidery hand,

Mother: Helena Lewis
Father: Not Named
Born 10th June 1873
Name: Sybil Helena

Idwal held the letter and the document in front of him, looking in blank amazement.

'Oh, Daughter what did you do? Why did you not tell me?'

The sound of horses' hooves drawing to a stop in front of him, brought him to his senses. Edward Meredith dismounted from his cob in something of a flurry, mouthing words at him in consternation.' Cave! baby, Helena!' He handed Idwal the saddle bag. 'You have a grandchild – but Helena – Helena…. he never finished the sentence. I must go back.

Curtains had twitched as the village awoke to the commotion outside the Inn. Edward's horse was surrounded by curious neighbours all intent on finding out what was the cause of the to-do!

'No!' The cry left Idwal's lungs like the cry of a wounded animal.

'Take me to her, man, why did you leave her there.

Edward handed the saddle bag to Mrs Hughes, one of the more responsible villagers, one who knew what to do with a baby, her having five of her own.

Then with Idwal riding behind him on Copper the cob they set off back up the mountain to the cave. Edward tied Copper to the same gorse bush and both men made their way into the cave. The sun had moved, and the light no longer shone in through the entrance.

There, was the Druid stone, immediately inside the narrow entrance of the cave. And there lying by the remains of the small fire was – nothing. The cave was empty. No sign of Helena, no sign of a body.

They searched the cave, this did not take long – there were no hiding places, few nooks and crannies and no way out other than the entrance.

'Are you sure she was dead?' Idwal asked Edward.

'She was lying there, white as stone, wrapped in her cloak. The babe was crying but she didn't move to see to the child, she had the look of death on her.'

'She can't have gone far, we must search, call the men out, search the mountain!'

The men of the village turned out and, organised by Idwal and Edward, they searched the mountain side as best they could, working in small groups, each with a small area to cover. By dusk they had all returned to the Inn, all with the same news. There was no sign of the landlord's daughter.

CHAPTER 9 - THE HOUSE AT PEN Y BANC
1873 - IDWAL

The last time I had heard from my daughter had been when she had taken employment with the Witch of Rhayader for that is all I knew of Mrs Eliza Jones. Maybe she would know at least where my daughter was headed, for scandal or no scandal I would have her at home.

I determined to ride to Rhayader. On a borrowed horse I rode into the town, it was market day, the main street was filled with stalls selling their wares, the sheep market was in full swing, the inns and hostels were full to bursting but every enquiry after Mrs Eliza Jones and Pen y Banc House was met with stony silence. Had my daughter ever worked there, did the place even exist?

Eventually Joshua the Ostler at the Bear Hotel broke the web of silence. Joshua was a bright lad who had been born in the north and posted to the area with the army, he had been discharged when he lost half his right hand and half his right foot in an accident with a cannon.

He said that he knew Mrs Jones and spoke well of her, she had treated his hand, still hoping to retain his fingers, she had re set the bones for him, painful at the time but now at least he could flex them and could still write and hold a set of reins when required.

He enthused about Mrs Jones, but his enthusiasm came with a warning to be careful how I approached the Jones house for she was wary of visitors.

I rode down East Street and out of town, heading for a house described as at the top of the long hill, surrounded by a high wall and trees and with huge iron gates. The very sight of the house made me uncertain of my welcome. The gates were open, I dismounted and led the horse up to the large green front door, tethered her to the post at the bottom of the steps, took my heart in his mouth and the large brass door knocker in my hand and knocked.

It seemed like an hour, but it was only a few minutes and the door opened slightly. A maid dressed in a smart burgundy and cream uniform ushered me in to the hall and instructed me to wait, while she told the mistress I was there.

I sat on the hard wooden seat a bit like a naughty child waiting outside the headmaster's office and listened to the tick of the long case clock which stood under the sweeping staircase of this impressive house.

As I sat, I heard the clock chime the quarter hour twice and then heard its baritone voice as it marked the hour. Only then did I hear the rustle of old silk and petticoats at the top of the stairs.

Eliza Jones was a harsh looking woman, tall, thin, and gaunt. Her black hair scraped back in a severe bun and topped with a square of lace held in place with a hair pin with an ebony bird at its blunt end.

Her eyes were as beady as a raven's, she was dressed in a high-necked dress in black silk which rustled as she walked. A chatelaine of keys hung at her waist, and a silver barrelled shotgun was held broken over her left arm. It was loaded I could see the gleam of the cartridge in the barrel, likely only with bird shot, but you couldn't be too careful!

'Mr Idwal Lewis?' She enquired, the voice was cultured, very English in its accent and precise in diction.

'Come in, welcome to Pen y Banc, may I offer you refreshment, some tea perhaps' without waiting for response she snapped her fingers and the maid appeared as if by magic 'Hannah, see to it will you'

Hannah, for that was the maid's name, disappeared through a baize door concealed under the stairs and out to what I presumed was the kitchen.

I was ushered into a room at the foot of the stairs at the front of the house. The furniture was dark wood and heavy dark green damask and velvet, the room itself had high ceilings, but the curtains were closed allowing little light. My eyes grew accustomed to the gloom, and I could see along one wall a Welsh dresser the upper part a bookcase filled with books, there was a piano in the centre of the room and in an alcove by the fire a Welsh Harp gleamed with gilded decoration.

Mrs Jones bade me sit by a small table near the curtained bay window. She sat down on the overstuffed chair opposite.

'I have come in search of my daughter.' I opened the conversation.

'I know why you have come, Mr Lewis', came the reply.' I am afraid I cannot help you. Your daughter is gone.'

'Was she here then?' I asked, wary now not to disclose what I thought he knew of this fearsome lady, who was obviously not telling him everything.

'She came here, yes, a lovely girl but not suited to service, too headstrong, not willing to do as she was asked, quite wild in fact. She had a talent though, for my art. I would have taught her – I am a healer you know in my own right but then I had to let her go.'

'Why did she go?' – I asked, head in hands, knowing the answer before it came.

'It became obvious that she was with child, The words hit the atmosphere like blocks of ice. '

'I could not have such shame in my house – she would be shunned, shamed before God in the chapel, any house sheltering her would suffer the same fate.'

'She asked me if I could rid her of the child. That is not my business, for shame, I could not do what she asked, it would be a sin before God.'

'So where did she go?'

'I do not know, she left before dawn the following day, she came with nothing and left the same way.'

'How could you, turn a child out to starve, and her only sixteen years old?'

'I presumed she would go home, wherever home was. I would not have taken a girl had she not been from good family, she came with references from Isaias Rees, I expected her to go back to St Harmon, she left some months ago, has she not returned!'

Idwal rose from his seat as the maid appeared with the tea things. He made to leave but was waved impatiently to sit, by this imperious woman.

'Sit, Mr Lewis, take tea with me, I do not have many visitors since my husband went away. People seem, well, loath to come here, things were so different before. The path to our door was well trodden then. But I live amongst superstitious people, who thrive on gossip and rumour. I have no doubt you were warned not to come here. '

I was handed a cup of tea in a bone China cup. It rattled on its saucer in my large work worn hand, I was offered a plate of dainty sandwiches and my host began once again to speak.

'What I tell you now, must go no further, it may help you find your daughter for she is not dead. When Helena told me that she was with child, I laid hands on her belly, I sensed that the child would be safe. I also sense that your daughter is alive, but she is gone. Your wife - her mother – she disappeared many years ago, did she not? She calls her daughter to her from her own place in time, where she will be safe. I have seen this when I gazed into the crystal, I felt the child in your daughter's belly, I sensed that she is also of these people. Your wife and daughter they are not of this world, and neither is your granddaughter, for years they have sought one with your granddaughter's talents and they will seek her out when she is of age, '

Eliza Jones seemed to have drifted into some form of trance, her voice had assumed a monotony which lulled him towards slumber. What might she have put into his tea?

In panic and fear I put down my cup and saucer and ran from the room upsetting the tea table in my haste. I found the maid already waiting with my coat and my horse still tied and waiting patiently outside the door.

I left Pen y Banc at a gallop, not even thinking about what I had been told.

CHAPTER 10 - MEANWHILE BACK AT THE INN

Mrs Davy Hughes had unwrapped the very vocal bundle which was stuffed unceremoniously into Edward Meredith's large leather saddle bag.

She had established that the child was a girl. She had not seen the birth certificate which had been left with Idwal. Having a young baby of her own and still breast feeding, she fed the hungry scrap and had settled her down in a drawer removed from the large chest of drawers in Idwals bedroom.

She was a tiny scrap of humanity, well-formed though with evidence of a head of curly red hair sprouting through the crown of her head in a dark red fuzz. Her eyes were blue and fixed Mrs Davy with an intense gaze, as she fed and then closed as the child breathed deeply in contentment and went to sleep.

The drawer was placed a discreet distance from the warm fire in the bar of the inn, it fitted nicely on the settle in the alcove between the chimney and the bar counter. Convenient for Idwal to watch over and quiet enough not to be woken by the noise. In the night it was moved upstairs to the room above the bar where any cries for attention could be heard and attended to without too much disturbance.

Mrs Davy sat with a mug of beer and watched the sleeping child as they waited for Idwal to return from lord knows where. In his absence Edward Meredith was running the bar and Mrs Davy had sent word to the neighbouring village for anyone who could wet nurse the child. She herself had no intention of taking on another infant.

Amongst the folds of the red blanket in which the child was wrapped was a small leather pouch, it contained a perfectly spherical opalescent moonstone, blue and purple in hue, polished to a shine and about the size of a man's fist. The birth stone for June.

Edward Meredith sat on the stool behind his friend's bar counter and turned the stone over in his hand. He mulled things over in his head and the only word that came from his mulling's over was.

'Tis Witchcraft'

He looked at the bible page which had been with Helena's note and then at the sleeping baby. He saw the beginnings of the red hair and had looked into the blue eyes.

He muttered to himself as he read the papers before him 'Sybil Helena – whose child are you!'

The door crashed open and Idwal walked into the bar, he was dishevelled and appeared terrified.

Edward passed him a tankard filled to the brim with the strongest of ales and watched him as he sat down, placed his head in his hands and wept.

CHAPTER 11 - MY CHILDHOOD - SIBYL

Time passed, years came and went, I became part of the daily life of the Sun Inn. I learned to crawl amongst the legs of the furniture and to walk by holding on to those same chair and table legs.

My grandfather Idwal had engaged a number of the older girls of the village to look after me while he worked, but I had grown up amongst the chatter of the bar and the consumption of ale. I was taught my numbers by a series of uncles using counters, dominos, and a pack of cards. I learned arithmetic from Grand da Idwal's accounts book, I had learned my letters from the news sheets of the day, when one could be had and from the big family bible which was written in Welsh and kept under the bed in what had been Idwal's wife's own room.

I was not allowed in the room itself; it was my grandmother's and was kept that way in hope that she may return.

My first word was "beer" or according to Idris Jenkins who sat in the corner every lunchtime, it was. He was a kind old man crippled with age and aching joints, he taught me to read from the books which Idwal kept behind the bar and my numbers from a pack of playing cards.

By the time I was five and ready to go to school I could already read and knew how to do basic mathematics. I was a tall girl with a shock of dark red curly hair the colour of a squirrel's tail and I was old beyond my years.

CHAPTER 12 - GOING TO SCHOOL - SIBYL

The local school in St Harmon was very small, well there were only about a dozen children of school age in the village. By that I mean between the ages of five and sixteen. There were more in numbers than this, but several were kept home to help on the land and do chores.

We spoke Welsh at home, all of us, but school was taught in English – there was a punishment for speaking Welsh in school. Anyone caught speaking what the English called a barbarous language would be made to stand at the front of class with a board on a piece of string hanging round their neck. This board bore the letters WN – Welsh Not! The head teacher, Mr Edgar would humiliate the wearer, if he was in a bad mood then the offender would get three stripes of his cane across the hand as well, just for good measure.

In general Mr Edgar only taught the boys, they got the worst of him. There were many sore backsides from his cane by a Friday, and many of the lads seen disappearing up the mountain to nurse their wounds and cry in privacy.

We girls were taught by Miss Williams, Jenny Williams, she was lovely, all smiles and kindness and taught us our letters and our numbers, reading in English of course and also in our own tongue though books in Welsh were hard to come by. Beyond this, girls were just taught to be decorative and learned to keep house and home. Cook, clean, get married, raise a family. Was that really all I could be expected to do. This was not a life I wanted.

I loved the countryside, the wild hills around the village, I was drawn to the mountains, never happier than roaming in the woodland which followed the valley up to the flat field at the top of the mountain which seemed to run endlessly on into the distance. All the way to infinity.

CHAPTER 13 - OWAIN - SIBYL

Owain the Mountain, Owain y Mynydd made his home in an old out building at the end of the village just down from the Church yard, the building had once been used by the gravediggers as a store shed. He had been found wandering by Mrs Old Mrs Pryce just outside the village at about the age of five years. He did not know where he had come from only that his name was Owain, though it was suspected that his parents had been from one of the villages nearby which had been ravaged by the blazing shits, as dysentery was known.

The Pryce family lived in a bow top caravan in the same field and made a living by dealing horses and ponies which they bought, broke in to be ridden or to pull a cart and then sold on. The Pryce family had arrived in the field at the far end of the village when I was five and set to go to school. Owain had wandered into our community a few weeks later.

The Pryce family had been one of several families who had made their home in the field. All but the Pryce's had moved on and they had gladly taken on the abandoned urchin who was Owain. It was them who had given him the name of y Mynydd, for he was of the mountain. He had spent several months living with them in the Bow Top before constructing his own makeshift shelter in the gravediggers' shed.

Mrs Pryce, Magdalena, or Ena as she was known was a large lady with a huge bosom and a friendly manner. She cooked over an open fire outside their caravan, all manner of things, always filling and mouth wateringly delicious, she was a great cook and I loved to stay to eat with them. It made a change from Grand da Idwal's efforts, usually burned offerings.

Owain was slightly younger than I. Though we were both five years old, he was new to the village and the other children were suspicious of him. They teased him for his strange accent and his house in the shed.

Tommy Pryce wanted him to go to school, and Owain dearly wanted to go, so when Tommy Pryce brought him to the Sun Inn one morning as I was leaving to walk to that house of education, I took him by the hand, and we walked together.

Dark haired with intense green eyes which sparkled when he laughed, and the runniest nose in the village, he and I hit it off straight away. He was fiercely independent and thought that he knew everything. I helped him with his schooling when he needed help for he was a bright boy, quick at numbers if a little slow with his writing. He could add and subtract in his head like lightning.

After school he would show me the snares he had set in the woodland to catch rabbits, introduced me to his mongrel dog Jack who he took hunting with him, using him to flush out the rabbits from their homes.

And not forgetting Fergal, a wriggly slightly nasty looking ferret, pale yellow in colour with pink eyes and long sharp fanglike teeth. Left by one of the older Pryce lads, Fergal did not like to be handled and had been known to bite ferociously, and he stank, like a polecat, appropriate, for that is what he was. Fergal's main aim in life was to escape from his master's custody and disappear down the nearest rabbit hole.

It was Owain who taught me to shoot with a bow and arrow, to catch and skin rabbits and cook them and I taught him how to ignore the children who taunted him, for he had a swift temper and would fight any boy big or small who called him tinker, or paddy or other bad names about the Irish. He may live with Ma and Pa Pryce, he said, but he was not Irish. Where he actually came from was a mystery.

By the time we were both twelve years old, Owain had grown to be a tall well-built boy with broad shoulders, a handsome face with a broad smile and still the deep sparkling green eyes. Now he dealt horses with Tommy Pryce at weekends, travelling with him to the horse fairs, and our adventures were curtailed unless I helped with the handling of the smaller ponies.

That summer we had spent riding the newly broken youngsters around the valley and the hillside. We had shared our first kiss together and become closer than ever before. As the nights became lighter, we stayed out later into the evening, cooking what we had caught over an open fire, drinking from the clear streams higher up in the hills and playing in the secret waterfall which was at the head of the rocky valley above Hengwm. I think I fell in love with Owain then, he was my soul mate, though nothing ever went any further than the most decorous of kisses, I knew that I would be tied to him forever by some form of invisible string which was attached inexorably to my heart.

I wished that summer could be endless but after haymaking had finished and it was time to go back to school, Idwal decided that my days of wandering the hills must come to an end.

I was now a woman, my courses had started, Owain became the devil in Idwal's eyes, so protective was he of my virtue. Always in the back of his mind the fate of my mother.

Owain had decisions to make as well, he had no people of his own so when Tommy Pryce offered him a job and a family to call his own, Owain took the chance with both hands.

CHAPTER 14 – AN ILL-ADVISED ADVENTURE – SIBYL

Before my adventure to Aberystwyth, Mrs Pryce had invited me into the bow top, and read my palm.

What she told me made no sense, I was destined to travel, I would go far and live long, and then she gazed into her crystals and told me that there were those who would seek me out, that they were far away, but could see me and hear me, as I would hear them, that they meant me no harm, to follow my heart and use my head and never be afraid for there was one who would always watch over me.

I believed that she was referring to the Lord Jesus and that he would watch over me as he watched over me as he watched over all children.

Then she told me that they were leaving, the family, she said, was to return to Ireland. In the morning they were gone. Maybe it was this news that made me trek over the hills to the coast. Maybe I thought I could see Owain's new home from my vantage point on the hill, get a last sight of the little bow top van pulled by the coloured horse as my only friend left me. Whatever it was, Idwal was not best pleased, and my life was about to change.

When Owain left I was bereft, I cried for days and when I had finished crying, I walked the hills on my own, visiting the places where I had been with my soul mate and my only true friend. If he was a friend why would he leave me, why wouldn't he stay, he could have lived at the Sun with me and Idwal, he could have found work on one of the farms.

Owain wasn't like that, he was a free spirit, with the Pryces he would be free. Maybe he would come back. I felt in my soul that he would. I just needed to see him one more time.

I had learned to ride almost as soon as I could walk, 'Uncle Edward', as I came to call Edward Meredith owned a herd of mountain ponies which grazed on the field at the top of the mountain. One of them was an old riding pony called ginger, he was at least twenty years old, steady, and sure footed as a goat. Uncle Edward had been given him by the local minister to be retired, he had been ridden by the elderly preacher's children and pulled the pony trap for The Rev Miles. He had also been ridden by my mother before she disappeared. One more adventure, just one more, maybe I would come across Owain and the Pryce family, maybe they would take me with them.

Riding Ginger I explored further afield, across the moorland all the way to Aberystwyth, I got into terrible trouble for that, but it was worth it – to see the sea crashing up onto the shore and look out across the endless ocean towards Ireland and then America. Places we had only been told of from books, and from my best friend Owain's tales of fairies and folklore.

I had left early in the morning, before the sun was up and headed West and followed the wind, there were few tracks across the moorland turf and, had I known it, I was riding across land peppered with areas of invisible treacherous bog. The weather could change in a heartbeat from the sunny skies and breeze I had set out in to howling winds and rain, or thick sea fog so dense you would never see a way home.

I had ridden all day, only stopping to rest Ginger and to eat my apple and piece of cheese, letting my mount graze for an hour and drink from the stream. It had taken me nearly half the day to get to the hilltop above the seaside town, with its promenade, the college and line of tall houses and elegant promenade stretching like a ribbon along the coast. I did not dare to ride into the town, I stood on the hill above with Ginger resting his old whiskered chin on my shoulder, and I thought about what it would be like to go to a real university and learn, to find a way out of what I was destined to be. I loved the land, I loved my life as it was now as a child but the thought of never venturing further than the village or maybe the nearest town Rhayader, well that was not for me. There is a great wide world out there,

66

and I wanted to see at least some of it. Destiny pah! I would make my own!

It was past dusk when I got within sight of St Harmon on my return journey, but it was not the lights of the village that greeted me, it was the lights of the search party.

Grand da Idwal, Uncle Edward and all the men were out, with lanterns calling out my name, sending their dogs into the woods to search, beating the bushes with their walking sticks.

Idwal had only ever taken the strap to me twice in my life before, and from the look on his face now, I feared that there would be a third time!

I winced in the saddle at the thought of it. The first time I had been eleven years old. Idwal had caught me climbing out of the window to play with my best friend Owain – Idwal did not approve of Owain.

Owain lived with the Irish family who had made their home on the common land at the end of the village, not far from the Inn. They had arrived. Owain was what Idwal called trouble on legs – he was always dirty, his nose running, his face covered in unidentifiable dirt, clothes always in need of repair, he was also light fingered. Tommy Pryce would take him into town most weekends and always on market day and set him to work stealing watches and wallets from the wealthy. He could also trap rabbits and fire a gun and shoot a bow and arrow.

Owain y Mynydd – Idwal said he could only ever end up on the end of a rope or being transported to

Australia. Which, in Idwal's opinion was the best place for him.

Owain and I were inseparable, and he was as clever as me. We were both streets ahead of our classmates, me the abandoned child and Owain the gypsy for that is what he seemed to be. We formed a bond which would never be broken, we looked out for each other. Idwal had issued six of the best with his belt that night.

The second time was when I had left the beer tap running in the cellar wasted a whole keg of ale, and flooded the place with it, another six with the strap for 'having my head in the clouds', and the rest of the day cleaning up the mess.

That had been only a few weeks ago, just before my birthday. Now as I saw his old, weathered face, ashen with worry, I feared the worst.

Ginger pulled up short at the head of the path, just as it dropped away into the woods, ears pricked he had snorted slightly seeing the lanterns coming towards him. I heard Idwal shout and saw him pass his torch to Edward and then he was running up the path towards me, pulling me from the back of a slightly perturbed Ginger. He stood me away from him, and then I saw that he was crying.

'Where on earth do you think you have been' and the onward litany of dangers and pitfalls of going alone across the mountains, and only twelve, and what about that poor pony, and how worried he'd been.' It all came burbling out in one breath.

Finishing with - let's get you home safe, we shall talk in the morning.

CHAPTER 15 - DISCUSSING THE FUTURE – SIBYL

We talked, all morning we talked. Idwal could see that I wanted more from my life than to take over the running of the Inn when he got too old, he could see that I wanted to better myself. But there were things he was not saying.

He refused to talk about my mother and why she had left, was she dead, I had always been told that she was not, that she might come back, every birthday I had waited for her to return, every Yuletide, every special occasion, but she had not. I had long since given up on tears for my mother.

I was twelve years old, I had four more years of compulsory school and then what. I told Grand da Idwal that I wanted to be a healer, I was fascinated with Mr Rees's apothecary shop in Rhayader, I wanted to see more of the world, go to college make something of myself. Idwal thought long and hard, no Lewis had ever aspired to do anything other than tend bar and serve beer and anecdotes to customers, he huffed and puffed and decided that I should continue my schooling.

Girls were not sent to the grammar school in Rhayader that was a boarding school for boys only, but he made enquiries with the school who recommended a lady who sometimes took on pupils at her home. Was this destiny or coincidence? The lady in question was Mrs Eliza Jones.

Idwal scratched his head and again thought long and hard about his last dealings with Mrs Jones. She had not been such a bad old stick he thought, a bit hard faced but obviously from her fine library of books and her educated ways, and from what Josh the Ostler had told him, she was a fine healer and not a woman who would allow a girl to stray into the ways of the flesh.

The school's head teacher further informed Grand Da that Mrs Jones had been married to Dr Richard Jones, who was an associate of Dr William Price of Llantrisant who believed himself a Druid.

Dr Jones, Eliza Jones' husband, had fled to the continent rather than face the authorities for his involvement in Dr Price's actions in cremating the body of his son. Both had also been involved in the supply of weapons to the chartist movement. They had been great pioneers for better working conditions in the industrial heartlands, advocates both for fair wages and better housing. Dr Price had been acquitted having made a case that cremation was widespread in other religions and was only a religious practice and not a criminal offence. His involvement in the supply of arms to the Newport rioters could not be proven and he had resumed his practice of medicine in his own fashion. Dr

Jones had not returned and was believed to have eventually made a new life for himself in America, leaving Eliza to fend for herself.

Grand Da was reassured that Eliza Jones, while strict, was a fair woman and a fine tutor who would teach me the sciences at which I excelled, as well as the knowledge of healing and herbal medicines I would need if I was to pursue my ambitions to be a healer.

I could never be a fully qualified doctor for that was thought unseemly for a woman. But I could be just as good as a herbalist and healer, as long as I did not get mistaken for a witch.

Mrs Jones would not take me until I was sixteen years old, until then I would have to do my chores, go to school, and learn what I could about herbs and their uses from Mr Rees, the apothecary in Rhayader, he had an opening for a girl to work at the shop at weekends and so I could ride over on Friday after school and ride back on Sunday after chapel. Ginger would be well looked after with the fine grazing in Mr Rees's orchard.

I'm sure Idwal thought that this arrangement would keep me out of trouble and away from Owain.

But in any case, Owain was gone, along with his family. I missed him dearly with all my heart. Before I went I had given him the birthstone which my mother had left with me. He promised that he would never forget me and that we would someday meet again. I felt my heart breaking as I saw the Pryce Family and Owain leave our village, Life would never be the same again.

CHAPTER 16 - MR REES'S SHOP. - SIBYL

Isaias Rees owned a shop on the Main Street in Rhayader, it was a double fronted property with two display windows, one either side of the front navy-blue front door and sign in jaunty blue and white above the door, proudly announcing Isaias Reese Apothecary and Purveyor of Herbal remedies.

The door opened inwards with the jingle of a bell to a dark cavern of a shop with a polished wood counter in pride of place with a flap through leading to the back room – the still room where Mr Reese prepared his remedies.

My room was at the back of the premises, above the still room with a window looking out over the orchard at the back, where Ginger now grazed happily under the apple trees. The far end of the orchard was fenced off with sturdy fence and was accessed by a gate. It contained the herb garden, and three beehives. The fence was covered with the brightly flowered climbing plants from which the bees loved to collect pollen.

Bees are essential, Mr Rees truly believed this to be true. He also believed we must always tell them the news, lest they leave, and a world without bees would be a terribly sad place indeed.

Was this an old wife's tale or is it just that there is something very restful about sitting in a garden near the hives and telling your news, good or bad to the busy little workers who are flying amongst the flowers. Do they take your news and spread your problems, is a problem shared not a problem solved? Mr Rees spent many hours with his bees, collecting the honey, telling them the town gossip, chiding them for buzzing too close to his face, watching them as they crawled up his shirt sleeves, he never seemed to get stung, the bees seemed to know he meant them no harm. I watched and learned and in time the bees came to treat me as their friend too.

Mr Rees was a lovely old gent, with a wide smiley face and bushy whiskers. He was short and slightly rotund and habitually dressed in tweed trousers with braces, a white shirt with no collar attached, collars were only for Sundays! His sleeves were pushed up with sleeve clips to keep them out of whatever liquid or potion he was dealing with.

If he was required to go out, then he would don jacket and waistcoat for the sake of respectability.

I would be expected to serve behind the shop counter, put up remedies for prescription written by the local doctor, and eventually to read the big receipts book, the book of recipes for the various salves and medicines which were made on the premises. I would learn their uses and how to make them. This book was always kept on its own table in the still room. It had been filled up over many many years and was in Mr Reese's opinion more use to man than the bible, but please don't tell that to the Reverend Edwin Davies, he really would not approve.

I began by familiarising myself with the jars and old bottles behind the counter. Some salves were dispensed in their own stone pots and customers would keep the pots and return them for re-filling. These needed to be washed clean and then put away in their own storage cupboard ready for re-filling.

Powders were weighed on a brass scale and dispensed in a twist of waxed paper.

Medicines, in glass or stone bottles again brought back for re-use by the patient.

Poisons were kept in a locked cupboard in the still room. Mr Rees had a good stock of deadly poisons used for killing vermin, a record of each sale of such things was kept in a separate register. Recording the buyer's name, address, the amount of the substance and it's intended use. Farmers usually, or the local innkeepers keeping down the rodent population in their storerooms. But there had been times when a wife or a husband had died suddenly in mysterious circumstances, and it was best to have a record for the constable when he came calling. I loved working for Mr Rees, I became part of the family, his wife, a quiet shy lady lived upstairs over the shop, and they had a son who had grown up and ran another similar shop in Newtown. William was ten years older than I, very like

75

his father in his ways, but a bit more formal in his attitude. Collars in Newtown were for every day, jacket was always required, in fact William Rees was a bit of a fashion statement. Smartly tailored suit and tie topped off with a jaunty hat. He would call in to see his father once a month and leave with supplies for his shop of those things he did not make himself, he arrived in a pony and trap and usually stayed for the weekend, returning on a Monday.

On these weekends I would stay and make myself useful, then tie Ginger to the back of the trap and have a lift back home with Mr William.

Time at the shop in Rhayader flew by and soon it was time to move on to Mrs Jones' tutelage.

CHAPTER 17 - ELIZA JONES 1889 – SIBYL

Pen y Banc was a fine double fronted stone-built house, set as the name suggests at the top of the bank, this being the hillside just outside the small market town of Rhayader.

It was set in large tree filled grounds, a gravelled driveway leading to a grass area in front of the front door large enough for a turning point for a horse drawn carriage, the driveway was bordered by large trees and the spring sunshine showed signs that crocus, daffodil and snowdrops dwelled in the woodland.

The double front doors were now painted a deep fashionable navy blue, with brass fittings, including a bell pull to one side and a huge brass knob in the centre.

While the house portrayed a very formal exterior, the interior was well worn and comfortable, a morning room of overstuffed cushions and chintz.

The wood panelled entrance hall with its formal chairs was about as welcoming as a trip to the headmaster's office she thought. The hall was the domain of the most marvellous long case clock. It stood taller than a guardsman at attention against the tallest wall in the stair well. It's tick could be heard throughout the house like a heartbeat measuring the pace of the inhabitants' lives. The clock was seemingly as old as time itself, passed down, Mrs Jones said, through the female side of her family, it was hers, passed to her from her mother, and her grandmother before that. Wound every Saturday, it marked each hour with a baritone 'bong' and each quarter hour with a melody of chimes. Mrs Jones polished and wound it herself not trusting anyone else with this task. Sad, she said that there was no one to leave it to when she died.

The kitchen was accessed through a baize covered door situated under the stairs, the province of Hannah who seemed to do everything other than care for the clock, it had a large range hung over with hooks for pots and kettles, a large scrubbed wooden table in the centre, and under the large sunny window which looked down the rear garden towards the herb garden and the still room, was a white stone sink.

The pantry was off to one side an featured a large stone, cold slab and hanging from the clothes airer which was pulleyed up and down from the ceiling were bunches of herbs in various stages of drying.

The only other room at the rear of the house, and with doors opening put onto the rear garden was the library. The library was glorious, only small it occupied the whole of this room at the back of the house, it's tall windows looking down the slightly overgrown garden at the rear, doors opening out onto the grass.

Where the rest of the house was slightly unkempt and dusty, this room gleamed, the huge desk under the window shone from hundreds of years of polishing, it's leather writing surface deep cherry red, marked with the occasional careless ink blot like the scars of life has left on an old friend.

Bookshelves lined three walls, floor to ceiling, leather bound volumes some hardly ever opened, some well-worn with use, but all revered and cared for.

Grey's Anatomy – four inches thick, leather bound and illustrated, diagrams of the human body and its organs, their function, drawn in detail for the student to see. Muscles and bones labelled with their scientific names; their workings detailed in print.

She ran her hand across the spine with reverence perhaps seeking to gain the knowledge contained there by absorption.

The Herball – published in 1597 a thick, ancient leather-bound volume detailing the uses of plants in medicine written by the herbalist John Gerard, illustrated with drawings of the plants, where they could be found, and their uses.

A copy of Richard Brooks family herbal all five hundred pages and only recently published in comparison – 1850 at least being in this century.

And even a book written by a man called Bartram – whose garden in the colonies of America was famous for its diversity of medicinal herbs and plants.

Book upon book, magazines and publications and other volumes. One written by Mrs Jones herself. bound in scruffy green buckram, handwritten like a diary, and filled with strange diagrams, it was called A Grimoire. A textbook of magic, instructions on how to create magical objects like talismans and amulets, how to perform magical spells, make charms and divination, and how to summon and invoke the supernatural, angels, demons, deities, and spirits.

Of these books there were two, the second being an altogether different style of volume thicker, nearly twice as thick and bound in expensive leather, with gold inlay, its pages were of old parchment, made from treated animal skin, the writing done with a quill and ink made from charcoal and tree gum. There was only a name embossed in worn gold on the front and the spine.

M de C.

I raised an eyebrow at this antique curiosity, no doubt my employer and mentor was a collector of such things, a fascinating read no doubt.

Alongside it on the shelf a slimmer volume, older but just as loved, the gold inlay of the title nearly worn away. The authors name hard to read, Fraser – yes that was it, Sibyl squinted at the spine Dr C.B.R Fraser – published 1778 Edinburgh. She drew the book from the shelf and opened the front cover, slowly as if the author might leap out and bite her. The printing was quality work, the fly leaf illustrated with an engraving by the noted engraver, A Bell, an image of the author, a woman! Surely not!

Now was 1889, medical school was not for women, though Mrs Jones - Eliza had told her of some ladies in

London who sought to change this, by setting up a school for the training of women. Some fifteen years ago Elizabeth Garret Anderson had established a medical school in London which allowed women to graduate. That was London not rural Wales. I would take the opportunities afforded locally and do my best with what was to be my destiny.

The face of Dr C B R Fraser leapt at me from the page, this was a practical book, well before it's time, a guide to good health, tips on how to avoid illness and disease, how to stay healthy, there were chapters of simple effective treatments for common illnesses using the herbs and products readily available to everyday folk.

The voice of Eliza Jones spoke to me from the library door – 'yes, 'it said 'she was very much before her time, she was English, but lived in America, in North Carolina, married a Scot, fascinating history, so far ahead of her time, many believed her a witch. The book came from a printing house in Edinburgh, it was one of a few special editions which the printer had kept, I acquired it when the shop was sold. There's a letter in the back, a record of the whole order, most were printed in affordable buckram binding and sent by ship to the colonies. It was a book to be used!'

The face of Dr Claire Fraser spoke to me from the pages of history, this book seemed to call me home. 'There is another book with it, I keep them together, it's altogether different, but still fascinating in its way'.

My eye went to the next volume in the line.

'Grandfathers Tales by J.A.M.M Fraser' it did indeed feel that these two books, published in the same year, were inextricably linked, not to be parted. 'Her husband?'

'Yes, I believe so', replied Eliza 'so I keep them together, I've read both, she was very capable, and he, well his tales will make you laugh'.

There were also books by Charles Dickens and Jane Austen and other authors of the time, I felt that I was at last at home.

I sighed. I would be happy here. Mrs Eliza Jones was not what everyone thought, at least not all of it. She lifted the bag which contained my few possessions and made her way up to her bedroom in the loft.

'Come down when you're ready' a voice called up the stairs 'Hannah has made supper. Oh, and call me Mother Jones or Mother Eliza or just plain Ma'.

I dropped my bag on the bed – making a cursory scan of a cosy room with a small bed, a chest of drawers for my clothes, a mirror, and a washstand. Luxury indeed compared to my room at the Sun Inn.

I was sixteen years old, and I was here to learn all that Mother Eliza could teach me, to make something of my life, even if I could not obtain the hallowed letters MD after my name, I would be the next best thing. I had all the knowledge I had gained from my work at the Apothecary in Rhayader, old Mr Isaias Rees had taught me the basics of how to prepare remedies and their uses, I did not know what exactly Mother Eliza would teach me, but I was here to learn. My days of running the hillsides were truly over unless it was to forage for plants.

CHAPTER 18 – ELIZA'S STILL ROOM - SIBYL

The still room was separate from the house, in fact it was in a building which had once housed the pigs. A long low building now adapted as what was to all intents and purposes a laboratory.

The brick floor was still there, now scrubbed hygienically clean, the walls were lined with wooden benches and large glass fronted cupboards filled with slightly scary and barbaric looking implements used in surgery. Tools for extracting teeth, amputation saws, a trepan for making holes in the skull to relieve pressure. Drawers filled with scalpels and knives, retractors and tenacula, curved needles stored ready threaded with silk thread in pots of alcohol for stitching. This had been her husband's realm before it was hers. And in pride of place at a raised plinth in the best of the light, her microscope.

The water pump was conveniently placed outside. And the windows had been enlarged to make a light and airy room from which one could see down the long garden to the house and into the kitchen. This was where Eliza treated the patients who came to her. Not so many nowadays after the scandal involving her husband and his partner Dr William Price.

Eliza's husband Dr Richard Jones had been great friends with Dr William Price of Llantrisant. The furore which had occurred after the Druidic cremation of Dr Price's son, contrary to all the social and religious mores of the time and their involvement in the Chartist movement seeking better conditions for the workers in the Iron and Coal works had led to both men fleeing the country for a period of time. Whilst William Price had returned and resumed his activities, Richard had disappeared. Eliza had neither seen nor heard from him for several years.

His disappearance had caused all manner of gossip and rumour in the locality. Superstition was rife, and Eliza once considered a fine healer, midwife and the good doctors able helper was now suspected of everything from murder to witchcraft. The latter being the far more serious crime in some peoples books.

These days the local folk would rather struggle through a dangerous birth risking death of themselves and their child than call on the services of Mother Eliza. Wounds which could have been healed with a few well-placed stitches and a salve were left to suppurate, broken limbs were left to heal in splints, un-straightened and healing twisted.

Maybe I could change things for her, make the townsfolk see her a little differently.

I was, after all, Mr Rees the apothecary's helper, folk would ask after me, and I would still be back and fore to the shop if not working there.

It was an all-female household, the only other resident being Hannah the maid who at the age of twenty did all the household chores, cooking, cleaning, and laundry – which I was expected to help with as part of my keep. I would stay with Mother Eliza for two years until I was eighteen and then I would be free to pursue my own future as a healer, wherever this might take me. I learned all manner of things from Mother Eliza.

I had been at Pen y Banc nearly two years when Dr William Price came to call on Eliza Jones. He was then a very old man - ninety-one years old. Though he did not seem that age. He came with news for Mother Eliza, he had had word from America that her husband, Richard, was now practicing medicine in New York. He had a fine practice and had finally written to his wife asking her to join him. Eliza was elated. Not knowing how his news would be taken he had written to his good friend and asked him to call upon his wife to beg her to make the journey to the New World.

There followed a flurry of activity, hasty plans to sell Pen y Banc, readily bought for a large sum of cash by Isaias Rees, it had everything he wanted in a home, and a large herb garden and surgery into which he could expand his empire. Hannah would stay, Mr Rees would employ her, and I would go to Llantrisant and continue my studies there. I was now eighteen years of age it was 1891. I had no plans to marry, I would learn what Dr

Price could teach me and, who knows, I might go to London. Maybe there would be a place for me in the newly opened college of medicine.

CHAPTER 19 - WITH THE SUN BEHIND ME - SIBYL

At the beginning of the year, before I left, I received news that Idwal had died. New people had taken over at The Sun Inn and I was cordially required to see to the removal of all personal effects from the property such as were not to be purchased as part of the business.

Idwal Lewis was buried in the churchyard at St Harmon. His funeral was attended by the whole village. There was not a person who did not come to pay their respects to the stubborn old fool who had kept the community supplied with ale and a place to talk about their woes for over half a century. A notice of his death was placed in the local paper for posterity and the reverend Miles waxed lyrical about his life, avoiding the minefield which was the absence of any family other than myself.

Edward Meredith was there, old now and snowy haired, great whiskers growing from his cheeks, he helped to carry Grand Da's coffin to its resting place and read a eulogy written as a friend rather than a minister of the church. It got to the measure of the kind and generous man who would do a favour for anyone he thought needed it, would give you the shirt off his back, a man who loved life, had loved, and missed his beloved wife, and had then lost his only daughter. Edward spoke of Idwal's pride in me, his granddaughter and all he hoped I would achieve whether I chose to stay amongst my people or move on to pastures new.

The funeral was on a Monday March 2nd 1891 at 11:30am I remember that well, the day after St David's Day. The daffodils were just blooming in the hedgerows and the crocuses beneath the trees, and Idwal Rees was lowered below the ground.

There would be money found for a headstone, there was precious little for the funeral, Idwal and his accounts not being best friends since I had left. Though, no one thought to ask me to keep an eye on them.

Edward would have, no doubt, but Idwal was too proud and stubborn to ask. Now truly alone in the world I climbed the stairs to the little loft room which my grandmother had kept as her work room. The key was stiff in the lock as I turned it. This was the one room at the Sun Inn into which I was not allowed. This had been my grandmother's private room, a room where Idwal said she went to read and to write in her diary. The last time he had been there was when Bron had disappeared leaving him to care for their daughter, my mother Helena. After Helena had also disappeared leaving me behind as an infant, he had locked the little attic room with a large padlock. He feared that in its contents lay some great danger, an evil beyond witchcraft. Now Idwal was gone, and the contents of this small room were mine and mine alone. I turned the key in the lock, it stuck a little then fell open and I removed it from its hasp and drew back the bolt.

I pushed the ledge and brace door inwards lifting the catch as I did so. Cobwebs hung from the ceiling and decorated the furniture of this small intimate room where my grandmother had kept her books and her needlework.

It had no proper window only a skylight in the roof and a tiny window looking out towards the rear of the building and up towards the hillside, a piece of glass which Idwal had fixed in place of one of the slates. It was under the eaves of the living quarters above the inn next to the big chimney which held the main fire in the bar and above the ceiling of the room where she slept with her husband Idwal. The man she had married when no other man would have her.

I pushed back the cobwebs brushing them from my arms and face, 'It's all yours.', I could hear Idwal's voice over my shoulder. Talking to me from beyond his grave.

There were books piled on the floor, some novels which Idwal had bought her seeking to keep her happy or if not happy at least contented with the life he could give her. Some though were older leather bound with hand drawn pictures, books of ancient herbal remedies and yes spells.

The family bible was there, in it written the births deaths and marriages of the Lewis family down the

generations. I flipped through the pages to the back
flyleaf.

Idwal Lewis married Bronwen Rowlands

Helena Lewis born – 5th June 1857

Rowlands – that was a strange name for the area, my
grandmother was not a local girl then. And Helena –
yes, I could do the sums – She was born only six months
after the wedding.

Idwal had spoken often of that evening that Bron had
walked into his life, Idwal Lewis bachelor of the parish,
landlord of the Sun Inn. Idwal, homely looking,
personable, funny even, always a story or an anecdote.
Friend to most people but not afraid of a fight. Idwal
who was happy in his life and had no wish to be
married.

She had fallen in through the front door of the Inn
one winters evening, soaking wet and freezing cold,
wrapped in that most amazing of creations, her beloved
cloak. She was petite and curvy with long silver hair and
cornflower blue eyes. Dressed in a simple brown
woollen dress belted at the waist with a thick leather
belt, she had sat by the big fire and warmed herself,
steam rising from her clothing, she had no belongings
and had begged a room for the night. She had no
money, and would she said work to pay for her room,
she would do anything, she said. Cook, clean, serve at
the bar.

And so, she had done all those things, for once he
was not short of a clean shirt with no holes, for she
mended, and patched and laundered. He did not go

without meals when the bar was busy as either she would cook, or she would serve his customers.

The Inn positively sparkled, the windows were a new standard of clean, dust was dusted away, brass was polished.

She was charming and funny, she got on well with his regulars especially Edward Meredith with whom she seemed to have a bond. Though Edward insisted that he had never seen her in his life before.

After a month or so it became obvious that she was with child, did he want her to leave, no he didn't, damn her – he wanted her to stay, for ever.

On the child's father she remained close lipped. They married three weeks later on a sunny summer morning in the local church. Edward Meredith had walked Bron down the aisle, the wedding breakfast had been held in the yard of the Inn, the whole village had celebrated with them.

A week later the chest had arrived. Idwal had not questioned where it had come from, the carter had delivered it whilst delivering ale in barrels to the inn – it had, he said, appeared on his load the night before. His job was just to deliver it! Not ask questions.

Bron had had it carried up to her little work room in the eaves and there it had stayed apparently unopened by the look of the lock. There was a comfortable Windsor chair draped with Welsh blankets for warmth and padding in the recess alongside the fire, the red of the dye in the blanket faded to an orange over the years.

The embroidered cushion also faded from deep purple and vibrant greens in thread work to dull greys, though the intricacy of the stitching was still evident. Along the wall under the one small window filling the wall from end to end was the coffer as big as a man's coffin. This too was locked but the lock was fragile and broke easily under a slight pressure revealing its contents.

At one end was a partitioned box. Filled with thin leather-bound books – diaries. In the main body of the trunk were a bundle of what I thought to be clothes. The first item I removed was a cloak, heavy, velvet, deep blue nearly black in colour lined with animal fur, in the pelts of many different coloured species, the grey brown of rabbit, the red of squirrel and fox. It had a hood edged with ermine the black and white speckles adding a sumptuous look to this otherwise country made garment. It was fashioned from material salvaged from other places, curtains perhaps, or the cast-off dress of a great lady, the lining hunted and skinned, and the occupants probably eaten for their pains. Not a cloak made by a tailor or professional seamstress then.

Under the cloak was a bow made of willow and a quiver of arrows, a pair of breeches, a linen shirt with no arms, pair of light leather boots and a sturdy leather jerkin, well-worn and supple and very very old.

The coffer had arrived after their marriage, Idwal had said that Bron had spirited it away upstairs, and he had assumed it was her belongings, after all a bride must have belongings, mustn't she?

He had never seen the contents, he had asked, yes he had asked. Many times, out of curiosity, he had joked about what she might keep hidden in a box big enough to bury a man in and that he had no need to invest in a coffin for in that chest there was surely room for two.

In the days when Bron drifted off to her own world and spent days on end in her room, yes, he had asked. Then the child had been born, his Helena, she would always be his Helena.

Bron had loved her child, doted on her, Helena was a precocious child, tall where her mother was tiny, long legged, and broad shouldered for a girl, her hair was silver, blonde, like her mothers and her eyes a deep blue, deeper blue than her mothers, more like thunder clouds or a stormy sea than the azure blue of the sky.

She walked before her first birthday and grew up amidst the people of the village. Edward Meredith taught her to ride and gave her the old pony from the farm to ride as her own.

Helena made few friends amongst the local children, preferring to ride into the hills alone. She had a vivid imagination, in her mind she had friends amongst the fairies, she would meet them on the hillside, early in the morning before the sun had risen, would talk of the world beneath the mountain, where Eryr the fairy Prince lived and ruled and kept all things safe.

Wybren was a mighty warrior, with dark red hair. He had flashing blue eyes was taller than any man she knew, and he carried a longbow and a sword, he came above ground when the mountain was misty and flew on a great dragon, to survey his land.

She had met him. She had spoken with him. In the druids' cave behind Mr Meredith's farm. No of course he did not live there, he lived below the mountain.

With tears running down her face, Helena had sworn that it was true, why didn't her mother believe her, did her mother think her a liar. Just because she was different from the other children, she didn't want to be like them, she wanted to be a Faerie.

The following day, Bron had gone out early, while the mountain mists were still filling the valley. Idwal had heard the front door click on the latch, had seen his wife walk up the road towards the mountain. Others had seen her take the parish road towards Hengwm, Meredith's farm. Idwal never saw his wife again. Neither did Helena ever see her mother.

The village turned out, they searched but they had found nothing. The druid's cave was empty, there was no sign of Bron on the mountain and no word of her in any of the farms or villages close by. At the age of ten Helena Lewis had lost her mother, and the man who had been her father since her birth did not intend his daughter to go the same way. Her mother gone, Helena had put her mind to her studies, been a model pupil at school and then found herself a job as housekeeper to Idwal's best friend Edward Meredith.

Idwal was pleased at first, it showed that Helena could be hardworking, was capable, and industrious and though easily distracted and living outside of reality,

95

was normal. Helena was jokingly referred to as being completely 'away with the Faeries'.

She never completely forgot the Faerie Prince who her father insisted was completely in her imagination.

I had been told all of this by Idwal before I left for my education with Mrs Eliza Jones. I had been abandoned, the circumstances of my being found were the stuff of gossip in St Harmon, I could not help but know that I was the abandoned child of the wanton daughter of the landlord of the Inn. But I had always felt loved and wanted and somehow connected to the village of St Harmon.

There was always talk, mainly of Edward Meredith and the fact that his hair had been red, the same colour as mine, that he had always kept an eye out for me, had given me old ginger when I was a child, the same old pony my mother had ridden.

He was not my father. I knew this with all the certainty of youth. With my worldly goods removed from the Sun Inn, I said my goodbyes and left St Harmon to travel the fifty odd miles to Llantrisant.

PART THREE

CHAPTER 20 - LLANTRISANT THE TOWN ON THE HILL 1893 - SIBYL

The town of Llantrisant was built on the top of a hill, a small town of narrow cobbled streets nestled in the shadow of its castle, small compared to the massive fortresses on the coast and its neighbour at Caerphilly it was part of a network of fortified houses built around the Vale of Glamorgan.

The towns church was dedicated to three saints, Gwynno, Illtyd and Dafodwg.

The castle that once stood so proudly on the top of the escarpment looking out across the fertile green patchwork of the vale had long been demolished, razed to the ground by Owain Glyndwr in his attempt to rise up and rid the Welsh of their English overlords. The only remaining structure the ivy clad Raven Tower pointing skyward from the castle green and towering over the narrow cobble street and two up two down cottages tacked onto the hillside below.

The guildhall still stood outside the grounds of the castle with its tall medieval chimney and steps to the great room where the local magistrates held their court.

The arched area beneath which served as the corn market once a month, and the cellar dug into the rock below which housed its cells and a passage which had once connected them to the dungeons of the castle.

Dr Price lived in a house built on the top of the neighbouring Caerlan Hill. By the time I took up residence in his household he was the remarkable age of ninety-two years, his wife had long since left him and he lived a comparatively quiet life, still an advocate of cremation and still a popular local figure he had erected a tall monument to his deceased son named Iesu Grist in the field next to the house and had started calling himself High Priest of the Sun Grown Old.

He had all but ceased to practice medicine but still had an eye for the ladies and I found myself fending off the unwanted attentions of an old man seeking to sire more children on a virgin bride.

He cut a striking figure in his outlandish clothes, his hawklike eye and long aquiline nose. His beard was worn long and was snowy white as was his hair which he wore in several plaits down his back and topped with an animal skin hat. While in matters of medicine he could still conduct himself in a professional manner, those who knew him well were of the opinion that he was affected by the same disease of the mind which had affected his father before him. 'As mad as a box of frogs'.

Mother Eliza had inadvertently apprenticed me to an ancient lecher in need of a housekeeper and prospective mother to his future children.

I took to rising early and walking the short distance into the town in order to seek an alternative billet. My few belongings were stored at the New Inn, Grand da had known the landlord Samuel Spencer well and he had allowed me to store my belongings in one of his lumber rooms, all was packed away in the big chest belonging to my grandmother, including the books which Mother Eliza had given me on her leaving for America.

CHAPTER 21 - A LETTER TO UNCLE EDWARD - SIBYL

In frustration I wrote to Edward Meredith at Hengwm, if I could find no one else to help me, maybe Uncle Edward would know what I should do, I had never felt so alone in my life.

26th August 1893

Dearest Uncle Edward

After several weeks my position in the household of Dr Price is untenable, He is clearly not in his right mind; he refers to himself by a Druidic name High Priest of the Sun Grown Old and seeks to take a virgin to his bed in order to father a child of pure Druidic blood. I do not feel safe or welcome in his house, nor am I furthering my education.

I have made enquiries locally and may have found a position as assistant to the new local Doctor, he has taken over most of Dr Price's duties and seeks a capable nurse with experience. I have an interview with Dr Jack

Rowlands in the morning. I hope that this will afford me suitable employment and progress my studies as Dada would have wanted.

He holds his surgery in the back room of the Guildhall until he finds suitable premises, this is convenient for me as I have now taken a room in the New Inn, which I have use of free until I am paid, I understand that this is partly because the innkeeper Mr Spencer was a friend of both you and Dada.

The Inn backs on to the Castle green, and the Guildhall a pleasant place to sit in the summer, in the shadow of the old ruins, there are even beehives still kept in the garden by Mr Ferris Bees as they call him.

Everyone seems to have a pet name, Mr Ferris Bees, Tommy Pigs, he keeps such animals at his farm, Dewi Malthouse for that is where he lives and so on.

I so miss the village and the Inn and if all my endeavours fail I hope I may return there.

My heart will always have a home in St Harmon.

Give my regards to all the regulars in the tap room and say hello to Idwal for me, I know he can hear me in spirit,

Sibyl.

I inserted the heavy sheet of cream velum into an envelope and sealed it with wax, then went to leave it for the post.

CHAPTER 22 - A WALK IN TIME -SIBYL

Today I walked from Castle Hill, heading east across the top of the Caerau hill where there is a large dew pond on the summit of the hill, this top field is grazed by wild ponies and surrounded by the same windswept trees as you see on the top of the mountain above St Harmon, it makes me feel quite at home.

The mountain track takes me across the front of the hill and down into the hamlet of Rhiwsaeson where there used to be a flax mill, the ruins are still visible, and it is said to be haunted. I wonder if the ghost is called Dai Flax, or Dai Mill. I must ask when I get back to the New Inn.

On my way I passed a strange little place in the midst of the wood, a cave, but with a doorway, there were signs of habitation there, long since gone, a shepherd's hut perhaps, or the home of a hermit.

It seemed a happy place, someone had felt great peace there, my bones told me so, and I have never known my bones to deceive me.

This peaceful place is so deep in the wood and so overgrown that had I not been slightly lost and obliged to follow the stream on its route down the valley, I would never have seen it. I suspect I will never find it again, like some Faerie dwelling, it may disappear to prevent further discovery. Or does it only show itself to those it chooses.

But it was real enough, I looked inside, in the dark in the farthest recess I found a box, small and wooden and containing a beautiful gold ring, I have it in front of me, a thick ring of gold set with three clear stones, maybe diamonds, unusual in that they are pushed in to the metal. Not set above it as is the fashion. Is it lost, or was it left there by its owner who intended to return for it, in any case it has a home with me now. I shall look after it, it is too nice a thing to be left buried in the earth.

I walked back then up the cart track all the way to the South Gate of the town, up the cobbled steps called Yr Allt and all the way to the foot of the Raven Tower. Tomorrow, I start work as assistant to Dr Jack Rowlands.

CHAPTER 23- THE RAVEN TOWER - SIBYL

I swear I can hear it calling me, each time I move away from where I sit with my lunch, I hear it's walls, full of voices, chattering, talking, some singing and a harp playing. Now as dusk falls I smell fires and meat cooking, each time I sit here they get louder and more distinct. Now and then I hear a woman calling. I hear her now; she seems to be calling to me from the tower.

The doorway to the Raven tower is buried deep in an ivy-covered wall, the wood of the door rotted away long ago, the pointed arch of the entrance remains in the wall, it is now a doorway to nowhere. I have seen it in daylight and have walked through it, all that lies on the other side of that door is a roofless, wall less space covered in yet more ivy. The remains of a stone stairway protruded hopefully out of the opposite wall, it's crumbling stone steps leading upwards to nothing.

At the bottom of these steps another set leads downwards to a metal grill laid over their entrance, the steps continue downwards to what used to be the castle dungeons, these still exist I have been told, beneath the green and the Raven Tower there are

105

underground cells, where prisoners had awaited execution by hanging or burning on the green in front of the Tower. They connect by a tunnel to the cells under the Guildhall where Dr Jack holds his surgery.

Dr Jack, as he is called locally, my new employer, is a native of the town and knows the history of the castle, the connections to the Black Prince and the battle of Crecy, the archers of the town, the freedoms granted by the Prince to the heroes of the day.

'Are there ghosts?' I asked him

'Undoubtedly' he replied 'Do you believe in ghosts'

'No' I replied. 'I do not, I have never been given reason to'.

He smiled an enigmatic smile back at me.

'But have you ever been given a reason not to?'

CHAPTER 24 – IS THIS MY CALLING - SIBYL

1st May 1894 – Calan Mai

It is the middle of the night, lying in my cot bed in the tiny bedroom above the tap room in the New Inn. My bedroom is at the back of the property, its little square window looked out over the cobbled back lane which leads up to the Castle green.

The noise is unearthly, screams of pain such as you could never imagine, making the hairs on my neck stand on end and my arms bristle with goose flesh, they are coming from the castle green.

Dressing in a hurry, and from my meagre wardrobe choosing the breeches and boots I wear for riding, I let myself out of the back door of the New Inn and follow the cries which come from the castle green fearing that there is a murder in progress.

I am alone, no one else seems to have heard the commotion, or if they have they were not concerned to see what it was.

Emerging from the mist which had gathered in a rolling grey cloud over the town was the Raven Tower,

107

no longer a ruin, the door at its base was open allowing light to shine out onto the green.

Three figures stood outlined in the mist and the eerie glow. One much taller than the rest beckoned to me to go closer. I could not resist, my feet carried me where my mind said I should not go, all my senses on high alert my logical brain told me to turn and flee, but my mind was not listening. My body could not disobey the call in any case.

Before me stood a man, or at least a male in human form, immensely tall, red haired, blue eyed, he spoke with a deep melodious voice, the voice alone rolled over me like a wave of reassurance.

'I am Deargan welcome daughter, welcome home'.

He was the only one of the three apparitions to speak.

He fixed me with a piercing blue stare and a smile lifted the corner of his mouth and then travelled to his eyes.

'I have waited a long time to meet you Sibyl, Merch Goch,' said the male. 'Go now with my brother Eryr he has much to show you'.

Another apparition of similar stature but of much darker countenance and eyes the colour of green moss stepped forward.

Taking me firmly by the arm he walked me through the doorway of the tower and into a blaze of white light. I was carried on waves of sound and the feeling that my whole being was torn apart and reassembled, I heard the sounds of arrows in flight, the clash of swords and the screams of horses, I felt the wind of war on my face, the drip of blood on my hands and then there was nothing.

I came to lying on a bed of fur, soft under my body and warm, so warm, I wanted to stay in its cocoon for ever. Then I became aware that there were people standing by me.

'Good, she is still with us, let her wake quietly.

I listened from behind closed eyelids, feigning sleep for as long as I could, trying to gather my thoughts together. I did not sense danger, whoever I was with meant no harm to me, but was this a place I wanted to be, was I held prisoner, could I go back, back to my little cosy room in the inn, to my work with Dr Jack and the life I was making for myself.

The smell of food being cooked tickled my nostrils, the scent of fresh bread and meat cooking, the smell of herbs drying in a kitchen. I opened one eye.

The face that looked down at me was smiling, a broad white smile in a handsome chiselled face, his eyes laughed at me as he pushed a stray ginger curl back behind an ear. 'You cannot hold out forever. You are human, you will need to pee!'

I suddenly realised that I did.

He pointed to a screen in the corner of what I now realised was a cave, or a room hollowed from the rock, I was still fully clothed, so I swung my legs out of bed and went behind the screen where I found a privy, carved out of rock, smooth and comfortable, remarkably so.

Mission accomplished, I returned to my bed hoping to crawl back into my nest. But my minder had other ideas.

'I am Eryr, I am a Prince of the kingdom of Faeries. 'This is our home', he gestured grandly around the room. 'I am not human, what you see is my present form, my appearance changes depending on my need. I mean you no harm, only good. I do not seek to keep you here after your work is done, though you may choose to stay. You are one of us, you carry our blood in your veins as does your mother and your grandmother.

A grave mistake has been made in this place. Many years ago, the balance of the worlds was set askew, the freedom of the Welsh people put in jeopardy for ever, you have the power and knowledge and the skill to right it. The wrong was done by human magic, it can only be undone by one who knows the spells of the one who created the enchantment and how to use them.

We seek one of our own who can make a prophesy come true, we need your help Sibyl, the prophet, Merch Coch. The red one'.

He told me that he had the power to move back and fore through time, paging through it like a book.
He could go back to the past, but he could not re write history, but he could make small changes, for the benefit of his people and for the human world.

'Come, let me show you around, you must eat, and then you must learn our ways, I took the liberty of bringing a few things for you'.

It was then that I noticed that the chest from my grandmother's room at the Sun Inn stood against one wall.

'How?' I asked, amazed. 'How long Have you been watching me?'

'All your life' came the reply, 'we were there when you were born, we made sure that you were found when your mother came back to us'.

I opened the chest and saw that the original contents were still there, along with the books which Mother Eliza had told me to keep from her library.

The book by Dr Fraser, Grey's Anatomy, and the Grimoire of Margaret de Clare.

'Have you ever worn the cloak' he asked.

'No,' I replied.

'Then you have no knowledge of its power'.

This was said as a statement, not a question.

'Bring the Grimoire, we will need them'.

In a daze, I picked up the old leather-bound books with their musty pages filled with ancient handwriting.

I followed him through what seemed like miles of stone passages, lit by candle lanterns, the smell of beeswax hanging in the air, the light reflected from the crystal shiny walls. Eventually we arrived in a moderately sized dining hall, furnished with wooden furniture, dressed in fabric drapes in the colours of the autumn woodland, with the occasional splash of colour.

The long oak table was laid with breakfast, bread, honey, butter, porridge and thick rashers of bacon, there was a pot of tea and a jug of fresh milk. I had indeed landed in a land of plenty.

And there sitting across the table, the woman who had abandoned me as a baby, left me alone in a cave, deserted me. What did she have to say for herself I wondered, she seemed as if she was lost in a trance. She still looked a young woman, now in her thirties by my reckoning her skin was still clear and unmarked, she had few wrinkles of age, her hair was still silver blonde and curly, flowing down her back held in place at her temples by fancy combs fashioned from bone. Her figure was still trim, and she was light footed as a faerie. That word faerie resonated.

I took Eryr abruptly by the arm as he passed behind me and shoved him roughly towards a seat.

'Sit down.' I demanded the command came out as if I was talking disobedient dog.

To my great surprise and his, he did.

'What exactly am I?'

CHAPTER 25 - EXPLAINING FAERIES – ERYR

I looked him straight in the eyes and fixed him with my best blue stare. The one which brooked no argument.

'And after you tell me that, you will also do one more thing' I said determinedly 'you will tell me how in God's holy name I am connected to all of this'.

Eryr's eyes glowed that sinister shade of red, which betrayed his origins. He sat down across the stone table from me and started to speak.

'My folk are everywhere, he started, you will have heard the tales of fairies at the bottom of the garden, sometimes a fairy is seen, usually by a child because children are more open to belief. Mostly they remain invisible to man who by and large does not believe in us. Belief is strong in the Celtic peoples; they still hold on to their folklore and the legends of the auld ones. Our father Aegir is the King of the Faeries, he lives beneath the site of the standing stones at Waun Mawn.

Beneath those mountains and moorlands are the many caves and halls of the Faerie world. They form a network deep below the surface of the earth. There are entrances and exits to this world all over the planet, some are plainly visible, and others will only appear at certain times of the year. He is not the only leader of the Faeries; the Faerie boundaries loosely follow the boundaries chosen by man. Particularly in what you may know as the Brythonic countries. Each of those lands has their own Faerie ruler.

Every living thing has a fairy which cares for it, which inhabits it. These are all of my folk, these fairies are mostly hidden, in the flowers and trees, in the rivers, with the animals and such like. These are the land fairies our realm is not fairyland as you understand it. Ours is the land of the auld ones. They are my family. Call them cousins of the land fairies if you like.

Where the land fairies can only tend and care for things and can be destroyed by human events, the auld ones who live in the land below have the more subtle powers, some can appear in different forms. Some may walk through the time passages hidden deep in the earth. And some have sight of the future.

I have two older brothers, Wybren named for the sky and the heavens and Deargan named for his red colouring.

My full name is Adain Eryr, I am named for the Eagle, most call me Eryr. We are blessed with certain abilities, all three of us may appear as other beings, what you see now is my usual state, but you have seen me in other guises. In addition, I have the ability to walk through the threads of time. Both Wybren and Deargan can fly and Deargan is the tamer of Dragons. We have the power to influence life above ground, not to change things in time, we cannot change destiny, but we can perhaps bend it sometimes, direct events to a suitable conclusion, usually to preserve our own world.

The world of the auld ones is connected to the human world, there are those of us who live human lives. They are the conduits to the land of man. They are the watchers and the messengers between the human and the Fairy world, spies if you like to think of them that way.

Did you ever notice a person who seemed to have been around for ever? Well, they are probably one of the fairy folk. Some have been above ground for hundreds of years. They may move about or disappear for a period of years only to return maybe in a different guise and pick up where they left off.

Other families have been chosen to marry into the fairy family, to add human blood to that of our kind. This strengthens the Faerie blood and makes us less vulnerable to human frailty and human disease. Your family and that of the Meredith's are linked with us in that way, The Celtic peoples mix well with my kind, there is a certain bond between us.

He drew in a breath and gesticulated vaguely with a long-boned graceful hand.

'Your grandmother Bron was not born in the halls beneath the mountain she was from a small village on the coast called St Donats, her mother had died in childbirth. Her father was so grief stricken that he had walked to the cliff top at the Witches Point and leaving his daughter to the wind and the weather had jumped over the cliff and to his death on the rocks below.

The baby was taken into the Faerie world by my father Aegir, when he found her wrapped in a bundle on the cliff top. Her father's death was needless and tragic, his family had no connection with us, neither he nor his wife had any connection that way, but Aegir could not leave her there to die. He took her into his family and raised her among his own children, she learned all our ways and became as much one of our kind as a human can be.

His youngest son Wybren was a baby when Bronwen was adopted into the family. They grew up together and from the minute both could walk they were inseparable, by the time they were grown they were very much in love.

They lay together, an act which is not shameful in the fairy world, it is just seen as a natural event, Faeries do not need to marry, the word husband or wife is used purely as a matter of convention. They were both of age and in love. Wybren wanted her to stay but Bronwen felt the pull of the world above, so strongly that when she was older she ran away. Wybren always knew where she was, he saw her through the mists, and he made sure that she was watched and cared for. He loved her enough to let her go. He guided her to Idwal Lewis for we have a watcher in that place. She gave birth to a child, your mother Helena. Idwal always knew that he was not her father. Your mother, Helena, had Faerie blood running strongly in her veins, she is very

116

much a sister, very beautiful, very ethereal but also very flighty. She was towards our world from the start. Pulled by her blood. She was a child with great insight, but not of a strong mind. I believe even your grandfather believed her 'away with the fairies'.

She met my oldest brother Deargan on the hillside, they met first when she was a young girl playing in the streams and in the fields. She saw the land fairies and imagined that she was one of them, was drawn to the druids cave, which is a doorway for us, we have many hidden in the Welsh mountains. That imaginary fairy Prince she talked of was, and is, my brother.

There was one there who watched over her, would keep her safe from harm, a spy in human form if you like. Helena fell in love with Deargan, she would go down into the world of the faeries with him but was always bound to return home to her family. No one believed her when she said where she had been, she was thought to inhabit a fantasy world, she was thought deranged or fey.

She was seduced by the Faerie life and dearly wanted to stay, eventually she and Deargan lay together, she wanted so much to stay with him and go back to the enchanted halls below the earth. She knew all along that her actions risked her being shamed by her own people.

Her mother sensed what was happening and came to the druids cave, she pleaded with Deargan to leave her daughter alone. Deargan would have none of it, Bron came alone back to the fairy halls, she should not have

117

done so, having made the journey alone, she could not return. To come alone is seen as being willing to stay. The way back was closed to her.

Bron made her bargain not with Deargan but with Wybren she would give herself to Wybren in exchange for her daughters heart. She would not have her daughter live any other life than as a human. Your grandmother as you have seen is alive and lives with us, she may not travel with us, and she may not return to the human world. Not that she wishes to do either

Finding herself with child in the human world your mother Helena ran away, again she was watched and guided by our folk.

Your mother, she has the sight, she also has the mind and the soul of the spirit world. But she does not have focus, she cannot harness her power. She was helped by old Nan Jenkins; Old Nan is one of our folk.

Helena left you in the cave and ran back to Deargan, he called to her through the stones, and she allowed herself to be taken. Poor child she is trapped in her fantasy world and her gifts are lost to us, but she is now happy in her own way.

So that is your family. The family which calls you now to use your blood to save a people. Certain of our blood have the power of sight. To see and feel things in the future, to walk through time as through the leaves of a book. The book of time is written and cannot be changed, but the words may be interpreted in different ways.

You have that sight, and you also have the power of healing, both your grandfather and your father are of the blood, it is strong within you.

I am Eryr, I too can walk through the strands of time, and I may also take different physical forms. I have been many things to you over the years, watching you, keeping you from harm.

There is a prophecy which will be fulfilled, it's fulfilment will make the Celtic people free for a time, a time when they will be governed fairly and not subjugated by outsiders it will be a time when the Country will thrive, and the Faerie world beneath will thrive with it. There are those whose actions will foil the prophecy, not by intent, but by misadventure.

There is a man, Welsh born, the prophecy says he will become a great leader of men, he is vital to the cause, but in the pages of time I have seen his death. We believe that for the prophecy to be fulfilled, he must live.

His death is not natural, he will be struck down by a poison, only you will have the power to find the antidote. He is also the father of a child who will live for five hundred years. That child is the oldest of our watchers he is alive in your time and has been travelling since the dawn of creation, he has been born and reborn, should his father the archer die then his chain of life will break. He has been watching over you all your life as he has in his different forms watched over kings and princes. You bear his name. He is the oldest of the old from who we all descend. His line must not be broken. You know him as Edward Meredith. He drew in breath as he finished his speech, the silence rolled like tumbleweed along the table as he waited for my response.

'I am no relation to Edward Meredith, there were rumours about him and my mother, but I am no blood relative of his I spat this at Eryr.' How could I be?'

I picked up the glass of cool mountain water which he offered me.

'I see why you think not, you will find out that you are his blood, you are both of the auld ones in that way he is your kind, you will see, if we are successful in our mission and you return to your time, it will then be time for him to regenerate, he will die, and you will inherit all he has. He will move on.

'I do not want all he has, it just reinforces the gossip and the rumours about my mother, Uncle Edward, my foot. The whole village believes him to be my father'.

I heard footsteps approaching softly across the floor and a huge red-haired figure stepped out of the shadows, his hair was the same hue as my own but straight and glossy like sheet of burnished copper, it was hung loose down his back dividing over a huge pair of what looked like wings, he was shirtless and displaying a fine array of muscles running down a long athletic body to a slim waist and legs encased in black leather trousers and long black boots. His face was patrician, the nose slightly hooked, his eyes maybe a little too close together giving the aspect of a bird of prey. Standing alongside him was a woman with blonde hair in wild curls about her face who looked at me through eyes which had been the models for my own.

The voice when it came was quiet and firm and held the tones of Welsh honey, gold and sweet in tone but deep in flavour and texture. It was a voice that could be spread on fresh bread and eaten with large amounts of freshly made butter.

'I am Deargan your father, Sibyl, have no doubt of that, I have watched you grow, It was me who stole your mother from you and Idwal's wife from him, but she was never of the human world, and her only wish was to see you safe.'

He gripped me by the shoulders, Strong arms held me pressing me to his hairless chest, his chin resting on the top of my head, I also felt my mother's arms about my waist though she said nothing.

There was nothing left to say.

CHAPTER 26 – THE PROPHESY - SIBYL

When the dragon is released from its mountain of
fire. A warrior will live who will drink the blood of kings,
One born of his line will come from the hills
And the people will be led to freedom.
Adain Eryr
Few of the prophesies of old were written down,
most were passed on by the bards who sang them, from
father to son over hundreds of years. Mixed with the
tales and superstitions of the time the words became
muddled and obscured but through all the time and all
the muddle the message remained the same.

Eryr's face was suffused with enthusiasm, he spoke
with a zeal that made everything seem possible.

Eryr his name suggested a mystic being, one who had
come from another time. He could feel the stars
aligning, he knew that this time it would be right, the
prophecy would at last be fulfilled. We would be there
to guide the hand of fate.

He slowly listed the possible candidates for the job of
messiah to the Celtic people 'There is one, he said
already in France who fights for the French against the
English. Owain Lawgoch he is called'.

Another bloody Owain, I thought to myself. Were they all called Owain for heaven's sake. 'But he will not return to Wales, his very name says that he has blood on his hands, he will die. So not him then.'

The mellow voice enthused, 'I can feel him near, I know the time is right, but I cannot see the end, you must be my guide. If Gwyn ap Meredith is he, then he must not die'.

What's in a name, I thought to myself,' Sibyl, named for the prophetesses of Ancient Greece. Why on earth couldn't I have been called Jane.'

I know I have the gift of sight; I had been shown how to use it by Mother Eliza, maybe my own mother knew about my gift when I was born. Was that why she left me, did not take me to live with these mystical beings?

How does this man from under the mountain expect me to guide him, he's the mystic being after all, surely he can find his own way, or are his kind just as fallible as we humans?

If I could only stop hearing these voices in my head for five minutes, if only I could go back to my little room above the bar in the New Inn and to my new job as assistant to Doctor Rowlands. That was supposed to be my life, wasn't it?

I sat and listened as Eryr outlined what he knew of the past, of the history of the small Welsh village with a cave under its mountain from which he said he took his human name.

He saw my mind wandering, he saw me looking mentally for my exit door. He brought me back to him by showing me, making me look through that crystal wall, appealing to the healer and the humanity in me, would I let it happen?

He knew all along that I would go with him, He played with me like a fisherman plays with a trout on a line, he let my mind run to the end of the play, then he reeled me in, granting me slack only to stop me from wriggling free of his lure.

Green eyes with just a hint of Faerie red held mine across the great wooden table, I was lost in them, and they read my mind, my soul and all my being then he took me by the arm and with a vicelike grip on my biceps muscle to prevent flight, he walked me towards the doors of time.

CHAPTER 27 - CRYSTAL GAZER - SIBYL

I had not used a gazing ball, or crystals since my days at Pen y Banc, I was young then and did not take it all that seriously, this was the stuff of carnival fortune tellers.

Mother Eliza had told me that for it to work I needed to believe, I needed to feel the aura of the crystals, and I needed a crystal of the same aura as my own, moonstone.

Eryr placed it in front of me, it was translucent and vaguely purple in colour, a polished sphere which glittered in the light from the candles which surrounded it, I had possessed a moonstone once before, the one I gave to my best friend Owain. Only now did I realise what it had been for.

The truth dawned on me, the truth of the reading by Ma Pryce, Owain had indeed gone, but not, to Ireland.

More smoke and mirrors, more mind games, what else did they hold in store for me?

I ran my hands over its surface, feeling the cool beneath my hands, and the vibration of its molecules. Slowly the surface warmed and became transparent. I sat before the gazing ball, recalling what Eliza had taught me about using my powers of the sight.
Call to those who would hear you,

I lit the incense burner and inhaled deeply, emptying my mind of all thought, then by instinct I took the Grimoire of Lady Margaret and placed it in front of me. I willed myself to find her, told my mind to call out to her across the void of time.

Would she hear my call?

My mind cleared and suddenly the ball began to focus, I could see faces emerging from the mist. Amongst the faces, there she was, tall and stately, hair concealed under a cap decorated with lace and velvet, patrician features slightly worn with age but still beautiful in an ageless way. And behind her still slightly in shadow, a man, thinning blonde hair swept back over a narrow forehead, goatee beard pulled to a point on his chin and eyes like winter frost, cold cold eyes, cold and lifeless like the eyes of a dead fish.

The face of the third figure was in darkness, the only distinguishing feature was the crown.

So, this was Lady Margaret, niece of King Edward II, cousin of King Edward III, what web had been woven between she and I that now drew me inexplicably through its tendrils towards her.

I was aware of Eryr waiting at my shoulder, he could not see what I saw for the images were only for me, of

126

my minds making, but he would be the connection between the worlds, he had the power to open the door of time, and to take me by the hand and walk me through it.

Instinctively I opened the Grimoire, the writing was small and at first cramped in style, childlike with exceptional care taken over the letters, through its pages the writing evolved as had the author into a flowing elegant hand, befitting the tall, graceful lady who penned it.

Page upon page of learning, of charms and receipts used only for the good, a white lady then, not a witch, taught from a child by a master or mistress not to use the powers of darkness which lay latent in her being but to channel them for good. Whatever she had done, for I sensed that she had committed some terrible sin and that she had done it for a reason.

My hand felt through her writing the knowledge of a healer, a lady of strength not afraid to walk amongst the poverty and cruelty outside the bars of her golden cage.

What had changed her so?

PART FOUR

CHAPTER 28 - MARGARET DE CLARE,

Tonbridge Castle, Kent 1293

Mistress you have a girl, the midwife fussed around mother and baby, wiped her clean and wrapped her in a clean shawl of the best linen.

I was born on a stormy winter morning in the upper chamber of the great castle at Tonbridge.

My father Gilbert, Earl of Hertford one of the most powerful nobles in the court of Edward 1st of England, my mother Joan of Acre was a Princess and daughter of the King, King Edward I, the one they called Longshanks because of his great height. They called me Margaret and I was their youngest child.

As a daughter of the house of de Clare and being of royal blood, I had an upbringing of wealth and privilege, I was educated by private tutors along with my two sisters, while my older brother was trained in chivalry and warfare. I spent time at the royal court of my grandfather learned to dance and embroider and to behave as a lady, an idyllic childhood until at the tender age of twelve I was found a husband and became betrothed.

I was an attractive girl but not pretty, I had long dark hair as black as a raven's wing, silver, grey eyes now and the colour of the sea in winter in later years but in my youth they were alight and sparkling with humour. I was tall and elegant in bearing; I was considered witty and intelligent.

My second husband would remove the sparkle from my eye and the warmth from my soul.

At twelve I became a woman, my courses had begun, my mother had taken me to one side and told me that a husband had been found for me. I was to be betrothed to Martin de Milford. Martin was only four years my senior, my heart leapt, she had met Martin at court and liked him. I had half expected to be married off to a man older than my grandfather. My mother had done well for me. We were to be married when I was fourteen and he eighteen, thus my destiny was mapped out.

I married in the year of our lord Thirteen hundred and seven, my sister Eleanor was already married to Hugh Despenser, a strange mercurial man, and a favourite at the Court of the new King Edward II and a great friend of my husband though several years older, he and Eleanor had married the previous year. That too was marriage of political convenience.

In the year that I married, the old King Edward Longshanks had died whilst embroiled in a continuing war against the Welsh and the Scots. For several years Eleanor and I and our husbands were close, our husbands were favourites at court much to the chagrin of the Barons and the Marcher Lords who ruled for the

King in the wild lands on the border between England and Wales.

Eleanor's husband was ambitious, greedy for money and titles and overly friendly some thought with the King in whose eyes he could do no wrong. Martin de Milford, my own husband, was caught up in his thrall, towed along on Despenser's wave of greed and success.

The heir to the wealth of our family should have been my brother Gilbert de Clare but he had been killed at the battle of Bannockburn in 1314.

Eleanor as a female could not inherit without consent of the King and she being married, her inheritance passed to her husband Hugh Despenser. And so it was that Hugh Despenser became Lord of Glamorgan, he then sought to seize lands throughout Wales and the Marches from the Marcher Lords. He waged his own private war against the great barons who were the trusted nobles of the kingdom. Despenser was in the favour of the new King and had acquired more power than the old Barons thought fitting.

The trail of destruction which he raised across the Welsh Marches which bordered England only served to alienate him from the other Barons, they sought to distance him from the King Edward II with whom he was still a great favourite.

By circumstance Eleanor and I became distant, she was forced to live in Wales and follow Hugh Despenser with his household wherever he chose to live. Meanwhile the Barons petitioned the King to deal with Despenser and return what they considered their rightful lands to them, they wanted revenge on Hugh Despenser, they wanted blood.

Being unsuccessful in forcing their monarch to change and curb the excessive gifts he bestowed on his court favourite, the Barons and the Queen Isabella moved against the King.

He was captured by the Barons whilst visiting Despenser at the Castle in Llantrisant. He was first imprisoned and then tortured at Llantrisant itself and then secretly moved to Berkeley Castle the stronghold of the Earls of Gloucester. The Barons then set about arresting and charging Hugh Despenser with treason, murder, theft, and sodomy. Well, the Despenser Lord was very overly friendly with the King wasn't he, and the mud born of gossip will stick if thrown hard enough and from close enough range.

King Edward II was never seen again. I was told that he was executed in a most brutal and unspeakable manner involving a red-hot poker and the nether regions of his anatomy.

My brother-in-law Despenser was executed publicly, hanged, drawn, and quartered and his genitals cut off while he was still conscious, his entrails being burned in front of him. My dear sister was forced to watch.

My husband Martin de Milford was beheaded for treason guilty only by association. He had always been loyal to his King, easily led but loyal.

My dear sister died not long after the execution of her husband leaving me now aged twenty-eight, unexpectedly an heiress to the Gloucester estates and those of Glamorgan, I became again a pawn in the political game of marriage. My only daughter with Martin de Milford had died in childhood, I was extremely wealthy, though all my lands and property were forfeit to the King. I was still of child bearing age and a widow. I was also a niece of the new King Edward III. As a marriage prospect, on paper I was a great asset to be used as a husband chose.

CHAPTER 29 - A POLITICAL PAWN - LADY MARGARET

I listened to her voice across time and heard the story of her life.

I was still a young woman she said when my uncle the King sold me in marriage to Sir Hugh de Audley a man nearly twice my age.

Sir Hugh was a friend of King Edward II. He was desirous of more land and wealth and also of a bride to replace the one who had died childless of the smallpox.

The deal was that Edward would reinstate my portion of the Gloucester inheritance, in exchange I would marry Sir Hugh and Sir Hugh would for a period of time take over the stewardship of my father's estate at Llantrisant. We were charged with re-establishing order in the estate, making repairs to the castle, re-establishing the loyalty which had formerly existed between the people and the crown.

My Cousin the baron Despenser had burned his way through the Welsh Marches with such effect that the Crown had declared him a traitor and seized all of the lands we had inherited from our uncle Gloucester.

De Audley had grasped the deal with both of his miserly hands and set about spending what he believed he was about to receive. The King in his wisdom had given him my inheritance with conditions.

It was a long time since the family had done more than pay a courtesy visit to the Welsh hilltop town. Well placed to see approaching raiders from the coast and to fend off those who came across the moorland at the rear it was a stronghold of a house, cold, damp, and windswept. Not like the cosy manor I lived in at Uncle Gloucester's grace and favour. But Despenser had put paid to all that.

The people were friendly, Welsh speaking, not many spoke the courtly French which de Audley insisted on using. His lack of knowledge of this loyal but stubborn people only succeeded in alienating him from them, he was lost without his courtly friends with their lavish manners and expensive tastes. My new husband set about re-creating the court of Edward II in poverty stricken rural Wales.

Hugh de Audley, I despised him on sight, our wedding was an overly grand affair, even though he had not long buried his first wife. I walked down the aisle of the cathedral at Gloucester on the arm of my uncle King Edward III. I had only met my bridegroom once. He had looked at me then as though I was less than the dirt on his shoes.

He had been told that he was getting a bride with royal connections, educated in France, brought up at Court in the orbit of royalty. All of this was true, but while the other ladies of the Court of Philip IV of France had been happy to while away their time with childish games and constant rounds of sweetmeats and fawning over the squires and pages and young knights who danced attendance upon them, I preferred to read a book, or go outside of the palace grounds, to put on my cloak and go out amongst the people of the town.

I saw the want and the poverty in France, the sewage in the streets, the filth in the rivers which once teemed with fish but now stank like the devil. People who were taxed relentlessly to pay for war after war against the Spanish or the English, was this so much different, the people of this small Welsh town I found myself in were no different to the French, only the wars our King fought were against the Scots or the King of France.

My beloved sensitive delicate brother Gilbert had been killed at the battle of Bannockburn and for what. Why not let the Scots have their own government, be at peace with them.

But I was a woman and not allowed an opinion outside of the circle of French hens whose company I was forced to keep.

In France I chose to learn from the healers and the so-called sorcerers. I studied all manner of charms and spells, I found that I had a talent for the arts but vowed only to use them for good. I wrote all down in a large leather-bound volume my Grimoire; it became my bible.

And then I was several inches taller than his lordship, my hair not the Saxon Blonde he wanted, my eyes not the blue he expected. He should have married one of my sisters, or my brother, for I suspect that my lord has a taste for young boys if recent events are anything to go by. His taste is certainly for younger flesh than mine.

I am the image of my mother, tall, some say stately, with black hair and grey eyes. I would not describe myself as pretty, but neither am I unfavoured, I suppose striking would describe my appearance. But I am certainly not to his Lordship's tastes. Our wedding night was merely an act of convention. Yes, he consummated the marriage, there was no love and certainly no joy involved.

If a man could be accused of raping his wife, Sir Hugh would have a charge to answer. I did my duty as a wife as expected of a well born and respectable lady and duly provided him with a daughter, also called Margaret, named for me.

Where is Margaret now, she like all other young girls of noble birth has been farmed out, sent to Court to be sold to the highest bidder. My husband has assured me that she will be well married to some foreign prince and that I may never see her again.

I knew he had mistresses, he made no secret of them, no girl of age with blonde hair, blue eyes and an ample chest could escape his notice, in a way I was grateful to them, it meant that I could get on with my other work.

I went out amongst the people of the town; I spoke their tongue albeit I was rusty in its use and stumbled over the pronunciation of the long vowelless words and the strange guttural LL and FF sounds.

I set about educating some of the young women, daughters of the business people, the farmers, the millers, the tradespeople, taking them in as ladies maids and teaching them their letters, some maths, and other useful skills that could make their lives easier. The rudiments of herbal medicines, how to avoid illness, how to treat common sicknesses.

I became skilled as a midwife, despite my position in society I was called on to deliver babies when the midwife was not available. If a birth became difficult, I was called from the castle to assist.

My husband was only interested in furthering his reputation with the king. He recruited a new master at arms, Sir Kenneth Fitzsimons, a soldier, an organiser, and a trainer of men. Sir Kenneth had no land of his own, he had earned his knighthood in battle, he was a professional soldier. It was he who ensured that the men of the town and surrounding farms practiced their archery.

Sir Kenneth organised the tournaments where they competed against each other, and against neighbouring counties, with prizes and honours to be won. He created a scholarship which was offered to the best of the archers who competed in the tournaments, an incentive to practice and to improve. He started a training school for the most proficient, the best archers, those he would make squires, they would live in the castle barracks, learn the art of warfare, tactics, to use a sword and shield, to hone their skills with the bow.

By the time the king had decided on a fresh campaign in France, Llantrisant was the home of professional archers, trained soldiers, all received small stipend were not classed as serfs or vassals the King was impressed and of course very benevolent towards Sir Hugh de Audley, a man who was adept at receiving praise, for other people's work.

I have to admit Sir Kenneth has a way about him, he is a man who commands a great deal of respect in his way.

CHAPTER 30 - EDUCATING MARGED- LADY MARGARET

I recall well the day that Marged Owen arrived at the castle, I had been advised by others in my employ that she was almost feral, ran wild on the hills and since her mother's death had been totally out of the control of her father. Relishing a challenge and maybe seeing a bit of myself in the description, I sent for her.

She arrived on the tinkers wagon, barefoot as I recall and wearing clothes more fitting for a boy. Miles my footman carried her from the wagon into the Raven Tower and stood her in front of me, her blonde hair loose about her face, face set and eyes rebellious. She was filthier than the urchins of the town and had a turn of phrase to match one of Sir Kenneth's stable boys. She was pretty, and as I soon found out intelligent, industrious at tasks she felt worthwhile but stubborn and intransigent about those she thought beneath her.

Most of all she hated to be indoors, at the slightest opportunity she would be off into the grounds of the castle and as I found out from Sir Kenneth could be found most days practicing at the archery butts, where she was, he said, a very good shot.

Marged had also been taught, by someone she called Daithí how to suture and dress wounds, she knew the rudiments of treating cuts and wounds in animals, Daithí she said had been a shepherd.

After six months of failed attempts to train her in the more feminine duties of a ladies maid, I was forced to concede that any stitches she could sew were better placed in skin, her dancing steps were more like those of a hunter stalking prey or a swordsman sizing up an opponent.

When I told her I intended to teach her healing her blue eyes widened, a broad smile lit up her face, and her whole manner changed. She still went to the practice at the archery butts, and she still went roaming the mountainside on her day off, but archery practice was confined to an hour in the evening before dusk and she was suddenly clean, well turned out, timely and polite. I also found out from Sir Kenneth that I was not the only cause of her reformed character. Marged was in love.

The object of her affections was installed in Sir Kenneth's barracks, a trainee squire to Sir Hugh, and the finest longbow man that Sir Kenneth had ever trained, had I looked further into the tinkers wagon in which Marged Owen had arrived, I would have seen him for they arrived on the very same day.

PART FIVE

CHAPTER 31 – BRED IN THE ARM,
Gwyn ap Meredith

Born 31st April 1329

Was I born with a bow in my hand? Sometimes it seemed that way.

I know now that my family were poor, home was a one roomed cottage built in the shelter of the mountain. We shared our home with the sheep in winter, and the cow and the rest of the beasts except for the pig. Mother drew the line there and made dada pen the pig outside. A Smokey peat fire provided some warmth, it's smoke drifting upwards through the chimney in our only hearth. This fire cooked our food, warmed our bones, and burned our eyes.

The beasts occupied the space by the open door, they acted as a hairy barricade between us and the wind which whipped around the corner of the mountain when the gales came in from the sea. Their body heat rising and being blown towards us to add to the heat of the fire.

I had my chores to do, I milked the cow and drove the sheep out to pasture on the mountain behind our cottage, I stayed with them all day, watching against foxes and thieves. I was their protection.

As soon as I could walk, dada had placed a bow in my hands, a small one, but still as tall as me! Easy to draw, made of willow with a leather string. He taught me to aim it true, allowing for wind and the arc of flight, how to judge distance, and the proper way to kill an animal, cleanly with one arrow through the heart. For only one chance you got at a deer worth eating. As I grew in strength the bow got bigger and more powerful. He taught me well, I practiced while I looked after the sheep, bringing home rabbits or squirrel for the pot, and the occasional deer if I got lucky, as time progressed I relied less on luck, venison appeared more often on the menu in the Meredith household.

On Sundays I practiced at the butt – with da making me hold my form and not be sloppy in firing, he made me fire volleys of arrows, one after the other, all expected to hit their target. And most did.

I learned to cut and fletch arrows using straight hazel or ash sticks from the hedgerows and the woods. Feathers dropped by wild birds or stolen from the chicken coop.

By the time I was ten I could hit the centre of the straw butt dada had set up down by the brook on the flat piece of meadow. I never missed. I also learned to

144

throw a knife and fight with one, though never using it in the rough and tumble I had with the village lads on market day. My pride and joy was the slim bladed knife my father had given me on my tenth birthday, razor sharp and pointed, its blade had been sharpened many times, had I had any whiskers my father joked, I would be able to shave with it. It lived in leather sheath on my belt and went everywhere with me, its hilt was bound with leather and the pommel was brass, polished to a shine and inlayed with a piece of strange multicoloured stone.

I won my first archery tournament when I was ten, a local affair at the village fete. The prize was a jug of cider and a place in the tournament in Brecon.

By the time I was twelve years old I was shooting and winning at tournaments all over the county and was invited to the contest at Llantrisant. I won that too and caught the eye of his lordships master at arms, Kenneth – he recruited for the de Clare family the red lords of Glamorgan. I saw him take Da aside, they talked for what seemed an age over several pots of ale, Da was arguing a point, he was not awed by Kenneth. Then they both smiled and shook hands, a deal had been done, a bargain made.

Da called me to him, he introduced me to Kenneth. The huge man dressed in leather jerkin topped by an heraldic tabard in the de Clare colours winked at me with a hooded brown eye from his weather-beaten face, his hand was on my shoulder subtly feeling the depth of muscle in my arm. The hand that squeezed had the strength of many war campaigns in its grip. I squirmed in an attempt to free myself.

He laughed and let go 'you'll do' he said, 'with an eye like yours and a few manners taught, yes you'll do nicely'.

Da and I slept at the tournament field that night, making our bed under the stars, we passed the day watching the jousting and the sword fight, and a thing called the melee which was a free for all amongst the younger fighting men. They fought until the last man standing, hand to hand, toe to toe and no holds barred, the only rule was that you did not kill anyone – at least not by intent. I was fascinated, to be an archer was one thing, but I needed to use a sword too.

We left for home the following day – it would take us nearly three days walking to get home unless we could catch a lift on the tinkers cart.

As we walked my father told me of the deal he had done with Kenneth or Sir Kenneth as I would call him.

On my fourteenth birthday, that was in six months' time, I was to start training as a squire to the de Clare's.

I would travel back to the castle at Llantrisant and live there with other boys of my age, we would be taught to fight with bow, and also with sword and shield, learn the arts of warfare and to serve our master on and off the field of battle, to care for horses and weapons and also learn manners and etiquette.

I looked at my father dumbfounded, who would tend the sheep? My little sister could not she was far too young and well; she was a girl. Who would do my chores, why was he sending me away. Had I done something wrong that he wanted to send me away?

We sat on a wall about five miles from home and he bade me listen well while he told me as best he could of all that Sir Kenneth had told him.

'There is a war coming' he said, 'The King, Edward III is raising an army to go to France. All the men and boys of fighting age will be called on to go, I am too old now they will not call me again. But you will be expected to fight, better to go as an archer with training and skills than as an ordinary foot soldier. Bowmen are paid and well looked after, the men at arms are bound to service for the King or for their lord. The war they fight has been going on for many years, I fought with Sir Kenneth against the Scots at Bannockburn, I was a young man the like you, I was good with a bow and Kenneth, for he had not been knighted was a young nobleman with no squire to attend him. He took me under his wing, he taught me, and now he will teach you. You will have a stipend, money for yourself, not much, but more than our land will raise, and there will be opportunity, take it Gwyn, take it with both hands, do not waste it'.

147

'But Da, I want to stay with you, and mam gi, and Gwennie. Here is my place, please don't make me go.'

'Gwyn boy, please go with God's grace and make us proud.'

We got back to the cottage late that night, fell into our beds and I slept, I dreamed that night of banners flying in the breeze, of men singing, and the endless tramp of feet.

The next day I went back to my old routine, doing my chores around the farm and playing with Gwennie, all the while with a feeling in the pit of my stomach, nervous in anticipation of leaving home and all that I knew so well.

The day before my birthday, when it was nearly time to leave my home forever my father bade me walk with him up the mountain. Halfway through the woods he took a path which led away from the sheep pasture. I had roamed all over this land for the whole of my life, but rarely chose to use this path. We walked deeper into the woodland and right up to the face of the sheer escarpment.

There in the rock was a fissure, just wide enough for a man's shoulders and tall enough for a man's height. A cave. How had I never found this place, in all my explorations as a child. I knew of the druids cave, and it's magic stones, and never to go there at the feast times, but I had never seen this cave before.

My father lit a pitch torch using his flint and steel and I followed him into the darkness. At the back of the cave was a chest, it looked like a coffin, a man's height in length and a shoulders width for its whole length. He pulled a key from the pouch he wore at his waist and opened the large black lock to the chest, the lid creaked open, moving the dust and cobwebs of years. Reaching in to the chest he pulled out a bundle rolled in hessian. The hessian covered a cloak of deep burgundy wool, lined with rabbit fur, rolled in the cloak was a yew longbow strung with hemp, a leather arrow quiver, empty of arrows, its leather still soft from years of care, and the leather thumb ring of a longbow man,

Protection for a hand against the rip of the bow string. Then a gleam of metal and I saw the shining hilt of an ornamental hand guard, wrought with Celtic patterns, the scabbard was plain and black and hung from a plain black leather belt. Father drew the blade from its resting place of many years.

'I took this from the field at Bannockburn, a Scottish broadsword, the blade is Moorish steel, there is none finer, see the patterns made by the smith – he showed me the fine tracings along it length where the armourer had folded and beaten the steel into shape. Damascus steel. Perfectly balanced for speed and strength.

'It's owner had been a Scottish Laird of the Clan Macgregor. I dare say it has been used with great effect.

I hold it like a cow with a tooth pick' he handed me the bundle 'learn to use it well'.

Then he took my thumb and ran it down the still sharp blade and wrapped my bleeding hand around the hilt 'it must know the blood of its master – then it will not do you harm'.

Lastly from the bottom of the chest he pulled a cloth bag, reaching in he produced a silk tabard, a surcoat in the Kings colours.

'When the time comes, wear it my son, wear it with pride and take what it will offer you'

The next day I waited at the crossroads for the tinkers waggon and returned to the castle at Llantrisant, this time I would be staying there, perhaps for ever.

Llantrisant, the town of three saints, Illtyd, Gwynno and Dafodwg. Set atop a hill and escarpment small cottages and farms nestle round the church and the castle. The castle looks out over the fertile fields of the vale and the coast some twenty miles away. There is a Tower 'Hen Felin Wynt on the next hilltop a mill which grinds the grain for the town and also acts as a second lookout point separate from the Castle.

The land behind the town, is mainly rough grazing for sheep stretching for few miles then leading to the pretty hamlet of Castellau and from there to the grim village of Beddau, the graves, named for the gibbet which it set on the square, the victims of which who are usually robbers and thieves are buried under the roadway so that the people may walk eternally over their graves.

The castle is owned at the grace of King Edward III by the De Clare family, English earls of Gloucester and Pembroke, the young Earl had been killed at Bannockburn in 1314 and the Castle at Llantrisant had passed to his sister Margaret and her second husband Henry de Audley again at the grace of the King.

It seemed that much of what was Llantrisant was at the 'Grace of the King'.

The tinker's wagon dropped me off at the South Gate, after a short detour by the driver to conduct some business with the miller at the flax mill at Rhiwsaeson.

It was here that I first saw Marged Owen. In fact, she was part of the business transaction at the mill. Her father had arranged that she be taken on as a servant at the castle, in the service of Lady de Audley. The miller was a widower and quite ill equipped to cope with the wild young woman his only daughter had become.

As I watched a wild haired young girl was carried from the millers house dressed in a pair of boys breeches with a linen shirt and a jerkin, bare feet flailing against her father's ankles she was carried from the house and unceremoniously deposited in the rear of the tinker's wagon alongside me and my bundle.

Upon seeing me she stopped struggling to get free and run and I found myself staring into the bluest pair of eyes I had ever seen. Deep blue like a thundery sky and their blue centres rimmed with black, and lighter flecks highlighting the black at the centre. I fell in love with Marged there and then and, by the way she stopped her thrashing around and pulled herself together I think that she might have fallen for me in the same way.

The tinker drove his wagon along the lane at the foot of the Caerau hill through the cross roads called Cross Inn and up the hill towards the South Gate to the town, up we went towards the castle at the top. Taking the shortcut behind the Greyhound Inn up the cobbled street known as Yr Allt. We arrived at the huge wooden gates of home for the next few years.

It was the year of our lord 1343 I was fourteen years old and now considered a man.

Marged, for that was her name, daughter of the flax miller Dafydd Owen was also fourteen years old. Once she had calmed down she proved to be chatty and well spoken, the tinker drove up to the living quarters of the castle and Marged had reached her destination. One of the Castle servants came to fetch her and gave me first sight of Lady Margaret standing in the doorway.

Alas Marged could not hold her composure for any longer and resumed her previous kicking and screeching, forcing the manservant to carry her like a parcel in through the door which closed swiftly behind them.

I climbed down from the wagon and the tinker pointed me towards the small foot door alongside the great gate, I banged with my fist and a small sliding panel opened and a wizened gnome of a gatekeeper known as Twpsin asked me my business. I showed him the letter which my father had given me, a letter of introduction from Sir Kenneth the master at arms.

The gate house was a Spartan stone room built into the thick castle walls alongside the main gate. Comprising a small office for the gate keeper which also housed the mechanism for winding open the great gates and raising the portcullis. No comfort here for Twpsin, who would spend his duty time as look out from the rampart above and was also in charge of dealing with callers. It was no wonder his legs were so short and bandy, with the number of trips up and down those steps.

At his call a boy appeared, dressed in livery of navy-blue tabard and breeches, belted at the waist, with simple leather shoes and stockings. Smart but by no means lavish. Geraint he was called – another of the trainee squires, he walked me across an expanse of well-kept grass surrounded by a well-trodden stone path to the guardroom. Here I was shown into a dormitory of six beds, one was Geraint's, two belonged to William and Clarence. They, Huw told me were English, from the Earls household in Oxfordshire. Sons of the nobility here to learn, as we were here to learn. I would meet them later in the dining hall. There were two others belonged to Tally and Gilbert, Tally was as

Welsh as they came, and it was an unspoken fact that Gilbert was one of Sir Hugh's bastards.

Geraint was six months my elder, slightly built with elfin features and light ginger hair, his pale blue eyes were piercing in their gaze, I would find out that what he lacked in stature he made up for with his quick wit and intellect he also had a great talent with horses.

Looking me up and down with an appraising eye, half smiling at my farm boys clothing made from simple homespun, and then gawping at the pommel of the sword which protruded from the bundle strapped on my back, he disappeared into an alcove behind a curtain and reappeared with a pile of clothing.

I was tall for my age, even taller than my father,, he was a tall, graceful man with curly red hair and green eyes, my hair follows my mother, I have dark hair and my father's green eyes. I towered over Huw by a good foot.

After several expeditions into the closet for a suitable size, I was equipped with two pairs of Breeches one in good linen one in homespun, the former being for formal wear, two linen shirts both with long sleeves, a jerkin of Navy homespun two pairs of stockings one pair of leather slipper style shoes one pair of leather knee length boots and a bonnet hat also in Navy Blue. A short cloak in Navy Blue velvet completed the uniform. Geraint handed me an empty straw mattress to fill for my bed – I was to fill this with whatever Matthew in the stables was willing to spare in the way of hay or straw.

And two woollen blankets. My, my, this was like Christmas, I had never had such clothing.

I unrolled my bundle on the bed – where should I keep the contents; the sword was over three feet in length and the long bow which had been fathers was over six feet tall.

Under the bed then, I shook out the rabbit lined cloak, wrapped both items in it and slipped them under my cot. My archers leather jerkin and thumb ring I placed in the small cupboard alongside.

Then at Geraint's beckoning he ushered me from the barracks to the guardroom office where I was to be reintroduced to Sir Kenneth.

Sir Kenneth, Master at Arms, was in charge of the small fighting force, which was trained at the castle, every Earl had a duty to the king to be able to raise men for the army. He was also responsible for ensuring that in accordance with the law, all males of fighting age practiced with a long bow at least once a week. In this case every Sunday on the grassy area between the inner and outer castle walls. Here there was a set of archery targets or butts at which Kenneth put the archers of the town through their paces. Some of the older men had seen service in the Scottish campaign, they were hardened men now returned to their farms, they passed their knowledge to their sons and in some cases their daughters. Sir Kenneth was a huge grey-haired man well past his fiftieth year, hair cropped short and wearing a short goatee beard, he wore the colours of the de

Audley family over his leather jerkin, his britches were leather, and he carried no spare flesh.

'Welcome master Meredith, a baritone voice boomed, 'I hope Geraint has found you a bed and I see he has kitted you out finely, today, he will show you the layout of the Castle, where to go and not to go, the stables, the kitchens, and the refectory. The other two of your cohort are engaged this moment in learning to handle a sword, you will meet them at supper, God willing they haven't killed each other. Tomorrow you will begin at the Butts. Directly after breakfast'

Geraint duly showed me the layout of the castle, for the moment I was confined to the areas between the outer walls and the inner keep where the family apartments were.

The stables, which housed all manner of horses, from short stocky cobs used for farm work and riding, her ladyships fine palfrey, his lordships charger a well-built young chestnut mare called Blondell, part Percheron with a fine blonde mane and tail, well up to carrying the weight of a fully armoured knight but still inexperienced and unused to sudden noises and Geraint told me, with a terrible fear of pigs. Sir Kenneth's mount Trooper a large chestnut beast of unknown pedigree with a wild eye and a savage temper but as Matthew said, Trooper was unflappable when ridden and Sir Kenneth would ride no other animal. Matthew the groom showed me where the harness was kept and the feed and the way to the dung heap. Mucking out was often a task left to the squires in training. Especially as a

156

form of punishment. In time my back muscles would become well used to carrying the muck sack.

I would spend many an hour grooming these horses, learning to ride on them, practicing fighting from horse back with a sword and without.

'What is that?' I asked him pointing to the structure built nearly to completion just outside the castle green.

That said Geraint is Sir Hugh's new Guildhall, as we walked he talked further.

'His lordship found the castle in a great state of disrepair when he was sent here by the King. It was much damaged by the war with the Despenser's and by the raiding parties from the north. He has set about repairing it and finding that it has no proper hall for holding the Court of Justice and for keeping prisoners he has used a great quantity of Milady's money with the King's consent to fund the build of his Guildhall. It is a fine building, with a great hall for the Court and a cellar beneath, the arched area you see will hold the covered market and there is a cell block dug deep into the floor which connects with the castle dungeon. He is proud of it indeed.

CHAPTER 32 - THE MILLERS DAUGHTER - MARGED

'How dare he do this to me! My mother was gone and him the old devil would have rid of me, his only child.

Just because he needed a housekeeper, why should I give up my childhood.'

Mother had taught me all the skills, I could cook, wash, sew and keep the house tidy, I also kept his books in order and organised the mill. Was it so wrong that I wanted some freedom as well.

I remember that morning well. He gave me no warning; I had no time to say my farewells. Maybe he knew me too well, knew that if he gave me a choice I would run for my safe place, my sanctuary on the hill.

'Me!' I had screamed, 'Ladies maid, never.' I had kicked and screamed, but my bag was already on the wagon which was pulled up by the little bridge over the river.

My father picked me up bodily and deposited me like a sack of the flax seed he lifted daily, I landed in the back of the wagon, with my eyes closed, and still screaming in a not very ladylike manner.

Well, I wasn't a lady, I was a fourteen years old and I would not be replaced in my father's affections by that dried up old hag, Mrs Bryant. More about my father's housekeeper later.

When I opened my eyes, I was staring up the nostrils of a boy, a tall and very pleasant looking boy, with dark curly hair, a wide smile, and green eyes the colour of the moss on the west side of the trees. He was laughing, a boyish laugh, and he was laughing at me. So was the tinker whose attention was now on driving his horses. But I could see his shoulders shaking in mirth! All sorts of bad words entered my mind, but they would do no good. My eyes flitted to the tailboard of the wagon, the boy caught the movement and placed his hand on my shoulder. Looking me direct in the eyes a quiet voice said, 'smile lass, it's not that bad, is it?'. His voice seemed to drip over me like butter and honey through a crumpet, warming and pleasantly sticky.

A large, long fingered hand took mine in a pantomimic courtly gesture. 'Gwyn ap Meredith, at your service Milady' he kissed my hand. HE kissed my hand, how dare he, those eyes were laughing, again.

pulled my hand away and wiped the snot from my nose with the back of my sleeve and then wiped it on my breeches.

'Marged Owen', I launched back at him, 'certainly not at yours!'

I wedged my back against the side of the wagon, drew my knees up to my chest, rested my forehead against them, wrapped my arms around and took a deep breath in. I held that breath all the way to the cross roads, before letting it out in resignation.

'It's okay, she's breathing' Gwyn's voice called to the driver.

Then he turned to me, 'Castle, is it?,' and before I could answer 'me too', he replied. His accent was from the west. Lilting as if he was singing. 'I'm to be a squire, and you?'

'Bloody, fucking ladies maid' I replied.

'Language, Marged' he admonished, eyebrow raised and eyes twinkling with laughter.

'Her ladyship is going to love you' cut in the tinker, from his seat up front, he clicked to his horses urging them on up the steep hill 'I've heard she likes a job with a challenge'.

I could not keep my face straight any longer, I began to laugh uncontrollably, nervous terrified laughter, but at least it was laughter. 'Well, I can certainly be one of those', I jested back.

'Well, if you are stuck for company, remember, I'm new too' Gwyn added as the cart drew us further up the hill. 'I've heard that you shoot an arrow'?

'Shoot! I can fire a bow better than any lad in this county' I threw down the challenge, and I hoped he would pick it up.

Our conversation ended there, as I launched into my best wildcat performance for the benefit of her ladyship and the servants. Marged Owen was not coming quietly!

Miles, her Ladyship's manservant carried me bodily into the Raven Tower, I remember Lady Margaret following him in a breeze of fabric along the dark passage and up several flights of stone spiral stairs which led to her apartments.

He did not seem concerned that my head was close to bumping off the damp stone walls as he climbed, with me slung face down over his shoulder like a small child, I could see just her feet as they climbed the steps behind us, elegant feet, in elegant slippers, well she would get no elegance from me!

Miles dropped me unceremoniously on the rug before the fire in Lady Margaret's private solar. She did not inhabit the same rooms as her husband.

Lady Margaret followed us into the room and Miles took up a position by the door. I could not get out other than through the window which for one thing was covered by a draped tapestry to keep out the draught and for another was at least three flights of stairs up above ground level, had I looked out I would have seen that the drop was at least a hundred feet to the cliff bottom, for Lady Margaret had the Solar with a view, all the way to the sea at Witches Point.

Standing slightly away from me but still towering above me, this elegant but stern looking lady fixed me with a metallic grey stare.

'Marged Owen?' it was a rebuke and a question all in one.

'Yes' I snapped.

'Well, I was warned that you were a bit wild, come child sit on a chair at least and we shall talk'.
I rose slowly from the floor and took the proffered seat before the fire.

'Now dry those tears, they won't get you anywhere, and you will find that this is not such a bad place.'

I snuffled, if she thought my tears were sadness then she had me all wrong, mine were tears of rage, and of frustration.

'Good,' the clipped English voice cut through my thoughts. Was there perhaps a hint of French in her accent?

'Your father says that you are not without merit, that you know your letters and numbers well, and that you are a fair worker when you put your mind to it, I can teach you a lot, but you must want to learn. I will not tolerate slackness, or rudeness, first you will get cleaned up, then Megan my dresser will show you around and get you some suitable clothes. You will sleep in the servants quarters; you will eat in the kitchen, and you will start your training tomorrow. By the time you are sixteen you will be a competent ladies maid at least. Anything else is up to you.'

She smiled, this time the smile reached her eyes and her face lit up, 'Marged this is an opportunity for you, do not waste it'.

I could think of nothing worse than a life of mending dresses, dressing her ladyship, and attending to her every need, every day, a life making endless small talk to chattering girls playing parlour games and making pointless entertainments. I dearly hoped she didn't want to hear me sing, I thought to myself I am tone deaf. Even the off-key bleating of goats is more tuneful than I.

She clapped her hands and rang a small bell which was conveniently placed on the mantle shelf above the fire.

Miles disappeared as if he had melted through the wall, and Megan appeared. The epitome of a ladies maid, hair neatly coiffed and concealed under a seemly bonnet which was navy blue in colour and studded with pearls. Her dress was floor length in Navy blue with inlaid panels of cream material, small neat felt shoes protruded from under the front. She had a kind face, pretty in her way, round with a snub nose and a broad smiley face and hazel eyes.

Sullenly I went with her through a door at the back of the room, concealed by a wall hanging embroidered with pictures of flowers and herbs worked in wool on tapestry and into the inner workings of my lady's chambers.

The door led to an ante room which looked out over the castle green. It was furnished as a sewing room and hanging space for her wardrobe, the walls were arranged with rails and chests and cupboards full of clothing, from the rails hung gowns in many colours, long to the floor with long detachable sleeves with large openings at the cuff. Long flowing tunics worn over embroidered underskirts laced in front and sometimes trimmed with fur.

Sumptuous cloaks for winter, in velvet, lined and trimmed with white fur, was that ermine, or rabbit, I saw at least two, one in Navy blue and one in dark green. Luxurious indeed.

Wooden stairs led from this chamber up through the floor and into the room above, this was Lady Margaret's bedchamber complete with private privy screened off in the corner, a bath constructed of half a hogshead's barrel, and a curtain behind which was her bed.

Who carried the hot water up all those stairs?

I think I knew the answer before I even asked the question of myself.

Walls again hung with tapestries, keeping in what warmth was generated by the fire.

From this floor was another set of stairs.

Megan told me in hushed tones that these led to her mistress's private room. It was forbidden to go there. The mistress was clear about that. The room above led to the battlement and the rooftop. That was all that Megan knew. She did not wish to know more.

Pulling aside another draped tapestry, Megan opened a small door to the back stairs, these were the stone stairs which ran from the top to the bottom of the tower. The great door at the bottom led to the outside world of the castle green. A smaller door alongside it led to the servants quarters. The unseen stairs by which we would scurry back and fore unseen doing our ladies wishes.

Lady Margaret employed a ladies maid, that was Megan and two maids in training, Megan had her own room in our quarters, and I was to share with Sian who was now fifteen and coming to the end of her training.

Megan kitted me out with a homespun tunic dress with wool stockings and felt shoes, pointed me to the hot water cauldron on the fire and the soap and told me to clean myself up. She tried her best to confiscate my breeches and shirt, but I refused to part with them, threatening another outburst of temper if she insisted. As I rolled them into a ball and stuffed them under my bed I saw her making mental notes as to how she could remove them without my knowledge. At her peril would she try.

Attired in what seemed to be the Navy blue and cream uniform worn by all the servants and with my hair washed and secured under a muslin cap, we continued our tour.

Sir Hugh, she said had apartments in the main building, which was joined on to the tower on the second floor, the arch beneath led to the outer green where the archers practiced, and the squires trained at riding and fencing.

This area was accessed by a walk through which was gated off for safety, from stray arrows I presumed. It was also off limits to the ladies maids.

The kitchen and the great hall were on the ground floor of the main block.

The guest apartments were above Sir Hugh's. These were the ones used by visiting nobility and sometimes even the king himself. The king Megan informed me travelled with a great retinue and was always looking for likely members of his household, many of his lords were single and looking for wives. Megan announced this with a certain amount of glee in her voice. When he visits, there are great feasts and dancing, the whole place is alive with life. We hope to have a visit soon, she crowed, not the King this time bit his son, Edward, she nearly swooned as she uttered the words 'Prince of Wales'.

The Great Wall of the castle with its gate house surrounded the whole structure, the stables and the barracks being built off the gatehouse under the castle wall.

Sir Kenneth I was told, by my guide, was the Master at Arms and had rooms above the barracks. A gruff man whose bark is worse than his bite, but do not cross him, and do not think to distract his Squires in any way. He has the ear of de Audley and probably of the King himself.

The trainee squires occupied the barracks and Twpsin the gatekeeper had a room above the gatehouse. Everyone ate in the great hall which served as a dining hall for everyday use or in the kitchen if you missed a meal time. My guide had enthused about every minute of castle life, all I could see was a life of endless drudgery.

My stomach grumbled hungrily at the mention of the kitchen causing Megan to raise an eyebrow.

Come said Megan as we crossed the green towards the kitchen, let's find you something to eat.

CHAPTER 33 – SQUIRE IN TRAINING - MARGED

I saw him then, walking from the stables towards the barracks, a cloth bundle over his shoulder and another from which protruded what I could see was a longbow and, was that a sword. Both rolled with care inside what looked like a large sheepskin.

I could see now that he was tall, he walked with the easy grace of a youthful cat stalking prey on the hillside, his dark curls hung just to his broad shoulders. He raised a hand and turned towards me, sweeping into a long low bow, leg extended a bow which would look good coming from a courtier, strangely amusing being performed by a farm boy from the sticks.

His voice travelled clear as a bell across the ground that separated us 'Marged Owen, I am your servant ma'am'.

Damn he had recognised me! In a dress!

Flustered completely I dropped a hasty curtsy in his direction and replied in the same vein 'Gwyn ap Meredith, I am certainly not yours sir,'

He was wearing the navy and cream livery of the de Audley squires and another youth walked with him, ginger haired and freckled.

Both snorted at my response, both bowed again, and the Ginger haired boy muttered 'Touché' under his breath.

Both disappeared through the door of the barracks and out of sight, leaving me slightly breathless and red faced with embarrassment.

As we sat down in the kitchen and waited for the cook, Mrs Brassington, to attend to our hunger, I saw that Megan was chuckling, a deep throaty chuckle. 'My my, Marged Owen you have made an impression, be careful girl, and be mindful of his Lordship, his is attention you do not want'.

I spent the rest of that day with Megan, her name was Megan Prichard, she had been born not far from Llantrisant in a pretty hamlet called Castellau. She was the youngest of five sisters, her parents held a few acres of land and some sheep on the mountain behind and also ran an ale house called the Lamb and Flag, all her sisters were married and living away from home and being fed up with serving beer Megan had leapt at the chance to leave her home and work amongst the wealthy.

She told me she had not had much schooling, that Lady Margaret had taught her to read and her numbers and now she could read and write and add a column of figures, whilst she could sew a fair stitch when she arrived, she could now embroider complicated work skilfully, she proudly pointed out the screen in front of one of the fires in our accommodation, a work including brightly coloured birds and flowers, beautiful and intricate. 'That is mine', she announced. It was beautiful indeed.

She said that she hoped to stay with Lady Margaret and that she would find a husband with a fair living eventually, leave Wales and never come back.

Sian Jones was a different matter entirely, she was a simple girl, she tried her hardest to learn, she worked tirelessly from dawn to dusk, at the most menial tasks but was slow witted and clumsy. Her mother had died in childbed at her birth and Sian had been cut from her mother's womb by Lady Margaret herself. Sian had not thrived as a baby; her father had left her in Lady Margaret's care and her ladyship loved her like a daughter. Lady Margaret would have had Sian close to her always, would have been always kind to her like some form of pet.

Sir Hugh viewed things differently and had ordered that Sian work like every other maid. Sian's father had fallen into crime, had been arrested by the constable for stealing sheep from the mountain beyond Llantrisant and for poaching rabbits on Treharne's land near Cowbridge in the Vale. He had been hanged at Beddau Cross when Sian was only four. Sir Hugh was scathing

170

about his wife's care for the girl. He believed that she should be turned onto the street to starve. But if that was not to happen she must work.

In reality Lady Margaret felt guilty about her, she believed that she had not acted quickly enough, she had let the mother stop breathing before she made the incision, the child had emerged from the womb blue, it had taken minutes not seconds to get her to breath. Maybe it would have been better if she had not.

Sian was however a happy child, and a contented teenager, she was funny and amusing if never likely to find a husband she was good company and Margaret de Audley loved her like a daughter, Sian would never leave her service. Sian could sing, she had the voice of a song bird, she learned songs by rote for she could not read words properly and would never read music. Most times she made up her own words, fitting them to her own tunes. She played the harp by ear and played it well. Nothing pleased Margaret so much as to have Sian play for her in the evening.

Then Megan had asked me what I liked to do, what were my talents, what did I want to do with my life.

I told her of my love of the outdoors, of my life before I had been sent to the castle, helping my father to run the Mill, but always happiest on the hillside helping Daithí the shepherd with the flock owned by Mr & Mrs Bryant which ran the mountain.

I told her how I had learned to treat animals and repair wounds, how I had birthed lambs and goats and once a foal which was stuck in the birth passage. How I had learned to hunt and trap animals and to shoot with a hunting bow. All I told Megan were skills I did not want to lose.

I had no intention of being confined to the castle, and I intended to find myself a bow and continue with my archery.

Megan looked at me and smiled, 'Give me time' she said, what she meant I was not sure. Maybe she wanted to preserve her own employment when she subtly sowed the idea with Lady Margaret that my talents were better placed in healing.

That night I slept in my small bed in the living quarters, under a warm quilt and listening to the crackle of the banked-up fire in the corner of the room. I woke before dawn and dressed in my breeches and shirt with the stout pair of boots my father had thought to put in my bag from the Mill on my feet. I crept out of the tower and across the castle green.

Behind the big door to the outer green, I could hear the sound of footsteps and equipment being dragged. The door was slightly open and looking into the archers practice area I saw Gwyn, Geraint his Ginger headed friend and two other lads setting up the targets for the mornings practice. Against the wall was a range of bows in different sizes. While the lads were distracted carrying the targets to the far end of the range, I selected a small light hunting bow from the rack which was against the wall.

It felt light and well balanced in my hand. I felt around in the box of arm guards which was alongside a rack of arrows and found the smallest I could. My own had been left in Daithí's old shelter, I would need to go further afield to retrieve it, and for now I could not even get out of the castle. I waited in the shadows for Gwyn and his friends to return from the far end of the range, then stepped out into the dawn light.

I planted six arrows into the ground in line in front of me and as Daithí had shown me uprooted them one at a time, knocking drawing and firing in one swift movement. All Six into the far target and all six in the centre, a hands span between them.

'Gwyn ap Meredith,' I called to him across the grassy strip where he stood, an amazed and slightly shocked look on his face 'Follow that if you will'.

He strode across the grass, took up a Yew Bow at least six feet tall, strung it easily and in one swift movement launched an arrow at the target, he missed, the arrow seemed to have developed a mind of its own and flew off at an angle towards the big wooden door.

To cries of ridicule from his fellow trainees, he once again bowed 'Marged Owen, you have me at a disadvantage'.

All was interrupted by a loud clearing of a throat in the shadows and Sir Kenneth appeared through the very door the stray arrow was embedded in.

'Away with you child, your mistress is stirring, and the water will want fetching'.

Taking the hint, I ran from the archery butt straight to the kitchen where I asked cook for the jugs of water needed to fill the cauldrons for the day, the well was at the rear of the kitchen and surrounded by a wet muddy patch.

I was carrying them back across the grass when Megan found me, looking at my mode of dress she sent me straight to our room to change into my dress. On my way I ran straight into Lady Margaret, how was she abroad before dawn? I saw that she had a basket of herbs fresh from the garden over her arm. Seeing me once again in my breeches she raised an eyebrow in question.

'I have been for the water milady; I did not wish to get my fine clothes dirty'.

I saw the laugh pass across her face and disappear as swiftly as it had arrived.

'Go now and change, I trust this is the truth'.

Back at the archery butt, Sir Kenneth walked to the target and pulled out my six arrows, He placed a hand across the holes made in the target, grunted to himself, and called to Gwyn and his cohort whilst walking to where Gwyn's arrow was sticking out of the wood of the door.

'Something to aim at Lads, missed did you Meredith?

You are here to learn not to be distracted by a pretty girl's arse in boy's breeches'.

My day went as I expected, I carried food and waited at table, I learned not to spill the water as I carried it up the stairs.

I ate lunch in the hall and supper in the kitchen and tried not to stray across to the barrack room where I knew Gwyn might be.

CHAPTER 34 - A MIXED BUNCH – GWŶN AP MEREDITH

It was a Sunday, Clarence de Bone and William Tewkesbury strolled back to the barracks from the refectory, they had eaten lunch and devilled the cook about the quality of the bread and had flirted in their clumsy teenage manner with several of the kitchen maids.

Clarence, or Bone as he liked to be called had had his face roundly slapped for allowing his hands to wander and for pinching the very large posterior of Ceinwen the scullery maid, a very round older lady with a large arse and little sense of humour, in the opinion of the boys. They were in high spirits and up for mischief.

'This new boy' opened Clarence.

'What of him?' replied William.

'Farm boy if ever I saw one, what business has he being a squire?'

'That is not our business Bone, Sir Kenneth thinks a lot of him'.

'Sir Kenneth thinks what he's paid to think!'

'You are wrong there Bone, Sir Kenneth is a fair man, he won his spurs in battle, he will give every man his chance.'

'Well, I don't think farm boy will stick it here, I bet he can't fight in armour, or ride a proper horse'.

'Well Bone,' retorted his companion,' after two years, of learning neither can you!'

Opening the door to the long dormitory, Bone spied something protruding from the end of Gwyn's bed.

'What's that under his bed Will?'

'Leave it there Clarence, it's nothing to do with you'.

'But you know the rule, no weapons in the dormitory, let's see what he's got, things have been known to disappear you know. I lay odds they are not his'.

Clarence reached under the bed and dragged-out Gwyn's precious bundle, pulling the cords which held it closed, he spilled the contents carelessly onto the floor. It was hard to miss the six-foot bow which stuck out from either end of the rolled-up sheepskin cloak which formed the outer wrapping. The sword fell to the stone floor with a monstrous clang, leather belt wrapped around the hilt, damascened blade contained in a black scabbard. Clarence lifted it from the ground, looking at it in awe.

'What have we here? How does a Welsh peasant come by such as this? See, I told you they cannot be his.'

He drew the blade slowly from its sheath gasping in awe at the workmanship 'Scottish, if I'm not wrong, it must be stolen, we must....'

'And what's this ...... he shook the tabard out, creased from being rolled amongst the other contents of the bundle, it was still the Kings colours. We must ....'

Clarence was interrupted mid-sentence by Taliesin Bowen known as Tally, another of the Welsh boys, who was relieving himself in the privy bucket. 'Why don't you mind your business; we don't hold with sneaks..... or thieves for that matter!'

'So, what are you going to do about it. Go crying to your woolly friends on the mountain?'
He made a lewd gesture with his hips. 'We all know you prefer a mountain sheep to a maiden Tally.'

'How many girlfriends have you now Tally Bowen?' Chipped in Gilbert Fitz Hugh, who had been quietly napping on his bunk hoping to spend his Sunday afternoon peacefully dozing.

'I must have counted fifty in the back fields all sore from your cock or his lordship's'.

'At least I have a cock, which is more than you will have in a minute'.

Tally flew across the room at Gilbert, hand on the hilt of the small dagger he kept at his waist. He knocked Gilbert backwards off his feet and into the curtain which concealed their clothes closet, and the privy, the curtain wrapped around him like a shroud and the curtain and both boys fell to the floor like two cats fighting in a sack.

Tally's knife dropped on the floor in the struggle to free himself from the embrace of the enveloping cloth.

With Tally and Gilbert thrashing about in front of him, Will, always the peacemaker seized Tally's knife from the floor where it had fallen, removing it from harm's way, he seized Gilbert by an ankle and pulled hard, the two boys by now had each other totally entangled and were trying to strangle each other with the cloth of the curtain. Pulling an ankle was to no avail. The privy bucket in the corner being the only thing at hand, Will emptied its contents over the fighting boys.

Clarence drew the sword out to its full length and swung it round his head Claymore style, its destination being the back of Wills skull, how dare he tip a bucket of piss over an Englishman. As it reached the high point of its arc, his wrist was seized in a vice like grip concealed in a large leather gauntlet glove.

'Cease! 'the order brooked no argument. The other great paw of a hand removed the sword from Clarence's grip, his other arm now pinioned behind him.

Sir Kenneth drew himself up to his full height and held Clarence de Bone by his throat with his feet barely touching the floor. 'Gwyn ap Meredith, is one of us, you will afford him the respect you give me! and all the other trainees. 'He tightened his grip on the youths throat imperceptibly.

'I will not tolerate such unchivalrous behaviour amongst you, is that clear?'

The usually merry dark brown eyes were alight with fire, and the old knights face was white with anger, and only inches from the boy's face.

Taking a breath in, Sir Kenneth replaced Clarence on his feet.

'Have you scoundrels nothing to be getting on with, out of my sight now, Tally find Meredith and send him to my quarters!'

'I suggest you start by clearing up this mess'.

Picking up the contents of Gwyn's bundle he turned on his leather booted heel and strode the length of the dormitory and left, slamming the door behind him.

Geraint had been showing me around, I had seen the archery butts, the area where we practiced fencing and fighting on foot. The Quintain, that rotating stuffed dummy which was our opponent at the joust.
Geraint had dressed me up in a full suit of armour and left me lying like a stranded beetle on my back while he went to the kitchen for bread and cheese. Had I been able to stand I couldn't have moved to fight him, but all was well, he did fetch me some lunch as well.

That was just to see how it felt. We would only get to wear a breastplate and helmet while we were apprenticed to a knight. Full armour only came with knighthood, and that was a long way off for all of us.

Released from my metal shell, we sat with our backs to the archery targets taking in the sun on the clear blue Sunday afternoon. We had been to church and said mass, duty done for the day, once I had completed my tour the afternoon was ours.

'What are the others like?' I asked.

Geraint drew in a breath 'Tally Bowen, now he is from the town, he is Welsh to his roots and proud of it, he may be small, but he is fast, and once he is your friend he will always have your back'.

'Good', I said I had only seen Tally from a distance, he was small and wiry looking with mousy brown hair, 'Go on'.

'Then there is Gilbert Fitz Hugh, he is related to his lordship in some way and thinks himself above us all, he is arrogant and petty, he likes to tease and play jokes, but he doesn't like the favour returned, and he is a sneak, he pretends to be English, but everyone knows he is one of his Lordship's bastards, his mother was one of the kitchen maids.'

'Go on' I bit into one of the crisp apples which Geraint had brought with our bread and cheese.

'Don't mention the 'bastard' bit mind you, Geraint added 'her ladyship gets very upset by it all, and we all love the lady Margaret we would not see her upset.'

'Then there is William Tewkesbury, he is the only one of us likely to become a knight by right. He is proper nobility, he is easily led, but his honour and his chivalry are dyed in his bones he is a Warwick by blood. William is a diplomat and a peacemaker'.

'Hmmm', I said through a mouthful of cheese.

'And lastly there is Clarence de Bone, he hates his name, well it is Clarence, and prefers that we call him Bone. Clarence is older than the rest of us, he is nearly eighteen, but you wouldn't think it. He likes to think he

181

is in charge, and he is a bully. He believes in English superiority in everything, oh and he is a thief. Beware of him, he will steal like a magpie and hide what he steals in your bunk. It is fortunate that Sir Kenneth knows his ways'.

I finished my cheese and ate the stump of the apple alongside the last mouthful of bread.

'And I', he added 'am Geraint ap Robert, I hale from North Wales even further than you, my family too were farmers, my father also fought with Sir Kenneth at Bannockburn, so we have a bit in common. Though my family are all dead of the plague two years since'.

I looked him square in his bright hazel eyes and saw his lopsided grin quiver with emotion and his eyes well up with tears.

'Well then Geraint, I believe I always wanted a brother, how would you like a little sister as well? I'm sure my family will welcome you'.

'Come then' said my new found brother 'they should all be back from duties by now, time to meet them in person'.

We stepped from the outer keep where the training ground was and onto the castle green, through the door opposite the barracks. The green was quiet, the castle was at rest for once, the hubbub of activity was observing the teaching of our lord.

It was Sunday after all.

All of a sudden the peace was disturbed

'MEREDITH' the distinctive voice rang out across the castle, we both turned towards the bellow.

Sir Kenneth was standing in his doorway, holding a bundle in his arms like cradling a baby.

'MEREDITH, HERE, NOW!'

'Best you go there quickly brother', laughed Geraint jogging my shoulder with his. We both broke into a run arriving red faced and breathless in front of the Master at Arms.

'INSIDE NOW! – not you Roberts your new friend needs some instruction on RULES'.

'Sit Down Meredith' Sir Kenneth gestured to a hard wooden stool positioned in front of his desk.

'Meredith....', His voice softened 'Gwyn, there are certain rules which are in place here for all of your protection.

The first rule is that no weapons are kept in your dormitory. He indicated the bundle on his desk.

'I know that these were your fathers, and I know how much they mean to you, but the bow will go in the rack in the weapons store along with the rest, you will have your own space there for it and only you will use it, I doubt any of the others have the arm to draw such a weapon in any case. The sword, I will keep with my own, in here, when you are proficient enough to use it, you will get it back. But as long as you live in this castle it will not be kept about your person. If you win them, you will get the colours, they will stay with the sword'.

I sat staring at my feet, I felt my colour rising shamefully up my neck and to my face.

'Young man, under your bunk is not a safe place even for your own piss pot. Not all of your cohort have your upbringing, your sense of honour or your honesty.'

He handed me the sheepskin cloak which was all that remained of my bundle, 'you will need that, should your blankets go missing. Now go, I want no more fighting amongst you, God knows you will have enough to do soon'.

I left his office feeling suitably chastised and reduced to a height not much taller than the daisies growing on the green.

There was silence when I finally entered the dormitory, the door was open. Geraint was sitting on my bed waiting for me, a lopsided grin on his face. William and Bone were sitting on Williams' bed, Bone was looking shame faced and sulky. All had their feet up on their beds, the stone floor was clear of stools and other obstructions.

Gilbert and Tally were scrubbing the flagstones with the foul-smelling soap used in the kitchen, Tally was on his knees scrubbing and Gilbert was behind him wielding the mop. Cook had dropped some lavender oil in Gilbert's bucket, but it did little to cover the overwhelming stench of piss. As I walked in I felt them visually inspecting me, taking in my height, and size. I squared my shoulders and addressed the room.

'Gwyn ap Meredith, at your service sirs'.

I bowed low in front of them. I heard Geraint start to clap, slowly. One by one they introduced themselves, some with enthusiasm and some quite sheepish. Only

one refused my hand completely, Clarence de Bone,
well why would he dirty his hands on a Welshman.

CHAPTER 35 – A GLIMPSE OF FREEDOM – MARGED

By the end of the first week, I was badly in need of some freedom. I don't know if Lady Margaret sensed this but on Sunday after Matins which we were obliged to go to she took me one side 'do you ride?' was the question.

'Yes Milady, I do, I ride well I have done so since I was five '.

'Go and seek out Matthew in the stable, ask him to saddle Mildred for me, and to pick out a quiet pony for you, you will accompany me'.

I ran as fast as I could to the stables and did as I was asked. I was horrified to find that I was expected to ride side saddle. But this was freedom of sorts and I had good balance after all.

We rode from the castle out along the road towards Beddau, the Graves. Then took the track I knew so well down the side of the Caerau mountain and out towards my father's mill. Lady Margaret pulled her horse to a standstill,' go ahead and visit your father, he has been asking after you'.

I agreed readily, but I had no intention of riding to the Mill. I had only been gone a week, no time for my father to miss me. I turned onto the parish road and urging on the sturdy grey pony I had been given to ride, I cantered up the track under the trees and turned onto the front of the hill. I heard Lady Margaret call to me

'Meet me here at sundown we must ride home together'.

I spent my day on the hill, I rode up to the dew pond at the top and tied Charm to one of the bent old trees out of sight of the field then I lay on the grass of the bank looking out over the Vale of Glamorgan with the laces of my dress undone and my boots removed and relished the fresh air and the sunshine. The grass was warm under my back, and I was just dozing off to sleep when Charm lifted his head and whinnied. Over the top of the low hedge, I could see Sir Kenneth dressed in leather breeches and with his shirt open, Trooper was cantering easily, clearly enjoying the exercise as much as his master. Behind him came Lady Margaret on Mildred, hair freed from under her cap and eyes shining like silver in the sunshine. She looked twenty years younger than her usual demeanour suggested and truly happy.

Horses cantering in unison they rode down over the bank towards Rhiwsaeson. As I watched they slowed to a walk where the parish road changed to a track into the woodlands, they stopped, and Sir Kenneth handed her down from her horse. Both riders led their mounts up the path and towards where Daithí's hut was.

'I must go, this was a dangerous place to be, at the least I must not be seen' I murmured to myself.

Curiosity getting the better of me, I crept down through the woods beneath me and saw the top of Sit Kenneth's grey head dip to kiss the lady Margaret firmly on her lips and take her in an embrace which was far more than friendship. Then he took her hand and led her into Daithí's hut, my hut – Daithí had given it to me, if anyone looked under the rough bed at the back of the cave they would find my hunting bow and quiver of arrows. It was my sanctuary not theirs, wasn't it?
Not anymore.

What was it Daithí said, 'knowledge is power, and information is key'.

But I could and would say nothing until the time was right. I f I ever needed to say anything at all.

As cover for myself I rode down to my father's Mill to find that he was from home, the widow Bryant was engaged in cleaning the front step of the Mill. I asked after my father and asked her to fetch me my leather gloves from what used to be my bedroom as I would have need of them. This accomplished I had a cover story; I rode back to the end of the parish road and sat by the mountain gate and waited for Lady Margaret.

Milady appeared just before dusk, her hair and clothing were immaculate as always though she seemed a little out of breath. I told her I had been to the Mill and showed her my gloves as proof. We rode in silence back to the castle. Before she left me at the stables after handing Mildred back to Matthew she whispered

'If you are asked, we have been together all day, remember you are not permitted out of the castle alone yet.' So, I was her alibi, and she was mine.

I had just left Charm in his stall when Sir Kenneth came breezing in on Trooper, he called out to Matthew who was busy and then to Gwyn who instantly appeared from the dormitory. 'Strap him well Gwyn, he has worked hard this afternoon, then give him a mash and some hay when he is cool'.

Did these instructions apply to his rider I thought naughtily as I caught Gwyn's eye over the top of Troopers withers.

I saw the tell-tale twinkle of laughter in his eye and the lift at the corner of his mouth. Maybe I was not the only one who knew of this dangerous liaison.

My Sunday ride with her ladyship became a regular adventure, sometimes we rode to collect herbs and Medicinals from the nearby woods at Miskin, she showed me the ancient graves at Tinkinswood and spoke to me as we rode of healing and herbal remedies. I told her of my knowledge of healing animals but never mentioned my connection to the shepherds hut and to Old Daithí, my mentor.

CHAPTER 36- SIX MONTHS ON- MARGED

It had proved an impossible task, trying to teach me the manners of the Court and how to conduct myself as a ladies maid, after six months, Lady Margaret took me to one side.

During the last six months I had repeatedly flouted her instructions not to visit the archery butt, whether to visit Gwyn or to practice my archery.

Sir Kenneth was slightly tight lipped about it, he knew that I had seen him with Lady Margaret or at least he knew that I knew of the hut, I had arrived to practice one morning to find my own bow in the rack and my quiver of arrows hanging with those of the lads. Sir Kenneth also had some respect for my ability as an archer, in fact he liked to see me putting his boys, as he called them, to the test.

Neither William nor Clarence were half the bowman I was. Geraint could compete with me fairly well over a shorter range, the only one who could beat me hands down was Gwyn.

Gwyn had split my arrows down the middle more than once. Or put his own six arrows in amongst mine at the centre of the target. I found that there was one sure way to distract Gwyn, all I had to do was look at him from under my hair and swing my hips a little before he fired and he would miss completely, peppering the door to the archway with arrows much to the dismay of Sir Kenneth. To counteract this distraction Sir Kenneth had taken to getting Gwyn to instruct me personally. He would show me the best way to hold my bow for a shot, try and strengthen my arm to even draw one of the smaller Yew bows. Sir Kenneth's theory was the more contact that Gwyn had with me the less he would be distracted by it. It made archery practice a pleasant experience all round. It did not do much to dampen Gwyn's obvious distraction.

'Is that an extra arrow yer carrying Meredith' was frequently heard when I turned up for practice.

Lady Margaret sat me down in her Solar on the chair I had sat in on that first day in her charge.

'Marged' she said 'Oh Marged is there no hope for you, your behaviour is not that of a lady, you are tardy, unreliable, impolite to my guests and you persist in chasing that young archer. Must I send you home to your father or is there another course you would take?'

The words left my mouth before I could stop them.

'Teach me healing, I promise I will study hard, Gwyn says there is a war coming, healers will be needed, teach me please'.

'Marged, the road to being a healer is a long one of many years, you have the rudiments, and you know them well, but to learn my art needs time and patience. More patience than I think you may have. Come'.

I followed her up to the top floor of the Raven Tower where she pulled back a heavy purple damask curtain to reveal a narrow wooden door in a pointed arch in the wall. A large key on her chatelaine turned in a well-greased lock, the door opened inwards to reveal the private sanctum of Margaret de Clare.

The ceiling was painted with stars and the walls were filled with shelves of polished wood, carrying all manner of receptacles, a large pestle and mortar, a mirror of polished silver which was suspended over a shallow bowl to be filled with water, a gazing crystal smooth and round and cloudy for Marged to look at, and on a lectern at the centre of the room a large leather-bound book-marked Grimoire of M de C.

There were many other books detailing herbal remedies and potions for healing, there was another book in which were written the details of Lady Margaret's patients, their treatments, and the outcomes.

In a cupboard was an array of brutal looking instruments used for amputation of limbs and for letting blood. There were also specially made needles for suturing flesh. Longer than the ones which Marged had used for repairing wounds on animals and stored in raw spirit which she got from the brewer in the town before he reserved it to make the cheap gin which he served to his customers. 'Prevents infection' she said, 'preventing infection is essential, if you can mend the wound and it gets infected then the infection will fester and will kill'.

Here she said I would come to learn of her work, and I would accompany her now on her daily visits to the sick of the town.

And so, I did for the next eighteen months, in that time I practiced my archery with her good grace for an hour every morning, sometimes Lady Margaret would come and watch, an excuse perhaps to see Sir Kenneth. They often stood together on the side lines watching closely as Sir Kenneth's men, as he now called them, tried to compete with my accuracy over the shorter distances. And laughing at my feeble attempts to draw a longbow as tall as myself.

CHAPTER 37 - A ROYAL VISIT- GWYN AP MEREDITH

The Barracks Llantrisant June 1346

It was about a week before we were due to depart for France, Sir Kenneth strode into our quarters, he was slightly flustered, most unusual for a man as imperturbable as him.

'He is coming' he announced.

'Who is coming?' I asked.

'Who, Jesus Christ?' Muttered William, from under his blankets.

'The King?' piped in Clarence from behind the privy screen in the corner.

'The Prince, Edward,' chirped Geraint,' I saw the letter to his lordship yesterday, he is returning from Ireland and will stop to inspect us on his way to join the Kings army, he rides with us to Portsmouth. His lordship has been told to accommodate the whole of his retinue along with twenty good Irish horses.

Sir Kenneth raised his grey eyebrows 'And pray tell me Geraint how you came to be in his Lordship's quarters, and how came you to read such a document?'

'I was not in his quarters Sir, he dropped the letter sir, it was in the stable yard, I gave it to that soft headed boy who cleans his boots, told him to put it on his master's desk'.

Sir Kenneth's brows dropped from their elevated position into a frown, and he shook his head in resignation. 'He is a careless fool, and nothing will cure him of his carelessness or his folly'.

'Squires we must have all ready, your billet will be needed for the Princes staff, you will make shift in the loft above the stables, all the work horses must be taken to the stables at Miskin, all the spare stables mucked out and painted, move our harness room into the end stall, the feed room will serve as it is, I don't suppose his majesty will bring feed, he will expect de Audley to provide.'

His majesty is due to arrive in four days, his ship landed at Pembroke two days ago, the messenger was dispatched by fast horse straight away.

The orders came many and quickly and we four were kept busy in a flurry of cleaning, painting, moving equipment and making ready. The last task was to empty the stables.

Geraint and I were tasked with riding the work horses over to the stables at Miskin.

Miskin was larger than a farm, a small Manor House, it's occupant was an elderly noble distantly related to the de Clare family. His land was lush and green, being on the flat plain below Llantrisant, he kept only a pair of cobs which served to pull his plough and as riding horses when needed. His stables were fine accommodation for the castles working animals.

The only horses left at the castle would be Trooper, Blondell Sir Hugh's horse and Mildred Lady Margaret's palfrey. It took several trips, the last being made using Trooper and Blondell to lead the last two animals the four miles to their new lodgings. It was not often Geraint and I got to ride a proper charger, time for a bit of fun then. Sitting astride Trooper bareback and Geraint on Blondell we took the circuitous route home, along the bank of the river Ely, a long straight field nearly half a mile long, ideal for a race, I urged Trooper into a canter, sitting easily into his stride, I expected Geraint to be alongside me, Blondell was well schooled on the schooling grounds, though spirited and headstrong, Geraint who was a better horseman than I had ridden her often and got on well with her, not today. I turned my head to see Blondell launch herself from a standstill into a headlong gallop, she passed trooper with her head tucked in close to her chest, legs pounding and with no intention of stopping. Geraint clung on to her mane manfully, holding on until they came to an undignified and sudden stop in the river, where Geraint was deposited into the deep water, of the approach to Pant Mill which thankfully only came up to his chest. Geraint could not swim. He squeezed the water from his shirt.

Climbing back onto the delinquent horse, he cursed her quietly, she needed to be ridden more often, it was not her fault her master kept her fed on hard food and confined to the stables, no wonder she boiled over with high spirits. Geraint wondered how on earth Sir Hugh would manage her on campaign, he was not the best of horsemen.

Dunking over, we took the parish road around the hill and over the moor at the rear of the castle giving both horses a good stretch of their legs before our royal visitor arrived. Our route took us up over the hill called the Graig which had a fine view out over the road to the West.

'Geraint! Look! I reined in Trooper on the brow of the hill and pointed into the distance where I could just see a glint of sunlight on metal, 'He is early! They will be here before nightfall '.

We rode back to the castle at a canter, eager to tell Sir Kenneth our news. The old warrior took one look at the filthy condition of what he considered his horses and the even filthier condition of Geraint and his clothing, he took a deep breath in and very quietly, in a voice which exactly conveyed his displeasure.

'Wash them down, now, and bed them down, then wash yourselves, and get your good selves back here clean before I decide to wash you myself! Then bed down the rest of the stalls with deep litter ready for his majesty's string. Start a bran mash and shake out the hay. I am going to alert the household of His Majesty's imminent arrival; I hope her ladyship has her kitchens prepared in time. In the darkness of the hayloft where our beds had been moved, I heard two English voices whispering and laughing at our fate, they had not gone otherwise unheard'.

'And you two slack brains, get off your backsides and help, if you expect to get your colours before we leave.' Sir Kenneth turned on his heel, straightened his massive shoulders and strode across the castle green heading for the kitchens.

Sir Kenneth's visit, and his news of the Prince's imminent arrival generated an explosion of activity in the castles living quarters, beds which had been put out to air were hastily brought back indoors to be carried up to the Royal apartments, wall hangings were beaten clean of dust, privy's were freshened up with fresh smelling herbs, ewers and basins of water were carried up the steep stone stairs by a fleet of kitchen maids. Water was set to boil on every available fire.

Mrs Brassington the cook swept into action, the pigs carcass intended for the next day was speared with the spit and set to turn over the fire in the kitchen hearth, vegetables were set to cook in large pots suspended over the fire, pies and tarts made in advance were set to warm. A feast fit for a King. Or at least for a Prince.

Once we had washed down and groomed our two filthy horses and settled them down with a warm mash and plenty of hay for the night, Geraint and I found a cauldron of hot water and scrubbed ourselves with a bar of Marged's scented soap, scented with oil from lily of the valley and made from a recipe given to her by

Lady Margaret for her own lavender soap, Marged had tinkered with the recipe and the scent and had made improvements. We dressed ourselves in our best shirts and breeches and then headed for the lookout post above Twpsin's lair in the gatehouse to wait for the cavalcade to arrive.

We heard them before we saw them, even though the Prince did not travel with the pageantry of his father. He did not subscribe to being announced with the blowing of trumpets and banging of drums. Never the less we heard the sounds of the harness clinking and shod hooves ringing on the cobbles of the High Street. Round the sharp bend in the road, where it was at its steepest, and leading to the South Gate, nothing but his standard flying from a staff held by his page mounted on a palfrey at the front of the cavalcade.

The Prince was mounted on a light horse part Arabian and descended from the horses which the Spanish had gifted to his father. Black as were all the Prince's mounts but with a flash of white down his forehead. He himself was dressed in unassuming garb of black leather breeches and jerkin laced at the front and covered with a light surcoat bearing the arms of the King, no helmet, he wore a black velvet bonnet with a jewelled brooch securing a feather at the front.

Behind him rode his retinue of knights and squires similarly attired but wearing plain surcoats. The horses were in good spirits but plainly tired as were the riders.

Next came a wagon drawn by two draught horses as big as Blondell, straining in the traces to haul the load of equipment up the steep hill to the castle.

At the rear was what we would be concerned with, a number of grooms riding one horse and leading two more. The rear of the cavalcade consisted of twenty horses including the Prince's battle horse, all to be bedded down and fed.

The front group of riders including Prince Edward turned onto Yr Allt to take the short cut to the castle gates leaving the wagon which was too wide to easily negotiate this lane to take the easier route through the town.

Geraint and I dashed down the steps while Twpsin made ready to open the great gate and admit the Royal visitor. Outside the barracks I could see Sir Kenneth and the other Squires assembled in line along with a tall dark man in the Prince's colours who I had not seen before.

CHAPTER 38 - MARRY ME MARGED – GWYN AP MEREDITH

I had done the morning round of feed for his Lordship's chargers and the great black animal which was Prince Edward's chosen mount. It was a feisty beast, all teeth, and hooves and ill temper, but he was battle hard, nothing frightened him, this was a horse which would gallop through fire for his master, but you would have to master him first.

I had seen the Prince ride him on the jousting field, practicing with sword strokes on a straw dummy, all at a gallop. A warrior indeed, and to think him only a few months older than I.

Sir Hugh's flash chestnut Blondell was mild tempered and kind mannered, a pleasure to be around in the stable, I would not hesitate to let Marged climb on her broad back and take to the field, until the first salvo of shot. Then the mare would take flight, bred in France, the warm blood of Flanders ran in her veins, she would, in time, breed some fine stock, but the mare herself needed experience, she had never been away from the stables and the schooling field, had not heard the sounds of men screaming. Sir Hugh would need his wits about him if he ever got close to the fray.

I had mucked out the stalls and brushed down the cobbles of the yard, all that remained to be done was to clean the harness. Then I could go to the kitchen for breakfast and an excuse to find Marged.

I sat on an upturned bucket, unbuckling leather straps, checking the stitching of bridles, wiping them clean of sweat and horse grease, polishing and checking the great leather saddles used on the broad backs of the horses, reinforced with metal armour to protect both rider and animal they sat heavy on a horses back, once mounted it did not do for a knight to be unhorsed, for he would be stranded on his back like a beetle, with his legs in the air and an easy target for the kill.

I glanced up and there she was leaning on the door jam, watching quietly as I worked, a mug of small beer for me in her hand and a culf of bread and cheese with a dried apple for my breakfast. She smiled, her face lighting up the whole of the dim saddle room.

I finished my work and took the meal she had brought me gratefully; I was hungry, I had missed supper the night before and my stomach growled in anticipation.

She stifled a giggle, and broke off the end of my bread, and a piece of the cheese and popped it in my mouth.

'Will that quiet your insides! You sound like the slops running down the masters privy! '

I ate, concentration on the job in hand, and once I had picked up the last crumbs from the pewter plate with my finger, and licked them from the ends, I turned back to her.

On impulse I said it, though I meant it from my heart and was only waiting for the right time and place. There would never be a right time or place, so now is as good as any.

'Marry me Marged'.

'My father will never allow it'.

'Since when did you, ever do as that old fool asked?'

'Don't you need his Lordship's permission?'

'I do not! I am not a vassal, or a bondsman, I was invited here to be taught, I could leave tomorrow if I liked and take you with me!'

'You march to France when the weather lifts, what of me then?'

'Come with us, travel with me, your skills will be needed! Many women do, wives and such, not just the whores and the washerwomen!'

'I heard her reply, quiet and nearly lost amongst the munching and stamping of the horses '

'Gwyn ap Meredith, so help me, I will marry you!'

We were married two days later, in the small side chapel of the old church, amongst the banners of the de Clare knights, the candles casting a pale light over the names carved in the stone memorials, and the tomb of Sir Gilbert the Red Lord of Glamorgan. Father Marcus led us through our vows, and they were witnessed by

Taliesin Bowen my friend and comrade in the ranks of the Squires.

Margeds ring was fashioned from two horseshoe nails, twined together. For good luck. It was the best I could do at the time, and the smith had complained at the complete waste of good nails on such a sentimental endeavour.

We had nothing that would pass as goods and chattels, we had no home of our own, I had the clothes I stood in, and the uniform provided by his Lordship, and my weapons, my longbow, and the highland blade, taken from a fallen Scot at Bannockburn by my father. Marged had less.

I had not seen my family for nigh on two years, it was several days travel to my father's farm, Marged had not seen her father in that much time either, the mill was less than three miles away.

'Gwyn,' she said the day after we wed, 'I must at least tell my father, please, we must go and visit him.'

We walked there that Sunday, in drizzling grey rain, to be warmed only by the heat of the reception we received. The lane to the hamlet of Rhiwsaeson ran along the foot of the hill, it was an old stone parish road, worn by the wheels of many heavy carts hauling goods to and from the mill.

Turning right and over the stone bridge over the river, the mill stood on the right-hand side of the road, it's great wheel towering over the mill stream which turned it. The river flowed fast at this point in its journey to the sea, the sluice gate built to control the flow of water lay just below the mill house on the straight piece of water which had been utilised as the mill pond. It was a clever piece of engineering, built with minimal need for expanding the watercourse.

When Marged knocked on the mill door, the mill was turning, she could hear the huge stones grinding against each other and the tuneless humming of her father's bass voice as he went about his work.

The sound of footsteps approaching the door, the creak of the hinges, dusty with grain dust, and there he was, she flung her arms around his neck, 'Da Da! '

Quite taken aback, the old miller hugged his errant daughter, and standing back to get a better view of the young lady he hoped she had become, spotted the tall imposing figure standing behind her.

'Da Da,! This is Gwyn, he is one of his Lordship's Squires, his family has land in the west, and he is not an owned man, and we are married!'

It came out all in one sentence, one breath, one excited, joyous statement.

I regained my consciousness on the lane outside the door of the flax mill, the fist when it came was as hard as the stone of the road, thrown faster than a bird of prey stooping on a mouse. I rubbed my jaw and felt my eye socket, it would be swollen on the morrow, likely I would not see properly for a day or so. But no teeth loosened.

The miller glowered at me from the doorstep, then glowered at his daughter from under beetling brows dusted with flour and flax seed.

'You have got her with child I suppose' – it was a statement, not a question.

'No sir, I have not' – I replied, standing on dignity, gathering myself, balancing my stance so as to duck the next blow when it came. The elderly man saw the shift of my shoulders and decided against a further swing at my jaw.

'You want my money then?' She has none you know' He clicked his teeth and sucked on his bottom lip as if sucking on some invisible lemon.

'No sir, I do not want your money, we came to tell you before we leave with the army for France'.

'You made vows?' He seemed to be checking the validity of the marriage.

'Yes sir, in the chapel, with the good father, and witnessed'.

'Then there is nothing for it! She is your trouble now! Best you come in, there is at least her mother's jewels she may have – I will find them'.

I ducked under the low door lintel into the miller's home, Marged's old home, she followed, and we came into a homely but Spartan living room. There was a small fire at one end in a large hearth, heavy wood furniture, polished to a shine it's patina glowing in the dim light which came through the horn window pane, Marged looked at her father, eyebrow raised in question.

'Yes 'he muttered 'I have a housekeeper, and what of it, the widow Bryant does for me, she goes home at weekends'.

'You look well father; she must do well for you'.
Marged suppressed a giggle.

The miller stumped up the stairs to the upper floor
and I heard him opening and closing cupboards,
stumping back down the stairs carrying a small leather
box in his fist. He pressed it into Margeds hand – this
was your mother's, though she never had occasion to
wear them, maybe you will, one day! Marged pushed
the box into the leather pouch hung around her waist,
she did not open it.

'Gwyn, you said?'

'Yes sir'.

'Beware of de Audley, look to my daughter…. your
wife's safety for she is yours now, please look to her
safety, I hear the castle gossip, the man is depraved, he
has, and he will come after her'.

Without further words Marged dragged me out of
her father's house and we began the walk back to the
castle. She to the maids' quarters and I to the barracks.
We were married in name, anything else would have to
wait.

CHAPTER 39 – DAITHÍ'S HUT – GWÝN AP MEREDITH

Marged was having none of it!

Instead of taking the cart track which ran to the left and under the front of the hill, she took my hand and led me up the steep hill in front of us and then onto a narrow sheep track, up through the gorse bushes and onto a wide strip of green meadow. Looking out towards the back of her father's mill and down to the river.

The meadow stretched out across the front of the hill, folding around its curves like a green robe on a matronly lady, ending in a stone wall with a stile, then the path disappeared into woodland.

As it descended through the rocky gulley in the woods, we came into a clearing. Quiet except for the song of the birds, fallen leaves and twigs crunched under foot. At the back of the clearing against the rock wall of the gulley where the stream bubbled down to join its big brother the river was a building, it appeared to be some sort of shepherd's hut. A low door, roof thatched with ferns fallen through with age, not renewed for several years then. Marged pushed open the door and we walked in.

Ingenious, whoever had built this had built the hut onto the cave behind, the space was larger than expected, Marged put her hand into a notch inside the entrance, she knew it was there instinctively and brought out a tinder box and a bundle of rush lights. She deftly lit one and I saw a home, or what could pass for one, a table fashioned from wood logs, with low stools. A fire pit near the door with a makeshift chimney to draw the smoke away from the cave itself. And at the back of the cave a sleeping area, a straw mattress which was still filled with leaves and straw, animal skins stitched together to make covers, how many rabbits and squirrels had sacrificed their lives for such comfort.

Marged's eyes held mine, the look was one of promise, direct, uncompromising. Long slim hands roughened not by kitchen work but with the marks of the hunting bow across her fingers, cared for with oils took my stubbed face between them, she kissed me and walked me backwards to the bed.

We were both virgins, totally inexperienced in the practicalities, but, whispered Marged, the Lady Margaret educated her ladies in all things, told them how to enjoy their menfolk, not just to submit to their masters will.

In between kisses she explored my body with her hands and her tongue until I could hold back no more, turning her onto her front I began to mount her as I had seen with the animals of the farm, wriggling like an eel, she turned beneath me and with one swift cock of her hips, my over excited cock had been encased in joy. It was fast too fast the first time, I drove home hard, crying out, my balls nestled in the hollow of her thighs, my body seeking to burn itself into hers, she bit my shoulder to stifle her cries and echoed my own as the rush lights faded into darkness, stars erupted round my head, and I held her close to stop both our worlds from spinning.

We lay, we talked, we found each other, we nestled together on that old leaf mattress encased in covers of skins and before we slept we became one.

This had been Daithí the shepherd's home many years ago, she had been a friend to the old shepherd as she grew up, his hut had become her refuge from her father and his rules. There was room here to tie a pony out of sight in the woods, to bide unseen and unfound until darkness and Daithí sent her home. Daithí had entertained her with stories of the old ones, of dragons and witches, had taught her to trap animals, fire a bow and arrow, to cook what she had caught and to care for the land. She helped him to roundup the sheep from the hillside, counted them for him, rescued ewes from the entangling bracken, used her small thin hands to birth new lambs.

Then Daithí had gone, one day she had come to the hut and all his belongings were gone. Not that there was much to move, he did not need a wagon. All would fit in the pack he carried on his back. Too old they had said, he had been replaced by Mrs Bryant's son. Mrs Bryant who now kept house for her father. Old Daithí would have to take his chances at the hiring fayre or wander the land as a beggar. He had no family, that he knew of, the idle lad who took his job did not know about the hut, did not care to look for it, he would deign not sleep amongst the flock in winter or even be close to them on the hill. Daithí had left Marged to care for the hut, his note said so! In the year before her father sent her to the castle she had cared for it, repaired it, and hoped Daithí would come back. He never did. This was now our refuge, a home of sorts. We slept, waking to see more stars in a summer sky through the holes in the thatch.

'We must away, we will be missed'.

Down the steep stony track, in the dark, eyes unaccustomed to the night Marged found the way, she knew every stone and tree personally, then up the hill to the North gate of the town, on the road that led to Beddau, the graves. A jaunty good evening called to the gatekeeper, and I kissed Marged goodnight chastely and made my way to the dormitory and the bawdy remarks of my compatriots.

I did not notice de Audley as he let himself out of the Raven Tower, through the door from the Lord's apartments. But he noticed us from his place in the shadows, watching.

Marged would be walking that very path, to her ladies bed chamber as she did every night after evening prayers.

CHAPTER 40 - THE PRINCE'S PROGRESS – LADY MARGARET

Prince Edward had not only come to take charge of his fighting men, but he also had business to conduct on behalf of his father Edward III, and instructions to view what progress my husband had made in restoring order to the county of Glamorgan.

Before the army leave for embarkation at Portsmouth, he must ride out into the vale and see for himself, he would speak to the cottages and the farmers, he would see for himself what progress if any my husband had made.

He will ride, he says in company, I must ride with them, only fitting for the Lady of the house to accompany her lord, and we would take one squire and a maid servant to accompany us. And of course, Sir Kenneth would be there, whether he had finished making lists or not. No choice then but to go.

Marged was overjoyed, any chance of a break from the castle, and to her great joy, her husband Gwyn had been chosen as the Prince's squire for this royal progress.

I am not so enthusiastic, the thought of spending maybe a week in my husband's company is not a pleasant prospect. But I have been commanded, I hope Kenneth, the old rogue can be discreet, ours is a liaison which could never become public knowledge. It is accepted by society that his Lordship should take a lover, and mine has done so in spades, but a Lady, she should remain faithful and dutiful at all times.

It will take about a week to cover the ground the Prince wants to see. First, we ride west to the abbey at Margam and then back along the Roman road visiting the coastal castles at Ogmore and St Donats then to Ewenny Priory and finally the Market town of Cowbridge built by my great great grandfather Richard de Clare the then Earl of Pembroke. Then home via Miskin the tiny hamlet home to one of the larger mills in the area and its own Manor House.

Prince Edward is a shrewd man even if he is only sixteen years old, I pray he will see the steps I have taken to make life better for the people of the towns and villages, much as I detest Sir Hugh, it has been a long road to recovering my family's property from the grasp of the King and then under conditions. I have done my utmost to comply with those conditions even if my husband has squandered all the goodwill I have developed, by his high-handed manners and spendthrift ways. A chance as well for Marged and I to forage the herb gardens at Margam and Ewenny to re stock my store room, to dig for roots on the wooded hills behind Margam Abbey and to climb the steep slope to the tiny chapel high on the hillside above the abbey, used by the monks so that they may continue their religious practice without having to leave the flocks unattended on the mountain side it is a haven of tranquillity amongst the deer and the great leafy oaks, looking out over the sand hills and the wide bay with the white topped grey waves of the Severn Channel in the distance.

I suspect that the Prince will also want to hunt while he is at Margam, the abbey keeps a pack of deer hounds and the land stretching up and behind the abbey is rich in game and in particular deer. The Cistercian monks of the abbey are also known for their expertise in brewing ale and making wine. Margam is said to have a fine winery, if the Prince does not wish to sample its produce then I am sure that my husband will.

The Benedictine priory at Ewenny is a smaller concern being closely related to the cathedral at Gloucester, the Benedictine monks with their black habits were very active in the local community, running schools for the village children in Corn town and St Brides, certain of the brothers engaged themselves in copying books which were finely illustrated and kept in the library which was accepted as being one of the finest in the area. Ewenny also has a fine herb garden, planted in a walled are which runs from the fortified wall of the priory itself alongside a small brook and down to the Ewenny River. It is abundant in water plants and also in leeches. I also wish to consult with Brother Bartram who runs a small infirmary within the walls of Ewenny Priory and often develops new remedies and cures.

Bartram is one of the few of the brethren who is not superstitious of change, he tempers his belief and faith in our Lord with a good dollop of science, if the science fails only then he will resort to prayer. Thankfully he is extremely proficient in the science department.
I try to visit brother Bartram once a month to read his record of treatments and take tips from his latest methods. Radical indeed. On my last visit I distinctly recall reading one of his most daring remedies.

13th January 1345

The village of St Brides has been beset again by an outbreak of smallpox.

I have visited several of the cottagers of the village, given them advice, they must wash their clothes and their bedding, and cover their nose and mouth if they cough. Boil all their water and avoid touching those who have become infected. One of the cases has been brought to the infirmary.
The Patient:

Mari James is a woman with a small child, Evan, who is now ten years old, her husband has already died of the pox, and she has no one to do for her, her neighbours are distant as she lives in an outlying farm cottage close to the river. I have fetched her on the cart to the infirmary along with her son.

Day 1: Mari James has a high fever which I am trying to control with cold compresses and snow when we have a fall of it, she complains of an intense headache and can keep no food down. She says that her symptoms have been with her for at least a week. Her son has no symptoms so far.

Day 4: Mari James is now covered in the red rash, which is typical of the pox, some have come up into pustules. Young Evan shows signs of a sore throat and has ulcers in his mouth.

I have read in a parchment from ancient China that if I can introduce the contents of the pustules beneath the skin of a patient who does not yet have the full manifestation of the pox, then they may survive.

I have taken a sharp needle and made small incisions in the muscle of young Evans arm.

After a few days he has a swelling and blisters in the area, but his ulcers are no worse and he has developed no fever.

His mother, Mari, however, shows no sign of improving health. I have isolated Evan in a cell used normally as a store room and am watching him closely, he is able to eat a little broth and is no longer vomiting.

Day 20: Mari James has lost her battle with Petit Variole; I have washed the body and she has been buried in the Priory churchyard. Young Evan has had a mild case of fever and developed few of the terrible pustules which completely covered his poor mother's skin. He is eating well and shows all the signs that he will recover well. He has not yet been told that his mother is dead. The child though, now an orphan, is thriving and will be taken in by monastery.

Maybe catching a disease in small measure may prevent death from it in its greatest manifestation.

Good observation Brother Bartram, but don't broadcast your findings for many will call it witchcraft, in fact there are those in the nearby village of Corntown who have already branded young Evan James, for that is his name as a charmed child or even a changeling.

I look forward to seeing that homely face under his monk's tonsure, his merry brown eyes and hearing his lilting slightly high-pitched voice and his slightly un-monastic sense of humour. But then not all monks started off that way, I think.

Maybe brother Bartram has a secret past. Whatever he is, he has the best herb garden in Glamorgan, and also the best stock of remedies in the County.

I must introduce him to Marged, with her pithy wit and homespun humour they will get along fine. Thinking on it, I am quite looking forward to the 'Royal Progress'

CHAPTER 41 – ABBOTS AND PRIORS – LADY MARGARET

With the great gates of the castle behind us and Gwyn riding ahead with the Prince's banner, my husband riding alongside the Prince on that great horse of his, we head to the west across the Meiros Mountain towards Llangynwydd and then on to Mynydd Margam and the back entrance to the Abbey.

It is a full day's ride with brief stops only to rest and water the horses and to eat the food which is carried in saddle bags on the pack horse which Marged is leading from her mount.

My husband is starting to regret not swapping his vast warmblood heavy horse for something more suited to the terrain, Blondell is a fine animal but more suited to the open spaces and easy terrain of the English downs than the parish roads and narrow tracks overhung with trees of the Welsh Valleys. Even his majesty the Prince has swapped his great black horse, Bryn, for Dylan, a neat white animal, spirited, but compact and easy to ride along the heavily rutted parish roads, overhung with low trees and bushes. Sir Kenneth will only ride old Trooper, but he is not a tall horse though he is as broad as a table and has the strength to carry a fully armoured knight.

The weather is fine, even for Wales, as we set off but by the time we ride into the stables at the abbey a fine misty rain is falling, we arrive just in time to avoid the torrential downpour which descends into the rain shadow of the hill.

The Cistercian brothers welcome my husband, myself, and the Prince, we are accommodated in rooms suited to our status in the Abbots accommodation. Marged, Gwyn and Sir Kenneth are to sleep in the travellers' bunk house which is comfortable and warm but basic in its furnishings.

Tired and hungry we are well fed with roasted venison and a variety of game pies and mashed root vegetables grown in the abbey gardens. The wine produced in the winery and the beer from the monks' brewery flows and replete and exhausted Marged and I retire to bed, me eschewing my husband's chamber as I have done for many years now and opting to sleep in one of the cells kept for travellers.

The Prince and my husband along with Sir Hugh stay up late, discussing the King's business, though they have arranged to ride out early to hounds and hunt deer on the mountain behind the abbey.

It must be the small hours of the morning when I hear Gwyn ap Meredith crash through the door of his and Marged's cell and her roundly cursing him for his cold hands and feet when applied to certain naked portions of her anatomy. This followed by the familiar grunts and groans of the nocturnal activities of a couple obviously much in love with each other.

I wrap my blankets around myself and listen rather wistfully to the loud guttural snoring of Sir Kenneth, as alone in his bed as I am in mine.

When I awake in the morning the menfolk have already risen, how do they manage to eat and drink so much with so few of the after-effects I seem to suffer.

Marged too is as bright as a button this morning, eager to breakfast and either to watch for the men and the hounds returning or to at least spend a morning in the herb garden of the abbey, the winery, and the brewery, learning new skills and taking cuttings from some of the more unusual plants which the brothers grow in the glass houses alongside the vines.

Abbot Whiting is a genial if slightly sardonic host, he is tight lipped about the Prince's business on behalf of the King but with the impending military campaign to France leaving within weeks, I strongly suspect it involves the good abbot parting with a substantial amount of the abbeys hoarded wealth. For this is a wealthy abbey, its white robed brothers make a great deal of profit from the sale of their wares, and I fear that there is more profit than worship undertaken in this religious institution.

Marged and I decide to venture up the hillside to the tiny chapel which is perched on a rocky outcrop on the hill above the abbey, from there we feel that we may be able to see the hunt which is taking place in the woods below.

The chapel, truly a place of peace, we make our obeisance to the lady Mary to whom the chapel is dedicated and then sit on the large flat stone outside the building and listen for the sound of the hounds working their way through the trees below.

Here they come noses to the ground, the lead hound checks and speaks, then nose back to the trail breaks into a gallop, ahead on a rise in the ground I see the deer a fine roe deer buck. The hounds are on his trail, and he breaks cover and bolts across the open ground, pursued by hounds and then horsemen. Led by the Prince of Wales closely followed by Sir Kenneth, Gwyn and lastly by an empty horse. Blondell has emerged riderless from the woodland, reins hanging loose over her head and harness flapping as she gallops, her huge heavy stride throwing up great clods of mud behind her.

I take a shocked intake of breath and look in the direction from which she has come. There he is, a short blonde-haired figure, red faced and angry and so covered in mud that his features are hardly visible beneath the liberal coating of Welsh bog.

I look at Marged who is trying very unsuccessfully to suppress her mirth, her face is red, her mouth pursed tight and there are tears running down her face, she turns away from me shoulders shaking and dissolves into helpless laughter.

Within seconds I join her, and we are both lying in a very undignified fashion on a limestone slab warmed by the sunshine on a Welsh mountainside bursting our seams with laughter.

Horses and hounds disappear into the distance, and we hear the sounds of the huntsman sounding the inevitable kill.

The Prince will no doubt conduct the coup de gras and say the hunters prayer over the animal which has sacrificed its life for our sport and ultimately for our food for no part of the animal will be wasted.

Hopefully there will be a supply of gut to be had for use in our medical chests, long bones to be cleaned and shaved to use for splints. Gut is useful for suturing though I would rather use silk thread, but that is hard to come by and expensive.

Composure regained, Marged and I carefully navigate the steep and sometimes slippery path back down to the Abbey with its unusual twelve-sided chapter house, would that be one side for each apostle, I must ask Abbot Whiting before we leave.

As we pass the stable block, I see a very amused Gwyn washing down Blondell, and my husband wearing half a Welsh bog in his breeches berating him thoroughly for not having the horse well enough trained. The sight of Sir Hugh de Audley in a rage is not pretty, to be on the end of it can sometimes be fatal.

Sir Kenneth is frantically peace-making, drawing my recalcitrant husband away to where the abbot assures him there is a warm bathtub waiting and fresh clothing. Gwyn will see to it that Blondell is more schooled for her next appearance with hounds, it is after all her first time out. Maybe sir Hugh would prefer to ride Dylan tomorrow.

Another night of talks between the Prince and the Abbot, this time alone in the Abbot's private rooms.

We are entertained by one of the brothers singing and playing the harp, folk songs in the Welsh language rather than religious canticles. He has a beautiful voice, and I find myself drifting off into sleep with my head rather indiscreetly on Sir Kenneth's shoulder. Old rogue that he is he does not move and slips a protective and supportive hand around my waist, his left hand securely clamped on the left cheek of my posterior.

Sir Hugh has retired to bed early, exhausted, and slightly sore from his equine adventure, and also rather embarrassed.

Gwyn has been released from service for the night and has Marged seated securely on his lap, he does not intend to let a night off go to waste.

After breakfast and Matins, the following day, the Prince having been assured by the Abbot that the King's taxes will be delivered to Llantrisant forthwith bids us mount up and we depart in good spirits and head east along what passes for the road towards Ogmore.

At Ogmore castle, a further ten archers are pledged to the cause, similarly at St Donats and Barry.

They will muster and march to St Nicholas our first proposed camp on the road to Portsmouth and the ships.

The Prince inspects the infirmary at Cowbridge and the small school both of which have been set up at my behest, he approves of both, he meets with the local dignitaries who renew their allegiances to his father the King and further archers from the town are pledged to the cause.

We reach Ewenny Priory in darkness on the fourth day. Gwyn dismounts and rings the great bell to the East gate house, Ewenny is a fortified building similar to a small castle, most unusual for a house of God.

After several minutes the door is answered by a novice monk in black robes. Where is the Prior? Something is wrong that there is no one of rank here to welcome a royal visitor.

'Fever' gasps the brother, plainly terrified of being put to death on the spot, 'We are infected by fever, sire we cannot let you in'.

Marged and I ride forward, 'can we help brother, I have knowledge of healing, so does my maid, where are your sick?'

Sir Kenneth suggests we stay at the nearby Tavern, the Old Fox looks a welcoming place, he is sure that the innkeeper will find bed and board for His Majesty, a tale he could no doubt dine off for life. Marged and I are taken inside the gates of the abbey.

'Tis not the pox' says the young monk who admitted us 'all the affected have fever and sickness and then the blazing shits – sorry milady'.

'Are you boiling the water' I ask, 'where are you getting it, the brook or the well?'

'Aye milady, I am boiling all the water, I have made broth as Brother Bartram told me, but he took sick yesterday, I am cooling the fever with cold water and making them drink. '

'Who else is helping you?'

'No one ma'am, there is only me left'

'And your name brother?'

'I am not yet a brother, my name is Evan, milady, Brother Bartram took me in when my mother died, he cured me of the smallpox' I could see then in the light of the candle lantern the remnants of the pox scars which adorned young Evan's face.

'Evan, take us inside, show us what is to be done'.

Marged and I led our horses into the Priory grounds, the usually neatly kept yard showed signs of neglect, it was not swept clean, the door to the kitchen and refectory stood open and I could see the cauldron of broth hanging over the fire. Evan in his wisdom had turned the refectory into a ward, the sick brothers lay in their cots in two rows one on either side of the room, twelve in total. The abbey only had twenty inhabitants.

'Where is Prior Edmund?'

'He has fled,' muttered Evan,' after brother Benjamin died last week, he took himself to visit at the cathedral in Gloucester, he said he will return when he has news that all are well or dead.'

'How many have you lost?'

'Four of the brothers have died milady, Brother Peter, Brother Mark, Brother Silas, and Brother Benjamin. The Prior has left, and all the others are sick, including Brother Bartram.'

'Show me to him' I said, thinking that he could confirm my diagnosis of dysentery.

Brother Bartram lay on his cot, he was covered in a sheet and sweating profusely, but shivering, the acrid smell of vomit rose from the bowl alongside his bed, the contents a mixture of half-digested broth tinged with blood where his stomach strained against its emptiness. He was weak as a kitten but raised a smile when he saw me.

'Marged,' I said.' Bring me cold water, cold as you can.'

I offered him a drink from the beaker by his bed and supported his head while he drank.

'Evan is a good lad, Margaret, take him with you, he need not give his life to God just yet.'

'Tis the Flux, I pray that all who are still alive will recover, young Evan has worked miracles, alone.
It will be better with you to help him.'

I sent Marged with our saddle bags to find the cleanest of the monks' cells for us to retire to, if we were to have any rest. Then I checked on the vital signs of all the living.

In the last bed by the door of the refectory cum ward lay Brother Septimus, he had been old when I last visited, but sprightly and vibrant for his great age, now he lay a skeletal shadow of himself, his muscle burned away by fever and his breath wheezing tightly from his chest.

I could see his lips moving in the act of prayer as he recited to himself the last rights, and I held his hand while he made his peace with God and his kindly ancient soul quietly left its withered body behind. The door was already open for it to leave.

'Marged, we will lose no more', I told my helper.

And so it began, for nearly a week we cleaned the functional parts of the Priory. Kitchen, refectory and sleeping cells each cell given fresh bedding, Evan was given a day of rest, then I set him to burning all the soiled blankets and habits, breaking into the Abbot's store room to issue every surviving brother with new fresh robes.

Brother Bartram had given him instruction on how to pick the great lock of the Prior's door. I still have my doubts about Brother Bartram, he is far too worldly to be a monk! For proprieties sake Evan bathed each patient, while Marged and I kept up the endless round of boiling water, broth, and cold flannels. Raiding the Prior's private store of simples, I found a supply of ginger and turmeric, expensive ingredients, but necessary to use them, I had Marged make a vat of strong tea, with which we dosed our patients regularly. One by one they began to improve, little by little, there was less vomiting, less diarrhoea and more complaining, a sure sign of men, be they brothers of the lord or not, getting better.

As they became able, they were bathed, issued a new habit and re housed in their monastic cells to rest and recuperate.

After a week, Gwyn came to the Priory, Sir Hugh, his Majesty, and Sir Kenneth he said, had ridden on back to the castle. He had been given instructions to stay with us and ride back with us when we thought it time to leave. I immediately sent him out to walk the length of the Priory water source from the Ewenny River to the Priory and check for any source of contamination, likely the cause of the outbreak. There was none.

'Then check the well'. I told him sharply.

Evan, when pressed remembered that the brothers had started to use the stream for water after the first of them became sick. Marged and I watched amused as Gwyn attached young Evan to a long rope and lowered him the thirty feet down into the well. Then I heard him shout.

'Master Gwyn sir, I have it'.

Gwyn hauled on the rope and slowly but surely the head of Evan James appeared over the parapet, then one arm and then the other holding by the tail the lifeless body of Jezebel the Prior's pet cat. A hissing spitting antisocial animal in life, the large and elderly tabby monster had disappeared several months ago.

'So that where the old witch got to! 'Evan announced.

Brother Bartram got blamed for her disappearance. But he would never have dropped her body down the well, News then to give the Prior, should he ever return. Ding Dong! I thought to myself. I sat and dictated while Marged wrote up the case book, describing the course of the infection, the treatment, and the cause.
Gwyn and Evan sought out and mended the cover for the well, all the water would need to be boiled for

several months in any case. until the water source had cleansed itself, a gallon of the vinegar also found in the Prior's store room was sent down into the water to assist the cleansing process.

A week later than planned, we packed our meagre belongings together with a large bundle of herbs harvested from the garden, a large box of prepared salves from Brother Bartram's still room and the benedictions and prayers of the residents, we left Ewenny Priory. Accompanied by Evan riding behind Gwyn, on his horse, sad to leave Brother Bartram who I would find out had taught him far more skills than basic healing.

That night we slept under the stars in a field next to the tiny church of St Canna, and Llangan I curled up in my travelling cloak for the night and went to sleep listening to Evan regaling Gwyn and Marged with tales of his life at the Priory. Gwyn's deep chuckle and Marged's bell in every tooth laugh. I had no doubt I would be regaled with many an interesting fact on the last leg of our journey.

CHAPTER 42 - THE TRUTH ABOUT BROTHER BARTRAM – LADY MARGARET

Robert Bartram McGregor – or Brother Bartram as he was now known.

Born the eldest son of a chief of Clan MacGregor in the year of our lord thirteen hundred, he had been fourteen years old when his father was killed at the battle of Bannockburn.

Despite the MacGregors having fought bravely in battle, Robert the Bruce had decided to punish them for their nefarious ways by giving their lands to the Clan Campbell. The retribution by the Campbells was swift and brutal.

Put from their homes and now living on the land and their wits, young Robert had kept his mother and his younger sisters from starvation by lifting cattle and sheep and killing game on what were now Campbell lands. He was arrested and taken prisoner, kept as a virtual slave to the Campbells, then just after his fifteenth birthday he had been told that his family were all dead. His mother and sister had starved to death in the heather, and the broken-down cottage they lived in had been burned to the ground.

With nothing more to lose, he had escaped from where the Campbells held him by jumping from the parapet into the deep loch below, he had then taken to the road, living on his wits. From living rough in the countryside, he had gained a knowledge of what was edible and what was not, his digestive tract had become a testing ground for all manner of plants and fungi. His mother had given him a good knowledge of what was definitely poisonous, so he avoided mushrooms and foxglove at all costs and observed the animals, watching what they thought fit to eat.

His travels took him to Edinburgh where he had worked as an errand boy for an apothecary. There he had gained more knowledge, before getting caught stealing from the shop. The old apothecary had not only slung him out back onto the streets to starve. He had had him branded a thief. His name blackened he had left town.

Working his way south, Robert had picked pockets in every city and town from Carlisle to Cardiff before he was caught again. Placed before the Cardiff Assizes Judge Gwilym Williams had taken pity on the now sixteen-year-old prisoner before him. The huge booming voice of this most illustrious and progressive of Judges told him that had the power to sentence him to death, or to have his hand or his ear cut off, or to have him flogged up to two hundred lashes, then he deliberated in his rooms at the back of the court house, the prison gaoler came forward and spoke words in Robert's favour, the boy is not all bad!

Judge Gwilym Williams chose flogging, but with a condition. Having heard that the prisoner before him had some skill as a healer and was not completely a lost cause, the Gaoler had knowledge that he had treated several men in the jail during his incarceration. The judge chose to impose sixty lashes, some physical punishment was after all expected. The rogue in the dock had been in possession of ten stolen wallets had he not, and there was evidence that he was a very proficient if not proven house breaker. Yes, sixty lashes would be ample, the condition was that it would reduce to twenty if the prisoner agreed to stay at the house of a religious order for a period of five years, to learn a trade and reform himself. And so, Robert surrendered himself to the lash, he still bore the scars, now feint and hidden under his habit. Evan had seen them when he had bathed the brother during the fever. Then he had been bundled into a cart and given into the custody of the fortified priory at Ewenny.

If happiness or at least contentment was to be found in the presence of God and a herb garden, and the tutelage of Brother Septimus then Robert had found it. He had taken his vows at the end of his five-year sentence and used the name Bartram in the same fashion that Septimus had taken the middle of his own name when he had taken orders.

Mark Septimus Jones was also a brother with a dark past.

Although Brother Bartram sometimes pined for the adventure of the open road, he found himself complete. And yes, he told young Evan he had been in love, he had left his lassie, Christina Ellen Crockett, in Scotland when they were both fifteen, and that was many years ago.

And now Evan, you have asked enough questions of an old man.

And so, with my sleepy ears, I listened to young Evan James, relating the life story of my friend Brother Bartram no doubt told to Evan in preparation for his death, should he be about to die of the flux, but an expurgated version should the reaper not come for him just yet. An old rogue indeed.

How many of his nefarious skills had this tonsured teacher passed on to his young apprentice. Only the legal ones I hoped, but I had a feeling I would be proven wrong with time.

CHAPTER 43 - PREPARATIONS FOR WAR – GWYN AP MEREDITH

In the weeks before we left upon campaign there was feasting and merrymaking all over the town, it was not often that a provincial Welsh unit were hailed as 'the best in the Country', the long bow men of Llantrisant were to march at the right of the Prince on this campaign against the French who sought to steal his territory across the channel and eventually to invade our island.

Candles and rush lights lit the windows of all the cottages clustered around the base of the castle, Sir Hugh Audley and his knights kept vigil in the ancient church, before returning to the great hall of the castle for a farewell feast. The red and yellow of the de Audley colours hung proudly from the castle ramparts and red and yellow pennants decked every window. And in pride of place amongst the red and yellow hung the Princes Colour, the coat of arms of the Prince Edward also that of the King Edward III Three Lions Couchant on a red ground and Fleur de Lys on an azure ground on a quartered shield.

The archers of the town were now the Prince's men. And proud to be so. All had been issued with the Green and White tunics of the Town in which they would march. The highborn and the nobles feasted in the great hall where long tables were set out with food and wine and a great hog roasted slowly in the fireplace, turned above the flames on a massive spit by a team of hard working kitchen boys to keep it from burning, out on the castle green under the stars the rest of the town and its fighting men gathered, here too hogs and sheep were roasting over fires, ale and cider was being drunk, men sang and ate and drank or took their lady loves to bed and said goodbye for one last time before starting the long march to London and from there to France. Many would not return, such was the nature of war, but at least we bowmen were valued assets and the nature of our weapons put us slightly out of the field of danger. Our role to fire from a distance.

I walked around the castle green a jug of ale in hand searching out Marged, my wife, she was coming with me after all.

There she was now, walking from the side gate of the church yard, across the cobbled lane, I would know that walk anywhere, Marged did not exactly walk, she floated with a natural grace, practically dancing across the grass, dressed in her best pale blue homespun dress, low cut to show a hint of bosom, but not indecorously low as to seem common, her white, blonde hair hanging down her back in a thick plait tired with blue and red ribbons for the occasion. Elfin featured with deep blue eyes which danced with light, still the girl I had fallen for on sight.

Marged could never have been one of Lady Margaret de Audley's ladies' maids, my Marged had far more spirit to her that that, not for her the demure sitting around the spinning wheel sewing needlework samplers or primping her ladyship's gowns.

Her spirit of mischief still hadn't left her, I had often found her dressed in one of the kitchen boys' clothes out at the archery butts practicing with a bow, she was a fine shot but would never have the strength to draw a long bow. Not deterred she practiced hard, she would ride off on one of the ponies from the stable, usually a feisty grey pony called Minstrel, across the moor to the North of the town and up onto the hills, returning often with a string of Rabbits for the pot.

Lady De Audley despaired of her and had all but given up on trying to discipline the free spirit who breezed through her rooms with unrestrained joy. The fact that she seemed to spread happiness in her wake was the only thing which prevented her being sent home in disgrace. Seeing the free spirit in her Lady Margaret had taught her healing Marged had been a good pupil.

There were things to be attended to, weapons to be loaded into carts, all the trappings of war to be assembled, what clothing each man possessed to be bundled up and stowed on the wagons. Most only had what clothes they stood in, some more fortunate possessed a change of breeches and shirt. All were given a leather bowman's jerkin and a helmet and a tabard bearing the Prince's colours.

The Prince had commanded me to ride out with his party across the land behind the castle towards the smaller villages in the valleys, he sought pledges from those of the bowmen who thought themselves too old or infirm to fight. He would, he said, pay them all well.

So, I had gone with the Royal party, we had been gone for days as far north as Brecon where I had won my first archery tournee. Returning at dusk the horses had been left in my charge in the stables. Five horses to settle for the night and me alone in the stables, or so I thought.

I had gone to the loft for more hay for Bryn the Prince's horse, it was then that I heard her screams, it was Marged. The screams came from the stables. In one of the spare stalls bedded down for the spare horses I saw them.

Dress ripped, my wife was pinned under the body of Sir Hugh De Audley, his breeches undone and his member now hanging flaccid from the lacings. Marged's thighs stained with blood, her arms and face bruised where she had fought him. His Lordship also sported a long gouge mark across his forehead, Marged had missed his eyes with her nails by a fraction.

His Lordship was known to stray from his marriage frequently, and to take his pleasures as and when he wanted. I hid in the shadows as he straightened his clothing and left. I ducked back into the shadows He did not see me, to make myself known would mean certain death.

CHAPTER 44 – HIS LORDSHIPS PROPERTY – MARGED

Amongst the throng of people gathered on the castle green, I could not see him. Usually, I could spot my husband easily but today the crowd seemed to swallow even Gwyn ap Meredith.

Sir Kenneth was there at his post outside the barracks, poring over his lists, barking orders, marshalling the ranks of chaos. Geraint had worn a track from the armoury to the waiting wagons, loading arms and supplies, Clarence, and William, I had seen them too, going about their duties.

I had not seen Gwyn, had he been sent on some errand or other, he had been absent for days. In preparation to march with the army I had stowed my travelling box of equipment on the wagon, my clothing such as it was rolled up in a bundle and ready to be stowed in the same manner.

Where was my husband, I had felt the need for him sorely in the last few days, married we were before God but still sleeping at opposite ends of the castle. When could we find ourselves a cottage of our own, possibly somewhere in the town, outside the castle walls. Somewhere we could truly call our own or would Gwyn go back to his parents farm? He had told me so much about his family. His father Myrddin who had fought against the Scots at Bannockburn and his mother Anwen and his baby sister Gwennie who he had left to do his chores about the farm. And Hengwm, I pictured the long low house settled in the hillside. Maybe we could go there, he had a whole family that I had never met. I was pleasantly daydreaming of cottages and hillsides and all manner of distracting things associated with them when I heard the sound of a page sounding a trumpet at the main gate.

Then I saw them returning, four horses riding back through the gates. Their riders, Sir Hugh, the Prince, and Lady Margaret, and with them Gwyn.

They rode into the stable yard, the Prince handing Milady down from her horse, Sir Hugh dismounting stiffly from Blondell, and Gwyn.

Still mildly distracted I took one more turn around the castle green, allowing the party time to hand the horses over to their grooms and for the nobility to leave the stables.

I smoothed my hair and straightened my pale blue dress the only one left outside of my travelling bundle. It was laced low at the front and cinched tight at the waist with a leather belt which I had purchased at the market on the Bull Ring.

I caught sight of my appearance in the water trough outside the stable walls and pushing a stray curl back off my forehead, I wandered casually into the stables in search of my husband. The grooms were used to my presence, I had frequently whiled away an hour or two sitting atop the feed bin or the hay waiting for Gwyn to finish his duties. I could hear him now, talking to the horses his soft voice in tune with each animal, the clink of harness, the friendly slap on each animals quarters as he left it comfortable fed and watered for the night.

Candle lanterns hung from the harness room wall casting a warm mellow light and some shadows on the dark little room which held the horses tack.

I saw Gwyn fork hay into each of the horses mangers, his broad shoulders and long back handling the fork with practiced ease, finding that there was not enough hay in the shaken pile for the Prince's horse, he disappeared back into the barn for more, whistling to himself as he went, and giving a running commentary to his charges of his progress.

'Wait on now Bryn, yours will be in a minute' a big hoof struck the stable door 'hush there big lad it's coming, with extra if you wait' a whinny and a snort of nostrils and another stamp at the door then quiet.

'Good evening to you my pretty Marged'.

The voice assaulted my ears from the darkness of the harness room. Sir Hugh must have returned by the back entrance, what business did he have in the stables. Foolish question, they are his stables, he may do as he pleases.

'A grand night for a roll in the hay eh!'

'Good evening Sir Hugh, I seek my husband, he cannot be here'.

I turned to leave to find my path blocked by his Lordship. I tried to step around him in some form of parody of a dance, I stepped right, he shadowed me, then left, then he grabbed me by the wrist and flung me against the stone wall of the stalls passage.
The impact knocked the wind from me, I doubled up in pain and was dragged across the passage into an empty stall already bedded down for one of the spare horses.

'Know that you are my property girl, mine to do as I please, and I will have you, scream for help now and I will make you know what screaming is all about'.

His stale breath was in my face, I felt his left hand groping up my leg and ripping my clothing aside, I wore no drawers, I had only two sets and they were packed for travel. His right hand was undoing his breeches, I could feel him against me, rubbing his hand up and down trying to make himself ready.

His sour breath warm in my ear he whispered words more obscene than even I had heard amongst the soldiers of the barracks describing to me in detail what he would do to me.

He forced me backwards into the horses bedding, I felt him then as he forced his fingers up inside me and ground his half hard member into the front of my rucked-up dress. I raked him with my nails, gouging at his eyes and his cheeks seeking to mark him at least, show the world what he was, I tried to scream but no noise came from my throat.

Then he forced himself inside me pulling my thighs apart roughly with his hand and his knee.

I felt him spill himself over the inside of my leg.

His voice harsh and whispered in my ear 'Remember you are my property Marged'.

Then he rose, and adjusted his clothing and left as if nothing was amiss.

I knew that Gwyn was there hidden in the shadows, I knew that he was powerless to intervene, but would I ever forgive him for not.

CHAPTER 45 - THE TUNNEL OF TIME - SIBYL

I felt Eryr take my arm and usher me towards the doorway in the corner of the room, a misty portal glowing with ethereal light, the sounds of passing millennia echoed in my ears, the smell decades past mixed with the acrid tang of electricity, one step was all it took then silence.

I came round to darkness, sightless black, not one chink of light, my eyes searched for some reference point in the darkness, there were two.

I sensed him squatting Indian style against the wall, elbows rested on his knees, hands under his chin watching and waiting. His eyes which had been a deep blue when last I saw them, glowed red in the darkness, wolf like in their intensity, they fixed on me with a questioning gaze.

I ran through a mental check list, my body seemed fine, arms and legs working, breath in, breath out. I held one hand up in front of my face and rotated it slowly, flexing my fingers, yes, I was still functioning.

He moved, pulling himself nearly to his full height, unable to stand fully, his head cocked to one side, at this point I realised we were in a tunnel, or a cavern of some sort. I could now hear noises above, the clink of harness, the shuffle of many feet on earth, the movement of hooves on the ground, men calling to each other, women saying their goodbyes, curses as heavy items dropped clumsily to the floor, orders shouted in clipped English tones, rising above the friendly banter of the Welsh.

Eryr guided me through the darkness to the end of the tunnel, it grew lighter, and I became aware of barrels and cases stacked against the damp rocky walls, racks of newly fletched and pointed arrows ready loaded in their quivers, shields decorated in red and yellow and some with the lion and Fleur de Lys crest of royalty emblazoned on their fronts, pieces of chain mail and helmets.

We weaved a path through the chaos, which was unfolding in front of us, unseen to the men who at the command of their officers were slowly instilling order.

This was an army preparing to march to war, but an army comprised of townsfolk and farmers, not regular troops. True some, those recruited by Kenneth the Master at Arms and numbering only about fifty strong were trained in the art of war, they would provide guidance for the rest who had only been required to practice with their bows once a week, on a Sunday.

The commanding voice was that of Sir Kenneth Fitzsimon, directing the loading of wagons, overseeing the wagon masters, checking their inventories as each barrel, box and item was loaded. Everyone from Lord

Hugh de Audley to the boys who would keep the bowmen supplied with arrows, From his lordships valet to the whores who followed the men, doubling as cooks and laundry maids, everyone was mustered, counted, inventoried, and ticked off a list.

King Edward was going to war with France and Llantrisant the bowmen of Llantrisant must answer his call. Under the command of Prince Edward of Wales, the Kings son.

It occurred to me as we emerged into the dawning summer morn that firstly I was now walking in the 14th century, if my history had been taught well this was the year of our lord 1346 and it was July, and secondly, I was dressed appropriately for the period, but it hardly mattered because not one of the people we had walked past could see me! As if reading my mind Eryr's deep voice at my shoulder – 'I am invisible to all unless I choose not to be. The cloak you wear provides the same protection, wear it, and wish to go unnoticed and it will grant you invisibility. Or it can be just what it is, a cloak. Do not lose it.'

The cavern we had emerged from was beneath the Raven Tower, the, fortified structure was impressive when seen in its entirety. This was not the ivy clad ruin I could see from the New Inn window every morning. This was a castellated dwelling, complete with barracks, living quarters, a well-kept, grassy courtyard, a gatehouse. Everything a marcher lord could want, to defend his position from the marauding Welsh rebels. But that would come later, the lords and the King would become complacent in their treatment of my people, for yes these were my people, and in this time, 1346 they were proud to serve the King.

Eryr spoke again, 'what did you see, think hard on it, and carefully, who must we seek out, I can guide you and keep you safe, but I cannot see as you do, you can see their souls.'

I need to sit, I told him, he pulled me into an alcove, a stony nook carved in the wall of the castle, the slit window at its apex looking out from the escarpment and over flat land, rough grazing at the hills base, leading to more fertile green meadows fenced and cared for, small farms and cottages, fields where sheep grazed and cattle, then in the distance the grain fields of the vale, and all the way to the sea. Visible too were the castles at Ruthin and Sully, all part of a chain of protection which the English lords had draped around the neck of the Welsh countryside.

The land in this part of Wales was near to the border with England which naturally fell along Offa's Dyke running north through the marches, and the English heartland. From this vantage point the defenders of the town would fire their arrows at whoever sought to displace them. I sat in the archer's nook and cast my mind back, the Grimoire was no longer in my hands, well how could it be, it was with its author, but where was she? She would be in her rooms, or her kitchens, she would be about her duties no time now for her charms and her spells. There was Royalty present, looking up I could see the pennant of the Prince flying from the battlements alongside the red and yellow of the de Audley and de Clare standard a blaze of colour, the King's representative, come to take command of his men.

His Lordship sir Hugh would be in his private apartments with the Prince discussing the business of the campaign and the wishes of the King. My mind cleared and a girl came into focus, light footed, nimble, dressed in britches and jerkin, carrying a light hunting bow, laughing, and a youth tall and dark his arm about her shoulder, he was dressed in the uniform of a squire to the de Audley's. He was armed, a longbow over six feet tall hung over his shoulder, a quiver of arrows slung at his waist, and on his back, unusually for an archer, a sword. As I watched through time, they embraced, and he had reached into his jerkin and produced a ring, simple and made from two horseshoe nails twisted together by his own hand, in the castle forge. A page turned in my mind, another day, a church, this church, the small side chapel with its ancient banners and coats of arms, a priest, yes and a witness, they had married.

The page turns, the glass goes dark, I cannot see, I only hear screams, pleading, begging, please no sir, I will not. I hear the grunts of a struggle; a girls voice using the language of the gutter and then silence. Like the curtain falling at that part of the play where an act ends, and the main player waits in the wings, theirs is a darker role. For now, to watch, and plan their entrance, the act to follow. The butts, I mutter under my breath, they will be at the butts. We must travel with them, I look at the being beside me, he reads my mind, eyes no longer a sinister red, but a deep shade of green, and they are laughing, laughing at me!

'Yes, I can,' it is a bald statement, 'shoot an arrow' you were thinking.

As I open my eyes from my musings a squire stands before me, a royal squire, in the livery of Prince Edward,
'will this do?'

'How do I uncloak myself? We need to be seen.'

'Just think that way, a few times and you will get the hang of it, but don't think too hard, or maybe it's not just the cloak you'll be removing'.

The eyes twinkled, his being, changed and before me stood.

'Sure, ye've met Owain y Mynydd before, now meet squire Owain, servant and archer and indispensable to His Majesty Prince Edward.'

And you'd be Sibyl, Merch Goch a healer, come to travel with the army, maybe we should just call you 'Red'.

I will explain later, the voice of Eryr spoke, we have no time now.

He took me by the arm and guided me through a thick wooden door in an archway, the grassy area which met us was long and narrow, stretching out before us, at the far end was a grass embankment in it embedded targets, the length of the firing range for that is what it was, was marked in yards.

Eryr's or was it Owain's hand on my shoulder I stopped in my tracks as a tall dark-haired youth, no more than sixteen years of age flexed his wide shoulders, strung his bow, nocked an arrow, and let it loose, I heard the whistle of its flight, my hearing still fired up by intense thought. Then I heard the thud as it buried its tip in the straw target. Flights and stem vibrating with the impact.

Hidden from sight slightly in front of him another figure, slightly built and obviously female despite the male clothing drew back the string of a light hunting bow, her arrow buried itself point for point alongside that of the archer. Fine shooting, indeed.

'May I, or is this private practise?' Owain stepped forward.

'Feel free, to join us' replied the archer 'Gwyn ap Meredith, at your service' spoken in Welsh.

'Owain y Mynydd, at yours' the formal reply, also in Welsh.

In a few deft movements Owain, for this was his current guise, strung his bow, nocked an arrow and taking careful aim, fired at the same target.

The arrow whistled in the air, the sound of splitting wood, the thud into the target, the archers arrow split down its length, the girls arrow separated from her husbands.

Varlet! Gwyn's demeanour changed, he swung out with a fist at Owain, striking him hard and unchallenged in the face, Owain flinched but did not move.

'You seek to split us up, as you have split the arrow, not you nor your English master will do that, she is mine, he shall not have his way again'.

The sword was drawn with the speed of a striking snake, but Owain was quicker.

The knife at his belt drew blood through the leather jerkin, the sword fell to the ground and a piercing English voice put an end to proceedings.

'Hold fast in the name of your Prince. Good shooting, the best I have seen, archers. I need you whole, not cut up in pieces. You will put aside your differences, or I will know their nature. '

Before us stood an unassuming youth, no older than Gwyn, but with a presence, an air of authority about him, dressed in sumptuous dark velvet and with Sir Kenneth in tow, the men bowed and the girl and I both offered slightly clumsy curtsies to Edward of Woodstock, Prince of Wales.

The Prince turned to Gwyn and indicating the four-inch gash where Owain's dagger had cut through leather and skin, 'get that seen to, and stitched, then both of you are to come to my rooms.'

The Prince turned on his heel, and with Sir Kenneth fuming and fussing in his wake, disappeared through the door.

I turned to Gwyn 'I can'. But before I could finish the girl interrupted.

'But you will not, he is mine and I will heal him. You will not use your magic on him, I sense you are a witch, be gone woman'.

She ushered her man out through the door, making the two fingered sign of the devil's horns behind her back, we followed, after all best we all obey the Royal summons together.

'Marged, do not take on so! Gwyn interceded; she only offers help.'

'But Gwyn I will not have it, I do not know her, she has been sent, by him, I sense her, she is one of them!' By one of them I took it she meant the English.

We had by now come to the small building alongside the armoured room which served as an infirmary, Gwyn had been stripped of jerkin and shirt and was seated on a low stool, I could see that the gash in his bicep muscle was deep, but clean.

Marged had rinsed it with alcohol, using the dipper in the small barrel of raw spirit kept for the purpose, mishaps were not uncommon during archery or sword practice.

Then she pulled out a leather and canvas roll from under the bench, it's inside stitched neatly into pockets. She pulled out already threaded needle from its place and soaked it in more alcohol. Then began to stitch. Neat stitches, as neat and proficient as my own, and without the benefit of my curved needle, ten small stitches later she tied off the last, applied a salve and a light bandage to the wound and declared her husband mended.

Marged ap Meredith knew her trade.

CHAPTER 46 -AN AUDIENCE WITH A PRINCE. – GWYN AP MEREDITH

Edward Prince of Wales had been accommodated in the castles most luxurious guest chambers, situated in the main keep of the castle, above the apartment of the de Audley's, there was a solar looking out over the flat plain of the Vale and all the way to the sea at the witches point, and from there on a clear day gone could see all the way to England.

A stone walkway gave a view of the central castle green and also to the narrow strip of ground between the inner and outer walls where the archery butts were placed.

This strip of ground was also where the squires learned to handle a sword and ride a horse. It was the home of the 'tilt' a wooden dummy on a swivel, designed to test horse and riders' accuracy and agility.

The apartments themselves were furnished with dark wood furniture; the walls draped with heavy damask hangings to mask the cold which permeated the thick stone walls. The bedroom contained a huge four poster bed with thick warm curtains of deep dark green velvet, the bed was covered with wolf skins and animal furs.

The audience room was simple, a huge dark wood chair carved with the Royal coat of arms was positioned throne like next to the huge open fire. The room accessed by double doors in a pointed arch at one end.

The door was guarded by a liveried man at arms of the Prince's service. Obeying the Prince's summons, we four found ourselves climbing the stone steps up to the door.

The man at arms pushed it open and announced our arrival.

A youth sat upon the vast throne. Swamped by the huge piece of furniture.

A slight blonde youth, no older than Gwyn, his hair worn slightly longer than the fashion of the court, slightly wavy and curling over his ears. He had a narrow patrician face with a long straight nose slightly too pointed at its end, over a wide mouth which broke into an easy smile on our entrance, showing even and well-kept white teeth.

He wore dark coloured leggings and long leather boots to his knees, a long tabard of sumptuous purple velvet with long wide sleeves.

'Sit' he gestured to a padded bench. 'I have heard good things of you Gwyn ap Meredith, and I have seen that you have a good eye and are a fine shot with a bow, Sir Kenneth also informs me you can use a sword with some effect.'

'I can sir, I have been taught fencing by Sir Kenneth himself'.

'And you, you wear my colours,' he spoke directly to Owain 'I do not recall you travelling with me, I think I should recall one as shall I say distinctive as you'.

Thinking on his feet Owain replied, 'I was sent in advance by your father sire, I have been embedded in the household for several weeks, learning of the ways of this place, I now speak the local tongue and can translate if needed.'

'Ladies, you may leave us, I have duties for your men to perform, for we leave for France at the months end, and there is still much to do, your talents will also be needed, on this journey we undertake, the men will need your ministrations.'

Marged and I left, leaving Gwyn and Owain in audience with the Prince.

CHAPTER 47 - SIX GOOD MEN AND A FAERIE

'Sit'.

We both sat on the stools indicated.

Well, who wouldn't when it was a Prince issuing the command.

The personage before us had an inbuilt aura of authority exuding from his thick light blonde hair, through those dark blue eyes and into his deeper than expected voice. It was a voice which was cultured and educated with a slight French accent so similar to the intonations of Lady Margaret if you listened to her carefully. This air of authority permeated his clothes from the unfastened neck of his leather jerkin over a pristine white linen shirt, to his dark coloured breeches and long leather boots. Then, he smiled and turned into the teenager he was.

'Ah Gwyn, Sir Kenneth had me watch you, he tells me that you are the best of his crop. You must tell me more of yourself, where do you come from, what experience have you'.

'And you,' he looked directly at Owain 'you wear my Father's colours, how are you here and why? He gave me no word to expect a new squire, and I already have Elgan for a page, I do not require another, but you too are a fine bowman, and handy with a knife, you too will tell me what you are about.

I looked at Owain and he at me. Who would go first.

'Your highness' I began, 'I was sent by your father to assist you in your campaign in any way I can, I speak the local tongue and am also familiar with the country, your father felt that I may be able to be of use to you in that way'. Suitably vague, I thought.

'For a mere page you seem very adept in the arts of war, where did you acquire these skills.'

'In my home, sire, I was taught by my father and brothers in the mountains where we live,' Not a lie in itself but a stretching of the truth.

'Whatever, I can use you,' the decision was swiftly made. He then turned to Gwyn.

'I have been told of you already, but please enlighten me, who is the young lady who shoots like a man?

'My wife' Gwyn replied. 'She learned to hunt with a bow as a child, she is learning healing and such from Lady Margaret.'

'Very well, but don't let her distract you, and be careful of the 'and such' she is learning, it is said in court that her ladyship is not only skilled in healing'.

He sat, in a large chair opposite, and took a deep breath in.

'I have discussed with Sir Kenneth, and he agrees, with my plan. I mean to form a well-disciplined force of longbowmen to serve on this campaign. I have the numbers, we have recruited over three thousand archers from across the country, but none so effective as the Welsh. There will be about six hundred in number from this area, men and boys, old soldiers from who have seen action and their sons who have seen nothing but the farm and a target. There are six of you squires, trained by a master at arms, I now need you to act as leaders of men. I propose to split the archers into six groups, that will be a hundred men each. They will join our army as we march, many will muster here but most will join us in the villages and towns along the way.
I require you to train these archers to fire in volleys, as a unit, Over twenty arrows a minute. They will work as a unit, and the units will work together. I mean to create a wall of arrows thick enough to terrify, and accurate enough to kill foot soldiers at several hundred yards, and powerful enough to pierce armour. Owain you will coordinate the whole body of men and come to me for your orders, you will start training tomorrow, and continue as we march and as your men muster.
I expect a lot of such young men as you, I know you will not fail me. Sir Kenneth is briefing the others, we will speak again before we march.

Oh, and Gwyn if you are to address my archers, you had better wear this'.

He handed Gwyn a crumpled garment made of faded silk.

I hear your father distinguished himself, I am certain you will do the same. Wear it with pride, I will award you your own in due course. Now leave me, I have much to think about.'

We needed no second command.

At the bottom of the stairs, Marged and Sibyl waited!

PART SIX

CHAPTER 48 - THE POISON PLOT - LADY MARGARET

Marged and I had returned from the priory at Ewenny escorted by Gwyn and my new apprentice Evan. At least that is what Evan had professed to be. He had no wish to be an archer or a squire, he wanted nothing to do with weapons and reluctantly took part in the archery practice he was obliged to do every Sunday by law. Having observed him and his use of even the most lightweight of bows, I could see why.

Sir Kenneth despaired of him, describing his arms as being like two pieces of knotty twine dangling from a broomstick. This was in fact a fair description of Evans' wiry physique.

When pointed at the large target even ten yards down the practice field he caused allcomers to take refuge behind the nearest door so random was his aim.

So, Sir Kenneth had suggested that he could be useful to me when treating the men who were reticent of having a woman inspect their injuries or their illnesses.

Evans face had lit up like a new moon in winter when he was told of his new employment. He was, after all, a student of Brother Bartram; he would he said make me and Brother Bartram proud.

We arrived back at the Castle to find that my beloved husband had been in conference with the Prince for several days. The purpose of this lengthy discussion had been to curry favour with the Prince, highlighting the work which he had done in subduing the rebellious people of the area.

Rebellious, my left foot. These people were so poor and downtrodden that they had not the strength to rebel and lived in terror that the 'proper' rebels who lived in the mountains of the North would come calling on us, burn their town to the ground.

Once relieved of some of the burden imposed on them in extra and illegal taxes paid to my husband and allowed to earn a fair living from their trades and occupations they had proven to be hard working and loyal to the Crown.

I am informed that the Prince has taken to walking amongst the camp fires on the green of an evening and has been told of my husband's practices when it comes to the newly married women of the locality. The Prince has an ear for the people and has questioned my husband as to the truth of these rumours, which he vehemently denies. But then my husband is an adept liar, he has had a lot of practice over the years.

I must speak to Marged further, there was something which troubled her about our return, if what I suspect is the case is correct then I will do what must I do to be rid of him. Not to stop my own humiliation, for I fear I am well used to that, but to put an end to his evil practices for good. If only there were proof, if only someone were willing to speak out against him. But to do that would be to be arrested and imprisoned on some fictitious charge and eventually banished or put to death.

These stoic people would rather keep silent about their woes than risk the justice system, for there is no justice for the poor, the courts favour the wealthy, without exception unless the matter is one of treason.

I will give it some more thought, for there is more than one way to skin a cat. I have an idea, but will Marged do what I ask of her. She is the only one who could.

I went up to my still room and closed the door and began to search through the books and scrolls which I kept there.

There it was: Based in Valerian Root.

The charm comprised valerian root pounded to a paste with the blood of the intended victim and commended to the Efnisien the God of wrongdoing A powerful charm indeed. It would only kill its intended victim. In others it would induce a deep sleep from which the sleeper could be weakened with the antidote

Which was made from distilled foxglove. Mixed with three drops of blood from their first-born child. Commended to Taliesin the Welsh God of Sorcery.

I prepared the charm as a paste to load the tips of Marged's arrows.

I did not prepare the antidote. To do that would be to tempt failure and this mission must not fail.

I spoke to Marged took her into my confidence and into the room where I had prepared the paste and together we loaded the arrow heads.

But the antidote – that remained written in the book hidden beneath the floor and in my grimoire.

I ground the valerian root with care, it was almost paste like in consistency, the blood, well her Hugh believes that regular bloodletting keeps him healthy. It was easy to take the bowl from the physicians' hands to dispose of the contents, as any good and loving wife should.

Carefully I tipped the paste into the silver and jewel encrusted chalice and climbed the steps from my room to the battlements of the Raven Tower. Holding the chalice aloft to the night sky, I called on Efnisien the Welsh God of wrongdoing. Invoked his power and that of Taliesin the Sorcerer. I spoke the words quiet, but plain, taken from the Grimoire left to me by Morganna the ancient crone from whom I had learned the dark arts.

Morgana's Grimoire is a book which must never see the light of day. It is kept hidden in a space under the floor between the joists in my tower room. Should it be found by anyone who understands its arcane language, it would mean certain death.

Marged had taken the arrowheads from the armoury, bodkin iron tips for these arrows, not the plain tips she usually practiced with, heavier yes, but she would allow for that. Only the archers practiced with armour piercing arrows.

She had passed them to me wrapped in one of my silken scarves, together we anointed each of the four tips with the charm. Then I held aloft the arrowheads and called on the Gods once more.

Leaning on the stone rampart, she cleared her head of thoughts and looked out over the flat vale of Glamorgan, towards the sea.

How had she ended up in this Welsh backwater, was she not the niece of the King, her brother Despenser had ruined her inheritance and all their futures with his war against the Marcher lords.

Now she had become just a pawn to be married off by the King to the next of his favourites, but she was old now, her childbearing years had finished, all she could bring to the table was the wealth of the de Clare family and her share of their lands, and then only with the King's blessing.

Hugh de Audley had been the King's choice for her, a cruel choice, a cruel man, she had done her duty but produced only a daughter, doubtless there was a queue of bastard sons waiting in the wings to steal what was left away from her.

Marged would do what was asked of her, the girl had her own motives and good reason to act against him.

There it was, means and motive, all that was needed now was opportunity.

Lady Margaret turned from the view of the night sky, straightened her robes, and walked stiff backed down the spiral stone steps back to her reality. Pulling open the heavy wooden door into the grand hall she drew back the heavy draped curtain, clapped her hands and called for music.

Above her in the darkness, the Gods of her ancestors would weave their magic, and make all things well, or at least rid her of Sir Hugh.

She had watched Marged dressed as a boy, firing arrow after arrow from her lightweight bow, always hitting the centre of the target, the girl never missed. Had seen her with that squire, the one from the far mountains, they were in love, anyone with eyes could see that. The tall straight dark haired young man with his tumble of black hair hanging over his shoulders when not tied back with a leather thong, he had the deep brown eyes typical of the Welsh and a melodious voice which carried like birdsong on the breeze. He almost sang as he talked. He was over six feet to the girls five, towering over her as he adjusted her stance and gave her tips on the art of archery. He had already caught the eye of Sir Kenneth the Master at Arms, Gwyn ap Meredith for that was his name was from good stock, though his family were now dirt-poor farmers in the Preseli mountains. The boy had a strong arm and a good

266

eye, and he was well mannered polite and blessed with a good head for reading and figures.

The girl, well she had needed taming, running wild of her father's discipline for years, without her mother's guidance she was unaware of her looks. Totally oblivious to the way that the other young men looked at her, when pressed she was an adequate lady's maid, but usually she was tardy, grubby, and cheeky, she had the language and manners of the stables and humour of the barrack room. All blonde curls and blue eyes, a tiny figure standing alongside a giant, yet on her day she could out-shoot him.

Using her lightweight hunting bow she was one of the few who could indeed split an arrow in two. She would never have an arm strong enough to draw a longbow properly however much she tried. And it was funny to watch her trying, struggling with the power of the yew stave and the flax string cursing under her breath as her arm refused to straighten and the bow refused to bend.

She was also quick with a knife and as light on her feet as an elf. Lady Margaret had watched from her roost high in the tower while Gwyn and Marged danced around each other, two souls from the same place, two minds of the same thought two hearts beating the same rhythm.

She had once known a love like that, until duty, lineage and the quest for power took over. There was something to envy in these people's lives, in having nothing, they at least had each other and in that they had all that they needed.

Gwyn ap Meredith would go far in life, he could have a bright future, and Marged well if she could master her wild side, she too would go far.

Drawn back from her reverie by the haunting sound of the harpist and Sian singing she returned to the demands of the evening,

Lady Margaret lost the look of youthful beauty which had suffused her face minutes before, replacing it with her usual stern mask, she presided over the activities of the evening and listened to the preparations for a war to come.

At the end of the evening once the trusted nobles had finished their talk around the table and all, but Lady Margaret the Prince and Sir Hugh had retired for the evening Sian again took up the harp and began to sing, she sang in Welsh, songs which she made up herself, songs of her life and life at the castle and of the people of the town.

Sir Hugh could see her talent and had plans to sell her as a vassal to the Royal Court. How good he would make himself look for sending such a fine singer of songs to entertain the King.

No said Lady Margaret, Sian would never go to Court, she was Margaret's to care for and look after. She would never survive at Court. She was too delicate a flower and too simple in her mind to survive the taunting of the ladies jealous of her talents and the attentions of the men who would seek to take her innocence away.

If the Prince wished to hear her then he must come more often to the town. Prince Edward retired to the apartments above to spend one last night in a bed before leaving for France.

Sir Hugh was drunk, he had taken far too much wine and argued that Sian should be given her chance in life. The real truth was that he did not like the girl; he saw her as an embarrassment with her round face slightly clumsy ways and the birthmark on her face.

Would it not be better for her to go to London with the Prince after the campaign and sing for her supper. Lady Margaret refused to countenance such a thing, He too rose in poor humour and stated his intention to retire to his bed.

Sian put away the harp and making her goodnights made her way from the great hall back to the servants' quarters.

Her body was found at the base of the cliff below the Raven Tower the following morning by one of the slops boys emptying the privy. Her throat was cut, and her body butchered from her breastbone to her pelvis, her insides were pulled out, and there were the tell-tale bruises down her thighs and the blood stains on her small clothes which showed that she had been defiled. Poor Sian. Her body was laid in the small chapel where Gwyn the Archer had married his Marged only days before.

I noted the condition of her body and the injuries and wrote them in my journal, in lack of a constable Sir Kenneth logged the incident in the Castle log book, the Prince was informed of it but took no real interest other than to excuse me and Sir Kenneth from any formal duties that day.

My husband had viewed the body.

'There you are,' he had said 'You would not let her better herself, so she has thrown herself from the walls he said, 'Poor child she has been savaged by the wolves that live on the midden heap. She stood no chance; I pray that she was dead before they found her..

Sir Kenneth, that is what you will write.

'If you say so my lord' muttered sir Kenneth.
He made the requested entry in the log, but he did not sign it, nor did he place his seal against the entry.

Sir Hugh left, satisfied with the outcome.

'Pass me your book Margaret' he said to me
'And your wax and a quill'.

I passed them as requested and watched him write in his flowing hand underneath my record of the injuries to the body.

Ending with AND SO IT HAPPENS AGAIN then he dripped a good drop of wax on the paper and stamped it with the seal from the signet ring which he wore on his left hand. The seal with the head of the Wolf under a crescent moon.

He kissed me softly on the mouth and held me close, then set me away from him slightly and in a soft and serious voice told me 'Do nothing you will regret Maggie Dearest'.

Without lying I assured him that I would not. For I would regret nothing.

CHAPTER 49 -THE RIDE SOUTH - NARRATOR

Sir Hugh de Audley took up position at the head of the column, preceded only by two outriders carrying the red and yellow standards of the de Audley's and the royal standard of the Prince.

His chestnut mare, a Percheron cross with a golden mane and tail danced underneath him, her coat shining glossy as a conker in the low sunlight of dawn, it would be a warm morning and a warmer day. The mare was already sweating slightly, she was a young horse, only six years old and not long broken in, she had been ridden about the countryside by one of the young squires, but she was not battle ready, and her rider was not the best of horsemen.

Edward of Woodstock Prince of Wales reined his huge black beast of a charger up alongside him. The Prince turned in his saddle and looked back along the assembled line of wagons, fighting men and followers, some with horses, most not.

His officers were mounted on light horse, Sir Kenneth Fitzsimon on his own particular choice of mount, sturdy and sure footed but not imposing, and not what Edward had expected from a knight of the realm. But Kenneth rode with ease, could mount and dismount swiftly and he knew that his dark grey cob Trooper would carry him all day without fail.

More horsemen would join them on the ride south, by the time they reached Portsmouth and the channel the army would be at least ten thousand strong. His own contingent would comprise seven thousand archers drawn from the towns and villages of England and Wales and a small force of men at arms and foot soldiers. He had seen the Llantrisant men practice and had been impressed with them, the longbow men of the area were trained well, he could only hope the rest would be as good.

The great gates opened before them and the signal to move passed back along the column.

With a rumble of cartwheels and the shuffle and stamp of feet and creak of leather the march to war began.

Those not marching with the army had strung banners and flags the length of the high street, the town was decked in colour, children waved to their fathers from street corners and wives waved, wondering if they would see their husbands again.

Out of the great wooden gates of the castle and down the steep winding hill which led out of the town the procession of knights, men at arms, squires, foot soldiers and archers progressed, at walking pace.

It was a long road to the ships harboured at Portsmouth and then the crossing to France.

Edward of Woodstock lifted his feather trimmed hat and ran his hand through his blonde hair and cast an assessing glance at the man riding alongside him.

Neither man wore armour, there was no need, the garb of battle was stored on the wagons which carried the weapons and accoutrements they would need.

Woodstock wore black leather breeches and sleeved jerkin under light chain mail also black in hue with a tunic bearing the colours of the King proudly on display. Gauntlet gloves held his mounts reins lightly and he sat limber in the saddle guiding the horse mainly with his legs.

He had been lavishly entertained by the de Audley's over the last week when he had been in residence at their home. His father, the King had been generous to Sir Hugh in granting him the stewardship of Glamorgan, the condition that he live there rather than at Court in London had not been well received at the time.

Woodstock's grandfather, Edward II had allowed his Barons to be absentee landlords, many of them in the more inhospitable lands had chosen to live in comfort in London and only visit their fiefdoms when there was trouble brewing. This had resulted in the rebellious Welsh raiding the lands more often, and the debacle of the Despenser Lord who had run amok seizing everything he could lay hands on for himself.

The King had arranged Sir Hugh's very advantageous marriage and made him very aware of his duty to his King.

Woodstock had found de Audley, overly subservient and nearly grovelling in some respects but with an underlying arrogance of manner which at times ran dangerously close to the surface.

Woodstock was, even at his young age, a shrewd judge of character, he had sat at the Royal Council meetings since he was a child. He was used to the diplomatic words which promised much and gave nothing. Empty vessels with no substance and frequently containing nasty surprises.

Yes! he had Sir Hugh's character read and saw through him as through a pane of glass.

Sir Hugh liked to forget that his wife was the King's niece, and Woodstock's cousin. Lady Margaret had her secrets, Woodstock knew that well, but above all she was a loyal subject, an intelligent and shrewd woman, and not a sufferer of fools.

Woodstock turned back to his horse, guiding him around the last hairpin bend in the road and out through the South Gate of the town and down the steep hill that led into the countryside of Glamorgan.

The road they followed was little more than a well-worn track, it wound its way through hamlets with small farms at intervals on either side. These farms were only a few acres each, little more than small holdings really, subsistence farmers, making a pittance to keep themselves and their families and paying rent and tax to their lord of the manor. Woodstock had noticed that de Audley was sporting a bruise on the left side of his face, and what looked like scram marks down his cheek. The man seemed preoccupied with something and had said not one word to Woodstock other than a brief' Good morning your highness 'over breakfast.

Lady Margaret had been attentive to him, but frosty with her husband.

All was not well with the de Audley's, and if Sir Hugh could not bring his mind back to the task in hand, it would be a very long campaign!

'Ware! Sir Hugh,' Woodstock looked back jolted from his thoughts by Sir Kenneth, shouting.

De Audley did not respond!

'Ware! Swine! '

Before de Audley could take action his mare, nostrils flaring and snorting like a dragon had leaped off the track to avoid a huge sow and piglets basking in the roadway.

As the terrified animal bolted down the embankment putting distance between itself and the evil smelling creature blocking its path, Woodstock raised his arm and halted the convoy whilst several of the foot soldiers and the nearby farmer chivvied the creature out of harm's way.

The rest of the men could be heard whooping and cheering as de Audley regained control and re-joined the front of the line.

His lordship was red in the face and flustered, one hand gripping tightly to the reins and the other holding tight to the front of his saddle.

Yes, thought Woodstock to himself, this could be a very long ride indeed.

In the end it was Sir Hugh who opened the conversation.

'What orders do we have from your father my liege'.

'We ride to Portsmouth and take ship for France. We are to take a route through Caerphilly and Chepstow which will lengthen our route, but they have men and equipment at both castles. We meet the men from Gloucester before we turn south. Eight miles a day will be all we can expect to cover with the baggage in tow. We should make Portsmouth in two weeks.'

'Should we not ride ahead my Lord, we can make better time and find more suitable accommodation than the column, more fitting for your comfort my liege'.

'Fie, my lord, we will have no such, courtesy in France, best we get used to the feel of hard ground beneath us, I do not expect to sleep in a feather bed until our return'.

You are a young man, my Prince, I fear my old bones will suffer from the lack, I need my comforts these days, still there is a goodly supply of well-padded wenches in the column. He laughed a loud guffaw.

Woodstock raised an eyebrow and slowing his horse dropped back to speak to Sir Kenneth Fitzsimon who was riding behind them 'what say you Kenneth?'

'I ride with the men, I eat and sleep with the men, I may be their leader, but I am also a soldier Sir, it helps to know the talk in the camp. Many of my men have their wives with them, not all the women are whores my liege!'

The statement was loaded, intended to convey a message to Woodstock, asking him to read between the lines.

de Audley chipped in 'what woman other than a whore would choose to travel with an army, if it looks like meat, then it is on the menu Sir!'

'What women you say! Well, the ones that cook your food, wash your small clothes, tend your wounds and your fevers my Lord Hugh. They are mostly wives of the men. This is to be a long campaign, their talents will be needed, it is best not to cause unrest in the camp.'

'Rubbish man, most of them only have one service to offer, and that's a warm body for the night'.

In disgust, Sir Kenneth swung his mount away from de Audley and his Prince and cantered back up the column to talk to his officers.

Back in the ranks of the longbow men towards the rear of the column Gwyn marched in company at the head of his section, each of the Squires had been given charge of a section of twelve archers, these were the men who were not tied to the King, some were mercenaries paid men not vassals or in the service of the de Audley's. Most were the men from the farming communities who had by law practiced with their bows every Sunday from the age of seven.

Gwyn was tasked with forming them into a cohesive unit, firing as one, volleys of arrows to fall like a sheet of steel rain on the enemy. The wagons contained portable targets, he planned to set them up each night for an hour and have his men practice. Their lives and his may depend on it.

He had not seen Marged since they left the Castle, she was quiet and withdrawn, he longed to take her in his arms and sooth away the memory of de Audley, he felt guilty for not killing the man for what he had done, but that would have meant instant death for him, and a life of poverty for Marged. He knew she thought him a coward for not acting in her defence. Tonight, he would find her, he would find a quiet place to pitch their shelter, they would sit round the fire with the other men and wives, eat and drink and sing. He would try and coax her out of her sadness.

'Hey Gwyn', his attention was grabbed by an Irish voice from several ranks back in the line 'quit dawdling will ye, or we'll not make St Nicholas before dusk! It was then he realised that lost in his thoughts he and his men had slowed the pace leaving a gap of several meters between them and the officers' horses in front of them.

Sir Kenneth's mount appeared alongside him 'shape up Meredith, stop dreaming of yer wife and keep moving, if ye can't march and do it! Don't do it at all, it will make ye blind in any case!'

Gwyn raised his right hand and waving behind him shouted the order 'with me' and started to run, as a unit his men followed soon making up the gap and a bit more. 'Split the line' came the next order, and his section divided and jogged swiftly down the outside of the column, past Woodstock, and de Audley and then as one unit ran as far as the next crossroads, Twmpath Cross, once there they stoop line abreast across the road, bows at the ready.

So intent were they on their mission, Gwyn did not notice one of his men jab de Audley's mare in the hind quarters with a spare arrowhead. She was now spinning in small circles and bucking as though she had been stung on the arse by a wasp!

The laughter of the rest of the line, and the cursing of his Lordship filled the air. The reason seen only by Woodstock, and Sir Kenneth who resolutely bit their lips, and showed no sympathy with Sir Hugh's predicament. Once all had calmed down and the mare had been soothed to a manageable state again Woodstock pulled Sir Kenneth to one side and through gritted teeth and suppressed laughter muttered

'Commend that unit on their fitness and efficiency Sir Kenneth and have a quiet word with their Squire.'

Sir Kenneth de Audley was becoming the butt of practical jokes, and they had only been marching one day. If this continued, then there would be trouble, serious trouble, no one wanted to be put on half rations before they even made it to France.

The column marched slowly along the leafy parish roads from Llantrisant and Southeast through Miskin then Peterston and arrived at the Tinkinswood field just outside St Nicholas with enough time to set up camp.

Horses were tied neatly in lines, the women erected shelters and tents and gathered firewood, out of chaos order appeared, smells of cooking drifted through the air, as the tasks for the day were completed, the men began to relax, sitting on logs or large stones around the fires, talking, singing, inspecting feet not accustomed to such long journeys. The healers would be busy treating foot rot and blisters before very long. But for now, all was well.

I was deep in conversation with Marged when Gwyn and Owain appeared at the tailboard of our wagon. We were busy taking an inventory of our combined stock of salves and remedies, stitching needles, and bandages. Marged had been fascinated by the curved needles which I had brought with me and kept ready threaded and soaking in raw spirit.

As Mother Eliza had taught me, so Lady Margaret had taught Marged. She constantly waged a battle to introduce cleanliness and the use of soap into the lives of the soldiers.

To boil their drinking water, or stick to small beer, which most of them preferred to do.

Gwyn and Owain were still laughing at the antics of de Audley's horse, pulling faces, and having a contest between each other the see who could look most like his Lordship being terrified.

Marged and I were so far back in the column which was nearly half a mile long that we had missed all the action. I laughed at the thought of the man hanging on for grim death, Marged just shrugged her shoulders 'good enough for him' then she turned back to her work.

Gwyn put his arm around her shoulder, 'Don't fret girl, all will come right, it was not your fault'.

'Damn you Gwyn Meredith, I know it was not my fault,' she spat back at her husband, hissing like a cat 'so help me if he comes visiting again, I will do for him if you will not'.

'Marged, love, it must not come to that, he is not worth your loss, for you would die for your act. If I cannot join you then Red will stay with you, Owain has promised me'.

In the short time I had known him Gwyn had taken up Owain's pet name for me 'Merch Coch' red maid. Shortened to Red, it would be his pet name for me from now on.

I wondered how long Eryr could keep up his pretence, his alter ego, Owain y Mynydd was servant to the Prince, and dressed as such, yet his master never called on him. It was surely only a matter of time before Woodstock decided to spend time in the camp, would he acknowledge Owain as part of his entourage or question the role of the imposing figure of the archer dressed in his majesty's colours, we could only hope that Woodstock had so many servants he would not notice a strange one here and there.

Gwyn and Owain left us to our work and began to set up the archery targets. Gwyn's section would shoot for an hour every evening, keeping their eyes practiced and their reactions swift. By the time we reached France each would be able to fire twenty-four arrows a minute, deadly to a foot soldier at one hundred yards and to an armoured knight at sixty.

The other sections would practice but not with the fervour of Gwyn's men. Sir Kenneth and his father had instilled in him that his life and that of the men may depend on every arrow.

The quiver lads who supplied the archers with arrows, and who retrieved the spent arrows from the field of battle ran like hounds on their prey, Gwyn left nothing to chance.

He and Owain seemed of one mind in this, practice made perfect, or if not, perfect it would make each movement reflex, and each shot sure on its target.

I made my bed such as it was in the corner of Margeds tent, a large bag filled with hay laid out on ground as dry as we could find, covered with my spare shift and my cloak. I was becoming used to the ways of this fascinating fur lined garment, I now knew with confidence that if I pulled it round my body and pulled the hood over my head and pictured myself in darkness, then I could not be seen. It would prove a useful tool around the camp, I would not know how useful until we reached France.

CHAPTER 50 – MORE MEN AND EQUIPMENT – GWYN AP MEREDITH

The slow meandering progress south continues, like a vast river of men and equipment, servants, households winding across the Welsh border and into the Marches.

At Chepstow we were joined by the Earl of Warwick one of the King's trusted nobles and his retinue of men at arms, Hobelar light horsemen armed with short bows and his knights on their chargers. He brought with him his own entourage of servants, squires, and pages, they made a fine sight with their brightly coloured banners and surcoats, their fine horses, coats brushed to a shine and coloured ribbons hanging from their harnesses. More people to take sick or get injured, more to be fed and laundered and generally tended to.

He also brought with him a number of heavy weapons, huge iron tubes which when loaded with gunpowder would fire large iron balls at the enemy. The duke called them Bombards, So that's where Bombardier came from I thought to myself. The forerunner of the cannon but without the wheels. These were carried in their own wagon drawn by four huge Suffolk punch horses, impressive weapons but heavy and not easy to move, they slowed our progress south to the ships, as they would no doubt slow our progress in France. The column rumbled on at a relentless pace considering the time it took to set up camp at night, and to pack it away in the morning. Even rising at dawn, it took hours before a wheel turned. We were lucky to cover ten miles in a day, marching until two hours before dusk to allow for pitching our tents for the night.

All along the route the numbers swelled men from every county along with their lords, whether in the King's favour or not.

This was a community on the move, the fighting men marching in their units, honing their skills, practicing along the route with weapons and without.
Horses were schooled, archers practiced, blacksmiths forged armour and weapons as well as shoeing horses. Owain and I drilled our men, getting them accustomed to the orders which became a rhythm to their lives. 'Arrow, nock, draw, loose. Arrow, nock, draw, loose.' Until they could repeat it twenty-seven times a minute.

Owain spent less time with us now, he was drawn into the confidence of Woodstock, as the Princes squire he was required to carry messages between the Prince and his nobles, wearing his surcoat in the King's colours he rode up and down the line on one of the spare horses stopping occasionally to talk but most times galloping straight past with another dispatch for those at the rear of the line.

Of an evening he would find us, me, Marged and Red and eat with us, making his bed with us and returning to the Prince in the morning for his instructions for the day.

Sometimes he was accompanied by Woodstock himself, a slight blonde figure, no older than me, just about showing the stubble of manhood on his chin, slight he may be, but he was broad across his chest and shoulders and strong in the legs. On these occasions he wore no mark of his rank, dressed only in a thick wool cloak over his customary leather breeches, and a simple linen shirt.

Every morning he would practice with his sword, usually with one of the Master at Arms but now and then with Owain. Owain was a fine swordsman, better with a sword than a bow, the Prince was in a different class again, taught by the finest masters of the art. The Italian fencing master employed by his father was known to be the best in the land and his services were coveted by the King.

The Prince spent many hours around the different camp fires, making a point of seeking out his longbow men, listening to their complaints, joking, and drinking with them. There would, he promised, be honours and rewards for all if the campaign were successful.

He had taken a liking to Owain, I feared I may lose Owain from the ranks of the longbow to that of Princes standard bearer. I had better make sure that Geraint knew all the commands we used just in case he was needed.

CHAPTER 51 - TALES FROM THE FIRESIDE –
PRINCE EDWARD OF WALES

As more men joined our company on the journey south, the gathering around the fires of an evening became more gregarious, some men had brought with them their flutes or pipes there was even a small harp on one of the wagons, and storytellers a plenty.

Far better company was to be found around the camp fires than amongst the constant bickering of their lordships, after supper, we had been joined now by the Earls of Northampton and Warwick who preferred to take their ease over the chess board, when de Audley made his excuses to retire, Sir Kenneth and I would walk amongst the camp fires, often sitting amongst the men listening to the storytellers and the singers amongst them.

Amongst the Llantrisant men there is a young squire called Geraint, he loves to tell the old folk tales. In particular the one of his namesake.

It is a tale of the court of King Arthur, I have been told these tales by my nurse as I grew up, they are full of fair maidens and knights who joust for their honour, and of magical animals mystical spells.

Tonight, we make camp on the Welsh borders, it is a fine summers night.

'Welcome milord.'

A friendly voice greets us from the fireside, several of the men shuffle along the great log where they have made a seat, making room for us amongst them.

Geraint was sitting on a rock near the fire, waiting for the gathered men to lapse into silence.

He surveyed his audience and began, the hum of conversations around the fire suddenly silent as his soft melodic voice began.

Appropriate to the moment, for we were encamped near the very place, he began with ….

This is the tale of Geraint of Erbin a knight of great chivalry

In the days of the court of King Arthur. A court of great warriors and great chivalry, a great Prince as is the Prince who sits amongst us.

This for the benefit of those who would be accidentally disrespectful of my company, not necessary, but an observance of protocol at least.

With a breath in, and a sweeping look around his audience, he began in earnest.

For seven Easter's and five Christmases and one Whitsun King Arthur had held court at Caerleon, for the halls of Caerleon were easily accessed by land and by sea.

All his great Lords and Kings attended the festivals, such was the greatness of the gathering that thirteen churches were set aside one for the King himself and the other Kings of the lands and their guests, one for Gwenhwyvar and her ladies, one for the Steward of the house and his suitors, one for the Franks the freemen of the land and the others for the nine masters of the households. In particular for Cwalchmai the great warlord. For Whitsun was a great festival with feasting and celebration for a whole seven days.

And so, it happened on Whit Tuesday that a youth appeared at the court of King Arthur.

He was tall and fair youth, clad in a coat and a surcoat of diapered satin, and a golden-hilted sword and dagger hung at his waist, and shoes of leather upon his feet.

Geraint paused and took a drink from his mug of ale. The gathered men could be heard discussing the clothes of the knight and comparing them to the rough shoes which they themselves wore and the women remarking on the impracticality of wearing white. Geraint continued.

He stood before Arthur and spoke to his King 'Hail to thee, Lord!' said he.

'Heaven prosper thee and be thou welcome.' Answered the King.' Dost thou bring any new tidings?'

The youth was called Madoc a forester of the Forest of Dean, told of a white stag of great size and stately bearing, a royal beast indeed.

And so, Arthur gave notice to his huntsman that they would hunt the stag on the morrow at daybreak.

And Gwenhwyvar - that's Guinevere to the heathens amongst ye, - added Geraint in an aside. Asked of Arthur 'Wilt thou permit me, Lord to go to-morrow to see and hear the hunt of the stag of which the young man spoke?'

'I will gladly,' said Arthur. 'Then will I go,' said she.

'Lord!' Spoke up Cwalchmai the most warlike of the Kings men, 'Lord, if it seem well to thee, permit that into whose hunt soever the stag shall come, that one, be he a knight, or one on foot, may cut off his head, and give it to whom he pleases, whether to his own ladylove, or to the lady of his friend'.

And so it was that the King agreed to the hunt, of the great white stag.
In the morning, the King, and the Lords and all the attendants rose early for the hunt, but Gwenhwyvar was still fast asleep in her bed.

'Do not disturb my lady,' said the King, 'If she would rather lie abed than see the hunt then let her lie.'
And so, when the lady awoke, she found that all the hunting party had left without her.

Arthur had gone forth from the palace, when Gwenhwyvar awoke, and called to her maidens, and dressed herself. 'Maidens,' said she, 'I had leave last night to go and see the hunt. Go one of you to the stable and order a horse such as a woman may ride.'

One of them went, and she found but two horses in the stable, and Gwenhwyvar and one of her maidens mounted them, and went through the Usk, and followed the track of the men and the horses.

As they followed in the tracks of the men they heard the sound of galloping hooves behind them and a loud rushing sound through the trees, looking behind them they saw a young knight on a mighty charger a fair-haired youth, bare-legged, and of princely mien, and a golden-hilted sword was at his side, and a robe and a surcoat of satin were upon him, shoes of leather upon his feet; and around him was a scarf of blue purple, at bearing the crest of a golden apple. The horse was sure and swift and quickly overtook Gwenhwyvar and her maid. Recognising his fair countenance as he passed and saluted her she replied to his salute. He reined in his horse to ride with her awhile.

'Heaven prosper thee, Geraint, I knew thee when first I saw thee just now. And the welcome of Heaven be unto thee. And why didst thou not go with thy Lord to hunt?'

'Because I knew not when he went my head being cloudy from the festivities of the night,' said he.

Geraint raised his mug of ale which had grown empty with the telling, and cleared his throat, raising and lowering his pitch in imitation of the speakers was taking its toll on his voice.

A full mug of ale was hastily found, and the storyteller urged to continue.

In his best voice of Guinevere, he carried on his tale.

'I marvel, too,' said she, 'how he could go unknown to me.'

'Indeed, lady,' said he.

'I was asleep, and knew not when he went; but thou, O young man, art the most agreeable companion I could have in the whole kingdom; and it may be, that I shall be more amused with the hunting than they; for we shall hear the horns when they sound, and we shall hear the dogs when they are let loose and begin to cry.'

So, they went to the edge of the Forest, and there they stood. 'From this place,' said she, 'we shall hear when the dogs are let loose.'

And thereupon, they heard a loud noise, and they looked towards the spot whence it came, and they beheld a dwarf riding upon a horse, stately, and foaming, and prancing, and strong, and spirited. In the hand of the dwarf was a whip. Near the dwarf they saw a lady upon a beautiful white horse, of steady and stately pace; and she was clothed in a garment of gold brocade. Near her was a knight upon a warhorse of large size, with heavy and bright armour both upon himself and upon his horse.

Gwenhwyvar had never seen this knight before and did not recognise his surcoat or his armour or his Dwarfish servant.

'Geraint,' said Gwenhwyvar, 'knowest thou the name of that tall knight yonder?'

'I know him not,' said he, 'and the strange armour that he wears prevents my either seeing his face or his features.'

And so Gwenhwyvar sent her handmaiden to enquire of the dwarf, the identity of his master

'I will not tell thee,' Answered the tiny man.

'Since thou art so churlish as not to tell me,' Said she, 'I will ask him himself'.

'Thou shalt not ask him, by my faith'" said he.

'You have not sufficient honour to speak so to my Lord!'

The maiden turned her horse's head towards the knight, and made to approach this golden being, upon which the dwarf struck her with the whip that was in his hand, he struck the maid across the face and the eyes beating her until the blood flowed forth.

The maiden, through the hurt she received from the blow, returned to Gwenhwyvar, complaining greatly of the pain.

'Very rudely has the dwarf treated thee,' said Geraint. 'I will go myself to know who the knight is.

'Go you,' said Gwenhwyvar. And Geraint went up to the dwarf'

'Who is yonder knight?' said Geraint.

'I will not tell thee.' Said the dwarf.

'Then will I ask him himself,' said he.

'That wilt thou not, by my faith,' said the dwarf, 'thou art not honourable enough to speak with my Lord.'

I have spoken with men of equal rank with him and those of more honourable station.'

He turned his horse's head towards the knight; but the dwarf overtook him, and struck him as he had done the maiden, so that the blood coloured the scarf that Geraint wore.

Geraint put his hand upon the hilt of his sword, but he took counsel with himself, and considered that it would be no vengeance for him to slay the dwarf, and to be attacked unarmed by the armed knight, so he returned to where Gwenhwyvar was.

'Thou hast acted wisely and discreetly,' said she.

'Lady,' said he, 'I will follow him yet, with thy permission; and at last, he will come to some inhabited place, where I may have arms either as a loan or for a pledge, so that I may encounter the knight.'

'Go, but do not attack him until thou hast good arms, I shall be very anxious concerning thee, until I hear tidings.'

'If I am alive, 'said he, 'thou shalt hear tidings of me by to-morrow afternoon;' and with that he departed.

The road they took was below the palace of Caerleon, and across the ford of the Usk; and they went along a fair, and even, and lofty ridge of ground, until they came to a town, and at the extremity of the town they saw a Fortress and a Castle.

When at last they came to the extremity of the town and as the knight passed through it, all the people arose, and saluted him, and bade him welcome.

When Geraint came into the town, he looked at every house, to see if he knew any of those whom he saw. But he knew none, and none knew him to do him the kindness to let him have arms either as a loan or for a pledge. Every house he saw was full of men, and arms, and horses. The men were polishing shields, and burnishing swords, and washing armour, and shoeing horses.

The knight, and the lady, and the dwarf rode up to the Castle that was in the town, and everyone was glad in the Castle. From the battlements and the gates, they risked their necks, through their eagerness to greet them, and to show their joy.

Geraint stood there to see whether the knight would remain in the Castle; and when he was certain that he would do so, he looked around him; and at a little distance from the town, he saw an old palace in ruins, wherein was a hall that was falling to decay. And as he knew not any one in the town, he went towards the old palace; and when he came near to the palace, he saw but one chamber, and a bridge of marble-stone leading to it.

Upon the bridge he saw sitting a grey-haired old man, upon whom were tattered garments. Geraint gazed steadfastly upon him for a long time. Then the hoary-headed man spoke to him.

'Young man, why art thou thoughtful?'

'I am thoughtful,' said he, 'because I know not where to go to-night.'

'Wilt thou come forward this way, chieftain?' said he, 'and thou shalt have of the best that can be procured for thee.' So, Geraint went forward.

The grey-haired man went before him into the old and run-down palace, he followed the man into an upper chamber where on a great but ragged embroidered cushion sat a woman with old, tattered garments of satin upon her; and it seemed to him that he had never seen a woman fairer than she must have been, when in the fulness of youth.

Beside her was a maiden, upon whom were a vest and a veil, both were old, and beginning to be worn out. Geraint had never seen a maiden more full of comeliness, and grace, and beauty than she.

The grey-haired man said to the maiden, 'There is no attendant for the horse of this youth but thyself.'

'I will render the best service I am able,' said she, 'both to him and to his horse.' The maiden took his cloak and led his horse away and furnished it with a good bed of straw and corn to eat and then she returned to the chamber.

Speaking to the maiden again the grey-haired man sent her into the town to fetch provisions of meat and ale and whatever else she could procure.

While she was away Geraint and the man conversed. Some while later the maid came back and with her a youth, bearing on his back a flat bottle full of good, purchased mead, and a quarter of a young bullock.

In the hands of the maiden was a quantity of white bread, and also some manchet bread concealed in her veil, all this she brought into the chamber

'I could not obtain better than this,' said she, 'nor with better should I have been trusted.'

'It is good enough,' said Geraint.

They cooked the meat and when their meal was ready they sat down to eat.

Geraint seated between the man and his wife while the maid served them they ate and drank and when they had finished eating, Geraint again talked with the grey-haired man.

Geraint enquired of his host to whom the palace in which he now sat belonged and to whom the castle belonged and the town.

'Truly,' said he, 'it was I that built it, and to me also belonged the city and the castle which thou sawest.'

'Alas!' said Geraint, 'how is it that thou hast lost them now?'

'I lost a great Earldom as well as these,' said he; 'and this is how I lost them. I had a nephew, the son of my brother, and I took his possessions to myself; and when he came to his strength, he demanded of me his property, but I withheld it from him. So, he made war upon me, and wrested from me all that I possessed.'

At this point a grumbling of voices came from the men of the marcher lord Warwick who were sitting in company with the Welsh archers for whom this story was merely a fiction to entertain.

The nature of the story brought back to them the days when the Despenser Lord had wreaked havoc through the marches in his quest for property and gold and razed many villages and good properties to the ground.

`Geraint allowed the grumbling to subside and took a pull at his ale mug. Drinking deeply.

'It grows late my lord,' he addressed the Prince who was still seated with Sir Kenneth listening to the story with his noble hand curled around a lowly pot mug of beer brewed by the laundry women.

'I shall draw this night to a close'.

He began again

'Good Sir, who are the knight, and the lady, and the dwarf who came into the town, and what is the preparation which I saw, and the putting of arms in order?'

'The preparations' said the grey-haired man 'are for the game that is to be held to-morrow by the young Earl, in the midst of a nearby meadow, which is here, two forks will be set up, and upon the two forks a silver rod will be placed and upon the silver rod a Sparrowhawk, and for the Sparrowhawk there will be a tournament. And to the tournament will go all the array thou didst see in the city, of men, and of horses, and of arms. And with each man will go the lady he loves best; and no man can joust for the Sparrowhawk, except the lady he loves best be with him.'

With this Geraint ap Robert of the Llantrisant archers rose.

Milords, ladies, and all those present, my voice grows tired, I shall continue on another night, when you will hear more of the adventures of my namesake.

Sir Kenneth and I rise discreetly from our place by the fire and wander back through the camp to our tents, I do not know what the ladies of the camp brew into their ale, but I fear that I am forced to lean on Sir Kenneth and he on me, it has been a pleasant evening, much more so than listening to an endless discourse on my father's collection of taxes.

I see the healer Marged and her husband locked in an embrace under a nearby tree, barely out of sight of passers-by but just within the circle of heat cast by the dying embers of the fire. I fear that my best archer has been distracted these last few days, I must speak with Sir Kenneth as to why.

Gwyn placed his arm around Marged's shoulder holding her close to him as they stared into the dying embers of the fire and Gwyn stretched his legs before him and leaned back against the backrest of the huge log they had made their seat for the evening.

'Marged, would you have me be your Sparrow Hawk?'

She pulled his face down to hers and kissed him deeply on the mouth.

'You do not need golden armour or a great horse, nor a sparrowhawk, all I need is to have faith Gwyn, faith that you will do what is right.'

They stayed late at the fire that night, rediscovering a trust in each other which Gwyn feared had been destroyed forever.

In the morning we broke camp at Chepstow and continued south. It is slow progress, ten miles a day if we are fortunate in the weather.

CHAPTER 52 - THE KNIGHT OF THE SPARROWHAWK – EDWARD PRINCE OF WALES

The following night we made camp on the banks of the great River Severn. At the small settlement of Aust we waited for the whole army to be ferried across the wide expanse of water, rather this than face a further four days march to find a suitable crossing point to the North, and in any case the Lord Warwick had just marched his men south along that route and had no wish to double his tracks or that of his men.

We camped less than half a mile from the river, away from the stinking marsh flats that formed its banks, on an area of grassland, there was not much more cover than low scrub land and bushes.

At dusk we lit fires and prepared food from the meat we had saved from the hunting in the forest land we had travelled through and the rabbits which had been snared on our journey.

301

As the camp settled for the night, Geraint resumed his tale of his namesake Geraint of Erbin and the Knight of the Sparrowhawk.

This time sitting on the tailboard of one of the wagons, Geraint began:

Geraint of Erbin spoke to the Grey-haired old man who had offered him his hospitality and been a most gracious host.

'Who?' he asked, 'is the knight I saw; he rides with a Dwarf as his servant and with a maiden dressed in white and gold and on fine horses.' The grey-haired man replied:

'The knight that you saw has gained the Sparrowhawk these two years; and if he gains it the third year, they will, from that time, send it every year to him, and he himself will come here no more. He will be called the Knight of the Sparrowhawk from that time forth.'

'Sir,' said Geraint, 'what is thy counsel to me concerning this knight, I seek retribution for an insult made by his dwarfish servant to the maid servant of Queen Gwenhwyvar the wife of King Arthur, the maidservant has suffered most grievously at his hand.'

'It is not easy to counsel thee, in as much as thou hast neither dame nor maiden belonging to thee, for whom you can joust. Yet, I have arms here, which thou could have; and there is my horse also, if he seem to thee better than thine own.'

'Ah! Sir,' said he, 'Heaven reward thee. But my own horse, to which I am accustomed, together with thy arms, will suffice me. When the appointed time shall come tomorrow, thou wilt permit me, Sir, to challenge for yonder maiden thy daughter.

I will engage, if I escape from the tournament, to love the maiden as long as I live; and if I do not escape, she will remain unsullied as before.'

'Gladly will I permit thee,' said the old man, 'and since thou dost thus resolve, it is necessary that thy horse and arms should be ready tomorrow at break of day. For then the Knight of the Sparrowhawk will make proclamation and ask the lady he loves best to take the Sparrowhawk. 'For,' will he say to her, 'thou art the fairest of women, and thou didst possess it last year, and the year previous; and if any deny it thee to-day, by force will I defend it for thee.' And therefore," said the grey-haired old man, 'it is needful for thee to be there at daybreak; and we three will be with thee.'

Thus, was it settled. They slept the night and at dawn they readied themselves; and by the time that it was day, they were all four in the meadow.

The Knight of the Sparrowhawk made his proclamation and asked his ladylove to fetch the sparrowhawk.

'Fetch it not,' said Geraint, 'for there is here a maiden, who is fairer, and more noble, and more comely, and who has a better claim to it than thou.'

Up spoke the Knight of the Sparrow Hawk 'If thou believes the Sparrowhawk to be due to her, come forward, and do battle with me.'

Geraint went forward to the top of the meadow, having upon himself and upon his horse armour which was old and heavy and rusted with the weather and worthless, battered into an uncouth shape.

Geraint paused for a refill of his ale pot, he surveyed his audience and saw the cloaked figures of the Prince and Sir Kenneth listening avidly in his audience, Gwyn and Marged wrapped in Gwyn's cloak seated against the wheel of the healer's wagon, drawn up on the other side of the fire and there was Owain, his arm draped in familiar fashion around the slim waist of that strange woman they all called Red, a woman who seemed to have a knowledge of everything and a rare talent for disappearing.

Ale pot replenished, he continued

Then they encountered each other, and they broke a set of lances, and they broke a second set, and a third.

Thus, they did at every onset, and they broke as many lances as were brought to them. And when the Young Earl and his company saw the Knight of the Sparrowhawk gaining the mastery, there was shouting, and joy, and mirth amongst them. The grey-haired man, and his wife, and his daughter were sorrowful. The Old man served Geraint lances as often as he broke them, and the dwarf served the Knight of the Sparrowhawk. Then the grey-haired man came to Geraint.

'[Oh! chieftain,' said he, 'since no other will hold with thee, behold, here is the lance which was in my hand on the day when I received the honour of knighthood; and from that time to this I never broke it. It has an excellent point still.'

Geraint took the lance, thanking him.

The dwarf also brought a lance to his lord.

'Behold, here is a lance for thee, not less good than his,' said the dwarf. 'And bethink thee, that no knight ever withstood thee before so long as this one has done.'

'I declare to Heaven,' said Geraint, 'that unless death takes me quickly hence, he shall fare never the better for thy service.' This was last lance in his armoury.

Geraint spurred his horse towards the Sparrow Hawk from the furthest point of the joust, he cried a warning to his opponent then rushed upon him, bearing down on him as fast as his horse could carry him under the weight of the old knight's armour. The blow pierced his shield and broke it into two, then split girths on his saddle and unhorsed the Sparrowhawk over the tail of his charger, depositing him heavily on the ground.

Geraint dismounted quickly. He drew his sword and rushed fiercely upon his opponent. Then the knight also arose and drew his sword against Geraint. They fought on foot with their swords until their arms struck sparks of fire like stars from one another; and thus, they continued fighting until the blood and sweat obscured the light from their eyes. When Geraint prevailed, the grey-haired man, and his wife, and his daughter were glad; and when the knight prevailed, it rejoiced the Young Earl and his party. Then Geraint received a sword stroke to his helmet rendering him dizzy and senseless, he was fast losing the will to continue.

The voice of the old knight roused him 'Oh, chieftain, remember the treatment which you received from the dwarf; will you not seek vengeance for the insult to thyself, and for the insult to Gwenhwyvar the wife of Arthur!'

With this Geraint raised his arms and the great sword above his head and struck the Sparrowhawk on the crown of his head so that he broke all his head-armour, and cut through all the flesh and the skin, even to the skull, until he wounded the bone. Then the knight fell upon his knees, and cast his sword from his hand, and besought mercy of Geraint.

'Of a truth,' said he, 'I seek your mercy and your forgiveness for my sin which is the sin of pride, before I surrender to my Lord God, fetch me a priest that I may pray also to him for forgiveness, good sir grant me grace.'

'I will grant thee grace upon this condition,' said Geraint, 'that thou wilt go to Gwenhwyvar the wife of Arthur, to do her satisfaction for the insult which her maiden received from thy dwarf. Your current situation is recompense enough for the insult to my person. Ride from here until you come into the presence of Gwenhwyvar, to make her what atonement shall be adjudged at the Court of Arthur.'

'This will I do gladly. And who art thou?' said he. 'I am Geraint the son of Erbin. And declare thou also who thou art.'

'I am Edeyrn the son of Nudd.'

Then the Knight threw himself upon his horse, and went forward to Arthur's Court, and the lady he loved best went before him and the dwarf, sorely injured and with much difficulty they rode.

Then came the Young Earl and his hosts to Geraint, and saluted him, and bade him to his castle.
But Geraint refused to take the hospitality of the castle, preferring to stay with the old grey-haired knight who had been so generous to him on the evening before.

For Geraint was a knight who was loyal to his friends and would not abandon the old knight and his family for the offer of a more sumptuous accommodation with the Earl.

At this Geraint our storyteller broke for the night and those around the fire drifted away, the Prince and sir Kenneth rose, but instead of walking back to the tents set for the nobles slightly apart from the main camp, Prince Edward crossed in front of the fire and made his way to the healer's wagon.

Madam, he addressed Marged, do you have a draft which will cure a disturbance of my innards.
'I do your majesty' came the reply, 'but I fear it is packed away in the wagon;'

'Tis not an urgent matter, wait on me in the morning or send a bottle with your husband, I would speak with him of other matters in any case

307

'Gwyn, will you walk with me a while? '

They strode off leaving Sir Kenneth talking with Marged and Red at the rear of the wagon.

I spoke in earnest to the finest of my archers who was walking alongside me.

'Gwyn, I need your complete attention on your work, are there things amiss with Marged? I sense she is not as happy as before we left.'

'Sire, she is homesick, this is the first time she travelled, she misses the lady Margaret, and she grieves for the young maid Sian who died before we left.'

'A tragic event, why would one so young end their life like that?'

'Why indeed' replied Gwyn.

'I sense you are not telling me all Gwyn ap Meredith, I will find out in time, there is unrest in this camp, and I will have none of it.'

The Prince turned on his heel and summarily dismissing the archer, he strode up the rise to the circle of tents where his nobles entertained themselves.

'Warwick, Northampton, do you still play at chess my Lords. Where is de Audley? I would speak with him.'

Warwick lifted his eyes from the chess pieces 'Sir Hugh has gone walking sire, he was headed for the river.'

There was no sign of Sir Hugh all night, but he was back to camp for breakfast in the morning.

It took two full days to ferry the whole army and equipment across the river. Once across the river the long march South continued. As the last of the column disembarked from the ferry pontoon and the ferryman tied it up for the last time only Morwenna Bowen the daughter of one of the laundry women saw the body of the boy floating face down in the river, his tawny hair spayed around his head like some grotesque halo.

At Cirencester we were joined by the Earl of Oxford Sir John Chandos, he brought with him men trained in the use of a volley firing crossbow called a ribauldequin. An ingenious machine but slow to load and not accurate.

He also brought several more bombasts to add to the arsenal which was being assembled.

Then on to Silchester, a small town on the border of Hampshire, we set up camp in fields near the church of St Mary and rested there for two days, giving the masters at arms opportunity to list all the men and take inventory of the stores and ammunition, a register was also made of the camp followers and workers.

Sir Kenneth was insistent on this, he would have no one left out. Babies would be born on campaign, members of the camp would take ill and die, all would be recorded in Sir Kenneth's flowing hand.

He inspected Marged's and Sibyl's records, the books they recorded their patients' symptoms and treatments in. He thoroughly approved of their thorough records and their book of recipes for remedies, salves, and potions. While many of the men thought the two of them a pair of witches, they were grateful for relief for their ale induced headaches and for the swift treatment of their cuts and bruises. He laughed at their story of the foraging party who had waded into a stream to tickle trout and emerged covered in leeches. Four grown men ran in terror to Marged to have the demons removed by application of salt. Only to see their demons housed in a jar for future use on bruises and black eyes. A frequent sight amongst their patients on a Monday morning.

Marged and I, well she still would not let me close, when found privacy enough to make love, she was distracted, mechanical even, just doing it to keep me happy. She no longer took me into her body with passion. Her eyes no longer shone when she saw me, she no longer melted at my touch. Her sleep was restless, she often cried out, fighting some unseen attacker in the darkness.

She told me that she saw him, his eyes, cold like a dead fish, his hands pawing, nails over long for a man, clawing her flesh, Marged hated long fingernails. I did not know how to make it right. I spoke to the priest at St Mary's church, I made confession and sought his guidance, time he said would heal my Marged time and love, and forgiveness.

I knew she would never forgive. Her hatred of de Audley ran too deep for that.

Our lord and master is rarely seen amongst his men, he prefers to obsequiate himself amongst the trusted nobles, though he is neither of their status or of their import with our monarch. He struts about their tents like a demented peacock, rarely taking off the colours of his family. Talking in the courtly French of the old court.

He rides at the front of the column on Blondell by far the largest ridden horse in the whole army, hardly ever in full control of her and frequently carried off the road and into the undergrowth at her whim.

Sir Kenneth has offered him a more suitable mount, but he refuses. Blondell he says is his and he will ride her. At night he spends his time drinking with the nobles then prowling the camp fires, not to make conversation but on the lookout for prey, female prey.

Red and Marged have warned all the young girls, told them to be wary of his Lordship, I pray they all listened. Tomorrow morning, we break camp and head for Portsmouth, a further three days march away.

CHAPTER 53 - SAILING FOR FRANCE – GWYN AP MEREDITH

The harbour at Portsmouth was crowded with ships, great vessels either tied up to the quayside or bobbing at anchor out in the bay waiting their turn to be loaded with men and equipment. Seven hundred vessels in total, filling the harbour and the channel all flying the pennants and flags of the nobility and the noise which went along with them creating a scene of organised chaos.

The whole town was alive with tradesmen selling their wares, seeking to make a few pennies from the massive influx of civilians and soldiers.

Less than ten years before, the French had raided Portsmouth, coming into the harbour under friendly flag and burning the whole town, many of the wooden defences and thatched roiled of the buildings had been razed to the ground. No friendly feelings here for the enemy across the English Channel.

On every street there were hawkers selling their wares, everything from pies to pike staffs. The Ale houses were full to bursting with soldiers and seamen and were patrolled by the Constables of the town who sought to keep some semblance of good order amongst the mayhem.

The Kings army now numbered about 15,000 men 2,500 men-at-arms, 7,000 longbowmen, 3,250 hobelars and 2,300 spearmen.

Along with horses and wagons and the retinues of the nobles and the knights all this wave of humanity must be loaded onto the seven hundred waiting ships to make the voyage to the French coast.

The army was under the command of our Prince Edward and also of William de Bohun the Earl of Northampton, a trusted friend of the King and an experienced leader of men. The King was also in residence, installed on his flagship out in the harbour, there being no suitable lodging in the town.

We had been joined on our route south by yet more men and more wagons. Our cavalcade was now at least a mile long from end to end.

By the time of our arrival, it was impossible to find a place to set up camp within the town. Sir Kenneth found us ground on which to set up camp for the time it would take us to be loaded onto the ships. Prince Edward and The Earls of Warwick and Oxford who had joined us sought out their fellow nobles to find out what his grace of Northampton had in the way of orders. Sir Hugh along with them as head of our contingent.

We made rough corrals and lines for the horses making sure all the mounts were hobbled or tied and safe. It took several days for all to be loaded. It would take about fifteen hours to sail to our destination, wherever that turned out to be. It was likely a beach landing, and not close to any fortified town, the King sought an element of surprise. The French must know from their network of spies that we were coming, but they would not know where on the many miles of coast we would land.

Owain and I had helped with the loading of the de Audley wagons and supplies, the horses had travelled calmly, Trooper was an old hand at this and a calming influence on Blondell, the horses Prince Edward had brought had already made a crossing from Ireland and were seasoned travellers, as was the Prince's horse.

Duties done, we found Marged and Red and leaning on the rail at the stern of the great ship, we watched England disappear into the early morning sea mist. The crossing was largely uneventful, apart from two horses being dispatched and butchered. The animals had been confined below deck and not used to the movement of the vessel beneath their hooves and the dark, they had panicked, threatening to hole the side of the ship with their great hooves, one had broken a leg in its attempts to break free and the other could not be calmed.

This battalion would eat well for a few days, though two of their knights would be seeking new horses from the string which travelled with the King and the Prince.

We landed in France on 12 July 1346. The landing ground proved to be on the sandy stretch that lies between La Hogue and St Vaast on the coast of Normandy and the shortest distance possible from Portsmouth. Great ramps appeared from the bellies of the ships, horses which had been winched aboard at Portsmouth could be walked off down the ramps and either into the water or straight onto the firm sand. Wagons were manhandled up the beach lest they get bogged down, foot soldiers formed into columns, mounted men donned what armour they had to hand and gradually an army appeared.

To the clink of harness and the tramp of feet the army of King Edward III marched into France intent on taking the crown of France for himself. Philip VI of France would have other ideas. We had landed with an element of surprise, but it is very hard to conceal an army of fifteen thousand men and all that travels with it. As soon as we cleared the coast we found that the French sought to hinder our progress by laying waste to their land, destroying any stocks of food or grain. Our foraging parties were ambushed by gangs of French bandits when they hunted the French forests for game.

In response, King Edward sent raiding parties to burn villages and towns, he razed whole communities to the ground. Men at arms were sent in small bands to burn houses and loot. Chivalry and the code of honour that went with it seemed to have been suspended.

As Archers, we were the specialised troops that would be needed when we met the night of the French

Army, we were not deployed on these raids, though we heard about them in the campfire talk every evening.

This was war then, not an act of glory not a game played by chivalrous rules, a bloodthirsty vicious game between thrones. The masters of which usually stood back and let their foot soldiers die for the cause.

Our first major skirmish was at Caen on 26th July

CHAPTER 54 – THE PRINCE WRITES – THE PRINCE OF WALES

Chepstow July 1346

I have been riding with these people for some days now.

I have stayed at their home, been made welcome and truly welcome by the people.

Despite my title as Prince of Wales, they have treated me as they would one of their own.

I find myself at the head of a fine band of archers, I have seen the Longbowmen of the town of Llantrisant practice, they are the finest I have seen.

They volley at over twenty arrows a minute; they are accurate, and they are deadly over a distance of nearly half a mile. I am indeed privileged to have their charge. They are a proud and stubborn bunch, loyal to the King and proud of their heritage. Fond of a mug of ale and a song and a story of an evening. There is one amongst them who is exceptional in his skill, his accuracy and in his ability to lead men. I have spoken to his Master at arms and Gwyn ap Meredith will be rewarded. He trains as a squire under Sir Hugh de Audley, but he is not a vassal, he is a free man.

As we have journeyed south to meet the fleet my father the King has assembled to take us across the channel, I find that I value the company of these men more than that of the pompous fool who holds the Castle and lands at Llantrisant.

Sir Hugh is a strange fish indeed, he and his wife the Lady Margaret lead separate lives, she good lady has done what my grandfather asked of them when he returned her inheritance to the family.

It is down to her good auspices and management that the towns of the area thrive, the religious establishments contribute to the community and the people are no longer on the point of rebellion.
Sir Hugh on the other hand is adept at spending the King's gold, he is greedy for land and favour of the King and seeks a return to Court. I fear he may have a long wait.

There are rumours, I have heard them, his Lordship strays from his marriage, not that this is unusual amongst the nobility, the rumours are that he takes his pleasures with the newly married wives, and not with their consent.
Sir Kenneth, his master of arms, is diplomatic and guarded in what he says, but fears that rape may be the least of the man's crimes. The men do not trust Sir

Hugh, and I have heard that there are those who would see him dead.

I shall keep my council for the present, there is no room for such unrest whilst on campaign.

I have also acquired a new page called Owain. Sent he says by my father some months ago, whilst I was in Ireland.

He too is a fine archer and a swordsman; he will do well.

I must enquire of my father where he found this man, for none of the nobles from court have seen him before.

He seems to have the ability to be exactly where I want him without my asking, or to disappear at will and be totally absent.

July 12[th,] 1346.

We have been joined on our journey by the Earls of Northampton, Warwick, and Essex. And also, by my great friend and advisor Sir John Chandos.

De Bohun of Northampton is to command the army alongside me. Warwick and Essex come with their cohort of men and their heavy armaments. They complete our army.

All are embarked on the vast fleet of ships, surely enough to fill the distance to France if joined together from stem to stern.

We sail on the next tide. For Normandy.

Philip VI will demand no more gold from us, we will not be vassals to the French, if we have to raze every town and village in our path, we will show the French we are not their servants.

July 13th, 1346.

St Vaast The Coast of Normandy.

I have been to mass with my father the King and he has seen fit to create me a knight of the realm. We have commended our campaign to God as a right and just cause.

Tomorrow we march south.

My lord Northampton has been ordered to divide his men into raiding parties both to acquire food and supplies as needed, to seize all items of value for the benefit of the King and to burn what is left. No quarter is to be given and no persons spared.

He is to instruct his men that the common soldiers are not however to rape or abuse the civilian population. This I will not tolerate.

My division of the great army will do likewise, in this way we should accomplish our aim of total destruction of the French economy and commerce before we ever meet the army of King Philip.

22nd July 1346

The City of St Lo.

The great city of St Lo, a centre of commerce and finance, Northampton's men have taken up occupation of the city after a short skirmish. It's treasuries have been emptied, it's religious buildings looted of gold, silver, and precious stones. I have several wagons loaded to return to the coast and load ships to take this booty back to England.

I have dispatched part of my force to Torigny a small city but with an impressive chateau which may hold assets of value, this small force of knights and men at arms will then follow our main party to the capital of Normandy, the city of Caen

CHAPTER 55 - THE BATTLE FOR CAEN –
EDWARD PRINCE OF WALES

26th July 1346
City of Caen

The city of Caen looms in front of us, it's walls taller than any I had seen before. The colour of wet sand baked in the sunshine. Pitted by the weather and the shot from old battles. The great wooden gates are closed.

It has a great and heavily fortified castle manned by nearly one thousand men at arms and crossbowmen, but they are split to guard the whole city and the walls which surround the new town, which is built on an island in the middle of the river.

A city nearly the size of London, the bearing heart of Normandy.

All men will have a role in this campaign, I send de Audley as envoy to speak to the burghers and negotiate their surrender.

I have brought Warwick's huge canon to bear on the gates and ranged the longbowmen along the walls opposite the river bank.

The townsfolk must know we do not make idle threats.

De Audley is fluent in their language, over inflated popinjay that he is, he speaks the French of my grandfather's court and has the manners to go with it. If he does not succeed then nothing is lost to us, I shall just release my dogs of war on the city and leave nothing but rubble and cinders.

The Burghers are intransigent, de Audley informs me that they have settled the towns defences around the wealthy new town, leaving the castle to stand behind its old stone defences.

They have been very courteous in their refusal to surrender their wealth to us 'fils de chiens Anglais' and in particular to a 'Fils d'un batard Anglais' and they have asked me to tell you that they would rather 'faire bouillir leurs tripes dans l'heuile' than give you a single sou!.

The French have a strange sense of humour.
I send de Audley back with fresh terms, I do not want to destroy this beautiful city. I tell him to bring the chief burgher to me to negotiate in person. If I see Sir Hugh returning empty handed then I shall unleash my archers.

Nightfall
26th July 1346

The French did not surrender.

Having been stood at ready all day, my headstrong soldiers have pre-empted my orders to attack.

On seeing de Audley and the open gates of the city, they have charged before my command.

Archers and pike men together fighting waist deep in the river. The townsfolk managed to close the great gates leaving Sir Hugh stranded on the bridge outside. Lucky not to be impaled he has leaped into the water below in all his finery and then dragged from the water by the French who now have him imprisoned.

Raoul de Eu the Constable of France has put up a fine defence, my troops are peppered with crossbow fire from their garrison.

Warwick and Oxford are hesitant, but the men will not stand and be shot at, nothing will stop them in their intent. They smell gold.

They have breached the old walls and have defeated the garrison which was defending the new town.
The city is ours, there is much wealth for my father's treasury and booty for the men.

The reprisals are sweeping, in proportion to the resistance offered. The man have sacked this city, they are still looting the warehouses and merchants homes of the new quarter.

The butcher's bill is light on our part, more than a hundred injured, twenty dead.

The French dead number over two thousand including several hundred townsfolk who would not leave. The dogs have slipped their leash, they will come to heel only when they are ready.

27th July 1346

My knights report that many of the enlisted men have indulged themselves in drunkenness and there have been many women raped within the city walls. My most chivalrous knights have rescued many and taken them out of the city to safety. We are not barbarians. They have searched for de Audley; he has escaped his captors but cannot be found. One Llantrisant archer, Iolo Bowen, reports seeing him making for the woods beyond the town in the same direction as the escaping women.

My knights have captured Raoul of Eu. He will remain a prisoner but be given the courtesy due to a person of his rank. Even if he is French. He will be a great loss to the French in his role as quartermaster general of their army.

Sir Kenneth and the other masters of arms must discipline their men. The reckless manner in which this town has been seized will lead to our downfall.

I will have discipline in this army.

28th July 1346

Today I send four wagons of gold, silver, and precious metals together with bolts of cloth and other goods of value to the coast. Our ships have been shadowing our progress and once loaded will take this treasure to England.

We March for the River Seine to find a crossing point.

Where are the French hiding, we have seen no great French Army. But it is here, somewhere, the French will not go easy, maybe they are just biding their time.

My orders to Warwick and Oxford remain the same. Sack and burn the towns, take what we need, drive the people into the countryside, destroy their way of life and their economy.

De Audley has returned, dishevelled, and bloodstained he says that after he had fought his guards for his escape he spent the night hiding out in the woodland and then found his way back to our camp on foot. He is most concerned that his horse is missing. She is a fine horse indeed but more suited to the shafts, she ran back to the horse lines alone and is happily pulling one of my wagons towards the coast. Maybe this will steady her flighty nature.

He is shifty and evasive and bears marks on his neck caused more from a woman's claws than from any fight to gain freedom from his captors.

But he is a man of honour and a Peer of the Realm if totally incompetent and a reprehensible character. I must reserve judgement.

CHAPTER 56 – A SKIRMISH AT ABBEVILLE

Crossing the Somme – Prince Edward

21st August 1346

I knew we would meet them eventually; the French would not continue to hide like curs in their forests and woodland.

They have drawn their line of blockade at the great river called the Somme. It is indeed a sleepy river, great and wide and seemingly calm in places. Where it is calm it is too deep to cross, and where the water is not still she flows too fast for us to wade.

My men are hungry, food is running out, we have marched the length of these riverbanks in both directions, mirrored by the French on the other side, taunting us. They have food a plenty on their side where we have only burned fields and starvation.

For days we have made no ground but to go sideways along this infernal river.

Some of the men talk of desertion, I hear it around the camp fires at night. When they have enough wood for a fire, discontent grows like bindweed around my army, silently choking it into submission.

My advisors have no ideas other than to wait, my Lord Oxford has suggested firing his bombasts at them, but the river is so wide. they will not have the range to hit the other side. The banks on our side are thick with trees and scrub, we are plagued by biting insects. My instinct is to send some men to scout the river further to the west, closer to the sea.

22nd August 1346

Last night I ordered Owain to send a party of his men to scout the riverbank unseen, to follow the river towards the sea. To find a crossing point for this army, while we stay here and occupy the French.

23rd August 1346

Owain reported that two of his men have found a crossing point, there is a ford across the river just before it widens to its estuary. There is a small town there, but it does not seem well defended.

I have given the order to strike camp, but quietly and we move at night.

We will leave signs of a camp in the cover of the trees to distract our foe and give us some distance. Then we will move.

Taliesin and Gilbert will lead us for it is they who have found the route.

The march will be long, some twenty miles, I plan to halt for that day striking distance from the river and we will cross under cover of darkness.

24th August 1346

We have crossed the Somme.

We are camped and will take some rest after a heavy skirmish. There is celebration of a victory in the camp and the men deserve some respite.

My archers have commended themselves again. If not for them the result would have been so different. The scouts went ahead and reported a fair force of French soldiers themselves camped on the opposite bank.

The French were not so stupid as to leave this place totally defenceless.

But darkness brings with it the element of surprise, and with my bowmen firing from the midst of the river we have routed the French. They have sustained many dead and wounded and have turned tail and fled back towards their main column back along the river towards Amiens.

We will rest here and take stock.

Crecy seems a fine town, there is a great church here, maybe father and I should say a prayer of thanks to our lord for our victory.

CHAPTER 57 - THE GHOSTS OF THE FUTURE - RED

Our route has taken us northwards, though we have been following this great river's course now for several days.

Sleep has become a stranger to me, not even the refuge of invisibility can silence the sadness held in this soil.

When I close my eyes I see them, not the mail and leather clad soldiers I march with, armed with bow and arrows or sword and shield, but men dressed in grey or khaki, strange uniforms lying trampled in the mud, the cries of wounded men, some already in tunnels below the ground. Ground churned into endless mud and strung with mile upon mile of razor-sharp wire.

This other ghostly conflict I sense is more terrible than the one my earthly feet walks amongst.

They fight with weapons which kill without being seen, they fight from fortified holes in the ground, all manner of deadly devices have been invented for their destruction. Bodies lie tangled in this infernal scene, more bodies than I have seen in any of our battles so far, men running to meet certain death. And in the middle of it all, a horse lies injured, Amongst the carnage and butchery two men once intent on killing each other crawl amongst the blood and the bodies to free the trusting animal from his bonds of steel. They share their tools to cut him free, one holding the proud equine head to the floor, quieting the animal while the other works.

Freed from his bonds and his harness the animal bolts towards his destiny, a regimental pendant still plaited into his mud smeared mane. The gunfire has ceased, no order was given. For humanity is not quite dead, just suspended. Run I urge him, do not get caught again.

Are these ghosts of the future, more ghosts I must see but cannot aid.

Where is sleep when I need her most,

I feel the blankets lift and Owain slides invisibly into my world, his strong arms fold around me, holding me against him, warming my body from behind, his lips nuzzle my ear and my neck, and my senses start to stir in response.

I turn over in his arms and return his kisses, pulling open the soft leather of his jerkin my teeth nipping at the golden faerie skin beneath, smooth, and hairless and enchanting to my touch. If not sleep, then at least there will be release, maybe both, if we are lucky. I hope this cloak also renders us unheard as well as unseen in the darkness. I cling to the reassurance of his warm solid body until the dawn calls him once more to the side of his Prince and the duties of the present.

One more hour and then it will be time to break camp again and search for a place to cross the great river Somme. If it is like our crossing of the Seine then the French will have burned all the bridges well in advance.

CHAPTER 58 - MURDER ON THE MARCH - RED

24th August 1346

Morwenna Bowen was one of the laundry girls, her mother Gwenllian was in charge of the laundresses, her father Iolo was an archer in Gwyn's section, Morwenna was cheeky, she was pretty, devoid of any of the social graces, she could curse like an arrow boy, and fight like one.

Outside of times of war, Iolo was a carpenter at the castle, he made furniture for his Lordship's rooms and also the rough stools and benches which furnished the houses of the poor. He also fletched a superb arrow. Iolo was a vassal to the de Audley family, as his father had been before him. His talents should have raised him out of penury and poverty, but Sir Hugh kept a feudal hand on Iolo's neck, and his nose permanently in the dirt.

Gwenllian had married him some twelve years ago, also bound to the family by feudal ties, she ran a laundry just outside the castle walls, she was a large boned tough woman, her skin reddened by steam, her arms and bosom strong from wielding the tools of her work. She was endlessly good tempered, always with a friendly remark, generous to a fault with the little she had, and also generous with Iolo's talents. If you needed a seat to sit on - don't worry, Iolo will sort you one out! Come back in a few days, I'm sure he'll have one for you.

Morwenna was their only daughter, now twelve years old, she helped her mother in the laundry, sorting through the dirty clothes and then folding the clean and taking it back to the owner. Most of the soldiers had only one set of clothing, maybe a change of shirt or underclothes at best. The laundry was mainly for the benefit of the knights and the squires and their lordships.

It had been two days before they eventually met the French at Crecy. 'Wenna, as she was known had spent all day helping her mother, Marged and I had chatted with her and her mother while we patched up the seemingly endless queue of minor injuries which arrived at our wagon. Burns were salved, blisters dressed, a dislocated finger re-located, a blackened toenail removed, and a broken wrist set.

As dusk fell and the men at arms who had been out scouting the location of the French returned to camp, they reported that food would be scarce as all the standing crops had been burned in the fields, barns of hay and grain had been destroyed. We would be relying on our foragers.

'Wenna had picked up a bundle of clean garments to return to Sir Kenneth and Sir Hugh, her mother told her to return them, then look for her father, Iolo, he should be with one of the hunting parties. She slung the bundle over her shoulder and had disappeared towards the pavilion tents where their lordships were billeted.

Iolo returned from the hunt along with Gwyn and Owain, no boar or venison tonight, only rabbit and squirrel. Marged was collecting skins to line a cloak, she dearly wanted one like mine, she didn't know it's powers and I was not going to tell her, to her it was just the epitome of warmth, she had already stitched the outer cloak from an old drapery Lady Margaret no longer wanted. Deep blood red velvet, heavy and already warm, lined with skins it would be glorious. Had Iolo seen Wenna on his travels?

No, he had not, 'where the bloody hell was the girl' it was late and they were pitched next to the battalion of convicts, who knew what manner of rogue was working his freedom and sleeping by the next fire!

Iolo resolved to give his daughter an hour before he started a round of the various camp fires to look for her. Iolo searched, he with Gwyn and Owain searched at every fire side, they asked all the section leaders had they seen her, they searched the tents of the convicted men, but they could not find 'Wenna.

Beside himself with worry Iolo sat all night by the dying embers of the fire, waiting for enough light to dawn so that he could continue the search for her. He found her body near the river bank, in a small clearing of brambles, no wild animal had killed her, well at least not a boar or a big cat nor even a wolf for there were wolves in the French forests, he heard them at night calling to each other. Some other beasts had robbed his daughter of her life.

She lay on her back on a grassy bank, her throat had been cut, blood congealed in the earth beneath her neck, her clothing was ripped from neck to waist showing her young full breasts, bruised, and bitten by some vile thing. Her legs were spread wide and her thighs bloody and bruised where she had struggled. 'Wenna his child had been raped and murdered.'

Iolo's anguished cries alerted the camp, the Master at Arms, Sir Kenneth, was called, and the Constable in charge of disciplining the men. The only clue to the identity of the beast amongst them a tiny scrap of cloth trapped between her teeth, and a strand of yellow hair wrapped around her fingers, pulled from her attacker's head as she had fought for her life. 'Wenna's body was carried back to the camp on a hurdle and she was brought to our wagon, mine and Margeds for us to wash her and prepare her for burial.

John Smythe the Constable at Arms dourly examined the body. He had come to see her along with Sir Kenneth Fitzsimon the Master at Arms for the de Audley's. They drew the canvas closed at the rear of the wagon and I could hear them talking in hushed tones, muttering under their breath.

'He crosses a line' Sir Kenneth's deep voice addressed the Sergeant.

'It would be a brave man to accuse him outright sir'.

336

'We fight a war John, we need the loyalty of every man, the troops will get restless, her father deserves answers'.

'But we have no answers, no proof, Sir, until then we must wait'.

I pulled back the tent flap, entering the tent with purpose, I faced John Smyth and addressed him directly.

'No proof, then what is this? At least grounds to ask questions! '

I placed before him the clump of yellow, blonde hair, and a scrap of red and yellow fine silk cloth which I had removed from the body. 'And' I added there was blood under her finger nails, she fought and fought hard. Whoever did this stuffed the cloth in her mouth to silence her screams, and she fought them tooth and nail, you owe her justice Sirs, whoever this beast is, he will bear the marks of her nails, and he will strike again'

Sir Kenneth held my eyes with his own deep brown ones, the expression in them bid me be silent.

John Smythe spoke 'madam would you tell me my job, there is no more I can do, would you have me hold a trial in the midst of a war. This matter must keep until later, until then you will say nothing, nothing, you hear me?'

He strode from the tent, Sir Kenneth in his wake. That very day we arrived at the small town of Crecy and made camp on the rise overlooking the river.

For once we had found the French land bountiful, their army had not burned out the farms, driven off the livestock or poisoned the water sources. Our foragers found food in plenty, the forest across the river from the town was rich in game, soon the camp was alive with the smell of meat cooking, beer and wine flowed in abundance, darkness fell on 25th August 1346 to the sounds of Welsh voices raised in song with their comrades in arms, and around our fire Iolo and his wife joined us to mourn their daughter, Iolo was not a man to forget or to forgive, he had not recognised the pattern of the cloth, his grief had been too much for him to focus, but his wife had, she knew it well, it was a pattern she had laundered too often.

There is a small church yard just outside Crecy where a murdered Welsh girl is buried, her grave marked with a simple stone bearing the hastily carved name Morwenna and under it the word Cariad.

We buried her at dawn, Iolo had fashioned a coffin from wood salvaged from the crates containing arrows in the baggage train.

Sir Kenneth had read prayers and Owain and Gwyn had dug the grave.

In the distance we could hear the French setting their lines for battle, there had been small skirmishes along our route through France so far, but now we could hear the might of the French in the distance.

CHAPTER 59 - RECONNAISSANCE – TALIESIN BOWEN

In the early hours 25th August 1346

Owain called us early from our beds, it was well before dawn. In fact, it was the middle of the night.

'Tally, Gilbert, dress quickly, and come with me'.

I pulled on my breeches and shirt and my jerkin over the top, smoothed down my hair and wiped the sleep from my eyes. Gilbert and I followed Owain through the camp to the tent where the commanders were deep in conversation.

There was Earl Northampton the Constable of the whole army and Warwick his deputy, and there too was Prince Edward.

'Are these you two fastest, and most stealthy? For I need runners to go quietly, they must be unseen.
The Prince spoke to Owain.

They are milord, replied Owain. Both can walk in the dead leaves of autumn and a grazing deer will not hear or see them.

'Lads' commanded the Prince 'these are your orders 'you must go into the woods to the east, go now, my spies say that the French are encamped on the other side, they are many in number, but in disarray as their Constable the Count de Eu was taken at Caen and is still a prisoner.

There has been much movement in the woods overnight, go, see how they have deployed, I need to know their strength.'

The forest to the south east of our camp was thick and green and grew on wet ground alongside a river, there was mud underfoot, the ground was soft and would churn up under horses' hooves.

Gil and I took handfuls and rubbed it on our skin, to hide our white faces amongst the dapple of the trees in the moonlight.

We followed the tree line along and saw that the road which ran along the wide river valley following its course was blocked with the French, many of them. Their baggage train stretched back for miles, there must be a hundred wagons.

And men, thousands of men, but not organised as we were, they were stretched in a line along the road with the baggage and supplies, no one had made shift of a proper camp, the horses were loosely corralled or hobbled and tied to trees, men slept under the wagons where they could.

We found a small crossing point and crossed the river, Gil can speak good French, he had a courtlier education than the rest of us, perks of being his

340

Lordship's bastard! If we are challenged, then he will speak for us.

I know that the French have crossbow men. I have heard the older archers who have fought before describing them, in their war stories around our fires at night.

They are not French but Italian, from Genoa, and fine marksmen, but slower in volley fire than us. Their weapon is heavy and cumbersome. They fire from behind a shield held by others to give them protection while they load, much in the fashion of the Roman legions. They wear little in the way of mail or armour, or even the padded leather with which we are equipped, the old soldiers say that they are not brave men, if they have no protection then they will run. They prefer a good strong castle wall to an open field.

Undercover of the darkness we lifted covers of wagons and there in amongst the general baggage of the army was a wagon neatly stacked with large shields, far larger than any knight could carry, too heavy for a foot soldier.

I hooted like an owl to Gil and called him over, we had passed a small barrel of gunpowder, I thought I had smelled the slight stink of rotten eggs which came from the barrel.

'Fire, Gil, we must burn the shields.

Finding the barrel, I prized off the lid, I nearly vomited at the smell, damn it all, it is pickled eggs! Silently we collected what we needed, to set a fire, kindling, plenty of dry stuff and a pitch torch, that would do. It would burn slow, and no bang at the end, but the damage would be done. Gil is good at fires, it's all down to the draught he says!

We left the smouldering pile inside the wagon, comfortably drawing a draught through the stacked shields. Then we made our way back into the woods.

He came out of nowhere, one random soldier waking for a piss and watchful enough to arm himself with a loaded crossbow.

As I rounded a great oak tree on the edge of the woods, there he was, right hand directing the stream from his cock, the crossbow slung over his shoulder, loaded and ready to fire.

I was so close, he pissed on my foot, and I smelled the garlic on his breath, and saw his unshaven face.

Run Gil, I hissed, and we high tailed it into the woodland.

We both heard the click of the trigger releasing in the darkness and hiss of the arrow through the leaves of the dense woodland, it was a random and unaimed shot.

I heard Gil yelp like a wounded hound, I grabbed him by his arm and dragged him

'My leg! I'm hit in the leg.'

Shouts could be heard as the French were being roused, we heard the cries of the sentries, caught napping waking the guard. All their focus on the path we had taken into the forest. Good I thought they have not checked their wagons.

Back along the riverbank, up through the woods, I dragged and carried Gilbert, I could feel the short crossbow arrow in the back of his thigh, he dragged his left leg behind him, and the blood oozed out from the wound running over my hand as we fled.

Noises in the bracken, in front of us. How so, our pursuers cannot have made that much ground on us.

Hide! I pulled Gil into a natural hide beneath the brambles, where they arched over each other, amongst the thick thorny stems. 'Lie still friend while I check'.

I crawled on my belly, careful not to disturb the brush beneath me, moving slowly closer to the panting sounds of heavy breathing in a nearby clearing, then I saw him.

Sir Hugh de Audley, there was no mistaking him, his blonde hair thinning and the shiny skin of his head with its balding pate glinting in the moon light. There was a knife in his hand and a body at his feet, he was covered in blood, blood soaked him and dripped from his hands, and from his face. His clothing was.... He wore no clothing he was naked.

At his feet was the body of a girl, I recognised her instantly even from this distance, I had kissed those breasts and that giving mouth many times since we left England. Morwenna. She could not be alive.

I returned to Gil, my mind on the living, we waited in silence. I bound his leg as Marged and Red had showed us, to stop the bleeding, we waited until daybreak and then limped into the camp to give our report.

My mind was racing with what I had seen, who could I tell, Gwyn perhaps, or Owain? To confront the man would mean certain death. Yet there he was large as life discoursing with the great earls and applauding the good work 'his men' had done! Taking praise for himself, and still with her blood under his well-manicured fingernails!

In the French camp a wagon slowly burst into flames, slow burning embers kindled to life and licked up the sides of the canvas cover, drawn by the draft from underneath they grew bigger and more powerful.
I smiled to myself, 'no shields for them then.' For an instant I was back on our farm in North Wales, with my parents, my mam made sure we all knew how to set a good fire!

I had left Gilbert at the healer's wagon in the capable hands of Marged and Red.

I would not tell him what I had seen, he would not believe me anyway, he so wanted to be recognised by his father.

As I washed the mud from my face and went to find my breakfast, I heard Gwyn's deep voice 'Bite on this Gil and hold tight this is going to hurt'

CHAPTER 60 - CHECK THE RECORDS -OWAIN

Owain's duties in his form as one of the Princes' squires took him far closer to the nobility than I or any of the others could get.

The Nobles had their tents set up slightly away from the main camp, the King, and his whole entourage. had joined us on the road to Portsmouth.

Whilst the Prince had deployed him with Gwyn and the archers because he wore the colours of the King he could move freely around their little enclave. He carried messages to and from the Prince.

John Smythe the Constable at Arms, in charge of discipline amongst the soldiers, was also in charge of the campaign records. While Sir Kenneth had his endless lists of equipment and stores, and the lists of the men themselves, John Smythe kept a daily record, a diary of notable events in camp.

The first few pages contained the lists of men and their numbers.

A large leather-bound volume, it sat on a campaign trunk in his pergola tent, every evening before he retired to bed he wrote in it, his tidy hand scribing the entries legibly and carefully, each one dated at the top and bearing the date and the location where the army was encamped and also where the event of what had happened.

For the most it contained records of minor disputes amongst the men at arms and the archers' fights which had resulted in injury to a man or loss or damage to equipment.

The physical injuries often included any treatment either I or Marged had given.

The Constable had taken office when the whole of the army had assembled at Portsmouth, until then our Welsh contingent had been under Sir Kenneth's good auspices.

Owain having business with the Prince and finding the Constable absent from his tent opened the cover.

We had taken ship on 12th July

The Kings Head Inn Portsmouth
11th July 1346
Evening time
Man at arms – Harry Brace – injured – broken hand
Harry Brace man of the Duke of Gloucester's company involved in riotous behaviour at the Inn, he having drunk more than his fill of ale and been thrown out of that same Inn has punched a hole through the shutters trying to re-join his companions.
Removed by his Sergeant at arms, damage to be made good on the morrow, hand strapped by the healer.

Harry Brace confined placed on short rations for 2 days. And to repair damage at his own cost.

Signed John Smythe.

Owain turned the pages, the constable was thorough in his note keeping, even adding small drawings where appropriate.

He noted incidences of sickness, drunkenness, riotous behaviour, theft and damage, and death.

All documented along with any fine or punishment given.

There it was, on the last page,

Crecy en Ponthieu, Picardy, France
25th August 1346

Before sun down.
Morwenna Bowen laundry maid, fourteen years of age. Daughter of Iolo Bowen, longbowman of Sir Hugh de Audley's men, and part of Gwyn ap Meredith's section. Her mother being Gwenllian Bowen our head laundress. All from near the town of Llantrisant.
Found dead by her father on the river bank, having left camp after delivering laundry to his Lordship sir Hugh de Audley.
Death due to having been attacked by wolves. I have seem the body for myself and have never seen such wounds before to her throat, limbs, and body. An awful

misadventure. Let this be a warning to all not to stray alone at night from the confines of the camp.

Body washed by the healers Sibyl Meredith and Marged Owen.

Buried by her family in the graveyard of the Church of St Severin. Crecy en Ponthieu.

May she rest in peace

Signed John Smythe.

There would be no promised enquiry into her death, here it was writ in ink and quill. On parchment for the official record.

Owain was incensed, his eyes flashed with the red of his inner soul. We had come to prevent a tragedy, and to protect the ancient blood lines that connected the Faerie kingdom and the people of Wales.

Tomorrow there would be a battle, the French were close by, he could smell their camp fires, his sharp hearing could hear their tongue.

This chapter must stay shut for now, but for how long could he keep the cover closed.

Who else knew its contents, certainly Iolo did not. And Sir Kenneth, trusted by all, loved by his men, would he see them betrayed in this way.

The surrounding tents were resplendent in the colours of the trusted Nobles, and in the greatest of them the highborn lords of England and the King himself Edward 3rd dined with his son Woodstock and the great

English Barons the trusted nobles, At the foot of the table were the lesser nobles including de Audley. Picking up the scraps from their Sovereign's table.

Owain drew back the flap to the great tent, bowed low towards the top table and waited to be summoned. The Prince would be sending his orders for the morning.

PART SEVEN

CHAPTER 61 - A BATTLE IS PLANNED

24th August 1346: two days before Crecy

Sir Kenneth Fitzsimon pulled back the tent flap to see Prince Edward poring over the maps and reports laid out on the table in front of him

A tray with several gilded drinking vessels stood on a tray at the end of the table with a decanter of wine.

'Come', the Prince waved a beckoning hand without raising his head, he was dressed in his usual black leather breeches and boots but only wore a linen shirt, his surcoat was laid over the back of the large chair which was positioned behind him.

'What news do you bring Sir Kenneth?'

'Sire, there has been talk of the death of the laundry maid, many do not accept it was a misadventure.'

'What is it that is said, Sir Kenneth?'

'There is talk now, amongst the archers of de Audley, it is not the first time he has been spoken of in this way. And the healer, the one they call Red, she was treating one of the men who says that they saw the girl Morwenna molested last night, by Sir Hugh.'

'We are on the eve of battle Sir Kenneth, I cannot deal with this now, there are plans to be made, the French are on the other side of the hill, in great numbers. Tomorrow there will be more deaths than a laundry maid if we are not wise in our tactics. Find Owain, tell him what you know, have him calm the waters. Say nothing to Sir Hugh. Go quickly and return for I will need your council – I expect Northampton and Warwick directly.'

Sir Kenneth strode from the tent, it was Owain who had told him what the two squires had seen. It would not be an easy task to quiet the rumble of discontent amongst the bowmen.

He walked quietly through the camp seeking out Owain and talking to the men.

All through the camp men sat sharpening blades, blades of all kinds, swords, knives, axes, pikes, and with each swipe of a whetstone some shook their heads in disgust and cursed de Audley. They did it quietly, curses in their Welsh language about 'bastard Saesneg' fell hurriedly silent as he passed.

Dusk was falling he found the small camp where Marged and Gwyn were openly arguing.

Sir Kenneth knew Marged to be a feisty and outspoken woman, but Gwyn was not easily riled, he had never heard the man shout and particularly not at his wife.

Sir Kenneth stood out of sight not seeking to intrude on the quarrel, all the men were on edge, there would be a battle tomorrow.

Marged was angry,

'Damn him, is there nothing that stops him, another poor soul this time dead at his hands, and I'll lay a pound to a pinch of sugar that Sian did not throw herself from that wall. Yet they do nothing, is he untouchable? Is there no justice, the man should hang, by his balls if I had my way'.

'Quiet woman, hush, you cannot be heard talking this way, Owain has told Sir Kenneth what was seen, we must let the Lords deal with it themselves, it is their place to see the law kept. I fire the arrows, and you stitch the wounds, that is the order of things, now rest, Tomorrow we will all have more than enough to do'.

Is your memory so short Gwyn, mine is not, I can neither forgive nor forget his hands on me! You stood and watched him paw me, and you, my husband, you did nothing!

The words spat from her lips as her hand snapped out and struck Gwyn on the face, the slap rang out.

Marged's wrist was seized in a vicelike grip, fingers that pulled a bowstring wrapped around her slim bones and she found herself with both her arms pinioned above her head and her husband's face close to hers, his eyes blazing with anger and frustration. Her back against the trunk of the oak tree from which they had hung their tent.

353

'Enough, I have had enough of this, what must I do, what would you have me do, should I have killed the man there and then, would you see me hanged, or should I do it now, and save being killed tomorrow, tell me Marged before I feel the need to silence you for good'?

Tears welled in her blue eyes and ran down her face, rage turned to racking sobs as she buried her head in his broad chest.

'Marged, Marged,' his arms wrapped around her, 'I love you, it will all come right, have faith, his sins will find him.

He tipped her chin upwards and kissed her, softly at first, she answered him in kind, nipping his lips with her teeth, her hand now firmly on the tight cheeks of his arse, she pulled him to her.

'Dieu Marged, I need you'.

Sir Kenneth turned and walked away, as Gwyn lowered his wife to the soft mossy ground beneath the oak tree and lifting her skirts buried himself as far as he could inside her giving body. He was still within earshot when he heard the cries of their lovemaking,

In the Prince's marquee their Lordships were gathered.

Sir Kenneth joined them, helping himself to the proffered goblet of good red wine, one of the benefits of a French campaign he thought, savouring the smooth powerful aromatic taste as it swirled over his tongue.

'The pits have been dug then and the Caltrops placed?'

354

'Yes Sire, there is a hot reception waiting the French cavalry'

'What news from the men you sent through the wood?'

They report great numbers of French, more in total than us, but not organised, their equipment is some distance from their camp, they sorely miss our captive their constable, the count of Eu. He would not countenance such folly. They are stopped in a line along the river, there is no formal camp, they sleep wherever they can find space.

They have a large contingent of crossbow men, from Genoa but thanks to young Tally and his friend Gilbert they have no shields to fire from. We must target their position well for they will turn tail if pressed hard.

'How no shields sire?' Asked Sir Kenneth.

The Prince raised a blonde eyebrow and laughed, 'it seems your men are adept at raising a fire, one wagon of shields and gambeson burned to its axle trees, did you not hear the commotion from across the river?'

All four men chuckled loudly, Northampton and Oxford greatly amused by the thought,
Sir Kenneth raised a smile, well done lads he thought,
But maybe the consternation of the French had covered the sound of poor Morwenna Bowen screaming!

It was a matter which would need addressing, but not here and not now, he hid the look of disgust on his face as Sir Hugh de Audley entered the tent.

Sir Hugh was looking remarkably fresh and laundered, He bowed to the Prince 'your pardon sire, I took the opportunity of a hot tub, as there was one available, our laundresses are remarkably obliging in that way'.

The Prince grunted his displeasure and commanded the man to 'sit, there is much to put into plan'.

'My Lord Northampton what do you propose?' Northampton bent over the table and started to indicate positions on a roughly drawn-out map.

We have dug our pits and Caltrops here; he indicated a line running between the small town of Wadicourt and Crecy en Ponthieu at the bottom of a south facing slope. Firstly, we will coral all the baggage and equipment at the top of the bank, we leave the horses saddled or harnessed in case they are needed, and we place a guard on the coral in case of French attack from the rear. Their army may have become split and chose to attack in two parts. I will position my division of men at the centre of the slope along with those of my Lords Warwick and Oxford. Your men will deploy alongside us forming a V at the centre of the slope, we shall deploy our archers to the front, and flanks thus protecting our men at arms and pikemen. Their flank will be protected from cavalry by the Caltrops. We will reinforce this by use of your bombasts my Lord Warwick.

Your Father's division, Sire will be formed up in the same manner across the top of the bank, his archers will have a firing range down the bank, as the French advance they will fall under their range to great effect. They will reinforce the line as the battle progresses.

'Our men are rested, but we shall deploy early in the morning.'

'Are your men prepared my lords?'

'Sir Kenneth, brief your archers, and make sure they are well supplied with arrows. We will need them firing at their maximum rate.'

'And Sir Kenneth, your excellent healing women, they will set up their tent in the coral area, out of range of the battle, they must expect to be busy, I don't expect the French to fall easily.'

'De Audley, I will leave you in charge of the baggage train, and the coral area, see to it nothing gets stolen by the French, you will have a dozen men at arms to post, and you will defend the casualty post if necessary.'

'Go to it my lords'.

Northampton refilled everyone's glasses and raised his own in a toast.

'My God grant us victory.'

CHAPTER 62 – CLOAKED IN PASSION - SIBYL

24th August 1346 – night time

Last night I dreamed, as I lay on my slightly damp, makeshift bed, wrapped as I was in my cloak, and invisible to all, was it the cloak which had filled my mind with images and sounds, or flashbacks to the awful events of our progress through the beauty of the French countryside.

For my dream was filled with screaming, the terrible heart-rending pleas for mercy, the screaming of women the crackling of fires, the mocking and taunting of an audience. I could even smell the dense smoke from the tar barrel and burning flesh.

The pyre stood centre stage on the castle green, piled high with kindling, slightly dampened by the Welsh weather. A crowd of hundreds had gathered around it waiting for the grand entrance of its victim.

I stirred in my sleep, pulling the warm cloak tighter around my shoulders, pulling my knees up into its folds, tucking my feet into the fur of the lining, anything for a scrap warmth.

Then I realised that the screams were my own. I woke suddenly to the feel of Owain, it was just before dawn, nearly time for the camp to stir and prepare to march for another day, the foot soldiers and men at arms had already left, Marged who slept like the very dead lay curled in Gwyn's arms on the other side of the canvas wall which hung down the centre of our tent.

Only Owain could have heard my dreaming, the sounds of the invisible would not be heard by those sleeping in the mortal world.

He slid under the cloak beside me, wrapping me in the strong arms of a bowman, holding me against the unfastened leather of his jerkin, his lips grazed my neck as he whispered to me in his own language, one I had not heard since we were children, calming me as he used to calm the terrified colts and fillies he and Tommy Pryce bought at the horse fair.

But there was no Owain y Mynydd, the lad I had fallen in love with was a device, his whole family was a fiction woven by Eryr to watch me as I grew up, I squirmed against him, fighting to get free, he whispered some more, this time running large strong hands down my body and turning me to face him, pulling me further into his warmth, I felt my body relax into him, and felt my dreams change.

We were riding across a mountain top, towards a great sea which shimmered in the distance, bareback, unbridled, I felt the muscles of my mount flex and stretch between my thighs as canter turned to gallop, my horses mane, dark and wild in the wind, the smell of his sweat as exertion broke through the surface of the dream, and then the screech of the gulls, floating above eternal waves, and plunging swiftly into darkness.

When I surfaced, we were still locked in each other's arms, his breath was warm on my neck, his long legs entangled with mine and his hands rested like fairies wings one comforting on the small of my back, the other very lewdly on the left cheek of my arse.

I squirmed, slightly more lewdly against him, feeling the last tremor of this dreamscape abate within me. 'Owain y Mynydd you bastard' the words firmed in my brain but did not form on my lips. This had been a long time coming, I could not regret it, my body betrayed me as my hips pushed against him in question and not only the dawn rose to meet me.

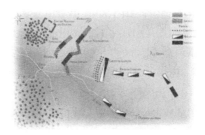

CHAPTER 63- TOUJOURS EN RETARD -- GWYN AP MEREDITH

Bloody French, they are always late:

We have been in position since dawn. Waiting
They are probably having a nice hot meal and a bottle of good wine before a fight.

The King himself is here, he and Prince Edward have gone to the church in Crecy to say mass and to pray for a victory.

I should rather trust my arm, and my bow.

The ground is damp beneath us, we have a good position on a grassy bank, facing south, the sky shows those clouds which indicate showers, and that is what we have had.

I have ordered the men to unstring their bows. The strings will stretch in the wet, reducing their power.
I heard the message pass along the lines, and I see the men act on it, bowstrings kept nice and dry in their waist pouches.

One by one I hear Tally and the others give the same order. All we can do now is sit and wait, below us on the bank I see the awful pits full of lethal spikes waiting for the French cavalry.

Behind us, the King himself has his section of the army, held in readiness for the last charge and to fill the line with reinforcements if they are needed.

The men are restless, all are concealed in the grass of the field, occasionally a head rises like a hare above the surface of the long green blades, peering around, ears and nostrils twitching, scenting the air for impending danger. Men stand to relieve themselves, not bothering to conceal their actions, but hurried lest the French be concealed nearby.

But no French arrows come.

I have eaten the two apples, the lump of cheese and the bread which Marged insisted I take with me. Wrapped in a separate cloth and slipped into my waist pouch with my spare bow strings. Now I am glad of her insistence for my belly is grumbling loudly with hunger and nerves.

Ah Marged – I lean back in the grass, arms behind my head, my bow lying beside me within arm's length, staring up at a French blue sky which is troubled only by the white rabbits tails of the clouds which will give us rain on and off all day.

I close my eyes and remember the warmth of her body, her touch on my own, her mouth on mine, her white teeth on my chest, her anger at me and finally her total surrender and forgiveness, I love Marged, she cannot be angry with me for long. I breathe out a long-contented sigh and picture her again.

'Meredith the Prince has orders'.

I hear the piping voice of Elgan Evans the Prince's messenger in my ear and am jerked sharply out of my reverie.

'I am to go with the lad who burned the shields, Tally is he called, he is to show me where to hide, I am to run back to the Prince when I see the French army move.'

'We cannot send Tally, he commands a whole section, we cannot spare him if all starts before you return he is needed'. See that man there – I point to a short stocky youth, dressed in the bottle green and white of a Llantrisant man, that is Delme, fetch him here. Keep your bloody head down boy!'

'Delme I can spare, every man on a team has his strong points, where Delme has arms which tire easily and cannot keep up volley fire for long, his legs are tireless, I have seen him run the five miles from his home at Miskin to Llantrisant in under half an hour. And he is a fine hunter, he will smell the garlic of the French before he sees them.'

I send him, lightly armed to guide the Prince's messenger into the woods along the river. He will bring news straight to us, as Elgan will take it to the Prince.

The Town of Crecy en Ponthieu has a fine church, l'eglise de Saint Severin, the Prince has heard mass there this very morning, it surely too has a fine bell in its tower, for I have heard it ring the hour many times since we took up position.

By my reckoning from the bell and the position of the sun in the sky it is about three o clock.

The men grow more restless by the minute.

Then there is movement in the grass, Delme falls into the little comfy nest I have made myself.

'They move Gwyn, the French are coming.'
We stay hid heads down in the grass, weapons concealed, shiny pike heads of the foot soldiers laid flat.

Below us on the flat ground in front of the Caltrops I hear the march of feet, orders shouted in a language foreign to me. Where is Owain, he would know what they say.

Iesu Mawr, it's raining again, big drops of a sudden deluge shatter on the floor at my feet, soaking my green and white jerkin through to the padded leather I wear underneath, if it rains much more we will none of us be able to move for the weight we carry.

Then as sudden as it started it stops and the sun is raising steam from the ground.

Suddenly Owain is at my elbow,

The Genoese are to our front. It will not be long now before we get the command.

I pass the order to my men to string their bows, dry strings mind. This rain is a bugger to stretch them. And stay low until the order comes.

And there it came on the stroke of the next bell, I hear the cry 'FUOCO'.

Then the click of the crossbow firing, and the rush of air made by their shorter arrows. The thud as they land, Iesu Grist they are all short of the mark.

With all my lungs I shout the order to stand, we rise as a unit, as I have trained my men to do, and along the lines, all the men of Wales do the same.

The order echoes along the line, 'Archers!, nock, draw, loose!' Each word carefully spaced; each arrow fired in the same moment. The first volley is fired.

I feel the arrows of the rank behind me fly over my head and hear the cries of the men on the receiving end of the first salvo. Our range is good then!

Again, and again, 'Nock, draw, loose' even Delme is keeping with the pace.

Then a command from behind, from Northampton himself.

'Advance!' – we advance a few paces down the bank 'Hold!'

Then again volley fire, a relentless hail of bodkin pointed goose fletched death rains upon the Genoese, they have few of their shields to hide behind thanks to Tally and Gilbert.

Then from Tally's division I hear the men shouting and cheering.

'Gachgi' Gachgi Gachgi they cry 'cowards' their volley fire has stopped, and their bows are raised in triumph. Then I realise through the steam rising from the ground that the Genoese have turned tail, in their haste they have run straight into the path of the charging French heavy cavalry of Count de Alencon. I see his colours flying in the breeze as his horse charges towards the caltrops. The Genoese are fallen. In the confusion, they are being cut down by their own knights. No time for pause now though.

We have not come off unscathed, the Genoese are fine archers and not all their arrows have fallen short. Delme! My runner appears, 'Delme, find the wounded, if they can walk get them back to Marged and Red at the wagon. If they cannot, send Marged or Red to the field to tend them when the firing stops'.

I am thrown to the floor by the crash of the Earl of Warwick's bombast firing at the French cavalry from the flanks.

The bottom of the bank has turned into a quagmire of thrashing and screaming men, horses and equipment, the Caltrops have done their work, poor animals, the butchers will indeed be busy later, but at least there will be meat aplenty. There will be little game in the forest after all this commotion, any sensible animal will have fled, faster than a Genoese archer before a Welshman!

'Advance!'

That is not Northampton's shout, his men at arms are already in the melee, that is the higher pitched voice of the Prince.

Hot headed idiot, too early, he goes far too early, de Alencon is still making progress up the slope.

Bryn his Black Charger crashes past me down the hill, towards the oncoming French, behind him his standard bearer on little Dylan the steady little horse I have brushed so often, carrying the colours. But he has little support, all his men are already fighting in the melee below and the King's men will not move without his father's command, he may pay for this rush of red mist dearly.

He heads straight for the John of Bohemia who alongside de Alencon heads the French charge, the French fly their Oriflamme colour the pointed red banner streaming from a golden lance, no quarter is to be given then. The French intend to take no prisoners. Edward knows the meaning of that flag and he will make us respond in kind.

The French King Philip has been unhorsed; his horse killed underneath him in the battle. A fresh horse is found, and he remounts. No one can accuse the French King of cowardice.

Then the French are upon us, our pikemen are fighting hand to hand, Prince Edward is thrown from his horse and lies helpless on the ground, his black heavy armour stranding him like a beetle. He rolls over onto his front with an effort and to his knees as the French bear down on him.

There is Owain, at his elbow surely it was not Owain with the colours, our work is done, we are out of arrows, I pull my father's sword from its scabbard which hangs down my back, between my shoulders and run down the bank to the aid of my Prince. And the strange man I have come to love as a brother.

Between us Owain and I hold off the blows of John of Bohemia and the Count de Alencon and drag Edward to his feet unhurt.

Steel clashes around us, we stand back-to-back with the Prince the three of us fighting for our lives, where is the help of the good English knights, they have left us to fend for ourselves, Blind John of Bohemia falls first. Just as we fear all is lost, the King's men step into the melee the French are fought back, many of their nobles have fallen, their chivalrous hearts preferring death in battle to fleeing and captivity.

Prince Edward of Wales has truly won his spurs today.

We are victorious! Owain leans on my shoulder the colours clutched in his left hand his sword dangling from his right and hanging just below my armpit. I am leaning on the hilt of the Scottish broadsword which has done good service today, a sword should know its master and I feel that this one has indeed guided my hand, I am not a skilful swordsman, but I have acquitted myself as such today. Prince Edward stands with us, helmet and armour dented and in disarray, we are surrounded by the dead and dying.

There is an eerie silence after a battle is over, the groans of men and the pitiful whinnies of injured horses, the occasional cry for mercy or help as a coup de grass is given or an unconscious man comes to and realises that he is not yet with his maker.

I see Red making her way amongst our fallen, Delme is with her, he and young Evan acting as her stretcher bearers, she and Marged will be busy with this evening.

The Prince breaks the silence 'Dieu merci, 'he uses courtly French, 'We are indeed victorious.'

Owain replies in kind 'Dieu ave Peutet a void avec ca.'

The Prince raises a blond eyebrow and a half smile,

Owain translates for me 'God had little to do with it, really Gwyn if you are to be at Court you must learn a little French'.

'a chi ychydig o ostyngeiddrwydd' I reply in my own tongue.

The Prince looks to Owain confused, not understanding.
Again Owain translates,' He says I should learn humility, sire.'

Putting up his sword into its scabbard, his attention drawn to further up the hill.

'Weapons away now, here comes my father and all his hangers on.

And sure enough here comes the Majesty of King Edward III in all his finery, and riding so close to his rear as to be joined to it is the golden figure of Sir Hugh de Audley, still pristine after his bath, and riding that totally impractical horse.

I see the Prince's eye raise to meet his father's gaze. Owain and I bow as deeply as exhaustion and weaponry will allow.

CHAPTER 64 – A CIRCLE OF WAGONS – RED

There is at least safety in numbers. Marged and I have set up our wagon and tent in a prominent place amongst the baggage carts.

We have employed a large red flannel blanket hung over the front as a flag to mark us out. They will at least know where to bring the wounded, and I fear that there will be a great many.

The laundry ladies have set to in boiling water and have rounded up a supply of blankets and straw mattresses. The girls have been sent out to collect filling for the empty ones, they go in groups of at least four, for the countryside is filled with danger, there are bands of French peasants who have been burnt out of their homes roaming the area, it is not their fault they have been reduced to living on their wits, but they are not the biggest danger the biggest one has charge of our encampment.

Equipment such as we have is boiled free of dirt and germs, needles are threaded with silk or gut, I have even found an old set of his Lordship's small clothes amongst the laundry and unpicked the silk thread from them, it will do nicely for small wounds and is a lovely colour purple as well.

Evan has busied himself in making one of brother Bartram's salves. Brother Bartram he says swears by its healing properties.

He has been grinding ribwort in a mortar with wild marigolds all found in the fields where we have camped over the last few weeks, ground with almond oil which he has acquired from somewhere – I have not enquired where!

This concoction smells heavenly, with a little lavender added, and mixed with beeswax would I am sure make a great cream for a lady's hands. But he does not mix it with beeswax, he has a large tub of foul-smelling grease which he acquired after the battle of Caen. Pilfered from an apothecary's shop there.

The label is worn off or removed, but there is a faded picture of a skull on the lid, and I can just make out the letters G and P in curlicue writing under its grinning face. Graise de Potence – gallows grease! Well Brother Bartram would know all about that ingredient.

The smell of the final product is tempered with lavender oil, but I will not tell the wounded of its origins should they ask. Evan is proving to be a master forager, and an accomplished thief.

De Audley patrols our small enclave like a caged bear, he knows he has been side lined, given the most menial job to do, he is not happy.

371

He has set his tent near the entrance to the stockade which is a barrier comprised of baggage carts. All are still loaded, the horses are all hobbled and tied for good measure, still in their harnesses. for this is a defensive position, Owain has told me that the King is not certain of the strength of the French Army and so has taken precaution not to lose our means of escape.

If the time is not right to fight, then he will move us on to fight another day. Sir Hugh watches everyone in and out, his cold fish eyes mentally undressing every female who passes.

He punctuates his watch with strutting up and down with his tail feathers ruffled, his lordship has watched intently as our women have gone about their duties. I thank God that Iolo Bowen is on the field with Gwyn, or there would be blood spilled for sure.

Marged is on a short fuse, she will not take her eyes from him, not in a pleasant way. Her best blue stare follows his back everywhere he walks. If she could mentally project some form of knife into the hollow between his shoulders then she would for certain.
She is stalking the stalker like a lioness stalking prey.

The passage of the day is marked by the bell in the church tower in the Town nearby. Midday has passed, the men are settled in their positions, we wait.
The wait is punctuated by brief but heavy rain showers, Marged observes in her dry fashion, 'I hope they've packed dry strings along with lunch and clean drawers, I'm sure some will be wearing the brown when the first arrows land'.

The girls return from the fields behind with full sacks of leaves and grass and other stuffing for mattresses. One has gathered a wooden bucket full of sphagnum moss, good girl.

Wrapped in muslin and used as a dressing it will help prevent infection, and it will absorb moisture keeping a wound dry.

Marged and I pounce on it with more glee than is seemly. Little things to alleviate the stress of waiting. Arwen, for that is the girl, will be of use to us, I will promote her from the laundry to the rank of assistant nurse. The cry goes up just after the church bell rings at four. We hunker down around the wagons, listening to the sounds of chaos on the bank below.

The volley order is called by – is that Gwyn's voice, or Owain, or Tally's or all in chorus, I have heard it in practice so often 'Nock, Draw, Loose'.

The arrow boys scurry back and fore they work in a chain, empty quivers filled by two boys no more than ten years old at the wagon in front of us, handed to the arrow boys serving the field, empty quivers left to be filled. They are fast emptying the wagon. Once all their stock is used they will scavenge the battlefield removing the arrows from the dead or from the ground and sort them into quivers for the archers to reuse.

After about twenty minutes a cheer goes up! A Welsh cheer something of importance has happened.

Who is this, a runner from the field, it is Iestyn Evans. 'I have been told to bring in the walking wounded ma'am, behind him I see a trail of bloodstained limping men supporting each other and their injuries using swords and bows as walking sticks and crutches. Leaning on each other for that last bit of courage it will take to reach our wagon. It will take all the courage they have to bear treatment for we have little effective pain relief except alcohol and a very small supply of laudanum, again liberated by Evan from the apothecary shop in Caen. I have a supply of leather strops to fold in half, for biting down on earplugs to defend against any of the soldiers' language which I have not heard before.

'Then when it quiets and is safe one of you to come and help with the other casualties, those who cannot walk and the dying.'

With this Iestyn scurries off back to the fray.

Then our work started in earnest, mainly minor wounds needing stitching. A few of the men have arrows embedded in their arms and legs, all treatable with laudanum and alcohol, a leather strap between the teeth and Marged with her specially made device for removing arrow heads from flesh.

Made by the smith in the forge at Llantrisant it is an ingenious device with serrated jaws which clamp over the broken off shaft and allow the user to pull the offending projectile from its resting place with the minimum of damage. The worst part of the operation is the look of fear when the patient sees what she is about to use.

The worst case we have seen is the unfortunate archer who has been blinded in one eye by a crossbow arrow. Like all the other wounds we have seen today, it does not seem as if the arrow impacted with any great force. While the man has lost the use of his eye, the rest of his face is intact, and the point has not damaged his eye socket. I have removed the eyeball and sewn up the socket, he will have a rather jaunty patch to wear in future but for the present a compress of moss and a smear of Evans' magic Salve will see him right.

All is entered in my record of treatment. His reads:

26th August 1346

Patient: Harold Williams (Old Harry English)
Division: Will Tewkesbury's Division of Archers.
Home town: Hastings
Wound: Arrow to the eye

Arrow and eyeball removed by my own hand, eye socket stitched closed, and salve and compress applied.
Patient highly amused and comforted that he has the same injury as his namesake sustained a previous battle against the French. He will have a tale to tell his grandchildren after all.

Arwen has left camp to look for more moss, I have sent Evan with her, I have not seen de Audley for several hours as it has been that chaotic in the camp. I do not trust that he is not lurking somewhere.
The queue for my services has shrunk to less than a dozen minor wounds, the laundry ladies have done a marvellous job of sorting the casualties into categories of

Very Serious – lots of very red blood and not much noise. Or no blood and no noise.

Serious – Bleeding but still screaming with no obvious bits missing.

Minor wounds – minor bleeding, no bits missing, walking, and talking.

Marged has gone onto the field to assist with the recovery of the seriously wounded with a spare cart and driver.

I expect her to return shortly with the first of the seriously wounded. I have treated no French for there were none in the queue, I anticipate that there may be many amongst the badly wounded.

I was just finishing off the bandaging of a badly blistered archer's finger and telling the man to 'Man up, I've had worse from a new pair of boots' when I heard the screaming from the treeline.

I ran as though the devil were after me towards the noise, it was a female scream, but I could see no one. I picked up Marged's arrow remover as the only weapon easily to hand and followed the noise.

Just inside the scrub woodland about fifty yards outside our circle of wagons I found Anwen.

'Thank God you've come.'

'Are you harmed?' I asked her.

'No, madam, it is Evan, he has taken Evan' she burst into sobs.

On the other side of the clearing, I heard the sound of groaning coming from the bushes, on the other side of a screen of brambles I found him.

Young Evan was lying face down, but he was breathing.

I turned him onto his back, terrified of what I might find, but he was undamaged except for his clothing, gripped in his hand was a stocking and enclosed in its foot was a stone about the size of his fist.

His nose was bleeding, and his left eye was swollen and blackened.

'I seen him madam, he tried to grab her, he tried to grab Anwen, but I stopped him, I swung it as Brother Bartram taught me and I caught him right in the stones, he'll not walk proper for a week.'

'Who Evan?'

'His Lordship, filthy bastard that he is'.

Arwen he told me, was bent over collecting moss in the stream, I was keeping watch but needed to pee so I had my back to her like every gent would madam. He came from nowhere, he must have been hiding in the bushes, like as not hiding from the battle and grabbed her from behind and started to push up her skirts like. While he was bending over her and couldn't see me I swung this at him from behind straight up between his arse cheeks.

I caught him a good one in his balls indeed. Then he swung at me with the pommel of his dagger and hit me clean in the bridge of the nose, then Arwen started with that racket of hers, she has great lungs for a small one.

'Indeed, she does Evan.' I walked back to the camp with them, no sign of de Audley, but his Lordship's horse was missing from the lines.

I wrote all down in my records and signed them; I wrote down exactly what Evan had said. Arwen said that she had not seen her attacker, she would tell me very little, she was so terrified that he would find her again.

Marged and I worked on into the night, it transpired that the casualties were either easily treated or likely to die from their wounds. There did not seem to be any half measures.

Those we could we treated and those we couldn't, we made comfortable in the small camp we had set up for our own use, with what ale we could scrounge from the main camp and a fire going to keep the injured warm at least.

It was decision time, after the dead had been buried and the wagons re loaded the army would likely split, the wounded and a small force of men to ensure safety would ride for the coast and embark for England, the rest would continue north, the King had his eyes on the port of Calais.

Marged felt that we should wait, I felt that waiting would achieve nothing, I knew what Marged kept in the tightly wrapped roll under her bunk, it was there for a purpose. It just needed the right moment.

It was gone midnight before Owain joined me at the campfire, he was exhausted and bruised, he came carrying a great plate of meat and a loaf of bread, and with Gwyn, who brought a leather bag of decent red wine obtained from the Prince's own stores, with his permission of course. Word that the Prince may call in later – when his father had finished telling him his orders and debriefing the day.

There were several French Nobles held as prisoners for ransom, but many had died on the field. The French army was decimated and had no experienced commanders as most had been taken, they were a spent force with no organisation.

The King did indeed propose to go North to Calais. We would know more in the morning.

We cooked the meat over the camp fire, well aware of the fact that we were probably eating best Filet de Cheval Francais. Courtesy of the French cavalry and the Calthrop pits.

Chances were that The King would send de Audley home with the wounded, he was more of a hinderance than an asset on the battlefield. Chances also were that The King and the Prince would send one of us with him. If that was Marged then there was no accounting for what might happen to her. If it was me then I could always disappear and remain conveniently out of sight. The King would not send his wounded home without sending a healer with them for care on the journey.

Owain and Gwyn had the ear of the Prince they would know first, and they would tell us.

CHAPTER 65 - WALKING INTO THE DARKNESS
- SIBYL

It was nearly dawn before we went to sleep on the night after the battle, Owain and Gwyn relived the whole event several times over for our benefit and for that of Prince Edward who joined us once his Father had had his fill of debriefing him, the King and the senior nobles had adjourned to their own entertainments and the Prince preferred company of those more his own age.

He came bearing more wine and more meat, the butchers had been very busy with the fallen horses. He was pleased with the men, determined that hours should be bestowed, and bravery rewarded.

There would be favour for all on our return home, he said.

Yes he confirmed, the army would head north, more than that he did not know.

So, we sat and ate and drank, Marged and I did one last round of the wounded who were bedded down in our makeshift hospital tent and curled up alongside our men whilst they talked longer into the night.

We heard of near misses with falling arrows, the hasty retreat of the Genoese under the lethal hail of arrows from our far superior long bows. The bravery of Will Tewkesbury and even Clarence Bone in rescuing one of the arrow boys from a Calthrop pit where he had fallen. Right from under the hooves of a fallen horse. The sadness then when they confirmed that Bone was amongst the fallen, not the best of swordsmen he had tangled with a French Knight who was on foot in the chaos after the Prince had shouted his advance. His basic skill with a blade was no match for one trained by the best fencing masters in France.

He had been killed swiftly by the great sword of the Count De Alencon. Proper order then that the Count had been slain by our own good Prince.

I fell asleep with my head on Owain's lap, and his ale mug balanced on my breast, listening to them reliving excitement of the day.

The dawn broke to another blue French sky with the same white clouds which heralded more showers. As we awoke, slightly later than usual, Sir Kenneth ambled into view. His surcoat slightly rumpled and his hair uncombed and his beard untrimmed 'I've lost the Prince', he said with one grey eyebrow raised.

'I'm here Sir Kenneth,' answered a bleary voice from a blanket under our wagon 'is there breakfast? Come breakfast with me my friends, there will be more than enough to go around.'

We made our excuses, Marged and I, we had wounded to check on, bandages and dressings to change, our men would bring us food when they returned, and so Owain and Gwyn went to eat with the nobles, maybe they would hear what the plans were for the next few days.

Our day passed peacefully enough, the dead were buried, the caltrop pits filled in and those poor horses which had been victims of the awful spikes were removed and they too were buried or butchered.

The nobles met in the King's marquee, they planned and discussed out of earshot of all. The men began stowing equipment for the next move.

Sir Kenneth began making his lists again.

He went round every division of men, calling the roll, making lists of the dead and the wounded. Confirming who was still with us and who was not.

The French Nobles were interviewed, then their ransom prices set. Envoys were dispatched to the Court in Paris to negotiate for their release.

Noon had passed before any news was heard.

Gwyn came back to the wagon park.

'We go north to Calais; he said I travel with the army. Owain too, you Red travel with us and Marged will travel back with the wounded.

You will take Evan to help you and Anwen. You will stay with the column as far as Le Crotoy. There the King expects reinforcements, from there we March on Calais. Sir Hugh de Audley is given charge of the wounded convoy, with Sir Kenneth as his deputy. He first insisted that he have both of you with him then relented but only if the King would allow him you Marged.'

Those last words were the only words of comfort in this news, Sir Kenneth at least was a man of honour. Marged was speechless, when at last she found her voice, 'I will not go Gwyn, I fear for my life, I will not go, I'd rather die than have him touch me again.' She set her lower lip in a determined line. Stubborn to the last, I feared that she would take matters into her own hand if she were made to leave her husband and put herself in reach of Sir Hugh, a man who believed that he owned her.

Tomorrow will be our last day in camp. Today we can rest easy. Tomorrow the Prince will honour the heroes of the battle, until then we must entertain ourselves.

Marged and I would not have much rest, we had wounded to care for. Those who would be fully fit within a week, would stay with the army, the rest would need to be made ready to travel home.

The men have gone for breakfast, Marged has gone into the woods with Evan and her bow to practice. She is venting her anger, she is angry with Gwyn for saying she must go, she is angry with me for not insisting that I take her place, she is angry with Owain for not insisting that I go, she is angry with the King himself for making the order, for it is one she cannot ignore without consequence for all, and most of all she is angry with the piece of lowlife excrement who is Sir Hugh.

I take a few moments to find a quiet spot under the wagon, with the cloak of the forest wrapped round me I curl up and try and get some sleep, the calls of the injured are quietened and I am just drifting nicely towards the oblivion I seek, when my exhausted mind hears them, there are two voices calling, one calls me by my name, Sibyl, the other as Red. They swirl in my head as I seek to make sense of either. Then they merge.

'Do it for her, you must do it, do it or she will die.'

Does my past play its games with me again, two women, one message, or is it really all just one and the same.

My mind clears and now I see it again, the castle green, the pyre, the jeering crowd.

Stop! Stop it both of you!

I throw off the fur cloak and desperate for rest wrap myself in the nearest blanket, it smells of horses and hay and bears further and more physical evidence that its last owner had four legs. Comforted by its aroma, I finally fall asleep.

I am woken by Marged and Evan returning, Marged is in high spirits and has a pot full of rabbits and squirrel hanging at her belt. Tonight, we will have a change from horse.

'Red, look, I've not lost my touch, get your knife out and skin these beauties, Red, Red, where are you hiding?'

Marged in full cry has woken our patients and Evan scurries off to assist those men who variously need their needs seen to.

Relieved groans and the sounds of men pissing, and farting signal a return to the daily grind. They are followed by calls for water, beer, or food in no particular order. Soldiers on the mend. Sleeping they are no trouble but awake, they are a recalcitrant bunch.

In my mental absence, no one has died, a few dressings and bandages have gone askew, and Iolo Bowen who has a splint on his leg has tried to walk unaided and fallen into a groaning heap by the fire. I make a mental note to get Evan to fashion him a crutch, Iolo will not lie still, he would still have revenge for his daughter's death, but I think it unlikely he can do anything until his leg is healed. And by that time, we will be back in Wales.

Here they come, the conquering hero's return. 'Beer for breakfast, was it?' Marged raises an eyebrow at Gwyn. 'Gwyn Bach, you will be the death of me, did you bring bread or is your wife to starve?'
Owain and Gwyn mutually supporting each other in their drink addled state, slide gracefully down the wheel of the wagon and with one of Owain's arms still looped in the spokes for support, they produce from their clothing all manner of goodies from the Nobles table and the Princes tent.

'I would never leave you hungry my lady, am I not your Sparrow Hawk, will I not love you until my dying day and then until my soul is burned in the fiery pits of hell?
I shake Owain by the shoulder 'I need to speak with you, 'emphasising you! 'Is there more news? '

Owain shook his head, to clear his thoughts. 'Only that we break camp in the morning at dawn, earlier than expected, we move north towards St Josse, there is better ground there away from the stench of the battlefield, there is fresh water not contaminated by waste and reinforcements have landed at Crotoy, they will meet us at St Josse.

They slept for most of the afternoon, while we tended our wounded. One by one during the day, many of our minor injuries declared themselves fit, not wishing to die of boredom or bedsores and limped or shuffled back to their divisions.

By the time the bells in the town chimed five o clock we had only three patients left. Iolo Bowen, awaiting a crutch to support his walking. Mansel Lewis who was blatantly malingering, playing on an injury to his foot caused by a dropped cannonball, and Billy Williams, known to all as Billy Simple, not due to any lack of brains for he was actually highly intelligent, he could read and write in several languages and also wrote music and played the flute. But both his names were William, so the men liked to keep it Simple. Billy was one of the few amputations I had performed, I had had to remove two fingers from his left hand, his third and fourth, both broken in several places and beyond my capabilities to re set them. He was lucky not to lose the whole hand, at least as he said, 'Miss if I never play the flute again, at least I can still draw a bow, and I can still hold my own cock to piss, though I really don't mind if you do that for me 'he winked at me suggestively.

'I bet you'll use that one on all the girls Billy'.

'Aye, I will, if you won't have me!'

I felt the large presence of Owain behind me, and a protective arm wrapped round my waist, 'This one's taken my Simple friend, save it for the wife, ay'.
For Billy was married, a fact he forgot frequently, an easy thing to do when you're in France and she's two hundred miles away, and no tales told on the Welsh side of the Severn.

I walked with Owain in companionable silence, were we a couple or not, I do not know, I love him to his bones, but I cannot ignore what he is.

'Tell me Owain, is Lady Margaret one of your kind?'
'No Red, she is not, she is truly a witch, she has power we can only dream of.

'And Eliza Jones?' I asked, 'are she and Margaret one?'

'Eliza was also a witch of some power, not in the league of Margaret, Margaret may be using her to find you.'

You need to use the ball again, tonight, before we sleep.

That night I peered into the mists of the Moonstone ball again and Lady Margaret showed me where I would find things, where she had hidden her books, how I should use what she had left. Then she showed me a forest clearing and a great tree with branches so low they nearly swept the floor, in full leaf green with natures clothing. All she said was Do what must be done, then she was gone.

Owain and I walked deep into the forest that night, far from the camp and away from the town, I told him what I had been shown. He had spoken of prophecies when we had started this journey, of a great leader who was endangered, why could we not just collect evidence against Sir Hugh and put him before a Court? Did there have to be more death? For once he could not explain.

It was dark as pitch, we should have had no light to guide us, yet every tree was lit in a pathway by a tiny glimmering light, each sleeping flower of the forest floor shone a different colour, and I could see them, there they were, as if they had escaped from a book I had read as a child. Elfin figures with wings like those of dragonflies lighting our way through the darkness. 'Listen' said my companion 'They are singing to us, they sing for their ruler, if you can see them then that means that they have accepted you as one of us, if you hear their song then they truly trust you to do what is right'.

I listened hard, and on the breath of the night time breeze I heard the melody, but I did not understand the words.

We made love to each other on the dry crisp leaves fallen under the trees, hidden beneath the cloak, unseen to anyone. He found a secret place, a hollow trunk of a huge tree, big enough to hide a man, or two of us, as if by magic the inside of the great oak opened up before us making a cosy, wood lined den. There he showed me his true self, gone was Owain the archer and squire to a Prince.

Dark haired, green eyed, broad shouldered and slim hipped, this being rippled with hard, animal muscle.

His back and chest were lightly furred with soft dark hair, his face was the same, only his features seemed more defined, his nose slightly longer, his eyes slightly closer together and having a red tint at the centre, their centres green but edged with black. He stood naked before me.

I inhaled, as he touched my cheek, with long sensitive fingers more gentle then gossamer, a faerie touch, my senses flew, he drew me to him on invisible threads, kissed my lips, my throat, and every part prom my breasts to my toes.

I was lying on an ethereal bed of clouds, floating in moonlight. It was then I heard what the fairies were singing.

Come with us, one night we pray,
Until the sun heralds the day
Deep beneath the forest floor
You know well our sacred door
Here is peace when all around
Wars trumpets are the only sound,
Lord of Eagles hear our plight
Before we all are put to flight
Help us heal our ravaged land,
Damaged not by Faerie hand,
Is she the one who listens still,
Far beneath our distant hill
A pardon seek for those who sinned
With dragons breath upon the wind.
With our hearts we light your way,

With our souls we beg you stay
Take what we would give you
Use our weapons well
Now go with one who holds your heart
Only you may break the spell

I felt him deep inside me and I heard myself cry out as my body arched under him, I was held by hands stronger than iron bands as I felt helpless through his firmament and back to his reality, when my senses returned we were lying together, my head on the shoulder of Eryr Prince of Faeries, and I knew I could never leave him. As if reading my mind, he spoke.

to love me would not be easy Red, I cannot live always in your world or even in your time, can you live the life of a wanderer, would you raise children without a father, in your own time. I am yours if you want me Red, but I cannot change.

CHAPTER 66 – MOTIVE, MEANS & METHOD

The camp was roused before dawn, by the time first light came the wheels of the wagons were turning.

The English army was on the move.

Our little wagon with its cargo of the last two non-walking wounded, Billy Simples, and Iolo Bowen both men's injuries making them so slow they would never keep up with even the snail's pace of the march. And its train of walking wounded behind was near the back of the column.

Marged insisted on driving, so I sat facing backwards keeping an eye on the patients behind and watching the world go by through the tent flaps at the rear.

Behind us I could see the stragglers of the camp carrying their bundles and belongings on their backs, we are travelling through light forest surrounded by small lakes, there is plenty of water, and I hope not too many mosquitos.

Just after the sun was at its highest, around noon, Owain rode down the line to tell us that we would be stopping in the next clearing. We have not come far, only a few miles perhaps, we will remain here for several days while the King in the guise of Sir Kenneth takes stock of our remaining supplies and men. Also, time for men to rest, the French have limped away, with their tails between their legs, but Calais should the King decide that this is his target, is another matter. It is a well-fortified port, with sea and marshland to one side and Great Walls around the rest. Many of the fighting men are paid, they are not bound to the King as vassals, their terms of contract are coming to an end, and they are restless to go home. Those that are not will want payment for their services.

Owain is riding alongside our wagon as we descend a long slope to a large grassy area surrounded by trees, there is a lake just within sight a source of water. At the top of the rise is a flat area, where the Nobles will set up the Prince's Marquee. The King himself together with Northampton and Warwick and a small number of men journeys on to Neufchâtel where he will stay and say mass at the church of Notre Dame.

He leaves his son and the minor Nobles in charge of his army. Owain tells me that the Prince intends to present colours to those who acquitted themselves well at Crecy. The names of all of the Squires of Llantrisant have been mentioned. I am listening distractedly to more tales of derringer do by the longbowmen of the town my eyes and ears only half tuned in to their surroundings' suddenly, there it was, the tree she had shown me through the crystal, a lone oak amongst the smaller leaner trees surrounding the clearing. Taller than its companions and with low slung branches. I did not betray my thoughts to Owain, he need know nothing of them. We drew our wagon into its customary location, amongst those the laundresses and the camp wives, a place we could always be found if needed.

Marged and I put Billy and Iolo to the light work of setting up our tent, we were well used as were all the army to the laying of a camp. All knew their place, shelters and tents appeared under trees and in quiet places out of the weather, foragers went out to look for food, hunters took their light bows and organised themselves to take larger game. What supplies that had come with the reinforcements were first counted by Sir Kenneth and added to his lists, and then what was needed was distributed to the men. A nearby farm was raided for corn for the horses and found to have a plentiful supply of wine, of which most was diverted by the Nobles for their own uses. The farmer was most obliging in surrendering his winter supply of cheese and preserves. Well according to Gwyn who brought us enough to keep our wagon in pickles for days he was.

When all was settling down, Gwyn and Owain were called to the Prince, Marged and I told to make ourselves presentable. Presentable for what?
Marged took herself to the lake to bathe, here it was, as the crystal had shown, here was definitely motive. I had means. I had been shown the opportunity.
Under pretence of following Marged to the lake, I pulled off my dress, and pulled my hunting clothes and Marged's cloth wrapped bundle from under her bed in the wagon.

Wrapping it all under my cloak, I disappeared into the wood, headed for that lone oak my stomach churning in fear and anticipation.

CHAPTER 67 – THE WRATH OF A PRINCE

He had wandered amongst the fires, spoken to the men, but all the talk was of the battle and the exploits of the archers, the flight of the Italian archers before the hail of Welsh arrows. The rescue of the Prince himself from near death by Owain. There was talk of Owain for no one seemed to know him well, he had no family anyone could recall, no childhood, he truly was from nowhere.

What had he told the Prince? He was sent by his father, the King. Maybe Edward would have to enquire whether this was true. The same applied to that red headed healer, true she was very effective at what she did, but there were rumours of witchcraft amongst the more superstitious of the men.

There was no talk of murder, or treason, no muttering or accusation of anyone for the death of Sir Hugh, and no rumours of any plot against his own life.

After completing his rounds, he strolled back to his tent and after some thought, decided on a course of action.

Sir Kenneth – he called the older knight into the tent, when no one appeared on the first shout he called again, then sent Elgan scurrying to find him.

Sir Kenneth appeared, half awake, clothed only in shirt and breeches.

'Take what men you need, do not use those from Wales, search the camps, all the tents, every wagon, I will get to the bottom of this before we leave for Calais. My father's campaign cannot be disrupted in this way!'

The Prince's fist banged on the table, making the discarded mugs and platters of supper jump. You will find the traitor; the camp will be rid of its scourge tonight and the culprit sent home for trial. Go to it man.

Finding half a dozen sober men was Sir Kenneth's first problem, most were already well into the casks of ale which had been liberated from the abandoned French baggage wagons.

'Sire! This is better done in the morning, at first light!'

Edwards face went red with rage, then paled to the white of seething anger, how dare his orders be questioned.

Sir Kenneth continued in a reasoned way 'Sire, to search now will cause more unrest than at dawn. The men are drunk, they will fight against this, to do it now is a recipe for disaster, let me make a plan and I will surely have your culprit by breakfast tomorrow!

'I will hold you to that Sir!' Came the reply, 'I hope you are not protecting anyone, do not fail me in this! I will need good news for his Majesty the King before we leave.

And Kenneth, I know there was no love for de Audley, but he was a favourite of my grandsire, my father knows him no better than that. Sir Kenneth Fitzsimons made his plan well, his six chosen men started their search as the sun rose over the forest, they were thorough, systematically looking through the men's belongings. Finding nothing, then searching through the laundry wagon, undoing the bundles of clothing, overturning the washing cauldrons, still nothing.

Iolo Bowen had been injured in the battle, he had cause to seek revenge on Sir Hugh, but was too wounded to have climbed a tree. But Marged Meredith, now she bore a grudge, and she had been taught by a great lady who also knew how to wield the charmed sword of vengeance.

The healer's wagon was shrouded in sleep, Marged curled up in the sleep of worry and exhaustion, where was Red, he could not see her anywhere, probably called away to another part of the camp.

Young Evan was there, sprawled under the wagon tree, a rough piece of sacking doing for a blanket, sleeping peacefully, dead to the world.

Then Sir Kenneth himself roused the sleeping Owain from where he lay entangled in his blankets, Red heard him rise to his feet and bid the knight good morning, yawning, and stretching as he did so and reaching for his clothes. She pulled the forest cloak around her, out of sight, out of mind.

The search did not take long for there was the evidence under Marged's bed, the last of the arrows, fletched in coloured feathers, identical to those lodged in Gwyn's shoulder and in Sir Hugh's chest. Under the wagon he found the light but powerful hunting bow, the very one he had seen Marged practice with on the butts of Llantrisant.

'Marged Meredith, I am arresting you for murder'.

'No!' I heard her scream, 'it was not me; I am innocent, it was another.'

Two of the guard seized her by the arms and tied them behind her back as she began to fight them, kicking and biting as only she knew how and screaming for her husband who could not hear her, and for me, who could not yet help her.

Owain kept his silence, deep in thought he reported for his own duties. Edward asked him no questions, in fact the usually open manner of his Lord had become closed and guarded, Owain's position was now to wait outside, like a dog who had disobeyed its master. He was treated with a covert suspicion, like a stranger.

Marged was locked away in a closed wagon, guarded against those who demanded instant justice, a hanging, or even a burning, for such as she was surely a witch.

CHAPTER 68 – THE TRIP GOING HOME - GWYN

I heard it first, I had heard very little else since the battle, the residual sound of an arrow in flight, death on the wing.

I sensed it's path, the Prince, it was headed straight for his unprotected flank.

Reaching up I grappled him from the horse, as my arms closed around his torso I felt the iron tip pierce my leather jerkin at the back of my shoulder.

A thump like I had been kicked by a mule, a jolt of pain which seared through my back and down my left arm, my head filled with waves of colour mixed with bright speckles of light and I fell to the floor, the body of Prince Edward underneath me, the hooves of his horse pounding the ground to dust on either side of us.

Hands gripped my arms and legs, and then nothing. I felt a feeling of lightness as I was carried, I was face down only seeing the dirt of the floor and the feet of those that carried me.

A tent! His Majesty's tent, the echo of instructions fade into the distance, my head spins and there is only black.

Face down still, I feel my surcoat and jerkin cut from my back, no! Do not cut those colours, they are those y

father gave me, too late, I feel the cool of air on my back. The draught from the tent door. I am unable to fight back, my muscles no longer move, my mind is yelling instruction, but no messages get through.
Pain, sharp pain in my shoulder, no, don't touch it, don't pull. I know the arrow is stuck fast in the bone. I can feel it grate as he moves it.

Snap! the shaft snaps.

I hear words but I don't understand them, they fade into white noise in my head.

Feathers, I see the colours, red, black, and white.

But it was not her.

I cannot speak to say the words,

A wave of sickness passes over me, shivering my whole being from the soles of my feet to the sweat soaked hair on my head.

'Jesu Mawr, what have you done.'

I sense Marged, but can no longer see, my sight is far away along with my hearing.

Firm hands pin my shoulders down, as if I could move in any case. I hear her voice, in control, clear cool commands, certain in her work.

I feel her probe the wound; the tool she uses grips the arrowhead close to the shoulder bone. I feel it's tip against the bone. She pulls, it burns but it is free. The sear of alcohol to clean the hole, and the sting of stitching, I count four in my mind.

Then nothing.

I feel movement, I am lifted again, more barked orders.

400

'Have a care do not drop him'.

I am on a hurdle, I get the sense of being carried, yet I feel nothing. Is this death? Is this what I will endure for ever? Purgatory perhaps, how many sins do I have to do penance for before this ends?

Is death not a dark and cold place, should my spirit not have journeyed to some ethereal waiting room?

I am lowered into a box, but I am not dead! Please God no, I have no voice, I cannot move, I am helpless to stop this. Oh God Marged do not let them put me in the dark, do not bury me I am not dead! There is no lid, not a coffin then.

My eyes can see the sky, and there is some comfort, a mattress of straw, rolls of cloth packed round my head to prevent movement. More movement, the sound of horses, I am moving.

The light to my eyes fades and I surrender myself to another wave of darkness. For many days it is the same. For now, there is only me and my thoughts.
There is one who comes several times each day, she turns me, one side and then the other, like some sort of hog on a spit, though I have not been placed above a fire.

She cleans me and cools my fever with cold cloths. Cold sweat runs down my naked body, for I am covered only in a linen sheet. A shroud! My mind sees death again. But I am not dead! Why am I not dead.

Another wave of lights, it is as if I see inside my whole being. Tiny worms infest my blood, is it they that cause the rushes of heat which come over me.

More cold wet cloths cool the rush. Applied with a practiced hand but She is not Marged, I would know Marged, where is Marged. The cooling hands are not shy, but they are not Marged. I must find Marged.

I feel my breath drawing in and out, I hear it in my ears, along with the regular thud of my heart beat. The whoosh of blood, like the flight of an arrow echoing in my brain. I fall into the dark again rocked by the motion of the horses and the roll of the cart.

It is all I can do. My body is powerless, only my mind now exists, and that like a broken ancient puzzle box with half the pieces missing. In flashes of light, I see the face of another healer, she who cares for me. Her face is framed in a cloud of light, her hair is red, Merch Coch She travels with me, with another, I hear another voice.

A warrior's voice, I heard it last at Crecy.

And I feel the sense of death, there is death here, but it is not mine. I can smell it close to me.

There is the sweet cloying smell of human decay, different from the decay of beasts it hangs in my nostrils, if I could vomit then I would, the smell is so strong and so close.

How long can this last, how long must my mind endure the prison of my body. Is there no death for me? Am I to be locked in this prison of my own body forever?

I pray for sleep

'May the peace of the tallest mountain and the peace of the smallest stone be my peace. May the stillness of the stars watch over me. May the everlasting music of the wave lull me to rest.'

I recite it to myself over and over, it is a prayer to take me home. The Celtic prayer I learned as a child.

The caring hand wets my lips, I taste the sweetness of honey and the heaviness of opium mixed with the tang of French brandy, I welcome the oblivion this mixture will bring.

How long has it been now? I smell the sea, I hear the gulls call, I also hear men arguing.

'He is either deid, or not deid sir, now which is he to be? The one in the coffin, that's fine, get it in the hold and quickly, but I'll no have an open casket on my ship. Tis the worst of luck. If he's deid, put a lid on him man. If he is alive then let him travel out of his coffin and in the quarters below.'

A female voice – 'he is not dead, but he is put into sleep for the journey. He is drugged. And it is not a coffin, it is a bed.'

'Are ye a witch then? The only drug wielding women I ken are witches, yer a healer ye say.'

'Ye must get him back tae Wales on command of the Black Prince, pish.'

I hear the unrolling of parchment, the scratching of a beard. My closed and heavy eyes sense a face peering into my vacant world.

The gruff voice again, that strange accent.

'Put him on the deck then, if ye must. Mind ye cover him with a cloth mind or I'll have a mutiny on ma hands, and ye are tae stay wi him, hero or no, he looks like a

403

corpse. Oh, and any hint of a spell mind you and ye will all be over the side. I already have one witch a prisoner in the brig, I have nae room fer two, and she's a murderer as well'

He grumbling of the voice faded into the distance, more of the opium mixture, and the darkness descends again.

She sits alongside my lidless coffin and takes my hand.

'Gwyn, if you can hear me, you are going home, all will be well, I swear'.

She is silent and I hear the sound of heavy footsteps passing.

'I can't say much, they believe me a witch, but we are half way to England. France is behind us. When we reach Llantrisant, Owain has a plan, the Lady Margaret can bring you back from sleep she knows the way of it'.

She does not leave me other than to vomit over the side of the ship, she stays with me all the way to the English coast.

I feel that the sleep is getting deeper, there are less periods of wakefulness when I can at least hear my surroundings, is the reaper coming for me.

In the absence of a priest, I begin to pray again. In the absence of a priest, it cannot be wrong to say your own rites, surely not.

Lord Jesus, holy and compassionate: forgive me my sins. By dying you unlocked the gates of life for those who believe in you: do not let this soul be parted from you, but by your glorious power give me your light, joy,

and peace in heaven where you live and reign forever
and ever. May the Lord who frees me from sin save me
and raise me up.
Amen.

CHAPTER 69 - KNOCK KNOCK BACK FROM THE DEAD – RED

What a performance, that jobsworth stubborn Scot in charge of loading us onto the transport ship, a disreputable looking tub called the Deo Volente. God Willing it would get us back to England.

The man had complained about everything. After some negotiations and a large amount of money changing hands, I am now in charge of two wooden caskets, one with a lid, and one without. One is on deck in the fresh air, the other is in the fetid hold of the ship along with one French prisoner who has yet to be ransomed, and Marged who they have at least allowed to assist me while we are on the ship, though she is still wearing manacles and leg irons.

The French prisoner is Francois de Vienne is the son of Jean de Vienne the governor of Calais, he may be of use to our King as a bargaining chip in the months to come.

It is not a long crossing back to England, but today the grey seas of the La Manche are rough, the wind is blowing the white tops from the waves and the under currents are making the Deo Volente wallow from side to side, I have already vomited my breakfast over the rail and am sitting amidships with my eyes on the horizon, the only way I can stop the world and my insides from turning inside out.

I had just lost sight of land behind us, when an unearthly scream issues from below decks, followed by a stream of French invective,' Sainte Maria, mere de Dieu', il n'est pas mort! Il est Le diable!

Then Marged emerged from the hold, white as a sheet, eyes wide with fright, manacles rattling like some demented ghost, she grabbed me with both hands on my shoulders and shook hard. 'It is alive, Red, his coffin, it speaks'.

Marged was closely followed by our resident irascible Scot, 'what have ye had me do woman, I have taken the devil aboard ma ship fer there is nought but evil in yon box below!'

He was right of course, the contents were evil, but they were not supposed to be alive.

I scampered down into the depths of the hold, where Sir Hugh's coffin was wedged between the cargo and the brig where Francois de Vienne and Marged were confined. Poor Francois was kneeling in the darkest corner, staring up through the grating above, crucifix in hand frantically praying.

'Dante Maria, mere de Dieu, sauvez nous, Holy Mary mother of God save us.'

I approached the rough wooded box which contained what ought to be the by now decomposing remains of Sir Hugh.

I listened, I did not have to listen hard, there was indeed a faint tapping coming from within and a muffled cry of 'attend ici, aides mois,' then a more English 'help!'

This should not be possible, the man had all the signs of death when we had wrapped him in his shroud, he was still in that condition when we lowered him still in his shroud into the makeshift coffin which was now his home.

I shouted to the purser for a pry bar, and then watched whilst he prised open the lid. As the lid lifted, the cramped and bony hand of Sir Hugh emerged from its white linen covering, fist clenched for its next effort to free himself. Oh my god, I took a deep breath in, the smell was awful, the pungent smell of rotting herbs, the smell of an unwashed body, though we had washed him well before we packed him His eyes opened, still those of a cold fish. His voice, weak and hardly audible rasped from his lungs through the cloth winding which bound his jaw shut 'someone will die for this'!

I felt like nailing the lid back down and getting the purser to throw him over the side, the Scot whose name was Malcolm Macgregor was obviously of that mind. But I had an audience, Francois, though a very personable and polite French gentleman could not be trusted. He had seen everything. So, for that matter had half the crew who had been brave and curious enough to listen at the hatch above.

I put on my best surprised, sympathetic face, the one that said, 'This is all a big mistake, but you are in safe hands now'. I called for water first, then a little wine. Then I instructed the Malcolm MacGregor the purser to have the box and contents carried to the deck for fresh air. I moistened Sir Hugh's lips and removed the winding sheet from his jaw. I covered his eyes with a light cloth, for he had not seen light for several weeks.

As the fresh air reclaimed his lungs, his breathing became less shallow, and his colour started to return. By the time we gained sight of land he was fully conscious but weak. There was no food to be had on board save what the crew ate, the rough weather had closed the galley, so there was nothing warm to be had, the revived corpse must wait until Dover.

Marged, looked on in horror, then in abject grief tinged with anger 'He was alive, her man was still asleep'.

CHAPTER 70 - ONLY ONE JUGGLER

The Deo Volente docked in Dover, and we were unceremoniously unloaded, the irascible and grumpy Malcolm MacGregor thoughtfully arranging to get us off his ship first before his crew could become any more mutinous. We were after all still part of the returning army, even if we were now regarded not as wounded heroes but with outright fear and superstition.
As part of the army and still under the aegis of the King, Sir Kenneth has used all his influence and a good deal of his available coin to find us a wagon and horses, for the use of Sir Hugh de Audley no doubt, there's nothing like a little name dropping to get what you need. Sir Hugh is still weak, thank goodness, though his strength is recovering rapidly.

Marged is still manacled and confined to the wagon but allowed to help me with care of the wounded and the sick. We left Dover behind on a rainy morning in early September, the sky is grey and a heavy mist hangs over La Manche. France seems like a lifetime away.

Our sorry little band now consists of Sir Kenneth, myself, Evan and Marged in her chains, Sir Hugh, and Gwyn.

All the Llantrisant archers declared themselves fit to march on to Calais in hope of more booty and pay for their services, the King is determined to win Calais for England and secure a strong port as a way into France for the future. Calais is vital to his plans.

Prince Edward rides with him and has taken Owain and most of the other men. The English wounded coming home have been discharged from service and disband as we leave the town, they will make their own way home.

I flick the reins at the horses and with Sir Kenneth riding alongside us and Evan sitting alongside me we start the long journey back to Wales.

Each night we set up camp alongside the road, there is not an Inn or an ale house which will accommodate a band such as we, Sir Kenneth could probably have found a bed as could I, but a seemingly dead man in a box, a recently revived corpse and a woman in manacles would push the best of hospitality to the edge. So, we drive on, stopping each night in a field or clearing alongside the road, making a fire, and living off what we have foraged, or Sir Kenneth has managed to buy from the farmers whose land we stay on. At night I sit and chat with Sir Kenneth, he is a fascinating man.

He was born in Yorkshire, on the high moors, the youngest of six brothers all living on the same small farm. When he was sixteen the army marched through on the way to Scotland, and the farmers boy who was handy with his fists and with a bow, and no slouch with a blade decided that farming was not for him. Whilst marching with the army as a foot soldier , he had become friendly with a Welsh archer called Myrddin ap Meredith, who was the grand age of eighteen they had marched together from North Yorkshire to Scotland, and both had distinguished themselves at Bannockburn.

Kenneth Simons as he was then served under Sir Marmaduke Thweng, who had made him a squire on the battlefield after the second day of Bannockburn. He had been captured by the Scots, but released when Sir Marmaduke who was known to King Robert had surrendered directly to the Scottish King.

King Robert had not ransomed Lord Thweng but had entertained him at his table and later released him along with his squire, the young Kenneth Simons.

He had trained as a knight in the household of Sir Marmaduke they had travelled with the army to France as mercenary soldiers and when the old man had died.

Styling himself Kenneth FitzSimons he had wandered into the service of Sir Henry Grossmont Earl of Derby. He had gone on campaign with Sir Henry to France and won his spurs at the Battle of Bergerac.

It was at Sir Henry's castle in Monmouth that he had met Margaret de Audley, he has been just plain Kenneth Fitzsimon then, Lady Margaret was by this time married to Sir Hugh de Audley, but Kenneth had fallen head over heels with this tall, graceful woman, she was intelligent, witty, and obviously not in love with her husband.

After that first campaign in France Sir Hugh had persuaded Sir Henry to allow him to take up a post at Llantrisant. Sir Kenneth had not objected.

While we talked by the fire Marged sat staring at her husband's still breathing but lifeless body. She talked to him endlessly. I heard her chattering away to his seemingly lifeless body about the mundane things we had done all day, did he hear the birds in the trees, how much she loved him, and she talked of their child, the child she carried inside her.

Sir Hugh mainly slept, his body was weak, though his strength was increasing daily. Food and fresh air were having their restorative effects on his body, though they were not improving his foul temper.

In a few days' time I anticipated that he would want to get up and start walking again, but for now, in his waking hours he demanded constant attention, punctuated with demands for justice and threats to the one who had sought to kill him.

I could not sedate him for much longer, I had run out of Laudanum days ago and valerian root was far too powerful to risk.

Sir Kenneth asked me of my past, where I had come from, how I had become so proficient at my work. I told him as little as I could in as many words as possible, of Sir Kenneth was too well travelled and too well read to suffer a fool. I must tread carefully.

PART EIGHT

CHAPTER 71 – THE LONG AND WINDING ROAD

As we made our slow progress along route home, most nights we made camp alongside the road, sleeping in rudimentary tents, drawing water from the streams which I insisted on boiling, much to the amusement of Sir Kenneth.

'What is the point of boiling it, to let it go cold again lass, tis a waste of time and firewood.'

'To make it safe to drink.' I told him 'We have no small beer left, and Sir Hugh will not drink the local brew in any case he thinks it beneath him, not that I care what he thinks, but we have to at least keep him alive. Maybe you could send Evan to the next farm to see what he can persuade the farmer to part with, he's good like that, very persuasive'.

We were travelling on the winding lanes of Somerset, not far from the village of Norton, not far from the spar town I knew as Bath. The farms here were prosperous and many made their own beer and cider. I was sure that Evan could be relied upon to replenish our supplies.

In anticipation I made him a list and gave him instructions on what we might need. Taking Sir Kenneth's horse leaving the knight of the realm seated alongside me on the wagon, he headed for the farm we could see ahead of us in the distance, it's location amongst the rolling fields marked by a slim spiral of chimney smoke rising into the late summer sky.

Evan returned from the farm at Norton bearing fresh supplies of crumbly tasty homemade cheese which melted in your mouth, fresh bread which must have been straight from the oven, for he had pinched the corner off the loaf for himself on the way back, half a flitch of bacon, we would be eating bacon for a month! And a small cask of cider which proved to be amazingly drinkable and also quite strong.

He was assisted in his mission by a tall and curvaceous girl with hair as black as a raven's wing and eyes to go with them, her skin was the olive of the Mediterranean, her name was Lucia and her father Silas Woodbridge farmed home farm at Norton for the nearby monastery at Hinton.
She came with invitation to us to move camp to their orchard where our horses could rest without hobbles and where we might find more shelter, or even have use of the barn if we wished. Grateful for the invitation, we followed her and Evan who now rode with her two up on Trooper to her father's house.

The sandstone building with its tall chimneys rose from a yard awash with chickens, the door was open, and a squat dark-haired lady dressed in a red homespun dress with a brightly coloured yellow and blue cloth tied around her hair, and a large sack cloth apron tied around her expanded waistline was busily sweeping down the flagstone floor.

Lucia slid gracefully from her seat behind Evan where she had been holding on for dear life in a rather indecorous manner. A manner which it was obvious from the grin on his homely face that Evan was rather enjoying.

'Mama! We have visitors!

Mama replied in a language I had not heard before, spoken rapidly it was not French or Breton, neither was it Gaelic or Welsh.

At the conclusion of this avalanche of words, Lucia disappeared at speed through the door yard and to the rear of the house, going around the outside to avoid her mother's clean floor!

I heard her shouts of 'Papa! Visitors! As she ran. 'Basque' interjected Sir Kenneth 'I have heard it on my travels, I also speak enough to get by – what did you say the farmers name was? '

The Papa! in question strode out to meet us from the rear of the building, he was the tallest, and probably the thinnest man I have ever seen, well over six feet tall he walked like a crane on legs which seemed too spindly to carry the weight of a body above them. His face was gaunt, wasted to emancipation but I could see that he had once been a handsome man from his fine bone structure and the long once dark hair which hung in a tail down his back, now streaked with a distinguished grey. His looks were reflected in his daughter who had the same angular beauty as her father. His shoulders were broad, and his once strong arms hung like those of a quintain on a jousting field. He carried in his right hand a large spotted handkerchief, which as he stopped to greet us, a broad smile across his haggard face, he coughed, a cough which racked his body from head to foot and caused his breath to suck in so far that I feared he may not breath again. Silas Woodbridge was not a well man. I pulled the wagon to a halt, and Sir Kenneth suddenly leapt from his seat alongside me!

'Silas! Silas Woodbridge! As I live and breathe man it is good to see you'.

The dark eyes of our host flickered in recognition and his face broke into a cadaverous grin, the laugh which came with the grin prompted another bout of coughing, but through his wheezing he gripped Sir Kenneth by his forearms.

'Silas Woodbridge – you old rascal, I thought you dead my friend. You, a farmer, how has this happened?'

'Kenneth my friend meet my wife, Gabriella and you have met my daughter Lucia. Come in, come in and welcome, my let us talk of old times. You must tell me of your life, are you wed, do you have children?

The gaunt frame shook with emotion and as the two old soldiers disappeared into the darkness of the house, I could sense that one of them at least was crying.

Gabriella followed them into the house, calling back over her shoulder in broken English.

'Lucia – show them the orchard and the barn, they may stay for as long as they need.'

I climbed back onto the wagon and drove to the orchard at the rear of the house, a small field punctuated with old apple trees, heavy with fruit waiting to be picked before the wind spread them over the floor.

I followed the tall figure of Lucia Woodbridge with the wagon and its remaining occupants to the orchard at the rear of the house, Evan followed Lucia Woodbridge with his eyes, his bottom jaw hanging open as he watched the gentle sway of her hips atop her long legs under the dark blue cloth of her skirts as she walked through the green grass of the meadow and bent to open the gate to the orchard where we were to stay.

We set up our camp beneath the apple trees, turning the horses loose in the meadow, watching over the gate as they galloped free for the first time in months and drank deeply from the stream, then rolled for sheer joy of scratching their backs on the earth, hooves in the air, grunting and snorting in pleasure.

Oh, that life could be that simple, that a roll in the dust and a drink of fresh water could bring instant happiness.

A short time later we were re-joined by Sir Kenneth, and Sir Silas, there was one introduction which Kenneth had realised that he had forgotten. He then went to the rear of the wagon and for the sake of etiquette alone roused the sleeping form of Sir Hugh and handed him down the step to the ground.

Sir Hugh de Audley, may I introduce my old friend Sir Silas Woodbridge, who gives us welcome to his home. Silas this is Sir Hugh Earl of Glamorgan and Governor of the Castle at Llantrisant.

Sir Silas bowed deeply 'your servant, your grace, my home is yours'.

Sir Hugh muttered a response, mustering only the basic formalities.

Silas, you must excuse his lordship, he is recovering from his wounds, sustained at the great victory of Crecy, added Sir Kenneth, diplomatically flowering the truth. If there is a bed available then it would be of great benefit to his grace, he has not slept other than in a tent for several months, I am happy to sleep outdoors Silas, we will not impose on your hospitality more than is necessary.

Marged had turned Gwyn in his bed as she did four times every day, she was religious in her care of him, she bathed him, massaged his hands and feet, and talked to him constantly. Strange, in all the weeks since he was wounded, he had not lost weight, nor shrivelled with thirst, his physical body seemed suspended in time. Just asleep, waiting, for some magic key to open the door back to life.

Would we ever find that key, was this man the leader that Eryr sought for the people, the one to lead them out of servitude to a tyrannical king? I was lost in my thoughts when Lucia touched my arm.

'Who is your friend Red?'

'How rude of me – Lucia, this is Marged, Marged ap Meredith she is a fellow healer, we travelled with the King's army to France, with the archers of our town.' 'This', I gestured to Gwyn's unconscious form 'is her husband Gwyn, he was wounded in battle saving the life of the Prince of Wales, he is wounded but not dead, we are taking him home to find a cure for his sickness.' I did not elaborate further, to hint at spells and witchcraft was to tempt accusations, and heaven knew we had enough of them to contend with.

Lucia reached in to Gwyn's box bed and placed a long-fingered hand upon his forehead. She closed her eyes, and when she opened them again, she looked straight at Marged.

'He hears you, when you speak to him, he is still there, sometimes he sees you as well, as though through a great fog, you are with child, he knows that, and he loves you do not give up on him.

Tears welled in Margeds eyes, 'How?' 'I have the power of touch, my hands sense things that are not seen, it is a gift from my mother' then she turned to me 'merch Goch' your man, he calls you, red maid, don't pine for him, he is near, when you are ready come to the house, you must meet mama, we rarely have guests, the villagers fear her strange tongue she is thought a witch in these parts, so father must work his farm alone, we have no help except from one of the brothers at the abbey. Brother Sebastian understands our language and speaks it well, he comes to help papa with the heavy work, and lets mama gather herbs in the Abbey Garden to make medicine for his chest. But he grows worse, far worse in the last few months. Some days he can barely breathe'.

Lucia said that she was now eighteen years old, her father sought to find her a husband, but she did not want to marry, she would stay and care for her father, until the end, and then she would go with her mother back to the Basque country. To her mother's family in the Spanish mountains below France.

She had heard stories of the village where her mother was born, the village just over the Spanish border from Gascony, it had been occupied by the

English in Gascony campaign long after the campaign had ended some of the disillusioned of English knights had stayed on, it was here in 1320 that Silas and Kenneth had first met. That evening we dined at Silas Woodbridge's table.

After we had eaten better than we had done for weeks, Marged made her excuses to tend to Gwyn, and the rest of us sat comfortably at Gabriella's hearth and listened while Silas and Kenneth told us of the day, they had last seen each other.

Silas was older than Kenneth by several years, he had been part of the failed Gascony campaign which had disastrously ended with the English army being driven out of France.

Kenneth had been a young squire then travelling with his master. Marmaduke Thweng, Silas was not of a noble family, he was a paid soldier, free to go where he chose, and he had chosen to stay, in the small village just south of Bayonne where he met Gabriella. Worn out from fighting and with no taste for the long journey back to England Silas had fallen in love with the country and with the tiny firebrand with the black sparkling eyes and the passionate temper which was Gabriella.

Gabriella was a fighter and no mistake she rode like a man and handled weapons with a frightening dexterity, particularly the vicious looking knife which lived in its sheath strapped to her back and hanging between her shoulder blades.

Silas told how he had left the English army on the French coast and ridden off into the mountains towards Northern Spain, the countryside was greener and the air fresh, he wore no colours to identify him as friend or foe and had only the small amount of pay he had managed to squeeze out of the army purser before he left. King Edward's coffers were empty and none of the paid men had any stomach for a war on no pay. His horse was exhausted, he had lost three of his shoes and was footsore with the hard dirt roads, Silas had dismounted and was walking along in the late summer sunshine. Making the most of the opportunity he had led the horse down to a stream which offered fresh water and plentiful grass for the horse and a pleasant resting place for a weary traveller.

Silas had hobbled the horse and left him to graze and had wandered upstream for a short distance where he found water cascading over a waterfall into a pool which seemed to be about waist deep to him. Ideal for a much-needed wash, I must have smelled like a polecat he laughed, a fleeing army has no chance for the niceties of a wash.

I had removed my surcoat and shirt he said and was about to remove my breeches in order to have much needed dip in the pool and a shower under the cascade of water when an arrow embedded itself in the tree just inches to the left of my head. It only missed because I was bending to undo my laces!

424

Diving into the undergrowth in the direction from which the arrow had come he had stumbled over the archer who had grappled with him in no small way, nearly getting the best of him save for his greater reach and weight.

The speed with which his assailant had pulled the knife from its sheath had nearly resulted in his death, had he not been able to hold the attacker at arm's length by the throat. It had been then that he realised that his attacker was a woman, as he twisted her away from him and took control of her deceptively strong arms and shoulders, and lifted the whole to a height of several inches above the floor his forearm came to rest on a fine pair of bosoms encased in a dirty linen hunting shirt which was tucked into a pair of curvaceously filled black men's breeches and belted with a thick leather belt.

The creature was uttering words which were by their very tone obviously blasphemous and extremely insulting but in a tongue which he did not recognise or understand.

Restraining her with one hand pinned at her back he had managed by means of gesticulating frantically with his spare hand to calm this she devil down, and all thoughts of a bath abandoned had marched her back to where he thought his horse was hobbled.

To his amazement he found that the old horse had been unsaddled and his remaining shoe had been

removed, the three sore feet had been encased in
sacking to ease the soreness and the old soldier was
happily grazing in the shade of a nearby large tree.

A wagging finger pointed at the horse and
admonished him for his supposedly bad treatment of his
old and faithful servant. Timothy for that is what the old
grey horse was called had put an end to the finger
wagging by shuffling his stiff old frame over to his
master and nuzzling into his shoulder in obvious
affection. At which point the woman threw her arms in the
air in a fit of gallic frustration and started to laugh. It was
then that he saw that her black eyes sparkled with life,
and she had the widest and whitest smile he had ever
seen in a person of the opposite sex.

He had pointed to his own chest 'Silas' he said then
pointed at the horse 'Timothy'.

His assailant looked him up and down with an
appraising eye and pointing to herself said 'Gabriella,
you come'.

She had beckoned to him to follow and leading
Timothy by the bridle and carrying his clothes he had
followed her to a small house on the outskirts of the
village of Sare.

He had stayed there while she had healed his horse,
he had in time fallen in love with this fiery young
woman who it seemed could turn her hand to anything
and who it paid not to argue with.

He had been living with Gabriella for about a year when another lone soldier wandered into the nearby town of Bayonne. An elderly knight called Sir Marmaduke Thweng, together with his squire the old knight was looking to give his squire experience of travel and an education. Sir Marmaduke was taken ill with the Grippe and Silas had taken both knight and squire back to Gabriella's home to recover before they both made their way to coast to take ship for England. Silas had taken to the young squire, and they had become firm friends. Silas recognised the lad Kenneth from the melee at the battle of Bannockburn they had fought together at close quarters and Silas would never forget a face.

These were hard times in the region, the English army had left with their tails between their legs, but they had run from a French army which fell into chaos leaving small bands of unpaid renegade troops seeking to rid their country of all things English and living off their wits and what they could steal.

Then one day a band of French renegades had returned seeking to rid the village once and for all of all the English outsiders.

Kenneth and his master Sir Marmaduke Thweng had been guests in the village, when the French struck, totally unexpected they had fallen on the village by night, dragging all from their beds. Villagers found harbouring the enemy had been slaughtered.

Gabriella's house was one of the last they visited and though they had had little time to prepare, Silas, Kenneth and Sir Marmaduke had fought back, Gabriella too had defended her home against the raiders. Armed only with slingshot and a hunting bow they had kept the marauding French at bay until nearly dawn. Overpowered and outnumbered Gabriella would not surrender, she had cursed them in the Basque language, mocking them and taunting them. She would not surrender herself to them. The French soldiers had fired her home, the four of them had fought until the roof caved in, the great beams falling on top of them.

It was Sir Marmaduke and his Squire that the French sought to capture, an English knight they might ransom. For they too were mercenaries, the disliked peace for it paid little.

Sir Marmaduke had dragged Kenneth from the building, and they had watched it collapse on their friends and hosts. Then Marmaduke had pulled him away, they had no horses and only the clothes they stood in, blackened with smoke and with Marmaduke bleeding from a wound to his head they had run under cover of the remaining darkness and made for the coast where they had taken the next boat home. The French renegades had left, leaving the little Basque village of Sare a heap of charred timbers. Sir Kenneth filled in on his side of the tale.

Sir Marmaduke and Kenneth had found a ship almost straight away and made land on the coast of England at

Plymouth after several days at sea. They had made their way back to the North of England where within a year the old knight had died. Silas coughed heavily and took up the story again.

When the beams fell, I was knocked unconscious, the French believed everyone dead so they left, they had not noticed my friend leaving thanks be to the lord or they would have searched further and found that Gabriella and I were still alive. It was the well that saved us. The rim of the well had stopped the beams falling to the floor and Gabriella had lowered herself over the edge of it into the water taking the bucket and rope down with her. When she was sure that all danger had passed she had climbed up the rope all thirty feet out of the well and found Silas apparently dead. She had dragged him into the fresh air and the application of several buckets of freezing water had revived him.

Silas's lungs, he said had been so choked with smoke that from that day off he had always coughed though these days he suspected that there was more that bothered his lungs than residual smoke.

Our home was destroyed, we had nothing left, not even old Timothy who the French had butchered for his meat. We too headed for the coast. We too sailed for England.

We were passing through Bath when I was taken sick with the cough and Gabriella who was by now big with child went to the Abbey at Hinton to buy herbs and seek a healer. They kept me at the Abbey in the care of Brother Sebastian for several months and once I was fit again they offered me this farm, it is owned by the church, I pay rent for it, but the Abbot is fair, and I make a good living.

Lucia was born here; it is the only home she has ever known. I fear that I will not last another year, the cough grows worse by the month, some days I can barely rise from bed.

He coughed deeply again and wiped the blood and phlegm from his chin. I can find no one to help on the farm for all the locals are afraid of Gabriella, she has never mastered English and with her other talents they suspect that she is a witch. She is not, I can assure you, there is only good in her, but she is fierce, and she is an outsider here. When I go I fear that my family will be driven out. Gabriella says that she will go back to her home land, but I would not have that for my daughter. This is her home and here she should stay.

In the end we stayed for several weeks with Silas and Gabriella.

Evan and Kenneth helped with the apple harvest and Marged and I helped with the pressing of apples into the large vat where Silas made his cider.

Marged and I went and visited Brother Sebastian and stocked up on our supply of herbs and simples and a variety of remedies which the brother recommended for wounds and ailments.

Evan and Lucia had become inseparable, he hung on her every word and followed her around like a lovesick puppy. He helped her with her chores and had become indispensable to Silas in assisting around the farm, he had mended the dry-stone walls which seemed to stretch to the horizon, he had cleaned out the ditches and the old well in the yard so that it once again ran clean.

For once Sir Hugh behaved himself he acquitted himself as a true gentleman, he was polite and attentive if obviously terrified of Gabriella, he made no advances to Lucia in fact he avoided all contact with her, preferring to either sit by the fire and recuperate or take the fresh air in the orchard. His strength was gathering fast now, and he was nearly capable of riding a horse though Sir Kenneth refused to allow him anywhere near Trooper.

On the night before we left we were all gathered around our small camp fire in the orchard, all was ready to leave in the morning.

That night we were all sitting replete around our fire, Sir Hugh was asleep, and even Marged had left Gwyn to his own devices. She had given her parole to Sir Kenneth that she would not leave camp, so he had removed her manacles.

I miss Geraint and his stories piped up Marged, do you know any good tales Red? I did not - though my life and that of Eryr would raise an eyebrow.

Evan cleared his throat, 'How about the tale of Gelert the faithful hound? I think I can remember it all, tis not so long as Geraint's great stories, but I like it all the same.'

Go on then lad, urged Sir Kenneth you have our ears.

I sat wrapped in the forest fur cloak, leaning against the wheel of the wagon, the sun was setting but it was still warm, the cloak gave me a secure and cosy feeling.

I felt him next to me, unseen in the firelight, a presence, undetected by anyone but me. I felt an invisible arm about my shoulder, drawing me to him. I squirmed closer to him, seeking his touch and yearning for his company. I heard his deep voice in my ear and in the wind 'I am with you, red one, merch goch, be not afraid'.

I let myself slide into somnolence and listened to the lilting voice of Evan as he began his tale.

In the mountainous land to the north where the mountains are snow covered in winter, and the forests dense with great trees, there lived many years ago, a great Prince of the north called Llewelyn. Llewelyn was married to a beautiful maid, and they were blessed with one son before she died. The child was the apple of his father's eye and the heir to the great lands of his father.

Llewelyn loved to hunt, he kept many hounds, all finely bred and swift on the scent of deer and boar. Amongst these hounds was one of exceptional faithfulness and a handsome hound indeed. A hound of three colours Black and Tan and white, with a fine silky coat, a soft muzzle, broad in his chest and with a flag of a tail. The hound who the Prince called Gelert was faithful and slept at his masters feet, keeping guard over the baby Prince's cradle, never straying far from his master save he was on the scent of prey.

432

One morning the Prince left his great house and rode out to the forest with his hounds, leaving his child in the care of a nursemaid. He called Gelert to his side and left to hunt deer to feed his household.

It was not long before the hounds took up a scent and a great stag was killed in the depths of the forest. The hounds were all baying at the kill, except for Gelert who was nowhere to be seen. The Prince blew on his hunting horn, he called out to the faithful hound, but no Gelert appeared.

Fearing his friend lost the Prince searched high and low for the animal, without success. Eventually with a heavy heart he returned home.

On his return he was greeted by Gelert tail wagging like a waving flag and with blood dripping from his muzzle. The young Prince's nurse ran distraught into the courtyard, crying in distress.

Llewelyn ran to his son's nursery where he saw the child's cradle upside down and no sign of the child. Fearing the worst and seeing the blood on Gelert's jaws, he flew into a rage of grief and took Gelert to the woods and with one arrow through his heart killed the hound.

Staggering back to his home he was greeted by his son's nurse, carrying the child who she had found hidden beneath the cradle protected by its sturdy wooden walls.

And, lying dead beneath the cradles ornate canopy, the body of a wolf, its throat torn out by the jaws of a hound.

Llewelyn had Gelert's body buried in the yard of the castle and a memorial made, to be a reminder to all. Never to judge things at face value and to seek all the facts before passing judgement.

The stone is still there, they say though the house of Llewelyn is long gone, and the baying of the faithful tricolour hound can still be heard on windy nights, calling for mercy from his grieving master.

Evan brought his story to a close, his arm wrapped protectively around Lucia.

Silas and Gabriella sat in companionable silence his back against the trunk of an old apple tree, and she nestled under his arm her head comfortably resting against his thin chest.

As I drifted off to sleep, I felt Eryr's grip tighten about me, I rolled under the wagon to where I had made my bed and surrendered my body to his invisible touch.

Listening to Marged sniffing back her tears, 'Oh Evan bach, that was wonderful'. And Sir Kenneth snoring peacefully in his blankets. I heard the wagon bed creak as Marged went to talk to Gwyn, no doubt his sleeping ears would hear all about Gelert.

In the morning Evan announced that he was not travelling with us. He would stay, at least until the end of the harvest, he hoped that Silas would consent for Lucia to marry him, but that was a long way off, he would have to show himself worthy of her hand first. And so, we drove on, without Evan heading inexorably closer to Llantrisant and inevitable consequences of that would follow.

CHAPTER 72 - WHAT GABRIELLA SAW

She placed a hand on his sleeping form and closed her eyes and muttered some words in her strange tongue.

As she spoke his breath seemed to draw deeper and the muscles of his eyes twitched but still he did not wake.

'He will live' she pronounced. 'He will live to see a Welsh King'.

'His fight is not over for his King will need him, take care of this man, when he awakes, he will see two hundred years before he can rest again'.

Gabriella had spoken in perfect English in a voice which both Marged and I recognised as being that of another.

She spoke in the voice of Lady Margaret de Audley.

She said no more but removed her hand and replaced the cover over the body of the sleeping archer.

CHAPTER 73 - PAYING THE FERRYMAN

We plodded on through Somerset eventually reaching the crossing of the Severn into Wales at Aust. Aust is a small place, everyone knows everyone else, and most of the people are related to each other. We had crossed from the other direction on our way to France and now, prepared to make the crossing back, this time we were alone, not part of that vast column of men and equipment marching off to a war. One wagon with four passenger and one man on a horse. Surely there could be no problems.

We pulled up at the jetty, the ferry was there, tied up and on the right side of the river, the tide was in, the river was full of grey water, no sight of the wide expanses of mud which bordered the banks when the tide was out.

I could see the ferrymen waiting to haul the pontoon across to the opposite side and Wales. Sir Kenneth had dismounted and gone to the hut alongside the ferry to arrange to get us aboard, there was no queue. But we had been waiting ages. Shortly the tide would turn, then we would have to wait, the tide was too strong to risk a crossing when the tide was on the turn. The river would drag the pontoon downstream, and the ferrymen would be powerless to stop it. The hairs on my neck rose, something was amiss.

A man was approaching! He was short and bandy, built like an ape, his arms so long and muscly his knuckles were nearly dragging the floor, he was brown, his hair was brown and untidy, his skin was brown and weathered and his clothes were brown and filthy. He ambled up to the wagon and grinned to show a mouth completely devoid of teeth except for one incisor in the centre of his top jaw.

He took hold of the wagon horses' bridle and looked at me with a distinct turn in one eye.

In a broad West Country accent, he said one word.

'Down!'

Marged and I got down from the driver seat.

'Open it'

Marged hesitated –

'Now my dear, if ye know what's good fer ye'.

Marged dropped the tail board of the wagon to show the man Gwyn's box bed and the hunched figure of Sir Hugh seated in the corner, huddled in his cloak, dopey from the Laudanum I had been sneaking into his food.

The man shouted over his shoulder to the six similarly appointed men who were making slow progress along the wharf. With Sir Kenneth plainly remonstrating with one of them who seemed to be in charge. And another who carried a rope.

'Tis him we want'.

I flung the tailboard back up and stood between it and the lynching party who approached.

'That man in there, he done Murder my son, left un ta rot in the mud, an' he done rape my dattur'.

Sir Kenneth pulled himself to his full height.

'You have evidence?

'That I do' replied the man.

When yon Kings army passed through, we gave ye every hospitality, and that great lord in there he came like a snake, he took my dattur, he said she were his by right, and her just marrit. He raped her an' she will say so, he left her for dead.

'After he threw her brother in the mud to die. He believed her dead, but she lived, her neck scarred fer life, and her voice hear gone, but she will speak.

We will have our justice and have it now!'

Tom Penny sucked in his breath and leaned on the tailboard of the wagon, his beady eyes on Sir Hugh, the coil of rope hanging from his hand.

'I shall ask un straight! Did thee rape my dattur?'

Sir Hugh who was on the point of losing all control of his bowels, tried to bluff it out 'I did not sir, a man of my standing would not lower himself to your level or that of your daughter'.

Tom Penny's face was less than inches from Sir Hugh's as he spat out his next sentence, strands of spittle flying onto Sir Hugh's beard.

'Did thee leave ma son ta drown in yon mud flat?'

'I did not!' Sir Hugh's denial did not sound convincing.

Sir Kenneth's stentorian voice cut in.

'Let the girl speak, I shall write what she says down, you may bring her to the castle in time and we will see justice done.

There were many soldiers also abroad that night, it was dark and no moon. How can she say who it was that defiled her?'

One minute there was no one standing with me, the next the tall imposing figure of Owain had materialised at my elbow. Dressed in his tabard of the Prince's colours, his sword drawn he placed the point of the sword elegantly under the chin of Thomas Penny. It's blade glinted in the half light, sharp enough to shave the man's fetid neck if needed.

Owain's voice was low and quiet but heard by all.

'I have word from our Prince in France, there are matters involving de Audley which are of concern to his highness. Sir Kenneth, you are commanded to place his Lordship in close confinement, in manacles and ensure his safe transport to Llantrisant, to await trial. Master Penny – Sir Kenneth will write down your daughter's evidence and it will be put before the Prince's court. There will be no lynching today.'

Tom Penny took a step back, as did the rest of his mob.

'Then take the girl with you, he said, she may speak in person and folk and your Prince may see what was done to her. I shall come too for I do not trust anyone of yers not to harm her further. I shall fetch her.' He turned on his heel and shambled off into the village.

We had missed the tide and would have to wait now a full eight hours until the river was full again. It would be a long wait for us, staring at the grey expanse of bottomless mud. Mud which had claimed the life of little Aaron Penny who had tried to save his sister.

Sir Kenneth placed his Lordship in the manacles once worn by Marged, 'for your safety milord' was all he said as he locked the cuffs around Sir Hugh's wrists. 'And for your safety you will remain chained'.

Sara Penny was not what I expected, she could have been a pretty girl, but at fifteen years old her face was scarred by the ravages of pox. Her teeth were already showing signs of decay, she had not washed probably for months, and she fairly stank. Her mouse brown hair was lank and greasy and hung in an oily wave over her shoulders, arranged across her breast to hide the vicious red scar which ran across her throat. Her eyes were the grey of the mud in the river and as dead. She did not speak, for she could not. When she tried, all that came from her was a cracked squeak. She carried her belongings in an old flour sack along with those of her father and placed them on the tail board of the waggon looking at me for approval and what I thought was a plea for help. I heard the rumble of wheels along the jetty, and the sound of horses' hooves on the wooden road. Turning I saw a small wagon approach, it's roof solid but its sides a prison of iron bars. It was a cage on wheels, drawn by a mule of noisy and unreliable temper who brayed constantly as he approached old Trooper who was tied to the rail of the jetty. Lifting his head snorting and stamping at the approach of this mobile gaol.

Tom Penny spoke 'he shall travel in there! I do not trust one of ye not to let un go! '

Sir Kenneth shrugged, resigned to the matter.

He did not like to be dictated to, but in this he seemed to have no choice.

Owain pulled me to one side while the prisoner was dealt with. 'I am not here to stay, call this an emergency measure', he kissed me a ghostly kiss on the lips, 'I will be back in time, with Prince Edward. The siege will be long, I must stay until it is won.'

'But there are other ways I can find you.'

'All will be well.'

I saw him mount a fine black horse it's long mane unmoving in the breeze off the sea and ride into the distance, knowing that neither horse nor rider were any more than an apparition. A timely device in a game I was becoming sorely tired of.

Would there never be a day without drama?

We crossed the river on the next tide. Our numbers swelled by Tom Penny, Sara Penny and Salty the mule. Marged seemed happy that Sir Hugh was now firmly locked away at night and kept manacled during the day. He complained constantly but got little shrift from Tom Penny who had appointed himself gaoler.

A further week's journey and as I drove our wagon round the corner of the Southgate and saw the walls of the Raven tower rising above us I knew we were home. What sort of reception awaited us?

CHAPTER 74 - NO MORE HEROES - RED

It was late afternoon when we reached the entrance to the Castle. We had driven along the high street unnoticed to the townsfolk.

We arrived without ceremony; without out riders and cheering crowds our return was not marked by the fanfare of trumpets or the hoisting of flags.

Sir Kenneth banged with his large, gloved fist on the great wooden door, and Twpsin the gatekeeper, roused himself from his afternoon nap. He had grown lax in our absence and no longer kept his watch from above. The hatch in the door was pulled to one side and Twpsin's beady eyes registered on his commanding officer, and he hurriedly straightened his clothing and tripped over his feet in his rush to open the gate and admit us to the safety of the castle grounds.

I drove in first, pulling the wagon to a standstill outside the infirmary where we would need to keep Gwyn for the time being.

The castle seemed deserted, no one came to greet us, no advance messenger had heralded our arrival. But within a few minutes, the Raven tower door opened, and Lady Margaret emerged into the sunlight.

Not, I thought. to greet her husband, and praise his exploits, her address was to Sir Kenneth who still sat on his horse and was looking down into her eyes with a look on his face which I could only see as sadness and reticence at the things he would be forced by his rank and position to do.

'Lady Margaret, it is good to be home'.

'Sir Kenneth, welcome back, how come you back so far ahead of the army?'

'Our men are at Calais with the King', he replied. 'We returned with the wounded, and with prisoners.
I must see to their accommodation, then we will talk. Madam we are all hungry, please send to the kitchen and see what can be provided.'

Lady Margaret hastened towards the kitchen, going herself rather than summon a servant.

The wagon containing Sir Hugh was pulled up alongside us.

We had unloaded Gwyn and placed him in his old bed in the barracks. I needed to speak to Lady Margaret alone, and soon. There was much that I had heard that only she could explain. Much that she needed to tell me. Marged could not help; it would be only hours before she was made prisoner again, for Sir Hugh was vocal in his protests of innocence and claimed himself the victim of a conspiracy. I pitied the man who would be forced to unpick this tangle of lies and intrigue. Sir Kenneth had his work cut out no mistake.
Tom Penny demanded justice for his daughter and his son,

Sir Hugh demanded justice for the attempt on his life, and his near death. He had not forgiven anyone for his journey in a closed coffin.

The Prince believed an attempt had been made on his life. He would see the culprit dead. And then there were the others, Marged would have vengeance on her attacker, Sianni's death was unpunished, Iolo Bowen would surely return and want justice for his daughter

For now, Sir Kenneth called the guard, two elderly men at arms came and escorted Sir Huw to his chambers.

'He is under house arrest, he is not to be allowed out of his chambers, his food will be brought to him, but he will be guarded at all times. All times mind you; do you understand me? He is arrested for rape and for murder, do not be slack in your duties'.

The guards nodded assent and taking Sir Hugh by his elbows dragged him from his waggon. Tom Penny started to speak; he had expected his Lordship to be flung into a dungeon at least.

'Master Penny' Sir Kenneth cut off the boatman's words. 'He is a lord, he must be tried by his peers, until the King returns from France there will be no court to try him! I must keep him alive until then. Besides the dungeons may soon be full to bursting.
Then he turned to Marged,

'Do not forget that you too are a prisoner. You have kept your word of parole but now we are at our destination, I must return you to a cell. You are arrested for witchcraft and murder, I am sorry lass, I have no choice.' Again, he called the Guard

'Place her in a cell with some light at least and make her as comfortable as you can. You will receive further orders later.'

Now Master Penny, I need to speak with your daughter. And both of you sir will take a bath before you enter my barracks.

He whistled through his teeth, summoning one of the young page boys from the kitchen.

'Find this man a tub and hot water, and soap if he can bare it, then find him clean clothes. Burn what he is wearing.'

Then he took Sara by the arm and escorted her towards a similar fate, at the hands of Lady Margaret's maids.

I ducked behind the wall which led to the barracks, anyone who had seen me would believe that I was visiting Gwyn, in the privacy of the wall I wrapped the cloak around me and pictured myself invisible. In my ear I heard an unseen being laugh and whisper, 'very nicely done merch goch' Then I followed the tall figure of Lady Margaret back into the Raven Tower

'The book Red, we need the book'. The voice whispered in my ear none too quietly.

'Will you shut up, she is scared, do you not realise, she expected to be a widow'.

I followed her into her solar where she sat in her big chair and stared out over the courtyard, her grey eyes blank of expression, deep in thought. 'What went wrong' she said to herself, 'why is he not dead, If he were dead then all would be well'.

I stepped out from my shadows, dropping the cloak.

'My lady, it would not, the wrath of the law would have pursued Marged to her death, you have at least the ear of Kings, she has nothing save her wits, who is it that is imprisoned – she is, yet she did not fire the arrow. I need your books milady, your Grimoire. The cure for Gwyn's curse, you have it.'

Lady Margaret pulled herself up to her imperious height and pulled on her ladies face,

'Red, I believe they call you, know this, I have no antidote to what ails him, for this endeavour is purely that of Marged Owen, she who sought to rob me of my husband'.

The lies came seamlessly from her lips, falling one upon the other, condemning my friend to her death.

'And what charms do you ply Merch Goch, appearing as if by magic in my private rooms, maybe you are the one they should be burning, for someone will burn, and it surely will not be me'.

Her arm waved to the door and cupped her ear indicating that we were being listened to. She pointed above her head and then to a curtain at the rear of the room.

Then she turned on me again and smiled and nodded her head slightly.

'Best you tread carefully Red lest your lies catch you out, my husband still has spies you know, he will find out who has tried to kill his Prince and who would see him dead and his good wife a widow and then heads at least will roll'.

Then the great lady of the court came to the fore, and she actually winked at me.

'Have you seen a traitors death Red, for that is what awaits an attempt on a Prince's life'.

She pulled back the curtain to reveal a flight of steep stone stairs, we climbed and eventually emerged into a small turret room the walls arrayed with books, the smell of dust, old leather and candles filled the air along with scent of herbs and spices.

'My husband has me watched; his spies have been watching me since the day you left for France. Nowhere but here is safe, the tapestry that now covers the door is like your cloak, only those with the true knowledge of what lies behind it may see those steps, to all others they lead nowhere but to a blank wall. Miles may be my servant, but he is my husband's vassal, and my husband has sway over his family. Miles will pass on the names of my visitors and what they say. Miles tells me this, for in his way he is loyal, it is a game we play. He tells what he hears, so he does not lie, but my husband hears nothing of import from my lips, but what Miles hears from you is fair game for the gossip mill my dear.'

While she was talking the great lady reached into a hole beneath the floorboards and pulled out an old green sharkskin covered book, older it seemed than time itself, the pages were old and well-worn and written in a spidery hand.

'This is the Grimoire of my teacher Morgana, what you seek is in the final chapter. It is a passage of verse and a simple charm, so simple a babe could bring back what is lost.'

I flipped open the back pages to see that it was written in strange letters, not a language or a script which I had ever seen.

'There, that is the page, that and there is an additional page which has fallen out with age, it is the loose leaf which is in the centre of the book,'
I stuffed the Grimoire down the front of my gown and turned back to Lady Margaret.

'And what will you do?'

'I will do what I must do', she replied 'do not worry for me my dear, I know where you are from, you have searched for me while you were in France, I felt you, be careful, do not be too bold with your talents, these are dangerous times to be of our kind. Now go, before Miles gets curious and seeks me out.'

I descended the stairs and under cover of my cloak I followed Lady Margaret from the tower and out into the sunlight.

Carrying my precious prize, I continued unseen into the Barracks and Infirmary building to minister to Gwyn. I could at least tell him that there was hope.

CHAPTER 75 - INTERROGATION - MARGED

As Sir Kenneth had instructed, the gaolers made me as comfortable as they could within the confines of a rat-infested cave in the ground. I had some light from the grating in the roof of the passage outside my cell. The castle lads did not drop waste or actively piss down this particular grating as it led to the passage where the guards sat. There was some sport to be had in pissing on the witch but not in anointing the head of Ned Prichard the head jailer, he could get quite angry and was quite willing to torture those he caught abusing his inmates. I was given extra straw for my bed, a stool, plenty of water and candles and I was allowed quill and ink, though I had no one to write to.

Sir Kenneth came in the morning with the bad news. It seems that Sir Hugh still has some influence, a messenger had been sent to the high sheriff at Cardiff who was sending his constable to interrogate me for my alleged offences.

Harry Finlay was a nasty looking man, he worked for the constable of the castle at Cardiff, he had been sent by Elias Gordon to thoroughly investigate the allegations made by Sir Hugh.

Harry Finlay was thin to the point of emaciation, he dressed in the manner of a country preacher, black coat and breeches and a white neck cloth and good black leather shoes with brass buckles. His nose was pointed, and his cheekbones protruded through his skin. His chin receded nearly as far as his hairline. His hands were long and skinny and appeared surprisingly strong. He brought with him a large wooden case in which he kept the tools of his trade. Almost identical I noted to the one which in which Red kept her surgical instruments. Everything about him screamed cruel.

Before he was allowed to remove me from my cell to the small room below the Guildhall where they conducted such interrogations Sir Kenneth came to see me, he sat and wrote on a parchment, he documented that he was handing me to this man fully fit and in good health and with child, though that was obvious or should have been even to a man like Harry Finlay. He would do his job anyway.

Then quietly he asked me to make my mark and sign the paper that this was correct. On a separate sheet of paper was written the words 'Tell them the truth, the truth will harm no one,' it was signed by Lady Margaret and sealed with her seal.

I opened my mouth to speak, and Sir Kenneth shook his head at me. 'My Lady sends her regards and begs you not to worry, she misses you but is sure all will be well'.

Then he folded his cloak around him tucked the roll of papers under his arm and left. Harry Finlay stood waiting in the passage directly under the grating which allowed in my only source of natural light.

For once I wished that one of the stable boys would get caught short on his way to the kitchen and relieve himself over this vile human being.

As if by magic a stream of acrid smelling liquid descended over the head of Harry Finlay, I could see no one but heard the loud whistle of one of the page boys calling Sir Hugh's faithful Irish Wolfhound to heel, the panting of a dog and the click of paws on the cobbles above. Well done, Merlin, good dog, there will be scraps for you if I ever get out of here.

CHAPTER 76 - THE TRUTH AND NOTHING BUT THE TRUTH - MARGED

'Mistress Meredith', the voice was that of a high-pitched snake, my name hissed from his lips. Was that a slight hint of a lisp to add to this man's unfortunate appearance.

After his impromptu shower courtesy of the dog, I was having trouble keeping a suitably straight face. The laughter when it came was just as much from terror as amusement, but laugh I did, until my sides nearly split.

'Mistress Meredith, it will not pay you to anger me, your hands if you please'.

He held up the manacles, indicating I should surrender my wrists to these iron bonds. No chain between the wrists now, these had a straight iron bar between the wrists and a long chain hanging from an eye at its centre.

I held out my wrists as requested, no sense in arguing, it would get me nowhere.

I moved towards the corner of my cell to get my shoes and stockings.

'Those will not be necessary'. The words accentuated the lisp. I stifled another bout of giggles.

'Marged,' I chided myself, 'this man has come all the way from Cardiff, he is not here for his health'.

He pulled on the chain, spinning me round and setting me quite off balance, I fell out through the door and into the passage, stumbling barefoot into the puddle of dog piss which lay at his feet.

The hood when it came, was a surprise, and suddenly my world was in darkness and I was led, barefoot and blindfolded down the stone tunnel which led to the rooms beneath the guildhall.

I heard a door creak as it was pushed open.

A stool was dragged away from a wall, a hand pressed my shoulder and I sat, before my rear hit the stool, the stool moved, and my arse hit the stone floor with a bump.

A clank of iron on iron, something turning, chains moving. Then my arms are pulled upwards by no human force, I am lifted bodily by the bar of the manacles, the locked wristbands cutting into my flesh, too tight to pass over my hands, I feel my wrists start to stretch, I try to get my feet under me to take the weight, but I cannot fight this thing, it is far stronger than I. When at last my legs are straight, I find that only the tips of my toes will touch the floor.

453

'Mistress Meredith, Marged, all I want is the truth, and all you will want to tell me will be the truth, won't it my dear?'

'Yes' I hissed at him, 'You have asked me nothing yet'.

'This is just a taster of things to come, I will need to be sure of your facts you see, certain you do not lie'.

I heard him walk to the end of the room, a bellows, I heard the puff of bellows, then the whiff of charcoal. A brazier, the bastard was heating coals. Footsteps, he returns, I can hear him, and I can smell him.

Heat, there is something hot by my face, I wince, throwing my head away from the source of the heat. I cry out as the cuffs bite savagely into my wrists. The heat disappears from my face, travels down my body, I hear metal drop on the floor, but I cannot say where.

I jerk my feet away, lift them off the floor.

My wrists scream in agony, I scream for them, my vocal cords straining in my throat.

'Mistress Meredith, I see you have got the idea. Now where shall we start?'

And so, I told him, everything, I left nothing out. Even when he played his games with me, lowering my feet onto his coals, to check his facts as he put it. I stuck to the truth.

Yes they were my arrows, yes it was my bow, yes I planned to kill him, yes I had help, and yes damn me I told him who had helped me. But no, I had not fired the arrows.

454

'Ask him', I pleaded, 'ask Sir Kenneth, he will tell you, if it had been me, I would not have missed I would not have shot the Prince, and I would not shoot my husband. I had only one target, but I did not do it'.

He checked his facts until my feet were raw, I vomited with the pain as he forced me to walk on my blisters back to my cell, then he threw me still manacled into the corner, doused my feet with the contents of my slops bucket and left me alone in the dark. Pain took over, and I surrendered gladly to unconsciousness. I do not know how long it was before I came to. But when I did, I was in the infirmary, the bed was soft beneath my bones, there were no fetters on my wrists instead I felt the cooling and soothing effects of Evans salve, and soft, clean linen bandages.

My feet stuck out from the end of the bed, and Red was examining them intently, tutting to herself and muttering expletives addressed to whatever sadistic fucking bastard was capable of inflicting this amount of pain and damage on another human. Loose dressings only until they dry, I heard her say.

'Yes ma'am 'I heard a familiar voice reply 'Evan! Evan! I strained my voice.

'Yes, it's Evan', he said, 'I am home, with my wife, and my mother-in-law. I will tell you all later, for now you must rest'.

I rested there for a week, then feet bound and hardly able to walk, I was sent back to my cell.

How was it that Sir Hugh could still dictate from his apartments when he was supposed to be under arrest?

Again, the order came from Cardiff.

Sir Kenneth had no choice but to humour him, but he drew the line at further interrogations. Mr Finlay would not play his games with me again.

When I was locked back in my cave, I found that I had company.

The cell at the opposite end of the passage was now occupied by Lady Margaret.

CHAPTER 77 - A GAME OF CONSEQUENCES – LADY

They came for me at dawn, I heard the heavy tread of marching feet on the paths outside. I peered from the solar window and saw them, hard faced and iron clad progressing towards my door from the gate house, did it really take four of them to escort me to my cell, for I knew that was my destination.

Marged was already imprisoned in the dungeon beneath the castle green, Sir Kenneth had told me that she had been brought home in chains from France, poor girl. He has said little else other than for me to prepare myself. Had she been tortured? I did not know.

I placed my Grimoire with its secrets under the floor of my still room, in the hide hole I had made there long ago.

That book would condemn me from my own hand. The other book bound in that strange green skin and written in language only known by the ancients would burn me for sure. But that I had given to Red to use as she would, I hoped I could trust her.

I could not hide my whole library, nor the vials and pots of my vocation, a lifetime of healing would be reduced to a word. Witchery. But at least there was nothing the wrong side of dark to be found in here. One last look around the room, all was in its place.

I straightened my robe, descended to the main solar took a drink from the glass of Sir Hugh's expensive French brandy and waited for the knock at the door. I could see the King's Constables crossing the castle green as I drank. The great oak door hummed with the thump of that great fist on its wood.

'We come for her Ladyship' the voice was loud and official.

'Stand aside'.

An unnecessary command, Miles had been instructed not to offer any resistance.

The Constable strode into my solar, backed by his henchmen, he was himself a scrawny ill-favoured piece of inhumanity, his pinched face and cruel black beady eyes betraying his sadistic nature. His voice was high pitched and grating when he spoke,

'Lady Margaret, I am commanded by his Majesty King Edward III to arrest you for the attempted Murder of your husband and for the crimes of witchcraft. And for the attempt to Murder his Majesty the Prince Edward, Prince of Wales. You will be taken to a place of detention to await your trial.'

'There will be a trial then?'

'In my view the evidence is clear, but yes there will be a trial, do you have a defence to offer?'

What point was there in answering this question?, there was only ever one result at a witch trial.

Miles already had his instructions. I held my hands out for the manacles and walked with my captors down into the bowels of the hill, to the caves beneath the green which had so conveniently been made into cells.

There was little natural light, torches and lanterns on the walls did little to relieve the gloom, along with what was admitted through the grating in the roof of the entrance passage.

A person would soon lose track of day and night in this place.

'Do not put them next to each other.'

So Marged was here then.

'If they talk, I want it heard and written down. The Constable gave his instructions'.

I was bundled roughly into the cell near the entrance, from here I could at least see the passing of the days. In the dim light I surveyed my new home, I was now the proud possessor of a stool, a rough table and a slop bucket and a straw mattress on the floor, I had no doubt I would have the company of rodents come nightfall if not sooner. With only bars separating me from the passage where the guard sat at his desk, there was no privacy, for me or for him. The charges ran through my head. That last sentence – the attempt to Murder his Majesty the Prince of Wales!

What on earth has happened?! How has this happened?. I have had no part in that certainly.

Attempt! That means the Prince lives, if this is so, he is a witness. Will I be held here until his return from France?

The Prince did not return with the small cohort of men he sent back from Crecy, he and the rest of the army fight on alongside the King and are besieging Calais. He may not return for years. They will not keep me prisoner indefinitely. I sat a while on the hard stool, waiting for my eyes to become accustomed to the dim surroundings. Maybe I will have to use my last resort after all.

CHAPTER 78 - THE SENTENCE

Lady Margaret de Audley. You have been found guilty of the heinous offence of witchcraft, in that you did by concourse with lucifer and the calling of the old Gods, make a charm to be used for the death of another.

As a consequence of your actions, an attempt was made to kill our most noble Prince, Edward of Wales, Your own husband our most gracious and good Sir Hugh de Audley was most brutally murdered.
And a brave man, he who has saved our Prince's life, now lies under the spell of this charm. The crowd took an audible breath in, anticipating the next sentence. The inquirer spoke on. Much has been said of your good work, your healing, and your teaching of our good folk, it has been said that there are those who ride with our Prince in France who could bring evidence of your good character, but they are not here now. You have admitted to your part in the act. You are a witch, and a witch cannot be allowed to live. You will suffer death by burning, to take place in one month. I grant you this one

month's grace, as a Lady of Nobility you will need to put your house in order.

The crowd erupted into a cacophony of noise, I heard amongst the rhythmic stamping and cries of 'Witch. Witch. Witch' the voices of those I had helped 'Lord bless you milady; may the Lord keep you milady'.

I straightened my back and drew myself up to my full height, and with all the dignity I could muster I walked between my gaolers back to my cell beneath the ground.

I sensed someone walking close behind me as I entered my cell, though I saw no one, the gaolers did not notice the slight disturbance in the air, the minute change in the temperature of the atmosphere.

I asked them for quill and ink, and I began to write. There was nothing I could write which would not be read, passed on to my captors and used against me or the notes bearer.

CHAPTER 79 – LADY MARGARET WRITES

Llantrisant Castle
5th May 1347

Sire

Cousin, for that is what you are, I stand condemned to die by fire, I do not plead for my life for I have admitted my guilt in the matter and accept my fate in the knowledge that my Lord God will pardon my sins and see them for what they are.

I have two requests of you before I die, and I hope that you will grant them.

On my death, I have no doubt that my lands will be forfeit, little matter for there is no heir to take on the mantle of governance of Glamorgan and its people. In time you may grant the lands to one of your choosing.

There is however one who I am told has distinguished himself in battle at Crecy and again at Calais.
He is a son of the de Audley house, albeit a bastard. He is a section leader and a squire in training at Llantrisant and acquits himself well in all things.

My husband should be dead, indirectly by my hand, your father arranged my marriage to a man who knew no bounds to his depravity. Indeed, I have wished him so daily for every year of my marriage.

I know him guilty of the murder of at least three women, and the rape of several more. I have documents to prove and witnesses who would testify to his guilt.

Sire, I would have you recognise the squire Gilbert Fitzhugh as the son of Hugh de Audley and grant him the rights of heir to the lands of Glamorgan, Sir Kenneth Fitzsimon will guide his hand until he is ready to act alone.

I would also ask a pardon for Marged Owen, she has sworn to me that she is not guilty of murder. She did not fire the arrow which killed my husband. That was done by another.

There was never a plot to kill your son. The arrow which struck Gwyn ap Meredith down was meant for my husband.

This brave man who took an arrow for his Prince will live; his wife is blameless in the matter.

I implore you, grant these last requests of a condemned woman.

Your Cousin

Margaret de Audley

CHAPTER 80 - THE KING REPLIES

Court of King Edward III
Calais
France
May 1347

Cousin
I write brief, your letter finds me perplexed.

On the first matter, I have spoken with my son, and he is in agreement, Gilbert Fitzhugh will be made heir to the de Audley estate and Sir Kenneth agrees to mentor him in matters he has no knowledge or experience of. I commend you for your wisdom in this matter. The lad having not inherited the reprehensible traits of his sire.

On the second, my son has spoken with many concerned, for they are his men. He has read evidence from a healer they call Red.

The sentence of death for Marged Meredith will be delayed for a year, if in this time the true culprit is found, then she will be pardoned. Sir Kenneth has also offered to stand as surety for her parole to the confines of the castle at Llantrisant until the matter be resolved either way.

Signed Edward III Rex

Sir Kenneth holds a copy of this letter should it not reach you in time,

May god be with you wherever you go
Cousin.

The package of correspondence also contained a further letter bearing the smaller seal of the Kings personal correspondence.

Court of King Edward III
Calais
France
May 1347

Sir Kenneth

My dear friend
The news from Llantrisant is most disturbing, I am concerned about the plight of my niece, she has always had more pride than was good for her. She does not ask for clemency, had she asked I would gladly have considered leniency. I have spoken to my son about the matter, and he has told me many concerning things, particularly about Sir Hugh de Audley. I have detailed much of this in my letter to Lady Margaret

I fear that the Prince is not able to return to Llantrisant until later in the year.

I fear too that I am too late to save the life of my Niece from her fate, but she appears to be unconcerned with her death.

In this letter I command you to delay any action against the woman Marged ap Meredith until such time as my advisors and the Prince have had opportunity to review the facts. I also instruct you to search your own records for any facts which may be pertinent to this woman's actions. Her death will in any case be delayed for a period of a year.

I understand that you have Sir Hugh under house arrest. He is to remain as such indefinitely and not to be made aware of our interest in this matter.

For your attention only

Edward

The letter was written as a man to his friend not as a King to his subject.

It was what the King had not said which troubled Sir Kenneth more. Lady Margaret had confessed to being a witch. The King had not chosen to refute this and had not chosen to use his power to pardon his niece whether she wanted pardon or not.

A witch it seemed was a witch her other talents were of no import.

CHAPTER 81– UNPICKING THE KNOTS – SIR KENNETH

Sir Kenneth scratched his old grey head with his quill leaving a copious ink stain in his hair, he ran his hands through his hair and spread the stain down his cheek, then he lay his head on his desk and sobbed. His tears mixing with the ink on his blotter and the wax seals which lay scattered around the pages before him.

The King suspected de Audley then, that was something at least.

Sir Kenneth in his own inimitable manner started to make a list, while he made his list he ran through in his head the people and the places where his own men had tried to tell him about Sir Hugh. Not just the men, Lady Margaret herself though she may have had an ulterior motive for disposing of her husband.

He took a clean sheet of parchment and dipped his quill in the ink.

The case against Sir Hugh de Audley

Victim

Sianni the Harp Player

Witnesses – none
Evidence – throat cut, defiled,
Circumstance – Sir Hugh wants the matter to be covered up.
False details recorded in my diary.
There is a different entry in Lady Margaret's records.

Victim
Morwenna Bowen
Witness: Taliesin Bowen (no relative of the girl)
Saw the act whilst on scout at Crecy
Evidence -Throat cut and body cruelly mutilated, defiled, his Lordship seen with scratches to his face on the morrow.

Victim
Arwen - The healers assistant
Witness: Evan James – now living in Norton
Saw the act and prevented further harm being caused.
He has assaulted his Lordship with a weapon. Arwen will say nothing of what happened out of fear.
All is written in the records of Red the healer.

Victim: Sara Penny and Aaron Penny
Witness Sara Penny
Her brother is dead and she so injured that she cannot speak. Her father has brought her to Llantrisant to accuse his Lordship.

Marged ap Meredith - raped

Witness Gwyn ap Meredith - injured after Crecy – still lying unconscious.

Marged was assaulted before ever we left for France. I have seen her shoot and I found the arrows and bow under her bed. She was a pupil of the Lady Margaret and now suspected of attempting to murder both the Prince, Sir Hugh, and her husband.

What foolery is this. If this was where it had all started then he needed to speak once more to Marged ap Meredith, should he show her what the King had written, at present she was with child and safe from the pyre, the Court would not condemn an innocent to death. Now she had the King's protection at least for a year.

He drew a rough line at the bottom of the page and walked out into the Castle grounds and across to the infirmary where he knew that Red would be tending to Gwyn ap Meredith. Tomorrow he would visit Marged in the dungeon beneath the castle green.

Tonight, he needed to speak to Lady Margaret, her guards had been doubled and they would not allow her unsupervised visits, most of the guards were terrified of her, maybe he could use that to his advantage.

CHAPTER 82 – WALKING THROUGH FIRE – LADY MARGARET

May 31st, 1347

I have been moved to the dark cells under the guild hall, from here I will be walked to my destiny. Kenneth came to see me last night, how he managed to get past the guards I do not know. They have removed all comforts from my cell, I am left only with a bed a stool a small table and a slops bucket in the corner. There is a very large man positioned outside my door at all times, mostly one of those with a most miserable and disfigured countenance. I am allowed visitors, but they are all searched before they are allowed to enter my dungeon abode and the guard sits outside the door obviously listening to all that is said. What more is there to say, I have admitted to all my sins, I have no need of a priest, what would I say to a man of God.

Yet a priest visited, a tall priest with short grey hair and merry brown eyes, cloaked in black robes of death and carrying the holy water and wearing the stole of his office and a cape with the hood up, lest he told the guard others may see him visiting the witch.

I heard him bless the guard asking him to show some compassion for a condemned woman and grant her the seal of privacy on her last confession. Then the door opened, and the priest strode in, with a stride more suited to a warrior knight, I sat on the bed and he on the stool opposite me, the little cell was dark there was no torch on the wall, and I was allowed no candle.

'What is this? I asked for no priest'.

Then I heard his voice, the voice that had held me in thrall for most of my adult life#

'Hush now my lady, let the Lord hear your last confession, go to him with a clear conscience'.

The hood was drawn back from that proud but ageing face and Sir Kenneth took my hands in his.

'It could have been so different' there were tears in his voice as he spoke to me 'Why Margaret, why did you not heed what I said?'

'Kenneth, do you not know me well enough by now? I could not tolerate what he was, and there was no other way to stop him'.

'Why did you not ask the King for pardon for yourself, he would have granted it, write again, it is not too late'.

He took me in his arms in a most unpriestly manner, his lips found mine and in faint mutterings of Latin prayer for the benefit of the guard stationed outside the door he kissed me.

'Do not worry, Maggie the guard has been well paid, he hears nothing'.

We lay together wrapped in his warm cloak happy to be alone and in each other's company. My head resting on his chest listening to the solid beat of his heart beneath his priests robe.

'Do you remember?' he started,

'I remember everything' I replied.

'The old shepherds hut, she saw us you know, Marged, she never said anything, except to her husband, it was their place before it was ours', He laughed,

I smiled remembering those days when I would go riding with him across the hillside, but he was wrong, I was always tied by blood to be a pawn of the King. If I had freed myself of de Audley's grasp then I would have been given to another. The wealthy do not have the freedom to choose a partner for love, or rarely so, and Kenneth would never be seen as a suitable partner for the niece of royalty, and he with his old-fashioned codes of honour would never think of us running away.

We talked for hours into the night, until there was a quiet knock at the door.

'Priest!, there can be little more to confess, the guard changes soon, you must be gone'.

'Kenneth, please, have no fear for me, I will be gone to a better place, there will be no bones in the ashes of tomorrow, believe me'.

He kissed me deeply once again and with tears in his eyes bid me farewell. He would not be on the green tomorrow.

I wake up on a bright May morning, May is the best month of the year, everything is green and growing, the birds fill the trees with song and the sun warms the soul to just the right degree.

I have written my letters and the messenger has taken them, I have faith that they were at least delivered, for I have received no reply. I have made my peace with this life; my course is decided, my requests were not for myself, for I am mistress of my own destiny, I will go where they may not follow.

I have listened to the hum of activity on the castle green for days now, it does not disturb me, the pyre is built, its tall central stake pointing skywards in an obscene gesture against life itself. There has not been this much excitement in the town since Prince Edward and my husband left for France taking the men of the town with them. Was that really less than a year ago. So much and so little has happened since they left. Was it folly to hope that we could bring our own justice down on the evil amongst us. In this world where only men's voices are heard must we accept that our lot in life is to remain unheard and unseen. If I have not made my mark in this life, then I hope to in the next.

I have said my goodbyes, I am ready, I have prepared carefully. Dressed simply, my gown of deepest purple, hair worn loose about my shoulders, my best shoes with the silver buckles, the silver and jet crucifix the old King himself gave me as a gift when I was a child. All covered with my black velvet cloak. Clear all fear from my mind, I cannot be afraid, my faith must be absolute. The words I must recite flow through my mind like a mantra. There

will be no book to read from, for that manual of deaths
is well hidden only one knows its hiding place.

'I call the gods to come to bear,
And powers of my own,
To fight the render of my flesh,
But surrender not my bone.
Death is for surrendered souls,
I seek power absolute,
A power that does not corrupt,
Not of Satan's root
I honour those who went before,
Life's sacrifice I send
Body tempered by your force,
I face my destined end.
Death upon first of feasts,
When souls of heroes rise,

Those born when the stars aligned
Have power as their prize.
I call on all my courage
To use this gifted night
To leave the grave and walk abroad,
To find the path of right
I build an image from the stars
I walk where few would tread
I seek live a life that lies between
The living and the dead.
I seek the one, so prophesied

His true life yet to be,
His power incorruptible
will help to set us free
He seeks one who will travel
A soul brave as his own,
One born of the auld ones
With power of her own.
I call you now as history says,
As prophesied by seers,
The child born of this true line,
Will cross two hundred years.

It started with the tolling of the bell in the church tower then the tramp of footsteps and the sound of voices as the great gates of the castle opened to admit the people of the town and the surrounding area to the castle green. I witnessed scenes like those I would walk through before, the carnival atmosphere, the children brought by their mothers to see a human being burned to death. The street vendors selling food the smell of roasting pig soon to be shrouded in the smell of burning tar and witch.

It was midday, on the twelfth stroke the door opened, and the Constable of Cardiff admitted himself to the room. He carried with him the warrant for my death, which he read out in a formal manner, then he held out his arm as all courtesy and charm and bid me 'Milady, please it is time'.

I took his arm and walked alongside him as a bride might walk alongside her father on her wedding day.

I baulked slightly on emerging into the sunlight, my eyes not being accustomed to the brightness of the day. I felt the wiry muscles of his arm tighten as I leant on him. Then I straightened my shoulders and looking straight ahead fixed my eyes on the path ahead and walked.

The cries of the people turned from a muted rumble into that of a pack of baying hounds

'Burn her, burn the witch,' and mixed in the occasional shout of 'God bless you milady, go with God, milady'.

The walk across the green was one I had made many times a day in freedom, now I knew that whatever the outcome I would not make this walk again.

I felt the first of the rotten eggs and tomatoes hit me as I ascended the pile of kindling and surrendered myself to be shackled to the central pole. The barrage continued as they poured the tar over the tinder dry branches and peat sods at my feet. I heard the priest, this time the genuine man of the cloth start his blessings, I closed my ears to them and began to recite my own. The first calling on Belenus for a barrier between my body and his all-consuming fire. Then I began my call to y Ddraig Goch. The Constable gave the signal, and the first of the lighted torches was thrown into the kindling. I felt the heat start to rise, the crackling and popping of the dry wood which surrounded me and the vicious heat rising from the peat under my shoes. The flames grew higher, they reached up as far as my chin, licking over my body but causing no harm. Then I felt the wind change, a steady breeze strengthening from the west, when the unearthly sound like a thousand crows wings beating in unison. A shadow fell over the castle green from the direction of the raven tower, the ravens took flight. He hovered just above head height causing the townsfolk gathered round to gloat at my downfall to throw themselves on the floor in terror. Gwynt y Ddraig the dragons wind gathered me up from the pyre and cradled me in its eddies as he rose above the land. I found myself seated between his great red wings, holding fast to his scales. As I looked behind me I saw the flames of the pyre consume the central pole and turn it to ashes.

All they would find when those ashes cooled would be a pair of silver shoe buckles and a Jet and Silver crucifix along with the manacles which had tethered my body to the stake. Lady Margaret de Audley was gone.

Looking down from my red perch I saw a familiar figure seated on old Trooper on the top of Hen Felin Wynt. I prayed that he would not grieve for too long.

The last thing which I heard as the great dragon's wings bore me more and more distant from that town on the hill was the cry of a new born child. Edward Meredith had entered the world.

CHAPTER 83 – THE SLOW WHEELS OF JUSTICE

31st October 1347

They came as fast as they could ride, but still they came too late for the Lady Margaret. She was gone.

Sir Kenneth in his grief spent more and more time with Marged and her baby, he seemed to find solace in the chubby little boy who had been born in the dungeon beneath the Raven Tower and had been called Edward for his Prince. The old knight had released Marged from her confinement to the dungeon on his own parole. She had moved into the servants' quarters with her son and between us we cared for Gwyn and the child.

Gwyn showed no sign of waking, I had read the Grimoire from cover to cover and could find no charm which indicated a cure for the curse which Lady Margaret had placed on those arrow tips. I had not seen or heard from Owain in months, and I had not felt his presence anywhere near, had he abandoned me to this time and place. I must have faith in my powers, I must learn to act on my own, but how.

Months passed and winter was drawing in, the leaves had fallen from the great trees, the horses were changing their coats from the sleek colours of summer to the shaggy long hair they needed for warmth in the winter. The Penny family lingered on in their hopes of justice and Sir Hugh remained confined to his apartments but still seemed to have an influence over our lives.

October was not just cold, it was freezing, it had rained solidly for weeks, the way it can only rain in Wales. A grey mist covered the hilltops making everything beneath it wet through and miserable. Daily life continued, Marged and I nursed Gwyn, tended to other patients who came to the infirmary.

Sir Kenneth took charge of the running of all things outside of Sir Hugh's grasp. There was no news from France or from London. Our company became more insular, the life of the town went on around us. There was no Lady to replace the Lady Margaret, so Sir Kenneth had charge of the kitchens and the laundry which he delegated to the head cook and to Miles, Lady Margaret's general factotum.

The clatter of horse shoes on the cobbles outside the great gate heralded the arrival of men on horseback. A hurried fanfare on a trumpet heralded that the visitors were of some import. It was still raining and cold when Twpsin roused himself from his position by his fire and went to the small window in the gate.

'Who goes there? 'he challenged half-heartedly.

'His highness the Prince of Wales's came the reply.

The gate was hastily opened to admit the arrivals. Twpsin frantically tripping over the detritus of left overs of his supper and accumulated rubbish which was quietly filling his cubby hole.

Here they came all mounted, sweating horses clouding the already misty air with the steam from their flanks.
Sir Kenneth, for once caught napping emerged from his office with baby Edward carried on his hip and Marged two steps behind him. They were home. Gilbert and Tally, Clarence, and William, and yes there he was tall and dark and soaked to the skin from the Welsh rain. Owain. And Edward Prince of Wales.

Sir Kenneth handed the baby unceremoniously to Marged and rushed to take the Prince's horse from him.

Instinct made him bark the orders more ferociously than he meant.

'Red – Marged – rouse the cook and the housekeepers and have chambers prepared. And food, the men will need to be fed. You squires must bed down your own horses, we have no lads here', all went with the army and are yet to return.

'Tom Penny' – he shouted across the yard – come and make yourself useful. The squat figure of the River Severn boatman appeared from the barracks where he was staying. And where is Evan?

Within minutes stables were bedded down for the horses and fires were stoked for cooking, rooms prepared for his highness, who would he said eat with the men at least, and quite happy to sleep in a barracks bed as long as it was softer that the ground he had slept on for the last year. Yawning widely, he strode towards the kitchens and food with Sir Kenneth trailing behind.

Marged and I went about our business then joined the squires in the kitchens for our own supper.

Owain found me later in the evening,

'Be prepared,' he said' Justice must be seen to be done, the Prince cannot be seen not to punish wrong doing, particularly where witchcraft is suspected, his father would have pardoned Lady Margaret had she confessed to him and begged his clemency. He has sent a letter of pardon for Marged at her request, and he has also sent his son to ensure justice is served'.

He took me in his arms and held me to him,' there is a way out for you, for us he whispered, but you could never come back.'

That night we forsook the cot where I usually slept and made our nest in the hayloft above the horses, listening to their contented munching and occasional whinnies and snorts.

It was Eryr who made love to me, taking me deep into his world on wings of fire burning my soul with his passion making my body want to meld itself with his never to be parted.

'What of you? 'I asked, 'Will you leave too, never to return?'

'Red, you know I will never settle anywhere, it is not in my nature, you will never lose me, but I cannot always be with you Merch Goch.'

'I would live below with you, take me there, my kin are there, they will look after me'.

'Red, were you ever one to be looked after, I think not, you were made to go your own way in life. Sleep now for they will come for you tomorrow to answer formally to the Prince'.

They did not come for me that morning nor the following morning, nor even the morning after that. Sir Kenneth visited my dungeon every day and told me the news, as he knew it.

Prince Edward had spoken at length to all those who had dealings with Sir Hugh, all their evidence had been written down and he had sent a deposition to his father outlining all that had happened and recommending that Sir Hugh be taken to London for trial. The messenger had been dispatched days ago and they awaited a reply.

'What will you do Red, there are serious charges against you? I fear that your life may be part of the deal which is struck.'

I heard the ring of horseshoes on the cobbles the following day, it was late, and the gaolers had just come round with supper such as it was. Pointless they said to feed one who was soon to be burned to ashes. I heard them jesting as they played their endless games of cards in the passage outside my cell. I heard the great gate open and the horse trot across the green above my head.

'I have news for the Prince' I heard the messenger shout.

He was swiftly ushered inside. Then there was silence. Sir Kenneth came to see me early the following morning

'There is news from the King. Some of it good, some not so'.

CHAPTER 84 - I CAN NEVER RETURN

Three days later, I stood on trial before the Prince for the murder of Sir Hugh de Audley, the attempted murder of Prince Edward of Wales and for the practicing witchcraft in that I did charm Gwyn ap Meredith with a sleeping charm.

The night before my trial, they had moved me to the cell beneath the new guildhall, for that is where they were holding the justice court. The cell beneath the courtroom was small, dark and had the usual four-legged companions in residence. There was a wide bench for a bed, with a thin mattress of straw, straw on the stone floor, a slop bucket in the corner. My belongings such as they were left in my old room in the servants' quarters, to be stolen I suspected, divvied up amongst the guards or their wives.

Much good it would do them, all that was left was a small bone hair comb, my pocket which hung from the waist of my dress, and the thick belt which would have held it in place.

Owain had told me that the Prince himself would hear the case, he would hear the evidence. I had witnessed the commotion in the castle when he arrived with his retinue. Amongst them Owain who had come to see me almost as soon as they arrived.

I had been given breakfast, a stale bread roll and a lump of very hard cheese, I seemed to have existed on bread and cheese for ever, maybe I could turn into a mouse. If all else failed!

I heard the bells of the clock chime the hour, ten of the morning, and right on cue the bolt drew back on the narrow cell door with its iron studs and small metal grilled window.

The court bailiff gestured to the stairs leading up to the hall, and I walked in front of him, the manacles they kept me in hanging heavy between my wrists, my knees suddenly shaking with fear.

The court room was empty! Save for a guard on each door armed with pike and sword. I was dragged into the room by my manacles and seated on a rough wooden stool at its centre. Then, there was silence,

I gazed upwards to the newly painted ceiling on the room, taking in the yellow and red detail of the de Audley and de Clare colours in its décor, the small shields with the coats of arms which punctuated the border around the ceiling. Then the main doors flew open and with three long blasts on his trumpet, Elgan the Princes page announced the arrival of Edward Prince of Wales. All action he strode purposefully into the room, dressed almost completely in black, topped with a rich blue and red surcoat, and a black velvet hat with three feathers pinned at the front. His blonde hair was trimmed neatly, and he was clean shaven. He strode down the length of the hall and took his seat behind the huge table which was set up on the dias. The constable of the town closed the great doors and twitching his gown of office over his shoulders straightened his clothing and prepared to speak.

Sibyl Helena Lewis you are charged with the attempted Murder of your Lord Sir Hugh de Audley and also with the attempted murder of his highness Edward Prince of Wales, how do you plead?

You are also charged with the attempted murder of Gwyn ap Meredith. How do you plead?

I took a deep breath in and the spoke out 'I am guilty as charged sire; In that I did attempt to kill Sir Hugh de Audley, but not, to any charge against your person sire or that of Gwyn ap Meredith'.

I directed my answer to The Black Prince. Owain stood to speak for me.

'This lady says that she has information which she would offer in mitigation for her crimes'.

The Black Prince spoke from his table.

'Well speak then woman, there is one who stands to face death for these very crimes, under these circumstances we need proof that it was actually you who acted, and that you are not just speaking to pervert the course of Marged Meredith's justice.

'Sire there is a witness, to my crime as there are witnesses a plenty to crimes committed by another which have gone unnoticed and un punished'.

And so, I told him my part in the events two days after Crecy and I begged for Marged's release.

Marged was brought to the court and asked why she had confessed her guilt. 'I confessed my guilt, lest they torture me, 'Marged spoke, 'I was tortured anyway, I told the truth in that I was prepared to kill the man who raped me, but I did not fire those arrows, why would I shoot my own husband and the father of my child?

I took a deep breath in and continued 'Sire, you were never the target, had Marged held the bow then there would only have been one arrow, but I am not as skilful as she and my first arrow missed its target. I am loyal to your cause sire and have served as healer to your army on the last campaign, I would never seek to harm you Sire'.

'Sibyl,' he questioned, 'That name means prophetess does it not? '

'It does sire'.

'Where do you hale from, for it is not from this town, there are those who call you witch, a white witch certainly but a witch non the less, what say you?'

'I am from the mountains of the west, I am a healer, as you know sire'.

'And what do you know of Owain. my Squire, he too is from the west, yet no one knows of him or his family, I have eyes and ears lady, both you and he are an enigma, I must take him on trust for he has done only good and brave deeds, but you, I am inclined to suspect that there is more to you than meets the eye'.

He raised an eyebrow and looked directly at Owain as if awaiting a response. Constable, take this woman to the dungeon below, I have much to do before I decide her fate. The Prince had spoken.

I was to be taken to the cells below the castle, I was allowed to take my warm cloak, the forest fur cloak. I would stay there until my fate was decided

The Prince spoke again, 'Marged ap Meredith, I have a letter of clemency from my father which releases you from your charges. You may thank the Lady Margaret for this. She asked nothing for herself.

Take your child and your husband home to the place of his father, he will heal better there. The place is his for as long as a Meredith shall live there, he saved my life both in battle and on that day, I shall pray for his recovery and his soul.'

Justice for me proved to be a swift decision. The Prince considered all, I was guilty, I was guilty of the offence and that was all there was to it, I had no mitigation, how could I explain why I had done what Marged was supposed to do and acted in her stead. To do that would be to admit to the darkest form of witchcraft one which had left Gwyn in a deathlike state. Was it Gwyn's predicament that swayed his decision?

By dusk I had my sentence I was to be taken to the Tower of London for my guilt to be confirmed by the King then I would no doubt be sentenced to the same fate as Lady Margaret. But I did not have her talent to call the auld ones, I would burn. We would leave in the morning.

Owain had a plan, unseen he came to see me.

'When they come for you in the morning, go with them, I will be there'. Wrap your cloak about you and make sure you walk between the jailers, one in front and one behind. That will be how they will take you from the cell. As you reach the daylight I will be there to take you from them. I will give them the warrant from the Prince which permits them to take you to London and will order your detention in the Tower. We shall walk up the steps onto the green and then you will use the cloak. Miss your footing, stumble a little and grab my arm, then use the cloaks magic. Tomorrow is all hallows the tunnels will be open to us. We shall both walk into the light of the Raven Tower and back to your time, we will do this together, but you can never return'.

What was I going back to, I had been gone a year, how would I explain that to the great and the good of the town?

CHAPTER 85 – THE AFTERMATH- MARGED

Take your husband home he had said. Take him to his father's place in the mountains, take your son and raise him well.

Sir Kenneth gave me the use of the smaller of the wagons and sent Gilbert and Tally with me for the journey back to St Harmon, a place I had never been to, to a family I had never met. Sir Kenneth had written a letter of introduction for me to give to Gwyn's father. The journey would take about a week given good weather and no hitches. I had a small supply of coin so that we could at least sleep at an Inn or lodging house occasionally.

The Prince was furious, Red had disappeared, seemingly escaped her guards, and run away with Owain who had also disappeared. The guard had been turned out and the area searched but there was no sign of either of them. The Prince felt his trust had been betrayed, he would see Owain and Red burning on the same pyre or at least beheaded on the same scaffold. I was relieved that my safety was guaranteed by the letter from the King, or the Prince's wrath might have reflected on me in turn.

Having read Sir Kenneth's gathering of evidence, the Prince had caused Sir Hugh to be removed from the comfort of his apartments and swiftly altering the warrant for imprisonment in the Tower, had dispatched him by closed wagon to London for trial. He had caused Sir Kenneth to take depositions from all the witnesses concerned and also petitioned his father that justice for Sir Hugh be swift and as requested by Lady Margaret, his lands, and the stewardship of the Castle at Llantrisant be given to Gilbert Fitz Hugh, his bastard son who would be acknowledged as heir to his estates. Young Gil was fortunate indeed, though he would need plenty of instruction on how to conduct himself as a Lord, and in a proper manner. No doubt Sir Kenneth would take on his tutelage and teach him well. For now, Gil rode alongside our wagon with Tally his great friend and comrade in arms, our destination Hengwm.

Apart from the incessant rain the journey went without incident, the Inns we stopped at welcomed us and the farms where we camped gave us shelter and allowed us to make use of their barns and orchards.

We drove up the track to Hengwm after a week's hard travel, as the wagon rumbled slowly around the bend in the steep track up to the cottage. I got my first sight of the long low cottage which had been Gwyn's childhood home.

As we approached, the front door of the house flew open and a girl aged about ten years old came tearing down the path as far as the gate, curly brown hair flying around her face and her skirts awhirl around her. She stopped at the gate and shouted back into the house.

'Mam, visitors, a wagon!'

'Gwennie, we are not expecting folk, go fetch your father from the top field'.

Round the corner from the yard emerged the figure of Myrddin ap Meredith, wiping the dirt from his hands on his britches.

Tally swung down from his horse and reached into his saddle bag for Sir Kenneth's letter.

'Sir, we come from Llantrisant, we bring your daughter in law and your grandson, and we bring Gwyn home.'

The old man kept reading the letter and walked to the rear of the wagon and peered in at the body of his eldest child, Gwyn, on who all his hopes had been pinned, then he reached up to the driver's perch and held out a hand to me.

'You must be Marged, welcome to the family cariad, go on in and be welcome, and you boys, go you in, I will carry him'.

Then he handed me down from the wagon and I walked up the front path of Hengwm carrying baby Edward in my arms.

He climbed into the rear of the wagon and extracting Gwyn from the box bed he picked him up as though he was a baby and carried him in strong arms into the house. Gwyn's mother Anwen emerged from the kitchen, dusting her apron clean of flour, she had been baking and the smell of fresh bread assaulted my senses and brought on a hunger that I never thought I could feel again.

Myrddin carried Gwyn further into the cottage and to his old bedroom at the rear and lay him on the small cot bed, he had long since grown too long for it and his feet hung over the end and the massive width of his shoulders completely filled its width.

'He's going to need a bigger bed', the gruff old farmer observed dryly. 'Now tell me what ails him.'

I told him everything, I left out nothing, I told him of Lady Margaret and of Red and Owain and Sir Hugh, well I didn't tell him quite all of that, some things should remain unsaid.

The old man rubbed his stubbled chin 'Let me think on it, there may be something we could try'.

That evening we sat around the fire at Hengwm, Myrddin in his chair beside the fire, Anwen sitting in her window seat, her mending on her lap and Edward asleep in Gwennie's old cradle which had been hurriedly cleaned and pressed into service. Tally and Gil sat on the floor, and I occupied the chair on the other side of the fire and Gwyn's father began to speak.

'Let me tell you of the home of 'y Ddraig' he started. 'Y Ddraig Goch, is a great red winged beast, it is the bringer of many things, it can either be of great good or wreak great havoc and damage to the land.'

Gwyn's father sat forward in his chair, and began,

'Y Ddraig Goch, there were tales told when I was a child, handed down from grandparents and the old folk of the villages, they told of the great red dragon which slept beneath the mountains of the north.

The old women said that the breath of the dragon as it slept could be felt in the caves under the mountains, that the distant thunder was its snoring, and the lightening was the echo of the fire from its nostrils as it hit the roof of the sky. There are caves you know, caves in these hills we live on that connect with the great mountains, in the days when the dragon slept in his lair, the ground was warm, the water in the brooks was no longer icy in the winter, the wells no longer froze, the ground stayed soft until deep into the winter, y Ddraig warmed our hearts, life seemed a little easier. It was not unknown for families to live in the caves when the winter cold came, for there was a warmth in the very stone around them.

All this was many years ago, long before even my grand da was born. The storytellers told of a great storm which ran across the country, a storm so great it woke y Ddraig, and the great red beast flew away. Then for many winters the hillsides were bleak and cold in winter, snow covered the mountains, the caves which gave the people shelter were as cold as the grave. Folk became sick and died in their hundreds, many families died out completely for nothing could cure them. One family it was said took all they had and walked deep into the caverns of the north, they followed the heat in the stones until they found a huge hollow lined with the bones of sheep and other animals and scattered with great red scales. They had found the lair of y Ddraig, they had no food left to eat, and were bone tired, the women of the family took some of the bones and boiled them for soup, and while the soup was cooking, they thanked the great beast and prayed for his return, then the family lay down to rest. When they awoke, they were in a small cave at the foot of a different hillside, the land which stretched into the valley below was green, the valley was lined with trees, and there was a stream running down towards a small village.

But all was strange, and when the man came back from the village, he told his family that they were no longer in their own time but had slept for many years. That family built a home for themselves, that family were my kin, and this is the home that they built home, the cave is still here.'

He paused for breath,

'At Calan Mai just passed we had a great storm, and since then I have noticed that the cave has been warm again, there has been talk that the stones of the mountain further north went hot to the touch. This is the dragon's breath, Gwynt y Ddraig, if the dragon cared for my family before, maybe his breath will heal my son now. I feel that we should make Gwyn's bed in the cave, let the spirit of the mountains warm his bones and make him whole again.'

He sat back in the chair, and looked around the room, Marged, 'what say you child?'

I nodded in agreement 'It is at least something,' I replied'

Was this where Lady Margaret had come to, that was too much even for me to take in. I knew the people of the hills believed in such things, Lady Margaret had shown me some of her art, but summoning dragons, if I had not seen it with my own eyes, I never would have believed.

She had led us all a merry dance, a dance of which she was still the mistress!

In the morning we carried Gwyn into the cave and laid him in the box bed which had brought him back from France. Myrddin sat with his son all that day talking with him telling him of all that had happened since he had left to train as an archer.

Gwennie and Anwen made a great fuss of little Edward who was just starting to crawl and to pull himself up on the furniture, Gwennie took him to see all the animals, generally spoiled him with treats of warm bread and fresh butter from the dairy. When Myrddin was busy on the land I sat with Gwyn. Myrddin was right, it was warm in the cave, the stones themselves

497

were pleasantly hot to the touch as if warmed by some source of heat coming from a great distance away.

CHAPTER 86 - LIFE AFTER DEATH - GWYN

How long have I lain here, If I am to die, I wish the good Lord would get on with it, make up his mind to take me, or not as the case may be.
I feel as though I have been run over by several herds of sheep, and a few cows as well, my very bones ache with lying still, and I can see nothing. I feel that I need to scratch the terrible itch which is starting at the sole of my left foot, but I cannot move my hand to attend to it.

It is warm here very warm, have the Gods chosen hell for me then? Is this, hells waiting room I am lying in? Surely, I have not displeased my God to that great an extent.

It is hard to tell night from day, all of time rolls into one.

I feel that there are others watching me from another place, another time even. There is a woman, there is red all about her, she glows with heat, her shadow is long, and she rises through flames. Behind my closed eyes I see scales of scarlet like a great snake slithering through my thoughts, something is changing, but I am damned if I know what it is. I hear too the sound of the wind, a warm wind, it warms my bones to the point of burning,

Marged if you are there, come to me, please help me, talk to me, tell me what strangeness is come over me.

I will never chide you for talking too much ever again if you will only come now and tell me my fate.

Sometimes there is another, she watches from afar, I sense she wants to be here, but she is held back, I hear the voice which tells her, 'You cannot return, you may never return,' she watches me through a glass, she searches in a great book, turning through the pages, seeking something.

One voice grows stronger, it tells me that I will not die, that I will live until a King born in Wales takes his throne. I feel my limbs warming and I find that I can see, the red scales have fallen away from my sight and the great red beast no longer lives in my head. But I am warm, too warm, I can feel the fever coursing through my veins. Cold cloths, I can feel cold on my forehead, gentle hands are mopping the sweat from my body. Yes, it is Marged.

My dry lips try and form the words 'Mar' my voice is weak and fades to a croak.

'Gwennie! Gwennie fetch your father, he is speaking, go Gwennie, go quickly'.

Where am I then that she is calling Gwennie, am I home, am I not in France still?

Marged is looking down at me I can see her face clearly, my eyes are open, she wets my lips with a little sweet water, her smile is so wide I fear her face may break from smiling. I hear the sound of heavy feet on stone steps and there is my father, followed by my sister.

I try and sit up, but my muscles are weak from being inactive for so long, but at least I am alive, and I can see and feel as I used to.

And who is this, Marged holds up a child so that I may see better, he is a sturdy child with long limbs and a shock of red hair. 'Edward ap Meredith', she says 'meet your father'.

'Gwyn, this is your son, I have named him Edward, for his Prince, the Prince whose life you saved and the Prince who granted me freedom.'
I am glad to be alive, all of a sudden the world is once again alive, I am welcomed back into the bosom of my family and half carried supported into the house where I grew up and there I find Gil and Tally, we have much to catch up on.

Yet something of the last few days stays in my mind, Was I dreaming or has a further curse been placed on my life. Am I truly destined to live until a King is born in Wales.

CHAPTER 87 – GOING UNDERGROUND - RED

Eryr had taken me by the arm and walked me through the light. I could not return to Llantrisant, how could I explain my absence.

Did I want to walk back out onto the castle green behind the New Inn and just carry on as before?

The light we walked into seemed to go on for ever, a tunnel of light, with endless doors and passages leading off it.

Owain was gone, replaced by his alter ego, my guide was there, in all his glory, dark haired and mildly satanic in aspect his green eyes with that red fire at their centre, the green ringed with black, hungry looking eyes which filled me at once with a terrible dread and a terrible hunger deep in my soul.

In an instant I wanted him to devour me with lust, to make love to me hard and fast, as I knew he could, to make me scream as my body melted into his, and also to flee, to run, as fast and as far away as I could.

'What will it be then Red, fight, or flight? Will you try before you buy, or will you do what your mind is willing you to do and leave me?'

In the midst of all the light I found that the tunnel did have walls he pinned me up against the rock, his long-fingered hands lifting my skirts to an unseemly level around my waist, I wore no undergarments, I had none, they were a vanity few of us had brought home from France and certainly not a luxury I had been allowed in the dungeons under the castle.

I felt him solid up against me, smelled the feral musk of his ardour, felt my insides turn moist in anticipation of his filling them, he lifted my hips and I opened myself to him and in one thrust the planes of my world spun out of control, his teeth bit my neck, hard, my nails raked his naked back and clawed at the globes of his buttocks. I felt him tease me, withdrawing slightly to the point where he knew I would lose all control, I wrapped my legs around him, drawing back into me, his tight furry balls nestled in the hollow of my inner thighs. We dissolved onto the floor still joined together. My eyes closed and I flew, my landing was cushioned in fur, soft warm fur beneath my naked body, Eryr was there sated alongside me, holding me close to him, partially pinning me beneath him, his long legs entwined with mine.

He raised himself on his arms and kissed my forehead.

'Fight it is then! You will stay, for a time at least, come let me show you around'.

'Where in God's holy name are we?'

'You are home, this is where you were born, the Druid's caves at St Harmon, not as you know them for, we are not in your time, we are still in Gwyn and

Marged's time, remember you cannot go back there, but we can watch and guide from my world and that is where you are. The time is theirs, but this place is ours. It is not grand, but it is my home, not the palace of my father, but well-appointed enough, we will do well here, for now.

I lay staring up at a rocky ceiling, it glowed with a million small crystals which shed their light over us, as my eyes started to focus I recognised that I was indeed in the Druids cave, the entrance was in front of us, the stone altar where I had been found as a child was there, but this was far more of a cave than I ever saw.

Stirring I swung my legs over the edge of what would be our bed, a wide stone ledge, lined with soft materials and the fur of many animals, hard yes, but not uncomfortable.

The floor was swept and clean, there was a passage leading off to the rear which I assumed went further into the hillside, there for us, but unseen to the world above.

Again, he read my thoughts, 'Yes, there is far more to the cave than you have ever seen, come, walk with me!'

It was only then that I realised that I wore no Clothing, I was naked.

'I gestured downwards and coughed, with that throat clearing noise that indicated a question.

'Just close your eyes and think yourself clothed' came the response.

My first attempt proved to be brown and dowdy looking, my second was thought too revealing and more fitting for a brothel, my third too prim and proper. On the next I just thought of Eryr.

I heard him grunt in approval and looking down saw that I was clad in leather britches, with knee length boots, and my top half in a leather jerkin fitted to the waist which accentuated my breasts quite nicely, it was worn over a white linen shirt, the top half did however sport two slits in the back which allowed a lovely cooling flow of air in and sight of a large amount of my back. With a smile, he touched the garment with one finger 'no wings' he announced with a laugh – the offending slits disappeared 'perfect' came the response.' Though how you expect me to show restraint when you've legs like those, below an arse like that, I really don't know, I've a good mind to undress you again right now, I can you know, and he did!' Without touching me he made my whole wardrobe disappear.

'Can I do that too?' I asked coyly raising an eyebrow.

'To yourself, ay ye can, and with a little practice, I may yet allow you to expand your repertoire, you are of the blood you know, you should know how to use it!'

He winked with one eye and reinstated my outfit, with a gracious bow, and gesturing to the passage at the rear of the cave 'After you madam'.

He showed me his home beneath the mountain. He had been truthful about where he lived, there was no great hall, with hanging tapestries, none of the grandeur of his father and his grandfather.

Eryr lived in a cave and would use his abilities and talents to create what he wished for in the way of home comforts. He still hunted and killed game for meat, and he still lived off the fruit of the land, he did not, he said, kill what human farmers raised, he did not take sheep or goats from their fields though he did occasionally take milk. If I chose to stay then would I be expected to live in the same itinerant manner, it was no wonder Owain had taken so well to the Gypsy lifestyle of the Pryce family. Again, as if reading my thoughts, he spoke

'Do not expect me to change, for I will not, I fear I cannot, I have chosen to live this way and it is a way which suits me, and which fits with the life of the land above. Can you live like this, with only the basics of life, in a world where you cannot visit your own kind. For in this time remember Red, you cannot be known for the wrath of the King will be upon you we are not so distant from the Crown that he will not take an interest, Gwyn was his friend and is a hero'.

I thought for a moment and then turned and standing on my tip toes, I kissed him on his mouth murmuring into his lips 'I will try.'

He took me deep into the mountain, through cave after cave all the way to a large opening in the side of the mountain which looked out onto the sea, it was night, the moon shone on the calm of the ocean.

Suddenly he took me in his arms and launched himself into the void beneath us, I had not noticed the great black wings, the wings of a black eagle which had emerged from his back, with his arm around my waist and my body held close to his we soared over the ocean, swooping low over the waves, then we turned to the

506

North towards the snow-capped mountains. He showed me the site great stone circle of Waun Mawn, the stones he said had been moved to the great plain at Salisbury, this was the place where his father held his court. Eryr had not been here for many years, he had chosen to his own path.

Then we flew back south and sat for a time invisible to all on the cliff top of the Witches Point, staring out to sea. Eryr spoke with passion about the human rulers of the day and of what he had seen coming, war upon war between the great houses. But there was one who would come from this great country, one not born to greatness but who would come from over the sea to rule over all of the islands.

'Maybe we were wrong, maybe it is not Prince Edward, he is a great leader of men but maybe it is not him the auld ones spoke of' he breathed deeply. 'She is not dead you know, and she has deceived us, she has power far greater than I have ever seen, the power to summon dragons is power indeed. What is she about? We must look, y Ddraig is back beneath the mountain, I can tell, the stone is warm again. Will she use him for her own ends?'

'Must I look through the veil again', I asked 'I will if you ask it, but it has done little good so far'.

As the dawn rose over the clifftops we flew back to our rocky home and I sat with the moonstone globe again, waiting for the clouds to clear and for something to come into view. I had both Grimoire open before me, the one I could read clearly, the other was written in an ancient language which not even Eryr could translate.

I sat with Eryr and peered across the void and into the world of men, or did I.

I saw Lady Margaret, she mirrored my actions, she too was looking across the veil, but her gaze was focussed, behind her in the gloom was a huge red beast.

Then I saw Gwyn, he was no longer at the Castle, he was in a place I had seen before but not in this time, it was the cave room behind Hengwm. How long had he been there, not long for sure. What is Lady Margaret about? I placed my hands on the sphere which grew hot under my hands and suddenly I heard her, she was invoking the breath of the dragon, Gwynt y Ddraig. I turned to Eryr,

'the caves in the mountain, they are all connected are they not?'

'They are, they are the caves which we walk through, the caves I call home, I can walk nearly the length of the land without breaking through to the surface.'

'And the cave at Hengwm – it is part of the same system?'

'It is.'

'So, if she can send the Dragon's breath through the rock to that cave then it will warm Gwyn?'

'Well, yes, as it warms everything in its path, now that y Ddraig has returned the stones are warm again.'

'She is using it to heal him, her charm will travel with the warmth, and he will be returned to life, but she does not do this from charity to him or to Marged, for she blames Marged for the failure of her first plan She does it for her own ends.'

CHAPTER 88 – RISK AND RETURN – RED

Time passed and Gwyn grew stronger, Gil returned to Llantrisant to find that he had an inheritance, and responsibilities, Sir Kenneth took him under his protective wing, and Gilbert Fitzhugh took on the mantle of Governor of the Castle.

Tally decided to stay at Hengwm and help Gwyn to run the farm, Myrddin was feeling his age and needed help with the heavier work, Gwyn himself needed to build his strength, it would take several months before he would regain his former strength.

Eryr watched them from beyond the veil, the family expanded, Edward was joined by a sister called Arianrhod, Aria for short.

Our own son was born, dark haired like his father with deep blue eyes, the colour of storm clouds. We called him Calon, It was a happy time for all, one whole year of peace.

For Eryr and I it was a time to truly know each other, he showed me the world from a different view, my faerie warrior also craved peace, he taught me how to use the faerie blood which ran in my veins, the power of thought, the magic the mind could create, and then how to make it real.

In these halcyon days, we roamed the mountains, flew on Eryr's eagle wings over the seas, Calon travelled with us strapped safely to his father's chest, loved and contented. But happy times will never last for ever.

What would I do when Calon was walking, when he needed friends to play with when he needed schooling and the company of others, I decided then that I would go back to St Harmon, back to the human world, there had been no visits from the Prince, all seemed to have died down. There was more to concern his highness than one runaway witch and suspected murderer, and after all, as I told Eryr, it was easy for us to hide if we needed to.

These times were harsh and harsher times to come, as a healer how could I sit back and watch what we had seen creeping across the lands to the east, across France where we had fought for our King only a year ago.

We had seen it, people dying in their hundreds, whole villages of people dead, piles of rotting bodies lying in the streets, no one to bury them, the great monasteries decimated, unable to care for the sick. I wondered how my friends in Margam and Ewenny would fare. Would they too succumb to this dreadful sickness.

For it would reach us, it's black fingers would reach into our home and hold it in a death grip.

I could not sit in my tower and watch it happen, I must at least try and lessen the blow when it came.

I told Eryr what I intended, he should come with me, a young family come from the villages to the west, fleeing the Black Death which was sweeping through the towns. We could find a home in the village, visit Gwyn, and warn his family what was coming, prepare them for the worst.

Did I say I told Eryr, well I didn't exactly tell him, we argued, it was too dangerous he said, people in the village would talk, what would he do, he was not exactly the grey man. Hard to be unobtrusive looking like he did, he told me.

He forbade me to go, he swore he would not let me take our son into a danger such as this. One that we could not prevent and could not control.

Did I have any idea what such a disease would do to the faerie kingdom if ever it crossed the veil into the world below ground? It would destroy it, there was no resistance to disease in the faerie world, the death would be magnified tenfold, it would be the end of his people. It was why they had married some human blood into their bloodlines, but not all his kin had this protection, little as it was.

Eryr was afraid, I saw it in his handsome face, in his eyes, his brow was furrowed, his eyes had a sadness in them which dimmed their glow. In his fear he raged at me, and I raged back.

I told him I would not live as a prisoner, for that was what he had made me, that I would leave him and never return to him. Then taking my son with me I ran to the mouth of the druids' cave and screaming for my freedom I wished the veil open and stepped out onto the green turf of the mountain above Hengwm.

Fearing that the wrath of Eryr would have him chase me down and take me back, I ran, Calon strapped to my back, down the valley and around the bend in the stream.

There they were, all of them, Gwyn, Marged, Tally and an old couple who I guessed were Gwyn's parents, with a younger woman, that would be Gwennie and there was little Edward, walking already, toddling around in the grass, and Aria in her mother's arms.

The whole family were taking their ease in the field alongside the stream, how I had missed their company. Talking amongst themselves, watching while the children basked and played in the spring sunshine.

I straightened my clothing and checked that I had attired myself in something suitable for the times, and had not left wearing garb, more suited to life below the mountain.

Adopting my best nonchalant walk, I strolled towards them, would they recognise me, how would they receive me, was I still a friend or had time and circumstance turned them against me.

It was Marged who saw me first, she froze, incredulous, then rose from her nest in the long grass of the meadow and ran towards me.

'Red, oh Red, you are back, you are alive'.

Tally followed 'Mistress Red, it is good to see you, where is Owain? Is he not with you? Is he dead?'

They hugged me and kissed my cheeks, both sides. A plaintive howl from my back, and Calon announced his presence, Marged took him from me, and laid him on her cloak in the grass where his chubby legs and fists punched at the sky in joy to be free of his bindings.

Gwyn rose to his feet, he took me by the arm, 'let us walk', he said 'I have much to ask you, and not a little to say to you'.

He turned to Marged 'look after the child Marged, we will not be long'.

We walked along the bank of a stream which would change little in five hundred years.

'Firstly, I forgive you' he announced 'I saw you plain as day, I know neither I nor Woodstock was your target, Secondly, it is not safe for you here, the Prince takes a great interest in our affairs, he was distressed at the way I came here, annoyed that his justice was not seen to be done. There is only one who he is more angered with, and he has faced a traitor's death in London. I may smooth your path, but his majesty may not forgive you as I do.

Next, where is Owain, for that is his son you have born, the child is his image, is he dead, or charmed as I was? Red, this is time for truth. I am alive, but I hear voices telling me of my life to come, that I have been destined to live, more years than a man should live. The witch calls me, for it was she that brought me back. But I saw you also, in my fever. Tell me now, what are you, and who am I'.

I told him everything I knew, I told him where and when I came from, I told him of who Owain was really, and what Lady Margaret was. I told him as much as I could remember from my school books about a King born in Wales, my memory was sketchy, but I was sure I would remember more if I thought hard on it.

'Live your life Gwyn', I told him, 'there are hard times coming, Eryr and I have seen it, you must try and keep your family safe. For there is no cure for the plague which comes, only to try not to get sick with it. That is why I came back; I could not watch you die again and do nothing'.

'And Owain, or Eryr as you call him?'

'Eryr can go whistle,' I said, knowing full well he would be listening 'I am neither his wife nor his slave, I will do as I choose, and I choose to be here, and now,' But my heart already missed him, my soul already bled for the hurt and anger I had caused him, but I did not yet have the words to say sorry. I hoped that he would find me again in time and find it in his stubborn faerie heart to forgive me.

We had walked the length of the meadow as far as the stone stile which led to the pathway to the house, he took my arm and we turned and made the walk back once again happy in each other's company.

I needed to find a place to live, Myrddin told me of a small cottage just outside the village, it was in need of some repairs, but it was built on the land which had been gifted to Gwyn after Crecy by the Prince. It had two downstairs rooms, two bedrooms and an attic, he said, a good garden and a large outbuilding, it would do well and Tally and Gwennie could help me fix it up.

Through the spring we worked on the cottage, repaired the roof, fixed the doors and windows, made it weatherproof. By Calon's first birthday in May 1349, I had moved in, the garden was planted with herbs and beans and my first small potato crop. I had pressed my first crop of apples to make cider and considering my future here, I had more room than I needed for me and Calon. I sensed an opportunity.

By the time hay making came around my second downstairs room was open for business, christened The Sun, it was open to sell home brewed ale and cider when the hay was made, and The Sun was out. There was no bar as I knew it, it was just a single room at the front of the cottage. Partitioned from my own accommodation by a wooden wall more suited to a stable than a dwelling. The Sun proved popular, and I was soon kept busy with the farm labourers from the village who came for refreshment on their way home from the fields, I had a home, and I had an income of sorts. The Meredith's had explained me as a relative who had travelled from the North in search of work. A husband, yes. I had one who would follow me, he was a soldier in the King's army they said, and still in service.

Calon grew like a weed, just after his first birthday he was walking and shortly after came his first word, Ed! He was besotted with Edward and treated him as his big

516

brother, I could only envisage the scrapes the two of them would get into later in their lives.

It was the late summer of 1349 word from the coast was that the sickness had reached London and that the dead were piled in the streets, the Black Death as it had been called was rampaging through the land spreading like wildfire from person to person in the cramped houses of the cities. There seemed to be no escape from it but to avoid contact with people, not to go where there were crowds.

The King's daughter, Joan, had died from the disease in London and the King had made a list of penalties and punishments for those who he thought were instrumental in spreading death.

The people were too sick to work, yet he still collected his taxes, so to pay their dues they took risks and fell ill.

In my own time my training had told me that the disease was passed by the bites of fleas which lived in clothing and in the bales of wool and cloth shipped in from abroad.

This far into the countryside we had few imported goods, we spun our own wool and flax for linen, no danger there then, as long as we kept ourselves clean and laundered regularly.

We would know the sickness because of the headache and fever, the swellings in the armpit the rash all over the body, turning gradually black, and then death. It would also spread by the racking cough which sometimes came with it, death came more quickly then, with the sick coughing and vomiting blood until they met their end.

All was well until the end of the summer when the time came for Myrddin to travel down to Brecon to the market to sell the excess from the farm and purchase stores of the things we could not grow such as salt for the winter. Myrddin and several other of the village farmers had driven the pigs the fat lambs before them to the market town and they had sold well, he had done his rounds of the market stalls and purchased the items on the list which I had given him and then he and the other men had adjourned to the Blue Boar on the high street to slake their thirst before starting the journey back. It was there that they had encountered the small, wizened traveller with his back pack full of carvings made by sailors come from the east, scrimshaw carved in the form of lace making bobbins, wouldn't Anwen just love these he said and after haggling a good price with the toothless old man he settled both on a set of intricately decorated bone bobbins and also a fine wool shawl edged in Flanders lace. The pedlar said that he had come from the North Counties of England and made no mention of any sickness, though he had a racking cough and was very short of breath. Myrddin shook his hand and embraced him, bargain made Myrddin, and men of St Harmon started the three-day journey back to the village.

He had been home about three days when he started to cough, a chill he thought, just a chill, then the fever started and the tell-tale swellings in his neck and under his arms.

I made his bed in the cave behind the house and kept him isolated from the rest of the family, Myrddin was a tough old customer and resolutely refused to succumb to this terrible sickness, he was sick for weeks until eventually the Black Death claimed the first victim in the Meredith family.

We buried him in the small field at the rear of the cottage, the field which would become well used for this purpose.

He was not the only victim of the sickness, little Edward became sick shortly after his grandfather, I cooled his little body with cloths and held him while he screamed with the pain of the headache, and I called on those that I had not called on for months to come to my aid.

After he had been sick for a week and this once robust child was reduced to a limp rag like form in my arms, I remembered my own roots, and took him in my arms and up to the Druids cave, I knew that he was dying so I placed him on the stone altar, and I begged the faeries to take him. I should have known that he would be there.

I sensed his presence on the other side of the veil, in this time but behind the walls of the mountain. I felt my being quicken as he stepped into the gloom of the cave, a tall dark, satanic looking being, red eyed and feral looking in the darkness.

Was this the Eryr that I had loved that I still loved, what had become of him. He was unkempt, his hair uncombed and loose, his beard untrimmed and ragged and his eyes rimmed with dark circles and pain.

Full of bravado, though I could see that his heart was not in his words he spoke.

'Why do you return Red? I have no need of you now'.

'I do not come for myself, I come for this child'.

'What would you have me do? '

'Take this sick child as a changeling, I beg you'.

'You beg me! Did I not beg you, Beg you not to leave, beg you to stay away from this terrible curse of death?'

'Please, for the love you once held for his father do this thing.'

'Merch Goch, do you think that we have children to spare, that we would just replace on a whim, you have forsaken your roots, and this child is not yours to exchange, I fear that I cannot'.

'Bastard! I called him, you could, you just choose to punish me, if I hurt you I am sorry, what would you have me do in exchange for his life?'

I made my bargain, I agreed that once he was grown I would return Calon to him to be taught about his heritage, I agreed that I would spend one more night with him before I returned to Hengwm.

I handed Edward's limp form to Eryr, he held the child close against his chest he stepped back through the veil taking the child with him.

'Where are we going?' I called after him.

'Waun Mawn, to see my father.'

520

I wrapped my old cloak around me and thought invisible, I could hear Marged and Gwyn calling my name in the valley below, searching for me, wondering where I had gone and what had become of their child.

It was dawn before Eryr returned, the dawn of 31st October 1349, the light flooded into the druids' cave and lit up the great stone altar, Aegir was there in person, a great flame haired presence floating in shadow above the stone. As he disappeared back into his own space and time I saw a bundle appear on the stone, a child, red haired as Edward had been, healthy and strong crying out loudly for his mother. I took him in my arms and from the bottom of my heart said a prayer of thanks for whatever had just happened.

Then he returned, Eryr, was there, his appearance had regained its usual form, dark beard trimmed to a heavy stubble hair brushed back and tied, his eyes still looked tired.

'take the child to his home, to them he will be the Edward they have always known, but he is and always will be a special child, and you should know this, the child who my father chose is your own brother. His father is Deargan, and his mother is Helena. He is a changeling and as with all of our blood he will live forever in one guise or another he may never marry outside of the Faerie kingdom, and he may never have children of his own. These are the conditions that my father has put on this bargain. Now go and do not forget that you too have a bargain with me, do not think I will forget'.

I reached up and kissed his lips and tried to draw him close, but he resisted, 'Go now Red, I am sorry, I was wrong, I see now that your folk need you, when you are done with this, remember that I love you and come home'.

'One thing more' I asked, 'what is his true name?' 'He is Bleddyn named for the Wolf'.

I met Marged and Gwyn on the path, 'I did it I found him'.

'Who?' they said.

'Y Ddraig' I lied, 'I found the caves where his breath was strong, and he has healed your son'.

I handed Edward back to his mother and we walked back to the cottage.

We lost both of Gwyn's parents to the sickness, Anwen died quickly, within days of the cough starting, it was merciful that she did not suffer as her husband had done. The rest of us, Aria, Calon, Gwennie, and Tal and myself all managed to avoid catching the plague which had killed whole villages.

We had not been to the village itself for months, I had stayed at Hengwm away from people and infection and isolation had worked.

The people of St Harmon were not so sure, many of the villagers had died from the Black Death, they wondered how the Meredith family had managed to survive, there was talk of Dragon's Breath, of strange goings on in the Druids' cave and as always followed these things, rumours of witchcraft. The finger was firmly pointed at me. There were those who believed that I was just a healer but there were those whose superstitious and uneducated minds could not see that we had suffered death in the family just as they had.

Who it was that had mentioned Gwynt y Ddraig to the villagers I would never find out, I did not like to blame Taliesin for having loose lips, but he did get talkative in his drink.

Christmas of 1349 passed without much celebration, there was after all not much to celebrate. By the New Year the wave of plague had washed over our mountain home leaving a trail of empty cottages, widows and orphans behind it, farms that had lain fallow for a whole season and animals who had gone half wild from lack of care. It was February 1350 when the messenger came from London.

It was Elgan, he rode up to Hengwm on a white horse who I recognised as old Dylan who had been in the Prince's stable at Llantrisant, he was filthy with road dust and glad to have found us.

Hengwm has few visitors and most of those are lost.

Prince Edward the Black Prince sent a letter and was travelling only a few days behind him. Should I run and hide or should I pray that he like most visitors gets lost.

CHAPTER 89 – A FLYING VISIT

I broke the seal on the letter and read:

Cardiff

Wales

February 1350

My Dear Gwyn

I write to you as friend and hope that you receive this letter as such. I have heard that you are now recovered from your wounds received at Crecy. I will always be in your debt for the service which you gave me on that campaign.

I find that I am again in Wales, but I do not propose to visit that hilltop hellhole called Llantrisant, except to converse briefly with another old friend.
I expect that you have heard that Sir Hugh de Audley was swiftly dealt with for his many crimes.

I am still curious as to what happened to your comrade Owain, a brave fighter indeed and another to whom I am indebted, when last seen he was assisting that convicted witch and murderer Sybil in her escape from justice. There is still a pyre with her name on it should she ever be found. But as with my cousin Lady Margaret witches can be hard to destroy.

I propose to visit you at your home, my reasons are two-fold, firstly I have legal documents which you will need to keep as proof of your title to the land, and secondly to seek advice from your good wife the healer Marged. I find myself suffering from a malaise of my intestines which I have acquired whilst on campaign in France.

I send Elgan with this message hoping that he is able to find you on your remote farm, I travel some three days behind him. I travel with only one companion and body servant and would make use only of one of your fields for my tent and horses.
Yours
Edward Prince of Wales

P.S

My travelling companion has been to your farm several times knows the road well. There is no need to send Elgan to meet us.

Marged flew into a fit of cleaning and polishing, how were we to accommodate a Prince, the cottage was tiny, only two rooms downstairs and upstairs, and only just with glass in the windows. By lunchtime the following day the old oak furniture gleamed, and the floor had been swept to within an inch of its life. Any occupants found trespassing on the newly mopped flagstones were likely to be skewered with my sword, which Elgan was busy cleaning and sharpening or beaten with Gwennie's rolling pin. Dirt and mess was not to be tolerated.

As far as we could with our meagre supplies left after the winter, Gwennie had baked enough pies and tarts to fill the larder several times over and Tally and I slung our bows and leaving Marged who swore that she was still a better shot at a deer than Tally, to look after Edward and Aria we went in search of game.

Red had made herself scarce, she had been quiet since Edward's illness and had kept Calon protectively close to her for weeks. I had heard the rumours about her in the village, but she had never-the-less opened the Sun for customers once more, and the villagers were getting accustomed to her again. Only I knew the true nature of her being and if there was a time for her to return to her former life then now was the time, given the contents of the Prince's letter.

Marged on the other hand had other ideas. Marged had been asked to treat the Prince's ailment, she was a well-practiced healer but was nervous of treating such an esteemed personage as the Prince of Wales, she had sought Red's advice and Red had disappeared for several days returning with several possible remedies for the Prince to try.

CHAPTER 90 – MEDICINE AT ITS FINEST – RED

Marged and Gwyn showed me the letter, I was not forgiven then, nor was I likely to be. Owain on the other hand would probably be greeted like the prodigal son. Elgan had described the Prince's symptoms to me, his bouts of sweating and shivering with vomiting and the blazing shits. He said that his lord would be free of this malaise for months but then it would return, and he would be forced to take to his bed unable to do much but curl up in agony or lie shaking and barely conscious with all about him fearing that he might die.

Malaria – he would have picked up the disease from the mosquitos of the coast of southern Europe, there was nothing I could think of which grew on our shores which I could use as a source of Quinine which would calm the fever and relieve the symptoms.
Could I ask a favour of Eryr, would he help Marged without expecting something in return. I could only ask him, I already owed him a debt, one more would not harm.

I went to the Druids' cave, and I called him, he knew I was there, he was waiting. Had he been listening all the time, reading my every thought, second guessing my intentions.

'Come with me then' he said, if I am to go to the ends of the earth for a Prince then you should at least come with me. How am I to know what to bring back. I am no healer, where shall I find your Chinchona Bark?'
He smiled his best lopsided winning smile and cocked his head to one side, right eyebrow raised in a question.

'Come with me Red, it will be an adventure, we have been short on adventure lately. Bring Calon, he can fly with us'.

I stepped into his realm once more and was swept up into his strong arms, no longer the unhappy, careworn being of a few months ago, he seemed happy or at least content. He kissed me and held me close to him, 'It is good to see you Red, since you took the child for Edward I have talked a great deal with my father, I have been harsh with you, he has made me see that. I will not make you honour our bargain if you do not wish to. But am I allowed to hope?'

I answered his kiss in the affirmative with my own, 'First we go adventuring.'

We flew across the great ocean and South over the curve of the earth to South America, not yet discovered by Christopher Columbus it had always been there, lying in wait for another hundred years at least, yet here we were thanks to my advance knowledge. The jungle was thick and swarming with mosquitos which pestered Eryr and Calon biting Eryr savagely on his arms and chest. Calon took shelter in his father's great black wings and pointed excitedly at the multi-coloured birds in the trees and the strange animals lying basking on the shores.

I found the trees and took what I thought I would need from their branches, stripping off the bark and placing it in a pouch slung over my shoulder for the trip back.

'Do Faeries have a weight limit?' I joked.

'Aye we do' came the reply, 'go easy with the trees could you, I can always come back'.

It was Eryr who suggested that we try taking a sapling for the Prince to grow in his hot house, for he had such a thing to grow oranges from trees given him by the King of Spain.

There and back in one day, I arrived back at Hengwm just before breakfast, we hung the bark to dry above the fire in the cottage in long strips. Before I made my exit to avoid the Prince I told her to how to make it into a tea, allowing it to steep and release the Quinine into the water, the Prince should be advised to drink the mixture only when he has an attack and then not to take too much of it. Tell him if the mixture makes hm feel sick then that is too much. It will calm his fever and his intestines. As a preventative he could take a diluted drink of it in boiled water every morning. This should stop the symptoms from recurring.

If you have need of me call me, send Gwennie down to the Sun, I will be there, but it is best I do not see the Prince.

CHAPTER 91 – A ROYAL VISIT TAKE TWO

As visits from royalty go it was a low-key visit, no
fanfare of trumpets, no advance party, just the
appearance of two horses riding side by side towards
the cottage and one solitary servant driving a mule and
wagon mule just behind.

The man who dismounted from the black horse
called Bryn was slight and wiry, weathered by hard miles
on the road, his blonde hair slightly unkempt under his
velvet bonnet, his face clean shaven, his eyes blue, but
tired looking and his smile as easy and welcoming as
ever. But the youth of 16 was now a man of 20 with the
look of a man of well beyond those years. It was hard to
see that he and Gwyn were the same age.

Was this the havoc that Malaria would wreak on a
body, the constant threat of an attack of fever and
diarrhoea, fear of eating anything that would bring on
the waves of nausea which pre-empted the agonising
clenching and voiding of the bowels with no control or
dignity?

His companion on the other hand rode a stocky
chestnut horse of indeterminate age, Trooper had been

carrying his master for many years, from the shelter of the tree where I watched I recognised the old horse, and the rider.

Sir Kenneth Fitzsimons sat tall in his saddle, his grey hair cropped short, his grey beard neatly trimmed and his merry brown eyes twinkling over a needlessly grim mouth which tried to hide the suggestion of a smile.

Elgan ran forward to take the horses, and the mule, Tally and Gwyn unloaded the wagon and began to erect the Prince's travelling tent in the upper meadow next to the cottage, Elgan untracked the horses and mule and turned them out into the lower meadow by the stream, where they happily dropped to the floor and rolled in the grass.

Gwyn gestured to the front door and ushered his royal guest into the building. Edward of Woodstock paused slightly, his attention caught by some movement on the path leading to the hillside.

I was about to take myself to my refuge at the Sun when I saw a figure strolling down the path from the mountain.

He wouldn't! He would never dare! it was Owain, I cut him off at the turn in the road, you cannot go in there, are you mad.'

'I will have it out with him, we have done him great service, saved his miserable hide many times, both in battle and from sickness and injury. For myself, I don't care but can he not pardon you as he has forgiven others, maybe he should see who I really am, am I not just as much of a Prince as he is, do I not deserve at least that much respect?'

He was in such a temper he lost control, Black wings sprouted from his shoulders, his eyes glowed feral beneath his brows, Eryr emerged in all his magnificence, just in time to see Edward Woodstock Prince of Wales emerge from Hengwm into the path before us.

He was unarmed, he was unaccompanied, unguarded, yet completely unafraid. He looked Eryr up and down, appraisingly, then smiled, the smile lit his tired face and his blue eyes sparkled with intelligence as they had done in the days before Crecy, before he became ill.

'Friend Owain, it is good to see you, it has been many months since your strange departure, welcome back'.

Eryr was lost for words, with some effort he brought Owain back to the fore and made a courtly bow before the King's son. Eryr would never bow, it was not in his nature, proud and stubborn Fae that he was.

The Prince continued:

'I always knew you were different, you came from nowhere, had no past, the men loved you, respected you, but no one knew you. You had no kin, no family, no roots. It becomes clear now, you were never of our world'.

'Sire? What can you mean, I am Owain y Mynydd, your humble and most loyal servant sir!'

'Faerie, you are far more than that, do you think your Prince stupid, I had schooling you know, I was taught of many things apart from Latin and scripture, I was taught folklore, superstition, what my people believe and what they fear, I believe that your kind exist, and not just in the minds of simple folk'.

'So, you saw then Sire?'

'Wings and all,' came the reply. 'Who are you truly, and where is that Red woman for she cannot be far away, is she of your kind too?'

'I am Adain Eryr, I too am a Prince, in my own place and my own time, my folk have lived in harmony with this land since time began'.

Owain disappeared and Eryr stood there towering head and shoulders above Edward, arms folded across a broad chest clad in snowy linen, long legs encased in black leather, black wings folded neatly away between his massive shoulders.

I stepped out from behind the wall where I had been hiding, I curtsied deeply, 'Sire, forgive me, my skills are at your disposal'.

'Walk with me' he said, 'both of you, I am a sick man, I do not wish to punish more than I have to, there must be a way for all to live and for some form of justice to be seen to be done. I cannot let you go unpunished, but now that Sir Hugh de Audley is safely dispatched from this earth, and with my father growing more moderate with age, there may be a way.

And so, we walked, and he talked, then he listened, and it was agreed.

Owain would serve him in his army, as before, and when needed Eryr would find the bark the Prince so needed to treat his illness. He would serve until the Prince's death, when required.

In return I was free to stay but banished from Llantrisant never to return, and as a human I was bound to live within sight of the mountain on the ground held by Gwyn Meredith or his family.

There were still things the Prince did not need to know about, and crossing the veil was one of them. He could bind me to nothing outside of his own time.

That night after walking the hillsides with us Prince Edward took a chill, his fever made his body shake with cold and then with heat in turn, sweat ran down his face and his body soaking the bed on which he lay.

I sat by his side pressing cold linen cloths to his forehead and cooling his limbs by soaking them in the water from the brook. I fed him sips of the Chinchona infusion I had made with the bark we had fetched from that, as yet undiscovered far away land. I had planted one of the saplings in the small wood behind the cottage and hoped that it would grow in the warmth provided by our underground resident. The earth was warm there and heaven knows Wales had enough rainfall to imitate the tropics.

The fever broke and then the vomiting and blazing shits started. His bowels were so affected that I began to believe that he was also suffering from dysentery, what food he ate either came straight back up through his mouth or hastened its way through the end result being a full slops bucket. It was no wonder he had become so thin; his body was getting hardly any nourishment from his food.

For four days he remained in his bed, gradually the chinchona bark worked its magic and he was able to eat without vomiting. My Royal guinea pig had been tested with varying strength of the infusion I prepared, to find a strength which stopped his symptoms but had no nasty side effects. Too strong a mix and he had started to hallucinate, seeing serpents and goblins in his sleep, clawing at his head with his hands and crying for mercy.

By the beginning of the second week, he was much improved, by the end of that week his strength had returned, he walked the mountain with Gwyn and Owain and Tally and Sir Kenneth, he played with the children, taking them on his knee and bouncing them, leading both Edward his namesake and Aria around the meadow on Bryn and Calon on Trooper.

He talked with Sir Kenneth late into the night, the old knight's health was failing him, he could no longer walk the mountain with his Prince and keep up as he used to. Yet he had lagged along behind them manfully, stopping to rest every few minutes, or excusing himself to take his own path.

He had found he said 'a cave of great peace, there he said he felt at home, would he said that it could be my final resting place.

The night before they were due to leave, Sir Kenneth went for one more walk on the mountain, he did not return, he had gone on foot leaving old Trooper in the meadow below the cottage.

The men of the village were called out and they searched for a whole day, the Prince postponed his departure until the search was given up as fruitless. The body of Sir Kenneth Fitzsimons was never found, and no sign of him was left behind. Prince Edward left the following day, he seemed unconcerned with his friend's fate, only saying to Gwyn and Owain, he is not dead, he is with her, and I wish him well.

Gwyn and Owain rode with him that day, off on another campaign to France. Yet more wars to retain a hold on land across the sea which in my view we could never reasonably call ours. Marged and I did not ride with them, I had agreed to be bound to the land at St Harmon and it would not do for me to be seen alive by the archers of Llantrisant. Many of them had branded me a murderess and a witch and would likely see me burned or hanged outright. I had my plans; I knew what I would do. Marged had children and a home to run.

Before they left I bid Eryr take Calon back beyond the veil, to begin his schooling, and I walked with him again this time back to my own time.

CHAPTER 92 – GONE NOT DEAD – GWYN

Edward was now as old as I had been when I left Hengwm to follow the Black Prince of Wales for the last time, after his visit to the farm I had kissed Marged goodbye, for what I know now would be the final time, I had held my children Edward and Aria close to me and felt their hearts beating close to mine.

I took my father's sword and my longbow from where they hung on the walls of that secret cave below the house and rolled them in my cloak. Packing what I needed in my bundle and travelling light, I mounted Sir Kenneth's old horse, Trooper, for he was in the field and pining for his master.

Owain had materialised from his mountain to join with us, the Prince had been long in conversation with both Owain and Red before he agreed to come. Red did not ride with us and neither did Marged.

We were all young then, I was twenty when the Prince of Wales came to our humble farm, he and I were of an age.

I had known that he would call on me again to fight with his army, both Owain and I would follow and be loyal to him until him until his death.

For nearly ten years we were away on campaign in various parts of France, we celebrated victories, and we mourned our dead all the time becoming more battle worn and tired. The King was a hard task master demanding ever more of his son in the way of conquest over the French, all of us longed for peace.

The Black Prince returned from campaign in France suffering more than ever from his malaise, the malaria as Marged had called it. The remedy which Red had made for him and which he returned to her for throughout his life had ceased to work and he became weaker and more debilitated by the fevers vomiting and diarrhoea it brought.

The Prince himself had married and now had two sons, Edward his son and heir, born in France and a candidate to rule over both England and France together. A lad destined to die before his seventh birthday. His second son Richard must take on that heavy mantle of responsibility before even reaching manhood.

In 1371 after the death of his oldest son and his return home from yet another campaign in France, he released me from his service, and I returned to St Harmon.

I arrived home to the news that the Black death had come calling and that both my wife, Marged, and my sister Gwennie, and her children had been taken, her husband Taliesin with who had fought alongside me at Crecy had also died that terrible death. They had taken their own farm nearby and should not have come back to see to Marged, where was Red when we needed her, banished by his highness, and gone. Had she been there could she have saved them?

As sure as the body of my Prince grows cold in his tomb, I feel a great tiredness come over me.

I begin to hear a familiar voice of old call me more and more often in my dreams, and my dreams became more filled with visions of that red scaled beast I had seen once before. I see her there now, that tall stately woman commanding the spirits to do her will, she calls me to an unknown destiny, and I must go.

We have little use now for quill and ink, but there is still a few sheets of parchment and a quill in Marged's old chest, and some water will soon loosen the ink which has dried in its pot. Marged, God bless her, she taught all the children their letters. I must write everything down for my Edward before I am called.

Hengwm
1376

Edward my son

I write because I may not have opportunity to tell you
what I must.

It is time for me to tell you of my life, much you already
know from the tales we tell round the fire; you know of
my great sickness and of how your mother and her
friend took care of me. How I recovered and how I was
called to serve once again in the Prince's Black Army.

My illness was no accident, and the price of my cure was
great, much of it has yet to be paid.

Deep in this mountain sleeps the guardian of this land,
with him lies the woman who will seek payment from
me. That time is coming, I feel a great tiredness in my
bones.

When that time comes, you will believe me dead, but I
am not. Lay me in the cave below the farm, leave with

me my sword and my bow, my weapons of war then seal up the entrance, for she will call me, and I must go with her.

I leave all that I have to you my son and to Aria your sister.
All that is listed in the parchment locked in your mother's wooden coffer was gifted to us by my Prince, for the loyalty of my body and my mind and the services of my bow. This is your land my son, care for it well.

Your father
Gwyn ap Meredith

As the ink left my quill I felt myself gone again and the ink which dried on the page closed another chapter of my life.

Later that day I heard the door to the cottage creak open, I heard Aria scream when she saw my slumped form at the table, I heard the muffled conversation between my son and my daughter, then I felt strong arms carry me to a place of darkness and for now a place of peace.

My limbs became heavy, and I slept, cradled once again in the warm breath of the dragon, waiting for her call.

CHAPTER 93 – EDWARD MEREDITH

I carried the limp body of my father down the stone steps to the cave, he was still warm and still breathing, though I could hardly see his chest moving. Already in the cave was the box bed my mother said he had been carried home in from Crecy.

I laid him in that bed like some form of ancient knight, with his arms crossed over his chest, the bed was lined with a soft cape of fur pelts, I pulled this around his shoulders despite the cave being warm, then I laid his sword and his longbow in the bed alongside him.

Aria and I both laid a final kiss of farewell on his forehead and then left the cave; I did not look back.

I shut the rough wood door behind us and before nightfall I had filled the stairway with rubble, no one should enter that cave again.

That night my sister and I sat in silent prayer before the fire.

'He was gone' she said, 'When I turned and looked back, he was gone, the bed was empty'.

In time my sister Arianrhod took to walking on the mountain in search of her father, she insisted that some magic had spirited him away. Eventually she moved from the farm into the village and reopened the Sun Inn, she never married despite several offers from local men. All people have an allotted time and Aria is buried in the graveyard behind the house with our mother and the rest of our kin.

It is now the year of our Lord fourteen hundred and forty-seven, it is the first of June and I have been on this earth for a hundred years. It is past my time to leave this place but there is something which keeps me here. The gossips in the village remark that I have not aged a bit in years and that I still look half my age. My hair is still an indelicate shade of ginger, my teeth are still in my head, top and bottom and my eyes are not yet cloudy with age. I look at my reflection in the water trough in the yard and wonder whether there were other things my father should have told me. I have no way to find out, and why worry about what I cannot change.

The farm is prosperous, I am still able to run it single handed, the cottage now has an extra room downstairs and has proper windows, I have built a byre for the cows and the goat, the Sun Inn of which I am owner is doing well and is being run by a local man who took over from my sister when she passed away.
All I can do is live from day to day and face each one as it comes. But I do wonder why it is that I am kept here

for longer than my allotted three score and ten. Maybe I am to be here forever, in the meantime while God decides what he has in store for me I shall walk down to the Sun Inn and take a mug of ale and a slice of their very good pie.

PART NINE

CHAPTER 94 - RETURN TICKET ST HARMON 1895

I stepped back into my own time, leaving Calon with his father, I must trust Eryr to raise our son.

No parting kiss, no chance to tell him, I walked through the druids' cave, turned and he was gone, did he know I was with child, did he sense it, was that why he had agreed I should come back.

Now here I was walking down the mountain path which led to Hengwm and then to the village. What would I tell everyone, life hadn't worked out in Llantrisant, keep it simple, that was best.

Sheep were grazing peacefully on either side of the path, a squirrel took refuge up a nearby tree as I passed, heading down the hill towards the house I had left 5 minutes and half a century ago.

And there he was, fitting the final stones into the top of a dry-stone wall, sleeves rolled up, shirt open at the neck, jacket hung on a nearby bush.

'Uncle Edward' I greeted him, lifting the broad brimmed hat I had selected from my faerie wardrobe, and waving it above my head.

His great white whiskers wobbled as his face broke into a broad smile, and his shock of white hair shook as he turned his head in disbelief.

'Sibyl, Sibyl girl, I never thought to see you back here, was Llantrisant that awful then, did that new doctor not treat you right? '

'No Uncle, I just felt, well, homesick, I missed you, I missed this place.'

I hugged the old man, squeezing hard, trying to settle in my mind that the man I called Uncle was really my brother and that he really was very very old indeed.

'You'll stay then, your old room is still there, and I still have some of your things from the Sun?'

'Only for a few days, I need to find work, I must go to Rhayader first thing'.

There is one thing about travelling through time, you travel light, no luggage, no belongings, only what you are wearing.

One of the advantages of being part Faerie is that you can dress yourself appropriately for your journey.

I installed myself in what was now Uncle Edward's spare room, in the attic at Hengwm, tidied my hair and went downstairs to find that the old man was preparing a meal for us, the griddle pan was on the range, and I could smell sausage and bacon cooking.

'Quick fry up, then down to the Sun and let everyone know you are back then'. His enthusiasm was bubbling over in an unseemly fashion for a gentlemen of his years.

The following day I caught Ginger from the field behind the house and harnessed the old boy to the light trap Edward used on Sundays and drove to Rhayader, intent on visiting the apothecary. I wasn't sure what I would look for when I arrived there, but I was sure Mr Isaias Rees would have some ideas.

Sitting up front on the seat of Edward's Sunday gig, I flicked the reins at Ginger's hind quarters and clicked my tongue at him in the way you do to an old friend. It's not a describable noise, it's just the squelchy click your tongue makes when sucked through your back teeth. He in turn flicked his handsome little inward curving ears, first backwards then forwards, groaned slightly then leant into his collar and pulled us into forward motion.

'Walk on! Good lad!' I encouraged as we set off along the road out of the village and over the mountain towards the market town of Rhayader.

Several hours later I was handing the reins to Joshua the Ostler at The Blue Boar and making my way down the street towards Mr Reese's shop.

The shop front had not changed, the small leaded windows still shone with cleanliness a thing totally next door to godliness in the apothecary's manual. The bell above the door still announced the arrival of a potential customer.

And there behind the counter was William, formally attired of course, no shirt sleeves for William, now sporting whiskers and a brisk business-like manner.

'Good Morning Ma.....' He had heard the bell ring as the door opened but had not yet looked up from his work. 'Sybil, is it really you, welcome back, come through, come through.'

He simultaneously lifted the counter flap, gestured me towards the back room and reached across to turn the sign on the door to closed.

We have missed you; I have missed you, there is so much to tell, how was Dr Price, we have heard so much about him in the broadsheets, he is quite the character!

I was swept through to the inner sanctum on a wave of gossip and boyish enthusiasm. William had not changed at all.

'How is your father?' I asked cautiously, for there was no sign of Isaias on the premises.

'Poor father died last year, of an apoplexy, it was sudden, one minute he was serving Nan Trenant with her new ague cure and the next he was staring sightless at the ceiling, dead as a door nail.'

'And your mother?'

'She still lives at Pen y Banc, I live with her, and we rattle around together in that big house, but she is well, missing Da, but well never the less, you must come and tame the herb garden for us, it is quite out of control, Da built a glass house to cultivate plants from the Americas, they seem to have colonised us in return and are now seeking their independence! Some fascinating and useful species! Jesuit bark in particular, most useful in cases of ague, ask Nan Trenant.'

We talked for the better part of the morning, and by the time he took me to lunch in the Bear Hotel, I was fully abreast of all of the more salacious gossip of the town. Who had married who while I was away, who was unmarried but with child, whose husband had run off with the barmaid from the Crown Inn. The scandalous price of cheese, and his need for an assistant, to start as soon as possible, and a gardener to suppress the rebellion in his herb garden at Pen y Banc.

Terms agreed, I could live in at the big house, bed and board provided, travel to town daily with him, help with the running of the shop, and manage the garden on my one day off and for performing this list of Herculean tasks would receive a small wage.

I was overjoyed, so overjoyed that I omitted to tell him that I would be expecting company in about six months' time. I would cross that bridge when it became necessary.

Ginger and I arrived back at Hengwm on a wave of hope for the future, to break the news to Edward. Uncle was matter of fact about it, positively phlegmatic,

'You know you always have a home here, you must choose your own path girl, but when it goes awry, you come home do you hear me?'

I heard him, loud and clear.

That night as I slept in my old cot bed in the attic, I heard more than Edward snoring, I heard the sounds of battle far away, horses screaming in pain, the whoosh of arrows fired in volley, the clang of swords and the grunts of men as they tried to end each other's lives, an unearthly animal scream ripped me to the core, and then silence.

I was shaking, I was sweating, my hand reached to my left thigh and found moisture, I cautiously put the hand to my nose and smelled the metallic smell of fresh blood, but not my blood, on further inspection my skin was unbroken, but there it was, a red stain on my palm, was he wounded?

I knew that Faeries bled just as humans bled, and that they could die, they were not totally infallible, hard to kill but not impossible.

I rose from my bed and sat by the tiny window in the roof and stared up at the stars, was Eryr lying helpless under a different sky?

I was lost in my thoughts and did not hear him, yet I felt his presence as I lay my head back on my pillow, head turned so I could still see the night sky.

Those tiny twinkling lights now seeming to be the only connection between us, what stars could be seen tonight.

'I see the same stars as you, Red, will you not tend a wounded soldier?'

There he was, in the doorway of the room, head bowed to avoid the low beams, leaning on the door jamb for support.

His right leg was dripping blood on the floorboards, cut open from knee to hip the long muscle lying open to the air, and the pulse of his femoral artery clearly throbbing beneath the thinnest layer of tissue.

Was fuck a word an apothecaries assistant should use? It was a word as old as time itself. 'Fuck!' I said it again.

'That bad is it?'

'Fuck' I replied.

He handed me a familiar bundle of leather and cord, my roll of instruments.

'Is this useful?' then he slid to the floor, his massive frame filling the tiny room and still bleeding on Edward's scrubbed floorboards.

I climbed over the prostrate form and descended the narrow stairs two at a time and reached into the bottom of the Welsh dresser for Edwards brandy bottle. Half full I noted.

Back up the stairs, I uncorked the bottle took a regenerative swig for the nurse, then tipped a good amount on the wound. Eryr hissed like an angry snake.

'Sorry,' I said then I opened the leather roll of surgical tools, 'bite on this' I placed the leather gag between his teeth. 'Now hold tight and think of Faerie land'.

I took a long-curved needle with a longer length of silk thread hanging from it like a tail, and I began to stitch, starting just above his elegant knee, holding the edges of the wound together with one hand and wielding the needle with the other.

I kept my needles ready threaded and had used three by the time I reached his groin. Two neat stitches held the muscle closed over the pulsing artery, then a final three stitches in the skin.

'Fuck'

I sat back on my heels and admired my work. The patient was coming round, and dawn was breaking. I heard Uncle stir in his room below and the familiar sound of footsteps followed by the flow of liquid into china as he took his morning piss into his chamber pot.

'What the hell is going on up there' he shouted grumpily before I heard the bed creak as he sat on its edge to reach for his stockings. 'I'm off out to milk the cow, poke up the fire when you rise girl, and get the kettle on'.

'Best I be off then,' Eryr kissed me on the forehead and with no further explanation he vanished as quickly as he had come, along with all traces that he had ever been. Except for the tell-tale roll of surgeons' tools. I really had not been dreaming.

'It's alright Uncle, I just fell out of bed, I shall be down in a minute'.

I heard the door click on its latch and felt the inrush of cool morning air as it drifted up the stairs, dispersing the mild odour of fear both human and not.

I started work for William Rees on the following Monday and moved my life over the mountain to Penybanc by the end of the following week. It was strange to be back once more in the house where I learned so much, and which held so many disjointed memories, Mrs Jones, my former mentor mixed with what I now knew of my family, and my blood.

Would I ever travel again, did I need the excitement it brought, or would I be content to just be human for a while?

The child growing inside me would be born in the here and now, of that I was determined. Boy or girl it's feet would be grounded in the human world.

As time went on and my condition became more evident, William brought matters to a head. In the few months in which I had shared his house, his shop, and his elderly mother, we had grown to be great friends, he was entertaining if a little gushing in his manner. He loved to talk, he was educated, erudite, we shared a common love of books and history. He was handsome in his own way, always clean shaven, neatly dressed in a colourful way, hair never out of place. Since the death of Isaias his mother worried that William had never married, she had no grandchildren, no one to continue the family line.

I had an inkling of what might be the problem, William, while he loved the company of women, had no interest in them sexually. He liked his life just as it was. Days of flirting harmlessly with the ladies who came to the shop, always a compliment offered about a new hat, or a lovely shawl, suggestions of what might suit their needs in the way of pomanders and other scented products, demonstrations of his latest range of perfumes, developed in Mrs Jones' old still room, using the scents he distilled from the flowers he cultivated in the glass house he had built, the very glass house he wanted me to organise. The ladies loved him.

There was indeed a queue of eligible young things who would love a turn around the park on the arm of the dashing and flamboyant Young Mr Rees.

Of an evening he might be found in the smoke room of the Blue Boar or upstairs in the private lounge with the gentlemen of the town, enjoying a brandy and a good cigar, and a bawdy yarn at the expense of the barmaid's feelings, maintaining his public persona. The gentlemen loved him too.

It came out of the blue, it was evening we were in the glass house, I was trimming and weeding, re potting and organising the delinquent greenery into some form of order. He was picking flowers from his favourite orchid plants; he loved their vibrant colours and the heady scent of vanilla and chocolate they produced. Later he would take the petals and steep them in jars of light olive oil, leaving them until the oils and scent had merged together, he would spend hours experimenting with different combinations of aromas, adding spices and aromatics until he had produced the bouquet he wanted to achieve.

The result was dispensed in small ornate glass bottles to his more discerning customers, who would have their bottles refilled on a regular basis.

He tailored his scent to both men and women and had acquired a device with which he could spray the smell of flowers around his shop. The effects were two-fold, a lovely smelling shop with lovely smelling customers, which made a change from the smell of the great unwashed, and increased sales for the apothecary.

William turned from his work and presented me with a beautiful orchid flower,

'Sibyl, will you marry me?'

I looked at him speechless! My jaw worked up and down, but no words came out.

'It makes good sense, I know you are with child, I have eyes, and ears, I hear you retch every morning, and I see you have gained weight in certain areas, that child needs a father. I have a nagging mother, I need a wife, on paper if nothing else, it would quiet my mother, and also silence the talk around town of my morals, and of yours, for I hear the gossips, by their very nature they are indiscreet. Marry me and I will raise your child as mine, mother will be overjoyed, she will know no different, and her pride would not let her say otherwise if she did. I will ask nothing about the child's father, unless you wish to tell me. What befell you in Llantrisant I expect you would rather forget – think on it – give me your answer in a few days'.

Speech over he raised my left hand to his lips, looked me directly in the eyes, kissed my fingers and walked purposefully into the still room in a waft of vanilla scented orchid.

Swelling bellies wait for no one, every night for a week I tried to bring the child's father to mind, but for once he was not there, he was lost in the mist of time, 'you bastard', I cursed him roundly 'you will not hold this against me, I will do what I think best'.

I closed my eyes tight and cursed him again 'Damn you, I will marry him, tell me now if you object, or have done with it'.

We were married as soon as the banns had been read, three weeks, there was no murmur from beyond. I walked down the aisle on the arm of Uncle Edward, he gave me away and was glad for me. As the service progressed and we made our vows, I froze when the vicar asked that question ending 'speak now or forever hold your peace.'

No one spoke, and I walked from the tiny church at St Harmon as a respectable married woman, wife of the apothecary.

But he was there, I saw him, standing beneath the yew tree just out of sight, sardonic smile across his face, blood-stained sword in his hand and a longbow slung across his back. He had company, in the shadows I saw the echoes of my mother and grandmother, as I passed beneath the litch gate they disappeared.

Mrs William Rees mounted the carriage on the hand if her husband and we drive back to town for celebrations at the Blue Boar.

Truly a time of peace my daughter Rhianydd was born six months later, blessed with wild red curly locks just like my own, the green eyes of her father and destined to be tall, she grew to be a child of incredible intellect. Her sister was born five years later, William's own daughter, the result of a very drunken liaison after the death of his mother.

In all that time Eryr had been dead to me, my life was now filled with children and business, a house which welcomed visitors, and which seemed to swell to accommodate them.

Passage of time was now marked by endless domesticity a settled life, as my girls grew into young ladies.

Rhianydd off to medical school in London, one of the first women in Wales with the letters MD to her name, William and I nearly burst with pride at her graduation.

Her sister Helena at ten years old already wanting to 'be like dada' a chemist.

It was 1905 old century had ended and the new was five years old.

CHAPTER 95- BLACKMAIL

The letter came from a lawyer in Rhayader, it had taken some time to travel the short distance from West Street to Pen y Banc.

Messrs Lloyd and Roberts
West Street
Rhayader
For the attention of Mrs Sibyl Rees
Pen y Banc House
Rhayader

6th January 1905

Dear Mrs Rees,

We have been instructed to act on behalf of one Mr Owain Mynydd who is the appointed executor in the matter of the affairs of Mr Edward Meredith of whom we have been informed you are his next of kin.

Mr Edward Meredith has been missing now for seven years and application made to the High Court in Cardiff for a presumption of death has been granted, and his estate has passed through probate.

Mr Meredith did leave a Will, which has now been read and is simple in its construct.

The sole beneficiary of his estate is Mrs Sibyl Rees of Rhayader.

We would be pleased to welcome you at our offices on West Street to finalise these matters with our Mr Lloyd at your convenience.

Yours faithfully
G Roberts (solicitor)

So, he had left, I did not believe that for one minute.

What hand did Eryr have in this? I smelled Faerie dabbling.

I showed the letter to William who told me to go to the lawyers' offices and tell them that I wanted none of it, that whatever it was I had inherited should be sold and the money given to the poorhouse.

But what then of Gwyn, that wandering soul will truly have no anchor, I had often thought of him, what would happen to him once Lady Margaret was through with him.

I kept the appointment, and I signed the papers and became the formal owner of the house and contents and the land of Hengwm.

For the first time in twenty years, William was truly angry with me, eventually he accepted the fact that the place was mine. But he forbade me ever to go there, in his lifetime or in that of his daughter.

In that, I obeyed him.

I found him, his body was lying in the glasshouse, amongst his beloved orchids. The cause of death was pronounced as heart failure, the local Doctor wrote the death certificate, he had after all been treating him for chest pain for some months, prescribing him small amounts of digitalin that powerful distillation of the foxglove which will cure or kill depending on dose.

It was hidden amongst the shocking news of the day, a short column of print amongst the announcement that the country was at war with Germany.

Brecon and Radnor Express
4th August 1914

It is with great sadness that the death is announced of Mr William Rees son of Isaias Rees, and apothecary of the town.
Mr Rees died suddenly on 28th July 1914 and leaves a widow Mrs Sibyl Rees and daughters Helena and Rhianydd.
Funeral will be held at St Clements Church Rhayader at 11am on Thursday 6th August 1914.

On William's death after the turmoil of sorting out his affairs, I found that I had been left more or less penniless. The house at Penybanc had been mortgaged many times over and was now property of the Bank. The business which on the face of things was doing so well was also mortgaged, surely not to pay for William's flamboyant lifestyle, his frequent business trips, his life of the eternal social butterfly in local society. This could not be true; William was a shrewd businessman. I had seen the accounts; I had been part of the running of the shop.

Then I found the letters, a whole sheaf of them in the middle draw of his desk. I had for a long time known that William was a homosexual, he had consummated our marriage and had fathered a daughter providing a smoke screen of respectability, a public face. But as he told me after Rhianydd's birth, when he began to sleep in his own rooms in Penybanc, he really did prefer the company of men, both socially and sexually.
I could not complain, he had after all provided me with the same mask of respectability as I now knew I provided for him.

The letters were not love letters, no billet doux from an ardent admirer, as I read them, the truth came starkly into focus. William was being blackmailed to the tune of hundreds of pounds, in fear of being revealed as a sodomite and imprisoned or worse.

The letters were post-marked Cardiff, the writing was untidy and scrawling, but the sentiment was clear. Did the writer know that his cash-cow was dead, or should I await another demand, the writer would get no money from me, and to hell with the threats. By my reckoning

563

another payment of £50 was due at the beginning of the month of September, I had much to do before then.

I did not get lost on my way to Hengwm, I had walked that path many times, overgrown as it was now. Edward would be spinning in his grave, if he has one, I suspect he has not, he has a memorial stone in the churchyard at St Harmon, but there is no grave beneath. The cottage had been left clean and tidy, everything in its place, as if he was only on holiday, away for a few days and coming back. Apart from nine years' worth of cobwebs and dust, the little house had not changed. It was like coming home.

Penybanc was sold, I had pennies in my bank again, the lawyers were to forward any post which arrived for William on to me at Hengwm, Helena had chosen to live with her sister in Cardiff, I did not blame her, at fourteen she did not want to change schools, her ambition to study chemistry was still with her and she was determined to go to university to obtain a degree and qualify as a pharmacist. William had enrolled her in a girls' private grammar school, with economies I could still afford this expense, she would have the education her father had promised her.

Alone again I sat at the scrubbed table in the kitchen and again read through the blackmailer's letters, I spread them on the table and put them in date order, I needed to find clues as to who this person was, how they were paid, and where. Had William paid them face to face, did he know them or was there some anonymous cache where he left the money?

April 1895

Mr Rees
I fear your conduct has been noticed, there is talk of your vile behaviour and salacious conduct in circles where you would prefer it not to be known that you are indeed a sodomite. I have in my employ one who would gladly testify as to your behaviour, a witness to your preferences.

To prevent this smoke becoming fire you may choose to pay me the sum of ten guineas per month to ensure my silence and that of my employee. In the cemetery at Roath there is a stone angel, a memorial to the dead of the Roberts' family, there is an urn at its feet, you may leave the money there on the first Saturday of each month at six in the evening before the gates close.

I should not want to read of your sexual exploits in the press, so please do the sensible thing.

Signed.   Black Cat.

From then the letters became shorter and more abrupt

June 1895

Apothecary, I thank you for your kind donation, but the price of my silence is now thirty guineas a month.
Same time same place.
Same consequence.

Black Cat

A few months of thirty guineas then another increase, and my William had kept paying. The consequence of not doing so was to risk ruin of his family and imprisonment.

Then a week before his death, a letter from the bank refusing more credit and calling in the loans taken out on the house and the business. He had taken the only course he could see to end the cycle. He had taken his own life. Had Dr Mostyn Jones MD known what William intended. He and Mostyn were the greatest of friends after all, friends since boyhood and perhaps more.

I withdrew an extra ten guineas from the bank each week and waited for a letter, sure enough there it was on the second week of September. Brief and to the point.

Apothecary's wife,

To save your shame and the humiliation of your family, you will leave fifty guineas at the feet of the stone angel in Roath cemetery, 6pm on Saturday next. As your perverted husband has done to ensure my silence.

Black Cat.

Eryr if I ever needed your help, I need it now. Wherever you are, whatever you are doing, hear me.

My head was in my hands, my elbows resting on the pine tabletop, paper spread before me.

As I watched, the papers lifted and ordered themselves into a pile, the fire in the hearth flared and became brighter.

I turned to the doorway to see my son, Calon standing where I expected to see his father.

My boy, tall and strong, smiling and reaching out to me.

'I have been sent to help, I cannot stay now, but have no fear, do as the Cat says, you will be safe, all will be well.' Then he was gone.

I dressed with care, in the closet where Edward had kept his guns, I found the knife I had not seen since my return from France, long bladed and with a moonstone set in the hilt it was perfectly balanced, too long for my purposes tonight, the small push dagger which Tally had left was there, that fitted nicely into the depths of my fur muff.

Black was the order of the day, a grieving relative, flowers to be laid at the feet of the angel. Then what, I would just have to wait and see, it would be getting dark by six, and cemeteries are strange places after dark.

I took the post coach from Rhayader to Cardiff the day before, I had booked a room in the Angel Hotel rather than spend the night with Rhianydd and Helena who must know nothing of this venture.

I spent the day browsing the shops and markets of the city, taking in the sights and the sounds, the stench of fish from the indoor market, the sounds of the market traders calling out their wares and prices, attracting customers, the aroma of hops and yeast from the brewing of the Brains Brewery, an acquired taste that, but better smelling than fish. Cardiff is a vibrant place, I walked the mile out of the centre up the Parade with its grand houses and along the road out of town to the cemetery, it's grand wrought iron gates were still open, the white stone angel stood at its centre, wings folded, bending in grace down towards the surrounding graves, arms outstretched.

I could feel the crispness of the bank notes I had folded in my reticule and the steel of the push dagger, which was concealed in the fur of my muff, my fingers wrapped around it's handle which fitted snuggly into my grip. The reticule hung from my wrist, and I held a single orchid bloom in my other hand.

Glancing all around me I saw no one except the hunched form of a vagrant sitting cradling his stone bottle of gut rot gin leaning against the trunk of one of the huge yew trees which shaded the grass beneath, his shoes were worn and his clothes a patchwork of mending and holes, slouch hat pulled low over his face. He was just the right side of unconscious, a few more gulps from his bottle would take him where he wanted to go.

I left my flower at the angel's feet and placed the money in the stone urn where others placed their candles or their posies. I turned bowed my head and said a prayer, slowly, ears tuned for footsteps.

My senses became aware of a figure at a nearby grave, there was someone, shadowy, not quite visible, tending to the plot beneath the trees at the edge of the grass.

Instinct told me to turn and walk away, slowly. I crossed myself, kissed the crucifix which hung around my neck, touched my fingertips to the angel's hand, and walked back towards the gate.

Seven o'clock passed, I heard it marked by the clock of St John's Church in the centre of town. The gravedigger came to start his work on a grave for tomorrow's funeral, digging after the gates closed gave him the privacy he needed and no need to intrude on other mourners. He closed the gates but did not lock them, I saw him plainly, he put the key into the lock, but did not turn it, then he removed it.

My heart leapt with that strange sick feeling which echoes through your intestines. Something was about to happen.

The Cat was a woman, she was old, old, and bent with age, but I recognised her, it was Eliza Jones – the woman who had taught me to use the latent power within me, she had passed through the gate unseen, she walked invisible in the gravedigger's wake. He had left the gate unlocked for her to leave. As I watched she took the money from the urn, removed one note from the bundle and shuffling up to the gravedigger, stuffed it into his pocket. She turned on her stick and continued towards the gate.

They were on her like wraiths, emerging from cover in the shadows, Calon and yes it was Eryr, son and father, Calon bundled the old lady into the neatly dug hole in front of the grave digger, Eryr neatly dispatching the gravedigger who followed her into the pit, his throat neatly slit by an unearthly weapon. Both disappeared down the same exit from the surface.

I watched in stunned amazement as the vagrant raised himself from the ground, put down his bottle and proceeded to use the gravedigger's tools to fill in the hole down which the rest had disappeared.

Then he straightened his clothing pulled his hat down over his eyes and as he turned to walk away, I caught a fleeting glimpse of his face Uncle Edward.

I hailed a horse drawn cab and paid the fare back to the Angel Hotel where I walked on shaky legs up to my room.

On putting the key into the door lock, the door opened before me, Calon and Eryr were sitting at the occasional table in the window. Both, in human attire, entirely appropriate for the situation.

'It is good to see you mother'.

'It has been a long time, you look well, has your father looked after you?'

'Do you think I would not?'

'I do not know what to think anymore, why have you not....'

'You did not tell me I have a daughter, you should have, Calon should know his sister.'

'And Edward, what on earth have you done to him? 'I have done nothing, Edward Meredith is not dead, he has returned to his place in the world below, with his kin, he will have care of Hengwm again in time. Folk were suspicious of him, there were those that would do him harm, so he is as you say having a break. It is your time to care for the mountain now, Hengwm is yours.'

'And Eliza Jones?'

'She is dead, as is her associate, the gravedigger'

Eryr handed me fifty guineas and a bag containing more gold sovereigns than I could count.

She will trouble you no more, her husband died, and she returned from the colonies with nothing but the clothes she stood in and her talent for medicine and took up with the gravedigger whose side-line is robbing the dead. He was doing exactly that when he came across your husband inflagrante with another man a male whore from the sea port, who he does not know. Unfortunately, Eliza knew William – she had been a customer of his for many years, and he had bought her house, had he not. She believed him to be wealthy, she knew he was vulnerable and weak.

CHAPTER 96 - A WORLD AT WAR.

Eryr and Calon left as swiftly as they came, out through the window of my room on the second floor of the Angel. The penny dropped about thirty seconds after they left, Calon was truly his father's son, he had needed no fatherly support, he too could fly. As I watched from the balcony, two winged figures soared across the face of the moon, over the streets of a damp Cardiffian night. One of them clearly showboating for the benefit of the drunks in the park. I could see them in my mind's eye staring upwards bemused and cursing the seagulls.

I slept in a cold bed that night, tossing and turning with every noise from the street below, had they not appeared, what would I have done, would I have killed her, or would I have been buried in the hole which had been dug for me.

I rose early, the journey home would be a long one, I do not have the gifts bestowed on my son!

At least now Helena's schooling was not in doubt, I could afford to make the repairs needed at Hengwm, and even to give William a suitable memorial stone. He was after all a good man, and he had been my husband. As I was dressing, I did not hear the quiet knock at the door, as I turned to pick up my bag and leave, I saw that a letter had been pushed under the door.

I stuffed it hurriedly into my pocket. No time to read it now, I would miss the coach. I would read it on my way home, I did not recognise the writing. If it was important then the writer would have waited, surely. I caught the Coach at Wood Street, I was the only passenger, but the driver said that he had stops in Cowbridge and Merthyr before making Brecon by nightfall.

CHAPTER 97 – WHAT OF UNCLE EDWARD

The door at Hengwm hung off the latch, I was certain I had locked it when I left.

There sitting at the table was Uncle Edward. His great white whiskers curling around his face, he looked old now, his hair snowy white under his old felt hat, his jacket tied with twine, his great paws of hands calloused and ingrained with years of farming now resting on the table before him, the right one curled around a stone mug which I could smell contained cider. He looked at me with his old blue eyes, the twinkle still there behind the frost of age, watery eyes and at the moment rimmed with red.

'Shibyl, how are you?' The question slurred from his lips.

Uncle Edward was drunk, more drunk than I had ever seen him.

'It is good to see you too uncle, I thought you were ....' I replied, walking to the pantry to check the level of liquid in the cider Jack. Nearly empty! It had been full when I left so Uncle Edward was now at least five mugs to the wind.

'I wish I were dead, sister, I have been alive far too long, but it seems I must wait for my father's return, whenever that may be'.

He knew then. He knew what he was. They must have told him before he helped them dispose of Eliza!

'Gwyn is not here, brother, and he will not return to this time, all you will find here is dust'. He looked at me with the eyes of a defeated man.

'She will bring him back though, once his job is done, he will come home, then we can both rest, so I must wait,' he paused, banging his mug on the table. 'Go you, leave me to myself for today, by dusk I will not trouble you further'.

So, I wrapped my cloak around me and walked the mountain, then, curiosity getting the better of my judgement I had returned to Hengwm.

The entrance to the cave beneath had been cleared, the stones used to block the door neatly stacked on the steps. Edward was always a neat methodical workman. The door was open, looking in I saw him sitting on my old three-legged milking stool, the one I use to reach the high shelves in the pantry, his head bent in prayer over the box bed where he had last seen his father, Gwyn.

'I see you Shhibyl, that cloak does not fool me, now block up the door on your way out, there's a good girl, leave me be.'

With tears in my eyes, I did as he asked. Would they have pity and take him home?

It took me all night to seal the cave again, then locking the door of the cottage I climbed the stairs to my room and pulled the curtains shut, I wrapped the forest cloak around my naked body feeling the softness of its fur lining on my skin and falling exhausted onto my bed. Before I surrendered to invisible sleep. I took out the letter and I read it

3 The Parade
Cardiff

10th August 1914

Dearest Mother,

By the time you get this letter I shall be in Scotland, well on my way to Inverness to be precise.

I am getting married, my fiancée is called Jack MacGregor he is a soldier with the 16th Rifle Brigade, I met him in London while I was on placement at St Thomas's hospital. His family is from Inverness, and it is his last leave before he re-joins his regiment.

With War having been declared, we see no reason to wait, and with father no longer with us and things being what they are between us, I would prefer you do not follow us as I know you would. Rest assured I am happy.

Your daughter
Rhianydd

PS. Helena is travelling with us, I would not leave her alone in these awful times.

Contained in the letter was a photograph of my daughter and a handsome man in uniform, tall with a short military haircut, a dapper moustache, fringe Brylcreamed back from an intelligent face with a wide smile and dark eyes under dark eyebrows. He wore the uniform of a private, with the crossed rifles insignia of a sniper sewn onto the arm. He looked so young.
He would be in the thick of it then, if not in the trenches.

I pulled the cloak up around my ears for maximum warmth   felt the breeze drift over my feet and my run like fingers over my cheek, the window was slightly open to allow in the night air of the mountain.

The dreams when they came did not wake me, they seemed to hold me under my consciousness like a drowning man, unable to reach the surface. I think I screamed, for I felt the sound rip my throat as it made its exit.

I heard the sounds of men shouting, horses screaming in pain, explosions, the sounds of war. I smelled the green smells of the forests of France, the smell of wild garlic mixed with the metallic smell of blood and the sulphur of gunfire and fear.

Strong as iron but gentle as the mountain breeze I felt his arms around me, holding me close to his body, offering comfort, long legs curled around my own,
As he soothed me into the darkness, I heard a voice calling, out of the darkness piercing the chaos in my mind, it was a voice I knew well, it was my own.

Who could I be searching for amongst the dead?

The only thing I could feel with any certainty was that whoever I was seeking and for whatever reason, this strange family of mine would somehow be with me.

It is the year of our Lord 1914 and the whole world is now at war.

THE END

EPILOGUE: Y MAB DAROGEN – THE SON OF THE PROPHECY

It was unseasonably warm, for January.

28th January to be exact, in the year of our lord 1457.

Edward Meredith noticed that the mountain soil was warm where it should be frozen, the spring bulbs had been warmed and started to show their heads above the surface in little green clumps beneath the trees. The brook where it should be icy was warm enough to wash in without shivering.

In the great castle of Pembrokeshire, on the West Coast of Wales a child was born to a mother far too young to survive his birth, a girl of noble blood given in marriage as a bargaining chip to Edmund Tudor 1st Earl of Richmond.

The child is a boy and history will say that his mother survived the birth and lived to see her son fulfil his destiny.

In a cave beneath the nearby mountains Lady Margaret de Audley wove her spells and called on her Gods and became in the instant of the young mothers death, Lady Margaret Beaufort.

At the same time the breath of the dragon Gwynt y Ddraig again flowed over the archer sleeping beneath Hengwm and once again he stirred.

It was all planned, a son even a baby should have a guardian, one to watch over him and guide him to his destiny.

In a country soon to be divided by war, a mother could never be too careful. Henry VII the first of the Tudor Kings.

He was born in Pembroke in the year of our lord 1457,

He was indeed born a Welshman, banished from his land at the age of fourteen he returned fourteen years later under the banner of the Red Dragon, he United the Celtic peoples behind him and in 1485 was crowned in London as King of England.

After many years of civil war, he stabilised the country and for a time there was peace.

Henry Tudor ruled as Henry VII and one hundred and the prophecy was finally fulfilled. It was fulfilled by a mother determined that her son should fulfil his birth right, a mother whose dogged determination refused to let the boy she knew was heir to the throne be swept away, Margaret Beaufort was a warrior indeed. A woman of tremendous foresight married too young be this time refusing to be a political pawn.

History repeats itself, maybe she had been down life's path before.

Before this arrival another Owain, Owain Glyndwr had carved a swathe of rebellion through the land, destroying all things English.

Today children play on the Graig hill below Hen Felin Wynt and carve their names in the stones of the tower at its summit. My initials are carved there for posterity, in the big flat slab over the door.

Wild ponies still graze the common land, that land given to the freemen of the town, descendants of the Black Army and, the castle at Llantrisant amongst others was demolished except for the Raven Tower which still stubbornly points its ivy clad finger at the sky in defiance. Listen hard and you may just hear the voices of the past calling from beyond the mist of time.

THE END

AUTHORS NOTES

Firstly, this is not a history tutorial, it is a work of fantasy fiction, none of the traits of any of the characters bear any similarity to any person of the same or similar name found in history.

Events in history have been researched and are believed to be accurate as far as possible and are used as reference points to anchor a story which also asks you to believe in Faeries, so a little flexibility and imaginative thinking is required when reading.

There is also reference made to books written by other authors, in the main these are authors whose work I have read and who have inspired me on my own writing journey.

Any reference to herbal remedies or concoctions and their ingredients as listed in this book as being used historically for medical or other purposes whilst they have been researched is no indication that they are either effective or harmless, many such preparations can be toxic and should only be administered by an experienced practitioner.

ACKNOWLEDGEMENTS

It is customary for authors to acknowledge those who have inspired them to write, and who have helped them along the way for various reasons. Often a small anecdote turns up in the acknowledgements. I recently compared writing a novel and getting as far as publication as being like sending a child out into the world, hoping that you have prepared it well enough to survive.

My inspiration for writing this book was initially, my great grandmother, Sybil Helena. I remember her as a white-haired old lady sitting in her chair, who I was taken to visit when I was about six years old. While researching our family tree, I came across her birth certificate, which was remarkably lacking in detail, and also the original Last Will and Testament of the man she called 'Uncle Edward'. This took me on a fascinating historical journey. The family called her Go Go which was a shortened version on Goch Goch – Red translated to Welsh for when young she had the most amazing Red curly hair! Thank you, Great Grandmother.

I also acknowledge the inspiration of the work of every author whose work I have read, and I am an avid reader, so thank you, Charles Dickens, Thomas Hardy, Jane Austen, Charlotte Brontë, Martina Cole, Wilbur Smith, Robert Crais, Phillipa Gregory and particularly Diana Gabaldon, without whose writing's lockdown would have been very boring.

Thanks also to the fellow author and poet Arthur Cole, a former colleague also with a passion for writing and literature which lay dormant until retirement. Your encouragement and enthusiasm have boosted my confidence in my work.

I also owe a great debt of thanks to all the friends and family who have helped with creative input both visually and editorially. Those who have 'test read' my efforts and been as ruthless in their opinions as I asked them to be.

So, thank you to my brothers Giles Morgan and Pete Morgan. Friends, Fran Evans, and Alison King for reading and critiquing. And to Nikki Sutton for editing.

My last mention goes to my husband, for phrases like 'when are you getting off that laptop. You need to take the dog out'.

And to Murph the Dog for making me get enough fresh air.

Also, to my daughter for promising to read my work one day, but I have a university assignment to do first.

I dedicate this book to the memory of my Great Grandmother, Sibyl Helena Rees 1873 to 1968.

COPYRIGHT

OTHER BOOKS BY THE AUTHOR

Ginger Like Biscuits - a short book for horsey pre-teens

Unofficial Droughtlander Relief.

The Droughtlander's Progress.

Totally Obsessed.

Fireside Stories.

Je Suis Prest.

Après Le Deluge

Dragonflies of Summer

Semper in Aeternum

Sia air Ochd

Intervallaqua

Facing the Storm

Reading Between the Lines

The Blue Vase - illustrated by Lyn Fuller

Mille Basia Volume 1

Mille Basia Vol 2

I hope the Princess will Approve – a book of COVID and Horse related poems.

A recipe for disaster - poems about the authors life

■■

TASTE OF THINGS TO COME

If you enjoyed An Arrow Through Time you may also like the follow on and second book in the series

A Bullet in the Mist

In 1915 both boys were sixteen years old, eager for adventure and seeking a way, any way to get out of their circumstances.

The enlistment posters filled every available space on the billboards of the city. The pointing finger followed them everywhere – your country needs you.
It was April the country had been at war for nine months, the army needed soldiers, St Pancras was raising its own company of riflemen, Frankie was up for enlisting, he was good with a rifle. Charlie was not quite so sure, but swept along on his friend's enthusiasm he agreed, it was the right thing to do.

After a short discussion between themselves, they had scrubbed themselves clean acquired two smart suits from the local pawn shop, on loan of course, Brylcreamed their hair, in an attempt to look older than their sixteen years, smoked several cigarettes to make their voices sound deeper and taken themselves off to the recruiting office.

The queue outside the working men's college on Crowdale Road filled the pavement and stretched around the corner for several hundred yards, it was mainly formed of young unmarried men who Charlie and Frankie knew from the streets, older men hoping to re-enlist and resume service in the regiments they had been in for the Boer War. Many obviously did not fall into the category of between 19 and 38 years old and over 5'3 tall.

Frankie and Charlie jostled their way into the queue behind a group of lads who they knew were only twelve or thirteen, hoping that the comparison in fresh faced boyishness, age and height would go in their favour. Charlie at least had some evidence of stubble on his chin, even if he was not yet shaving, and Frankie could fire a rifle, how could they fail.

Charlie had his brothers birth certificate and had memorised all the details, he would become Herbert Charles, but everyone calls me Charlie!

Frankie had no birth certificate he knew of, but Black Eric had supplied one at a price, Albert Frederick Baker now aged eighteen years. Born in Scotland of all places, Inverness, but I've lived in London all my life, sir, my parents are dead, and everyone calls me Frankie.

The real Albert Baker was buried under a slab of Scottish Granite in the graveyard at Grantown on Spey along with his mother and father, victims of a house fire, Albert had been six months old at the time.

The recruiting officer took one look at them, in their too big suits, Brylcreamed fringes and smiled.

'Come on then laddie!' His accent was broad and Scottish, 'Convince me!' huge hands like boiled hams spread across the table, in anticipation of the next implausible story.

Charlie was first to the wide table full of forms behind which sat a huge man with twinkly brown eyes, black eyebrows, short cropped black hair, a big bushy moustache, just like the man on the poster, a barrel of a chest bursting out of a Khaki tunic and Sam Brown belt. He was having a bad morning, he had just turned away half a class of children, six men well into their fifties and too old to fight, one girl dressed in her brothers' clothes, and he was not in the mood for nonsense.

Sensing the moment, Charlie stood to attention in the best way he knew how. Drew himself to his full height of five feet eight and threw out his chest. Placing the birth certificate on the table in front of the Officer he announced.

'Herbert Charles Turner, sir! Age eighteen sir! And nineteen in a few weeks.

'And I'm the Queen of Sheba, if you're eighteen I'm a monkeys uncle ye wee gobshite'.

'I am eighteen sir, ask my dad if you like,'

'Ye expect me tae believe ye have a dad as well then!' Charlie's dad had lost count of children many years ago.

'See it says so here'. Charlie pointed at the birth certificate.

'I din'nae care what it says there, sonny, ye din'nae look the age,'

He picked up the birth certificate and read it, humph'd to himself several times, and ye were born in Britain.

'Aye Sir,' Charlie's natural talent as a mimic picked up the officers accent, the officer raised an eyebrow at him, and half smiled.

'Are ye fit and well lad'

'I am so, sir, and I can fire a rifle!' He lied bravely. Hoping that Frankie would back him up or at least teach him the rudiments before they were sent to training camp.

'Get yersel through there then,'

He was ushered through to the next room where he was told to undress to the waist, his chest was listened to and found to be sound, his eyes tested, and his feet checked. A bit like a horse being put through its paces for the vet, he thought. Sound in wind eye and action.

The army doctor ran through a long list of diseases which Charlie swore he had never had,

Thank You for reading

Maggie J
2023

Printed in Great Britain
by Amazon

27903665R00334